Praise for Christine

"Heart-stopping action. (
emotions . . . [A] little bit
enjoys a solid paranormal

"With a Feehan novel you know you will get well-developed characters and an engaging plot, so when you add a dose of sizzling sexuality, you have an unbeatable mix."

—RT Book Reviews

"Heady, passionate, seductive . . . Ms. Feehan does a fantastic job of building up to the climax for a smashing finale that leaves you breathless and satisfied." —Smexy Books

"Readers . . . will be seduced by this erotic adventure."

—*Publishers Weekly*

"Another wild ride . . . enter the lair of the shapeshifters."

—Romance Reviews Today

"A passionate, jam-packed adventure."

—Fallen Angel Reviews

"The passion runs high and the sex is hot!"

—The Romance Readers Connection

"Sizzling and exciting . . . surprises erupt at every turn."

—Fresh Fiction

"A phenomenal story . . . Christine Feehan knows how to weave a tale of action, suspense and paranormal passion that has earned her so many fans and keeps bringing new ones."

—Romance Junkies

Titles by Christine Feehan

COVERT GAME
POWER GAME
SPIDER GAME
VIPER GAME
SAMURAI GAME
RUTHLESS GAME
STREET GAME
MURDER GAME
PREDATORY GAME
DEADLY GAME
CONSPIRACY GAME
NIGHT GAME
MIND GAME
SHADOW GAME

HIDDEN CURRENTS
TURBULENT SEA
SAFE HARBOR
DANGEROUS TIDES
OCEANS OF FIRE

LEOPARD'S RUN
LEOPARD'S BLOOD
LEOPARD'S FURY
WILD CAT
CAT'S LAIR
LEOPARD'S PREY
SAVAGE NATURE
WILD FIRE
BURNING WILD
WILD RAIN

BOUND TOGETHER
FIRE BOUND
EARTH BOUND
AIR BOUND
SPIRIT BOUND
WATER BOUND

SHADOW KEEPER
SHADOW REAPER
SHADOW RIDER

JUDGMENT ROAD

DARK SENTINEL
DARK LEGACY
DARK CAROUSEL
DARK PROMISES
DARK GHOST
DARK BLOOD
DARK WOLF
DARK LYCAN
DARK STORM
DARK PREDATOR
DARK PERIL
DARK SLAYER
DARK CURSE
DARK HUNGER
DARK POSSESSION
DARK CELEBRATION
DARK DEMON
DARK SECRET
DARK DESTINY
DARK MELODY
DARK SYMPHONY
DARK GUARDIAN
DARK LEGEND
DARK FIRE
DARK CHALLENGE
DARK MAGIC
DARK GOLD
DARK DESIRE
DARK PRINCE

Anthologies

EDGE OF DARKNESS
(with Maggie Shayne and Lori Herter)

DARKEST AT DAWN
(includes DARK HUNGER *and* DARK SECRET*)*

SEA STORM
(includes MAGIC IN THE WIND *and* OCEANS OF FIRE*)*

FEVER
(includes THE AWAKENING *and* WILD RAIN*)*

FANTASY
(with Emma Holly, Sabrina Jeffries, and Elda Minger)

LOVER BEWARE
(with Fiona Brand, Katherine Sutcliffe, and Eileen Wilks)

HOT BLOODED
(with Maggie Shayne, Emma Holly, and Angela Knight)

Specials

DARK CRIME
DARK HUNGER
MAGIC IN THE WIND
THE AWAKENING

LEOPARD'S RUN

CHRISTINE FEEHAN

JOVE
New York

A JOVE BOOK
Published by Berkley
An imprint of Penguin Random House LLC
375 Hudson Street, New York, New York 10014

ISBN: 9780451490162

First Edition: November 2018

Printed in the United States of America
1 3 5 7 9 10 8 6 4 2

Cover photos by Getty Images
Cover design by Judith Lagerman

This is a work of fiction. Names, characters, places, and incidents either are the product of the author's imagination or are used fictitiously, and any resemblance to actual persons, living or dead, business establishments, events, or locales is entirely coincidental.

For my friend, Susan Winding . . .

For My Readers

Be sure to go to http://www.christinefeehan.com/members/ to sign up for my PRIVATE book announcement list and download the FREE ebook of *Dark Desserts.* Join my community and get firsthand news, enter the book discussions, ask your questions and chat with me. Please feel free to email me at Christine@christinefeehan.com. I would love to hear from you.

Acknowledgments

I ran into a lot of problems writing this book. Sometimes that's just what happens. Many thanks to Brian Feehan for challenging me to write faster and always try for better. Thank you to Sheila English for going through the book looking for those loose ends. To Domini Walker, working weekends and when you were sick to get it done, you have no idea how much I appreciate you. To Denise Feehan for covering for everyone while we made the mad dash for the deadline—thank you very much! Special thank-you to Cheryl Wilson, a good friend who always comes through at crunch time!

1

TIMUR Amurov cursed under his breath using his native language, something his brother—and boss—strictly forbade. Striding from the town car with its tinted windows and black paint, he moved easily through those walking on the sidewalk. His trench coat swirled around his ankles, the inner lining filled with many loops to hide the weapons he carried.

People moved out of his way. It was the set of his wide shoulders, the scars on his face, his expressionless mask, the threat in his cold, dead eyes. He saw their reactions, and he knew exactly what they would do—step aside for him—so he never broke or deviated from his pace. He looked dangerous because he *was* dangerous. He looked like a man who would kill—and he was.

He didn't pretend to be anything other than who he was. A shifter. A bodyguard. A weapon sent out when it was deemed necessary. If he showed up at someone's door, they weren't going to see another sunrise. He looked the part because that was exactly who he was. A stone-cold killer, a legacy given to him by his father. And grandfather. And uncles. There was no hiding the truth, not even from himself, and he didn't care to. Life had handed him a shit deck of cards, but he was playing his hand until he couldn't take it anymore and then he would go out his way.

He didn't let down his guard for many people. First and foremost was Fyodor, his older brother. Fyodor had risked everything to save Timur and his cousin Gorya, a man brought up with them in their sick, twisted environment. Timur and Gorya had taken the position of bodyguards to Fyodor, but his brother just refused to stay out of harm's way. Fyodor was the head of a large territory and might as well have gone around with a target painted on his back. No matter what security measures Timur and his security team took, Fyodor seemed to just ignore them.

In his defense, Fyodor had been a bodyguard, a soldier, long before he'd ascended to the throne, but Timur considered that he should know how difficult it was to guard and keep safe a man who ignored every security protocol.

He loved his brother. Not that they talked of such things. That had been forbidden growing up. They'd been taught never to feel affection for anyone—especially a woman. Fyodor's wife, Evangeline, owned and operated a bakery in San Antonio, and that meant Fyodor worked out of it sometimes. Most times. He had an office in the back. And despite their upbringing, Fyodor made no bones about loving his wife. No bones about showing it either. The thing was, Timur loved her too. He loved her as a sister, but couldn't express it. A childhood of savage beatings had seen to that.

Timur yanked open the glass door to the bakery. He'd had the door replaced and bulletproof glass placed in it, along with the banks of windows that made up the shop's storefront. Evangeline looked up quickly and sent him a smile. His heart contracted. She was sweet. Beautiful. Perfect for his brother. More, she kept his brother's leopard from trying to break loose to hunt and kill. His own leopard raked and clawed, angry, violent, moody as hell.

"Everythin' all right, Timur?" Evangeline's little Louisiana accent always made him feel warm, like he'd come home. Her smile began to fade when he didn't return it.

Hell no, nothing was all right. His fucked-up brother was so smitten with this woman that he risked his life—and hers—every damn day. He kept that to himself. Fyodor wouldn't want him upsetting Evangeline, nor did he want to.

He gave her a curt nod as he moved across the floor, checking every table as he made his way to the restrooms. He scanned them quickly, around the legs, under the tabletops, to ensure no incendiary device or explosives had been placed there.

"Timur?"

Evangeline was being insistent. What was he going to say? Fyodor had received more death threats? That was a common enough occurrence. However, this particular threat he was taking seriously, but his brother wasn't—as usual. Timur knew they'd taken too many chances and sooner or later their luck was going to run out. His gut—never to be ignored—told him their luck was long gone and this time the threat was very real.

"Make me a double latte."

"A double latte?" She was clearly shocked.

He needed the caffeine. He needed her busy. He gave her another curt nod and shoved open the men's restroom door. He checked it carefully, every stall, making certain his brother was safe from any assassin, and then he checked the women's room. The moment he put his hand on the door to push it open, he knew, by the way his leopard went crazy, that it was occupied. He didn't care. He wasn't there to cater to anyone's sensibilities. He was there to make certain Fyodor wasn't murdered.

She stood in front of the mirror, lipstick in her hand, and

her eyes went wide when he strode in. Her eyes caught him first thing. They were almost too big for her face. A very light brown, amber really, like a fine whiskey you sipped at night when you just wanted to lay it all down. The amber was ringed with very thick, dark lashes, making her eyes stand out. Those lashes feathered down in long sweeps, curling at the ends.

She turned toward him, lipstick held slightly in front of her as if that could stop him if he came at her. He knew he was intimidating. He was tall, had wide shoulders and a thick chest. Ropes of muscle rippled along his arms, back and chest and down his abdomen. His heart thudded unexpectedly. Hard. An ache he'd never experienced.

She was beautiful. He could see her front, those breasts pushing at her thin tank. The small, tucked-in waist that wasn't in the least hidden by her shirt. She had hips and a very nice ass, which he'd noticed the moment he walked in. She filled those soft blue jeans to perfection. He kept walking right past her and yanked open each of the stall doors. It wouldn't have mattered to him had they been locked. He still would have made the inspection. Fortunately, they were all empty; she was the only occupant in the room.

When he'd stepped past her to get to the stalls, he'd inhaled instinctively. She smelled faintly of grapefruit and fresh-cut cypress. Who smelled like that? Evidently he liked it, or, more importantly, his leopard did. Usually, if he got too close to a human being, male or female, his leopard raged, wanting to kill. Needing to draw blood. For the first time, the cat had gone entirely quiet. That never happened. As in—*never.* Even when he was close to Evangeline and his leopard settled, the cat was never like this. Quiet. Almost purring.

"You are?" he demanded. *Shit.* There was no denying his Russian accent or his growl. Both came out overly strong.

He doubted if the top of her head came up to the middle

of his chest, but she narrowed her eyes at him in what, he suspected, was supposed to be a scary look.

"I'm in the *women's* bathroom, which is supposed to be private to *women*."

Sass. The woman had sass in abundance. Stupidity as well. He stepped closer to her, close enough that the tips of her breasts brushed his abs. She had to tilt her head all the way back to look up at him.

"You don't fuck with a man like me," he advised.

She nodded. "No, I won't. Not ever. Thanks for the advice."

Her voice was even enough, but she was totally fucking with him now, using his own words against him. He had to hand it to her, she kept a straight face and even managed wide-eyed innocence.

God help him, his body chose that moment to betray him. His physical reaction to her was intense. His cock lengthened and grew into a monster, roaring at him just the way his leopard always did, painful now. He didn't dare step forward or back. She had to feel it. There was no hiding it and he kept his expression blank, but he did a hell of a lot of inward cursing—and he used his own language too. Never once in his life had he had such a problem. Now, of all times, his body had decided to react on its own.

He took a breath and resisted the idea of patting her down. By now, Fyodor was going to be restless. He wanted to see his woman and he would just . . .

"Is there a problem, Timur?" His brother's voice came smoothly over the tiny radio.

Looking straight into her eyes, Timur answered. "No problem. Give me a minute." His men were up on rooftops, watching over the car and keeping Fyodor safe while Timur checked out the interior of the bakery.

He was met with silence. That could mean anything. Fyodor might decide to not give Timur any shit for once and stay in the car, or he could just come striding in. In any case, Timur had to get away from close proximity to the woman. She was wreaking havoc with him and his leopard. For once, instead of demanding blood, his cat was acting weird, rolling around and practically purring. It was not only annoying, it was throwing him off his game.

"Tell me your name."

"Ashe Bronte."

"You made that up."

"You're just the nicest man I've ever met." Sarcasm dripped from her voice. "If you don't like it, you'll have to take it up with my parents. Unfortunately, they're both deceased, so you might have a little trouble finding them."

She pushed past him, and he let her go. She had hair. Lots of it. It was thick and wild, a light blond that also emphasized her unusual eyes. It was only after the door closed behind her, and he was left to stand alone in the cool of the ladies' room, that he realized his leopard had been calm the *entire* time. *Silent.* There was no vicious raking. No demand for blood. Not even when his body had touched her body. For the first time in years he knew respite from his cat's constant fury. But the minute the woman was out of his sight, his leopard reacted, going insane, fighting for control.

This was what Fyodor had found with Evangeline. She tamed the beast in him just by being in close proximity. Timur refused to allow his heart to accelerate, or the adrenaline to be released into his bloodstream. Just because, for a few short minutes, his leopard hadn't clawed for freedom and blood, it didn't mean this woman would do for him what Evangeline did for Fyodor.

He turned abruptly and followed her out. She was walking across the shop floor, straight to the counter. The way she moved in her jeans was a work of art. His heart did a funny stutter as he watched her talk to Evangeline for a moment and then step behind the counter.

"Evangeline?" It was a demand. Nothing less. She

couldn't hire someone, as she'd clearly done, without following protocol.

Evangeline tried to win in a stare down, and it wasn't happening. She sighed and came out from behind the counter to catch his arm and guide him across the room, presumably out of earshot, although the bakery wasn't that large and he figured whatever she said was going to be overheard.

"I know. I'm sorry, Timur, but she needed a job and she has experience. I can't keep having your men, who break my things, try to pretend they're baristas. They aren't. I know why you want them in the shop, but they're losing me customers. She's fast, knows her drinks, remembers customers' names and doesn't glare at them or intimidate them in any way."

"Damn it, Evangeline. She could be anyone. What did she do? Just wander in off the street?"

"That's how most people come in. And she is someone," Evangeline sounded more defiant than sorry. "I need the help."

"You could have told us and we'd have found you someone. Fuck. Her name is a joke. Ashe Bronte? That's ridiculous. No one is named that. Maybe a fucking porn star."

"Keep making fun of my name and every time you order a drink, I'm going to put something in it you aren't going to like," Ashe muttered under her breath.

She said it softly enough he knew she didn't think he could hear. He hadn't bothered to speak that low, but still, she had good hearing. Her jeans were tight enough that he could see she wasn't hiding a weapon, but her breasts were generous enough that she might conceal a knife there. A garrote could be sewn into clothing, and she wore boots that had room for a gun.

"That isn't very nice, Timur," Evangeline pointed out. She lowered her voice even more. "Is she a porn star? Have you seen her in movies? She's gorgeous enough."

"How the fuck would I know? You think I spend my time looking at porn movies and jacking off? Why is it that I always get into very inappropriate conversations with you? Sweet God in heaven, woman, you're the bane of my life."

Abruptly he spun around and hurried out of the shop, swearing again under his breath when Evangeline's soft laughter followed him. He looked right and left, and then studied the rooftops before he opened the door to allow his brother out onto the sidewalk. The moment he did, Gorya slid out and flanked Fyodor, covering his back. They walked in step and Timur noted that Fyodor was getting used to having bodyguards. He was much more in sync with them than he had been.

They'd already gone through an attack on their family. Evangeline had been targeted. Mitya, a cousin, had been badly wounded when those targeting her tried to kill Fyodor. Timur knew Fyodor felt responsible for that. He had been a little more cooperative ever since. All of them knew it was a matter of time before the real enemy discovered where they were—hiding out in the open.

Fyodor had been living as Alonzo Massi, but after the attack that had nearly killed Mitya, he took his real name back. Timur was grateful for that. He was Russian and proud of who he was, but he was also a bodyguard; chances were, by taking his real identity back, Fyodor was going to have some serious enemies coming after him. They would be coming for all of them.

Timur opened the door for his brother, but stepped inside while doing so. He wanted to keep an eye on the newcomer. If she went for a weapon, she was dead. The idea of killing her didn't sit well with him and he kept his body between the new barista and Fyodor at all times. It was easy enough when Fyodor had eyes only for Evangeline.

She came to him immediately, no hesitation. Timur knew better than to look at them. He kept his gaze sweeping the sidewalks through the glass and then back to the new woman. She was looking at Evangeline and Fyodor, and color had swept over her face.

Gorya wandered over to the counter, pretending he wanted a coffee, but clearly what he really wanted to do was flirt. Timur stepped closer to her. At once his leopard settled, curling up contentedly and leaving him the hell alone. Even so, he could feel the leopard snarling, head up alertly. He might be content to be close to the woman he dubbed the leopard whisperer, but his cat didn't like her near his cousin.

"Baby, who is this woman you've hired? You know this is dangerous, not only to us, but to what we do," Fyodor whispered to Evangeline. "You said nothing about this woman to me, or to Timur. He's responsible for our lives. Can you imagine how he would feel if he failed in his job and you were killed? Or I was? Evangeline, you know better than this."

Timur nearly fell down he was so shocked. It was all he could do to keep his mouth from dropping open. Fyodor had never once indicated to him that he knew his personal security was a nightmare for Timur, especially since the attempt on his life as well as Evangeline's. His brother never reprimanded Evangeline, let alone in public.

He glanced up and met Ashe's eyes. The impact was just like a bullet through his heart. That intense. That visceral. She'd heard, and Fyodor and Evangeline were clear across the room, huddled together in a little corner while Ashe was behind the counter. Her hearing was more than excellent. She looked away first, ducking her head and concentrating on making Gorya's drink.

"I'm sorry, Fyodor," Evangeline whispered. "I really, really need the help, and none of the men you had working for me worked out. They drop things. They ruin the machines. Do you have any idea how much those cost?"

"Baby." There was a sigh in Fyodor's voice. "We can afford a new coffee machine. We can't afford a new you."

"She isn't a threat to me. Or to you. Please, honey, just let this one go."

Something in Evangeline's voice alerted him. Timur moved closer to the counter. Evangeline knew Ashe. There was some connection between them. He watched as Ashe handed Gorya his coffee and took his money. Her hands appeared steady enough, but they were trembling. Just slightly, but they were trembling all the same.

Timur didn't like puzzles, especially when it came to Fyodor's safety. Gorya signaled to him. His cousin had been raised as a sibling with him, and they had continued to be close as adults, although if he kept flirting with Ashe, that closeness might end. Timur was a little shocked that the thought went through his head.

He joined Gorya at the table his cousin chose. It was always the same one. It was small, a table for two, and it was positioned so that Gorya had his back protected and yet could see the front door and the sidewalks through the window, and still keep the counter in sight. Rather than take the chair opposite him that would put his back to the wall, Timur toed one around and sat straddling it, facing the door as well.

"She's scared," Gorya mouthed around his coffee cup. "My leopard went quiet, just the way it does when Evangeline is close."

"Maybe it's Evangeline," Timur pointed out, but he knew it wasn't. He knew it was Ashe. His leopard was practically purring.

"She has to be leopard."

Timur had to agree with that, and if they were both suspicious, that meant she was close to the emerging—a time when the female leopard's cycle and the woman's cycle synchronized together. "Where's she from?"

Gorya shrugged. "I asked, but she didn't answer. She didn't answer any of my questions."

The bakery was beginning to fill up. Fyodor slipped behind the counter to the back room he used as his office. Gorya went with him. They took turns, one up front, one in the back. Two more patrolled the alley behind the bakery, and two were on the front walkway. One was on the roof above the shop and another was across the street on the roof.

Timur watched Evangeline and Ashe work together. They were fast and efficient. They moved in sync as if they'd been doing so for years. They laughed occasionally, and when they did, Ashe's laughter seemed to move through his body, teasing every one of his senses. Again, that was so unusual that he didn't trust it.

His cat hated everyone. The leopard had been raised in violence, just as he'd been. His father had lived to control the world around him. He'd done so through fear. He'd liked everyone to be afraid of him. He'd *needed* that. Timur and Gorya, a few years younger than Fyodor, *had* been afraid. They hadn't dared befriend anyone because their father would have been very likely to force them to kill that person. It wouldn't have mattered if it had been a child, a woman or a man responsible for providing for his family—Timur's father would have laughed when he forced the young men to kill.

It had been impossible to be with a woman. Well, not impossible, but the risk had made it very difficult. When his need had become too great, Timur had found a willing woman in a bar, had sex with her and then left before his raging leopard could get loose and kill her. He'd talked to Fyodor, and his brother had the same problem with his leopard. Gorya had as well. Timur had suspected his other cousins Mitya and Sevastyan had the same difficulties when it came to women.

The leopards had been subjected to too much violence, too many killings at a young age. Timur's leopard had been forced to come out, to shift against Timur's will in order to stop the brutal beatings Timur had suffered at the hands of his father. The moment the leopard had come out, he'd been forced to participate in his father's cruel, sick games, training the cat to kill for pleasure. For blood. Human blood.

He tapped the table, watching the sidewalk. He wanted a home, just like any other man might want, but he knew that was impossible for him. Fyodor had found Evangeline, but they were still in a kind of prison and always would be. There was really no place anyone could hide anymore without being found. They'd all known it was a matter of time before their crimes caught up with them. Timur wasn't going to have a wife and children. He would never have a home or feel a woman's touch on his skin. Not again. Not when they were hunted like animals.

"Can I get you anything?" Evangeline offered during the next lull.

He'd been aware of her approach and knew she would attempt to fix things between them. He was upset with her for hiring Ashe without consulting with him. He needed a background check. He needed to know everything there was to know about the woman before he allowed her to get close to Evangeline or Fyodor. By hiring the woman herself, and then going to Fyodor, Evangeline had made certain that wasn't going to happen.

She slipped into the seat opposite him the moment he straightened with a small shake of his head. Ashe was watching them. She held herself a little too stiff, the smile fading.

"You don't want to do this with me right now," Timur said, his voice gruff. He couldn't control the rasp in his voice, the near growl. He wanted to shake some sense into her. "I'm angry with you, Evangeline."

"I know. I'm sorry. You have every right to be."

"Sorry doesn't cut it. You could get my brother killed. Or, you could be killed, and then what would he do? I don't want to hear your excuses right now. We're not in a place of privacy."

That should tell her he had a lot to say, things she wasn't going to like. As it was, she'd winced at the lash in his voice, especially when he'd rightly pointed out that it was Fyodor who could pay the price for her willfulness.

"I really am sorry. It won't happen again."

"I'm sure it won't. You can't know that many women who worked with you in a coffee shop." He kept his eyes on her face, although he really wanted to see Ashe's reaction.

Evangeline blushed. She glanced over her shoulder to look at Ashe.

"Don't bother to deny it, *mladshaya sestra*, that would just piss me off more. I don't like lies, and you're not very good at them."

"I don't want to lie to you," Evangeline admitted. "I just can't say anything. I'm really, really sorry, Timur, but she isn't a threat to us at all."

"You don't get to make that call and you know it. When you married my brother, that went right out the window. I make the call, not you. You want your friend to stay, you come clean with me. Make this right, because if you don't, she could disappear."

Evangeline's face went pale. "Timur . . ."

"Don't." He snapped the order at her, leaning across the table, staring her in the eye so she knew he meant what he said. "I'm responsible for you both. For your lives. I've spent a lifetime shaping myself into a weapon to ensure Fyodor's safety. And now yours and those of any children you have. That's my sole purpose in life. You don't get exceptions. You can talk to Fyodor, insist he fire me, it won't do you any good. I'll still watch over you both. Come clean about your friend or send her on her way."

The thought of Ashe leaving hurt. His cat protested with a mean snarl and a vicious swipe to his gut. That didn't matter. He'd meant every word he'd said, and Evangeline had better take him seriously.

"I'll talk to her. If she gives me permission, I'll tell you everything. If she doesn't, I'll tell her she has to leave. I promise, Timur, you'll either have that information by the end of the day or she'll leave."

Timur sat back in his chair and gave her a slight nod. She knew him well enough to know he meant what he said. His gaze was on the sidewalk outside. He noticed the two men approaching and a small sigh escaped. Cops. He knew them; they knew him. One, Jeff Meyers, had been undercover as Brice Addler, and had tried to steal Evangeline out from under Fyodor's nose. His partner had gone by Reeve Hawkins. His real name was Ray Harding.

"I never noticed before, but you're actually further gone than Fyodor was, aren't you, Timur?" Evangeline said softly, compassion in her voice.

He didn't want her sympathy. He didn't want anything from her that might somehow change who he was, because then he might not be as sharp, and his brother—or Evangeline—would pay the price for his weakness. He waved her back to work, jerking his chin toward the door. He didn't want Ashe serving either of the cops. They'd hit on her. Both were like that and he didn't want the woman telling them a single thing about his family.

Jeff strolled in like he owned the shop, Ray beside him, both in plain clothes. Timur kept his mask in place as they stared at him. It was impossible for either cop to win in a stare down and they knew it from experience, so they didn't try. They barely acknowledged his existence before they were at the counter, flirting outrageously with Evangeline.

Evangeline had wisely told Ashe to take a break in the back room. That allowed Timur to breathe easier. The last thing he wanted was for his leopard to make him any edgier or moodier than he'd felt the moment he'd seen the cops. They didn't like him, and he sure as hell didn't like them.

He kept his gaze on the street, but always had the cops in his vision. Hopefully, Gorya was standing in front of the door to Fyodor's office just in case Ashe took it in her head to be friendly and go talk to his brother, or worse, decide this was a great time to kill him, if she was an assassin. He nearly groaned aloud. Now he was worried.

"Keep your eyes on the new girl, Gorya," he ordered, talking softly into his radio.

"Eyes are on her," Gorya confirmed with a little too much enthusiasm for Timur's liking.

"I said eyes, not hands or mouth or any other part of your anatomy that I might have to cut off if you disobey that very direct order."

Gorya's laughter was offensive. Not because Timur didn't understand it, but because his attraction to Evangeline's friend burned through his body, making him so uncomfortable he felt surly and edgy even without the help of his leopard. He didn't trust himself to address Jeff and Ray and the way they flirted with Evangeline. Another time, he might have gotten up and broken up the flirt-fest, but right then it was far more important to sit in his chair, legs sprawled in front of him, and contemplate ways to kill them. He had already thought of at least fifteen and that was without really trying.

He breathed a sigh of relief when they left and told his leopard to calm down and stop making an ass out of himself. The cat answered with a snarl, a show of teeth and a pithy attitude, stating that was all Timur and not him. For once, Timur knew the leopard was right. Still, that didn't stop him from stalking to the counter and glaring at Evangeline.

"Have they seen or talked to her?" he demanded.

Evangeline didn't pretend not to know who he was talking about. She shook her head. "Not yet. If they caught a glimpse of her when they were walking through the door before I sent her into the back, they didn't say, and I think they would have."

"Try to keep it that way."

She nodded abruptly, and then the door between the kitchen and the main shop opened and Ashe stepped through. It was easy enough to see why her parents had given her that name. Her hair was a thick mass, colored ash and platinum with a little gold thrown in. He turned his back on her, but watched her in the mirrors he'd installed in strategic places throughout the large room. She didn't take her eyes off him until he was once again settled in his seat. There was some satisfaction in that.

The next hour saw a steady stream of customers. He took the opportunity to walk around, stretching his legs, keeping his muscles loose. He knew they needed a larger security force around Fyodor, but he wanted leopards and there were only so many. Shifters were faster, and if push came to shove, they could call on their animal counterparts to aid them. Every sense was far more acute and a leopard sensed danger and knew when other leopards were close—with one exception: females whose leopards haven't yet emerged.

He sank back into his chair, his gaze fixed on Ashe. She was making drinks and handing out pastries. There was always a smile on her face, but he didn't quite believe it. Each time the little bell tinkled over the entrance, signaling another customer, her eyes jumped to the door. She was worried. Scared. That presented an entirely new set of dangers.

If she was leopard—and he was certain she was—and her leopard hadn't emerged, it would be like his uncles to send her in to assassinate Fyodor. His uncles were reputed to be even crueler and much more vicious than Timur's father had been, and they had sworn to see Fyodor dead for killing their brother. It didn't matter to them that the kill had been justified.

Fyodor had walked in on a bloodbath. Their father had already brutally murdered their mother and had been beating Timur and Gorya almost to death because the two boys had tried to stop him. Fyodor had killed him and then gone after the senior members of his father's lair in order to stop them from killing the women. Now, their uncles were out for their blood. They'd put bounties on their nephews' heads, and now that Fyodor and his brother were no longer hiding behind false identities, the assassins would come to collect. It would make sense to send a female.

Timur studied Ashe as she worked. She was fast. Really fast. Sometimes he thought she would make a mistake, but she never did. Her handoff was smooth, and she moved with a fluid grace that seemed too honed to be entirely natural. As if she were in complete control of every muscle, every movement.

He really wanted to yell at Evangeline. Ashe made no sense at all, but she was strikingly beautiful. The more he looked at her, the more he thought so. She was model material, but then she didn't have the height. Her skin looked so soft he found himself wanting an excuse to touch her, just to see if it was as soft as it appeared.

She had tied her hair in some messy knot that kept falling out and she'd have to redo it. That told him she hadn't worked in the food service industry in a while, otherwise she wouldn't have forgotten to wear her hair back or covered. Instead, she kept pulling her hair up into that silly mess that had him thinking about bedrooms. Or sex. Or both. The bedroom didn't matter nearly as much as the sex.

The fact that her hair was so thick even though it was blond told him the odds that she was leopard were even higher. Leopards tended to have a lot of hair no matter what the color. The way she moved was an indicator as well. She suddenly looked up and stared right into his eyes. She caught up the coffeepot and came out from behind the safety of the counter, stomping right toward him. Not a good move.

"Stop staring at me," she hissed as she poured coffee into his cup. "I mean it. You're making me uncomfortable. I get that you're royally pissed that I'm working here. I get why now that I've seen Evangeline's husband, but I need the work, so please just back off."

He caught her wrist as she turned away. Very gently he

removed the coffeepot from her hand and set it on the table, just out of her reach. The last thing he wanted was for her to dump scalding-hot coffee in his lap, and he had the feeling that not only was she capable of it, she'd been considering it. He kept possession of her wrist. "You're better suited to be a bodyguard than a barista."

"Why do you say that?"

Her voice was strained. She sounded smooth, but he had a good ear and caught the stressed notes she tried to hide.

"The way you move. You're trained to protect yourself, and, I suspect, others."

"Maybe so, but I'm not in that line of work. I'm good at this, and I need the job."

"How do you know Evangeline?"

"Ask her."

"I'm asking you."

She sighed and glanced toward the counter. "I have to work. We're getting busy again. I know you need answers. Maybe after work I could meet you somewhere."

"I work until late. Where do you live?"

She hesitated.

Timur sighed. "I'm going to find out anyway. Just fucking tell me."

"I'm living in Evangeline's house. The one she used to live in."

He was glad she didn't argue about telling him where she lived. Tonight, he'd be with her. Alone. He even liked the idea, which was dangerous for both of them. He let go of her. She immediately rubbed her wrist as if he'd hurt her—or she was trying to get the feel of him off her skin.

The entire time she'd been close, his leopard had been acting like a complete fool, rolling around and making absurd rumbling noises, which, fortunately, no one could hear but him. He ran his finger down her arm to her hand and then indicated the coffeepot. "You forgot something."

Soft color raced up her neck to her face. She caught up

the glass pot without another word and hurried back to the safety of the counter.

His heart settled to normal again and he pressed his hand over his chest while he breathed away the hard-on he hadn't been able to control and, thankfully, she hadn't seen. Or at least he thought she hadn't. She'd kept her gaze studiously away from that portion of his anatomy. It had been far too many years since he'd had problems controlling his body. He had to put it down to his leopard and the fact that a potential mate was in close proximity.

Did she know? Most women didn't have a clue about their leopards, not until the emergence. Evangeline had known. She'd had a relationship with her leopard almost since infancy. If Ashe didn't know, then her leopard would as it rose, making her inclined to flirt with every man coming near her, including Gorya and the two clowns that passed for cops. That didn't sit well with him.

A man came down the sidewalk and passed the shop, barely glancing in. There was nothing about him to catch Timur's interest, but everything in him went still. His leopard snarled and came to attention. He lifted his coffee cup to his lips and kept his eyes on the man dressed in a dark suit. The man paused just at the edge of the window, glanced at his watch and turned around to go back the way he'd come. As he did so, he took a long look through the glass.

Timur cursed inwardly. He should have had that glass tinted more. The shop was busy, and there were a lot of customers, two deep by the counter. He watched as the man hesitated by the door and then went on past it.

"Man in dark suit. You on him? Tall, dark glasses, mirrored."

"Got him, boss," Trey Sinclair said. He was on the roof across the street. Timur had two more of his security patrolling the streets and another on the roof of the bakery. *Right in the crosshairs.*

"What about you, Jeremiah? Can you follow him with-

out getting tagged? This is important. You're not out in the jungle." He added the last because the kid needed to be a little humbler and a lot more vigilant. He was young and eager, and he wanted Timur to take notice of him. Timur didn't like sending the kid into dangerous situations, and he had a gut feeling this man was very dangerous.

"No problem, boss."

"Cocky little son of a bitch, you listen to me. That man will kill you if he spots you. Don't fuck up. You do, there aren't any second chances."

There was a small silence. Jeremiah might be cocky and full of attitude, but he'd learned that when one of them said something, it was worth listening. They'd grown up surrounded by danger, by vicious monsters; he hadn't. They had a built-in radar for danger; Jeremiah was just beginning to hone his skills.

"I hear you, Timur. I'll be doubly careful."

"I'd rather you lose him than get too close."

"I understand."

Timur could only hope the kid did, because even with the target out of sight, every warning bell he had was shrieking at him.

2

"YOU'RE going to wear a hole in that carpet," Gorya pointed out. "Pacing isn't going to bring that kid home faster. Either he's on his way or he isn't."

"I never should have sent that little monster," Timur said, shaking his head and stepping to the window. Habit had him staying to one side and looking from an angle, careful no one could see him looking out. Fyodor's mansion was enormous and the carpets were worth a fortune. Timur was fairly certain he couldn't really wear a hole in the luxurious wool, but he paced often.

"I like the kid. It's just that he's so young and eager to prove himself," he admitted. "I swear, if he gets home safe, I'm calling Drake Donovan and telling him to reassign him to someone else. Let Joshua or Elijah babysit him."

Gorya shook his head. "You're training him, not babysitting him. That's the problem, Timur. You don't see him as a man."

Timur had to agree with that assessment, but he'd be damned if the kid was dying on his watch. He couldn't chance texting the kid because if he was in a compromising situation—like being tortured for information—a call from him would make things worse.

He closed his eyes, seeing a river of blood and hearing the screams of his mother as she was so brutally murdered. He'd seen too many tortures. He'd participated in more than he wanted to admit and he never wanted to see one again. Right now, his body felt like it was watching one, a little in shock, adrenaline racing through his bloodstream so fast he had to work to keep his expression a mask.

He didn't want the kid's death on him. If he killed someone, so be it, but to send out the kid, when he'd known that stranger was no one to fuck with . . . that would haunt him to the end of his days. "Damn it, Gorya. Do we even have a way to track him? Let's put some men in the field."

"It won't do much good when we don't have a direction on him."

He swore and spun around. "I'm telling Fyodor we're putting microchips in our men so we can find them if there's a problem like this. Phones are no good because it's the first thing you get rid of, but no one would suspect a microchip in our bodies."

"He'll be back and he'll be in one piece. Five minutes in his company, if he's pulled this off, and I'll bet you'll want to kill him yourself," Gorya predicted.

Timur couldn't say he was wrong. The kid could make a saint want to choose hell over heaven. "What did you think about the new girl? Ashe Bronte?" He had to change the subject or he was going to start pulling out his hair.

"Wasn't Bronte some kind of writer?"

"That's right. Three sisters. Very famous." Timur wasn't going to risk his cousin giving him a hard time about knowing English literature. He'd had to study in secret so his father wouldn't beat the hell out of him.

"Well, no one can find anything on a woman named Ashe Bronte. I'm sure there is one, but it isn't this one," Gorya said. "She's got to be a plant. I hate saying that because she's got a body on her and—"

"Shut the fuck up." Timur all but snarled it. "I don't need you going on about her body. You think I didn't notice? I'm not blind. Every man for a hundred miles noticed. I'm just saying, she's off-limits, so quit flirting with her."

Gorya stared at him for a little too long. Timur refused to be the first one to look away. He stared him down, allowing his leopard to look through his eyes at the man who was more sibling than cousin.

"You're attracted to her."

"I'm attracted to a lot of women, and as you say, she's got a body on her."

Gorya shook his head slowly. "No, Timur, this is different. This one is the real deal. You're going to go after her. Your cat even may let you have some fun without trying to kill her."

Timur shrugged casually. There was nothing casual about the way he felt when he was close to Ashe Bronte. "That would be the hope. So, forget going in that direction. It wouldn't make me happy."

"She's not going to fall for your charms," Gorya said. "Oh. Wait. You don't really have any."

Timur flung himself into an armchair opposite Gorya. "She didn't much like me saying her name sounded like she'd made it up, and worse, that it sounded like a porn star's."

Gorya stared at him for a long moment and then burst out laughing. Timur had never had a lot to laugh at, so his answering grin was rusty, but it was there.

"Hell of thing to say when you're hoping to nail her," Gorya pointed out. "Just sayin', bro, your tactics need a little work. I think you haven't had much practice lately."

Timur wasn't touching that. He hadn't. There was no

getting around that. Picking up a woman was easy enough for him. Getting her out of her clothes was even easier. Controlling his furious leopard, that was something altogether different, and sometimes nearly impossible. The thought of being with Ashe, clothes off and bodies coming together hard, rough, the way he liked it, without his leopard demanding blood, was worth any price he might have to pay.

"Go to hell," Timur said and flipped his cousin off. He glanced at his watch again, and then looked to the window. If the boy didn't get back soon, he'd have to apprise his brother that there might be a problem, and then he'd move heaven and earth to find the kid and bring him home.

Jeremiah Wheating was a good kid. Overeager to prove himself, but he had all the right instincts. Drake Donovan had brought the boy with him from Borneo and the kid had spent time first as a bodyguard with Jake Bannaconni, a powerful shifter who had a lot of enemies. Jake could take apart a company and put it back together in a matter of a week. That made money, but also enemies.

After Jake, Drake had given Jeremiah other assignments, wanting him to be well-rounded in his experiences. He'd come to Timur's brother, Fyodor. The kid had been assigned to watch over Evangeline at the bakery, a job he hadn't excelled at. In fact, Jeremiah had detested the assignment so much he caused a few problems for Fyodor with his woman—something Timur didn't recommend anyone do.

Jeremiah had proved he was unable to work in the bakery and make it look like he was a barista. Timur sighed. If Jeremiah had worked out, Ashe wouldn't be in the bakery. Her sweet little ass wouldn't be parked in Evangeline's house. Evangeline had moved in with Fyodor at the main estate, but she had refused to give up her house. She'd bought it on her own, fixed it up and didn't want to part with it. Who knew she was going to use it to harbor a potential threat?

Timur had his people working to uncover Ashe's real identity, but a part of him didn't want to know if she was an enemy. If she was, he would be the one to have to take care of her, and that meant permanently. He pressed two fingers to his eyes. Hard. Wishing he was a better man. Wishing he'd at least had the chance to be a better man. He'd been born into violence and he knew damn well he was going to go out the same way.

"You all right?" Gorya asked with real concern.

Timur looked up and met his eyes. Gorya had been more of a brother to him than even Fyodor. They'd shared a terrible childhood and, thanks to Fyodor, survived it, but nothing, no amount of time, could erase those brutal, ugly memories for either of them. He nodded slowly. He wouldn't lie to Gorya. His cousin was the one person who would always get the truth no matter what. "She's stirring up things in me better left alone."

Like the need to have her under him. Like the need for those beautiful eyes to plead with him for release, for whatever he was willing to give her. Mostly, it was the worry that she might have to die and he would be the one to pull the trigger. If she was the enemy, he wasn't going to allow interrogation. She would die quick and clean and never see it coming. He could at least give her that much.

"You think they sent her, don't you?" Gorya asked. His voice was very soft, very quiet, no hint of the compassion Timur saw in his eyes.

Timur sighed again and gave another slow nod. "What other explanation is there? She's lying about her name. She turns up out of nowhere and convinces Evangeline to hire her without even telling any of us. She's that good. That persuasive. She even talks her way into Evangeline's house. Did you watch the way she moved? She's no barista, Gorya, as good as she is at making drinks. She isn't new at the job, but I'm not buying her act."

"Do you think Lazar sent her?" Gorya named their uncle. The name had come out in a hated, fearful whisper.

Timur shrugged. "We know he's going to be coming at us. This may be his opening move. We're strong and he knows it. He'd be smart to send a female assassin. We'd be looking for a male, but a female just going into the Han Vol Dan? Her heat would have every male leopard for miles going nuts. It would be easy enough, once she gets all of us into a frenzy, to kill Fyodor. Or us. He'll want our blood too."

"But especially Mitya's," Gorya said.

Timur had to agree. Of all of them living in that nightmare world, Mitya had suffered even more so than their other cousin, Sevastyan. It had been so bad that at times even Timur's father had risked Lazar's and his brother Rolan's wrath and protested the treatment of his nephews. That was saying something.

"He'll try to kill all of us. Even our women. Evangeline needs protection around the clock, especially now that this female has shown up and somehow managed to get in good with her. I'll be talking with Ashe Bronte this evening." He glanced again at his watch, frowned and then shook his head. "This is taking too long. Try him, Gorya."

"He would check in if he could," Gorya said. "Are you certain you want me to do this?"

Timur nodded, jumped to his feet again and began pacing. He had so much restless energy inside him he felt like he might explode if he didn't move. It was her fault. Ashe. He'd been resigned to his life. He would protect his brother and Evangeline, but he wouldn't be alive. There would be nothing for him. His sins were too great and he'd done little to redeem himself. He'd been born a violent criminal and he'd lived his entire life as one.

"He answered my text. He's alive, Timur." Gorya poured relief into his voice.

Timur's heart jumped and he found himself rubbing his chest. The thuds were getting stronger. The panic attacks closer. He couldn't afford either. He didn't want to show his elation because his cousin already knew how anxious he'd been.

"About damn time," he groused. "I'm going to ground that kid."

"Timur," Gorya cautioned. "Don't break him the way we were broken. We could never do anything right, although we both know that was an excuse to beat the holy hell out of us. Your father enjoyed making us feel like shit. Just be careful of following his patterns. I have to fight it every day, and I imagine you do as well."

Timur swung around, ready to do battle with Gorya. Every muscle in his body, every single cell, wanted to protest his words. He wanted combat, ripping and tearing at flesh, pounding it with his fists, anything to escape the thought that he could be anything like his father—and yet, there was the proof. He not only wanted those things; he needed them.

He stared at his cousin for a long time, seeing his father standing there, waiting for his son to fuck up so he could beat him. One wrong word. The lack of a word. One wrong move, or lack of one. It wouldn't matter, the pounding would start.

Eventually Timur liked those encounters because he could fight back. He knew his father would beat him within an inch of his life, but every punch he got in, he made count. He needed the satisfaction of knowing he'd managed to hurt his father with those blows. Every one of them.

He doubled his fists and stared down at them. "I liked hitting him," he admitted. Finally. Aloud. He'd said it and he'd meant it. "Sometimes I hated him so much that I would start a fight just so he would come at me. I knew he'd kick my ass, but I could hit him. I began counting how many good blows I got in. How hard I hit. I always used the maximum force possible. If I was as strong then as I am now, I would have broken his bones." There was satisfaction in knowing that. He would have liked to break his father's bones.

"I always wondered why you taunted him while I cowered in the corner. I hated those nights when he went after you."

Timur grinned at him, a show of teeth more than a smile. "You never cowered in the corner. The moment he laid his fists on me, you came out swinging."

Gorya shrugged, a casual roll of his shoulders. "That never lasted long. I was on the ground with my head ringing."

"It gave me the opportunity to punch him. I used that bastard as my punching bag. I actually pretended I was training."

"You still do. Train, I mean. Every day."

"We all do, you included. We know what's coming and we know the war is going to be gruesome. You don't like letting your leopard free, but that's the reason we have to, Gorya. You say I can't be like my father, but by holding your leopard at bay every second, we both are exactly like him. And like your father. And Lazar. Our leopards need freedom and, yes, the fighting as well. We have to train them until their skills are every bit as good as our own."

Gorya shook his head, sadness in every line of his face. His handsome features revealed in that rare moment the torment Timur felt. "My leopard is a killer, Timur. I'm afraid if I let him loose, he will kill everyone before I can take back control. Mitya has this same concern. I work at getting stronger, more disciplined, so that my leopard will have no choice but to obey me. I am not there yet. He's that strong."

Timur swore and turned back to the window. Gorya was

the most easygoing, good-natured one of them. He laughed more readily and would often calm Timur or Fyodor when they were angry with each other. He was the peacemaker, when they were the ones ready to fight at the drop of a hat. Yet now, seeing his cousin's stark, raw emotion, he knew Gorya fought, every single day, the same demons he did.

"There is no end to this, is there?" he asked.

"I don't know," Gorya answered honestly. "Fyodor and Evangeline provided a small window of hope for me. I thought if he could find a woman who would take him as he was, then perhaps I could do so as well."

"Evangeline." Timur breathed her name with reverence. "I thought her the enemy, that she would get Fyodor killed. Sometimes, because she lives her life so filled with joy and happiness, I think she still may get him killed. She refuses to see the ugliness in the world. She lived with her own set of demons as a child, and yet to see her now, you would never know anything ugly ever touched her."

"I don't like having only a couple of men watching her. And she insists they take breaks and go walk around outside. She's a bossy little thing," Gorya said.

Timur swung around, frowning. "They take breaks and walk around outside?" His gut began to churn when he saw the truth on Gorya's face. "Damn that woman. I'm going to talk to Fyodor. At least he's taking his security more seriously. You should have told me immediately."

Gorya nodded. "I just found out today and was waiting for the right moment. I knew this new woman was a big worry."

"Having Evangeline's guards leave her alone with Ashe when we don't know a damned thing about her is more worrisome."

Gorya again nodded his agreement. "You're right."

Timur glanced at his watch. "How far out is Jeremiah? Did he give you a time?"

Gorya consulted his phone and began texting. While his

cousin asked the more pertinent questions of the kid, Timur made good use of his phone, texting two of the shifter guards, Kyanite Boston and Rodion Galerkin. Rodion had followed Timur and Gorya from the lair after Fyodor had killed all the males. They all knew their uncles would retaliate. Rodion and Kyanite had helped burn the bodies before they'd left and then come to the United States in the hopes of disappearing. Like Timur and Gorya, there was very little they knew how to do, other than to kill.

Timur trusted both men implicitly—well, as much as he trusted anyone who wasn't part of his family. He pretty much considered both men in that category. He wanted them closer to home. They traveled with the team covering Fyodor, but he needed shifters covering Evangeline as well. The two men he'd had on her weren't from his home lairs.

He and the other shifters known to him had been born in the Primorye region of southeast Russia. There, the Amur leopard still had a valiant foothold, but was close to extinction. There was a reason for that. The lairs were made up of the Amur leopards, and instead of finding the women who could complete them, they made certain they didn't in order to show their loyalty to the *bratya*.

"Nothing like killing a mother in front of her sons to make men out of them, right, Gorya?" Timur whispered bitterly. He would never get over that nightmare. It would never stop moving through his mind, day or night. He didn't know how many times he'd replayed that gruesome scene in his head. His father's cruel smile as he'd killed her, making her suffer as much as possible, all the while telling Timur and Gorya they would enjoy this if they let themselves. He had tried to call their leopards out to feast on her blood.

Gorya leapt out of his chair and punched at the wall. Sheetrock and paint cracked beneath the powerful blow. "Stop. You have to stop thinking about it."

"You tell me how I'm supposed to do that," Timur said.

Before Gorya could answer, the heavy oak door swung open and Jeremiah hurried in. He had the collar of his coat pulled up as high as possible against the cold. A wind blew in with him, cooling the overheated room. Timur didn't want the door to close. The taste of his mother's blood was clinging to his mouth and staining his chest. The scent was in his nose and the horrendous sound of her screams in his ears.

He turned so neither man could see his face. Jeremiah shut the door hard enough that it was jarring. He bit down on his tongue, refusing to give in to the temptation to yell at the kid. Gorya was right. He didn't want to be anything like his father, and his father would never have waited to hear what he had to say.

"I followed him all the way into the city, Timur. It wasn't easy either. He spent a lot of time backtracking. I thought he might have made me at one point, but I was wrong."

Timur watched Jeremiah remove his coat and, with a small shiver, stomp over to the fireplace. He held out his hands to the warmth. He remained silent. Waiting. There wasn't going to be a lecture on safety, or any asking of questions such as *"Are you certain he wasn't onto you?"* He was going to be reasonable . . .

"You sure you weren't followed back here?" Gorya demanded. "Did you check?"

"Of course, I checked," Jeremiah defended, a note of belligerence creeping into his voice.

Timur sighed and gave a slight headshake toward Gorya, indicating to his cousin to back off. First, he'd given Timur a lecture about jumping the gun and sounding like his father, and then he'd done it himself.

"Give me whatever info you managed to collect on this man," Timur intervened.

Jeremiah gave Gorya another glare and then hurried with his report, the words stumbling over one another as he attempted to talk fast. "His name is Apostol Delov."

Timur's heart sank. His breath caught in his throat.

"The messenger," Timur and Gorya said simultaneously. They exchanged a long look.

Apostol Delov was a name taken by men—shifters—trained to track and find whomever Lazar pointed them toward. They found their prey and then called in the killers. They were men well trained in the art of survival. Timur thought of them as very cunning weasels.

Jeremiah rubbed his hands together. "Whatever he is, he's a scary son of a bitch. I watched him through the window. He stripped off his clothes and began working out. Doing forms made up of karate moves. He was smooth and fast, and he had muscles in places I'm pretty sure you're not supposed to have them."

"What else did you find out?"

"I snooped through his garbage can and his mailbox. No mail other than a bill for his electricity, which I brought back with me." He tossed it on the table. "That's where I got his name. I hung around, up on the roof of one of the houses across the street. His home backs up to a large field that runs into a park. It's just a street over from a little cul-de-sac and—"

"Wait. Wait. Wait." Timur spun around to stand directly in front of Gorya. "Evangeline's house. That's on a little cul-de-sac. What's the address, Jeremiah?" He snapped his fingers. "The address. Have you ever been to Evangeline's house?"

"Well, yeah, but Evangeline lives here now. Her house is empty," Jeremiah said.

The door opened, allowing the cold in, and Timur stepped into the draft. He liked the cold. He'd been born and raised in it. Jeremiah was from the humidity of the rain forest. He moved closer to the fire.

Kyanite and Rodion came in. Neither wore a coat, a testament to the fact that they preferred the colder weather as well. "Got your message, boss," Kyanite said, unnecessarily since they had come in answer to his summons.

"Pull up a map. Jeremiah, give us that address."

"He's staying at a house at 1222 West Elm."

"The house Evangeline owns is 320 Cherry Blossom," Timur said. "How close are those two streets?"

"Right on top of each other." Rodion had his phone out and showed the map. "One street over. You want to tell us who we're going to kill?"

That was always going to be the first solution they thought of. Timur detested that it had been his first thought as well. "We're not killing anyone yet. A man showed up outside of the bakery. I just didn't like the look of him and had Jeremiah follow him. He found a bill with a name on it. Apostol Delov."

The two men exchanged a long look. "The messenger," Kyanite said. "He's come."

"He works for Lazar." Timur gave Jeremiah an explanation about shifters taking that particular name. "Lazar always liked to send a messenger first, before he showed up. The fact that a messenger turned up when we have a new employee at the bakery, and that employee lives in Evangeline's old home, cannot possibly be a coincidence."

He hated that even more than the fact that he thought killing was a solution. He didn't want Ashe to be involved in any way. "Did she have any kind of accent that you heard, Gorya?"

Gorya shook his head. "Southern maybe. I didn't hear Russian, but then we all learned not to speak with accents."

"We can get it out of her if she's here because of Lazar," Rodion stated.

Timur's leopard went insane. He felt the itch running over his skin. His muscles contorted. The need to kill was strong, the leopard pushing for supremacy, the need to shed blood. Timur fought him back, just as determined to stop him. *These men are with us. Our friends. Our allies.* He tried to calm the raging beast.

The leopard's mind was frenzied chaos, so much so that

Timur couldn't break through to soothe him. He had to settle for pure brute strength and discipline to keep the leopard from forcing him to shift. Taking several deep breaths to help him fight off the cat, he faced the others. All of them had contended with a fighting leopard at one time or another, so they waited patiently, depending on him to keep the animal under control.

Part of the ability to control a furious, bad-tempered cat thirsting for blood was knowing one's companions in jeopardy believed you could. Timur settled the leopard with harsh skill and then looked straight at Rodion, letting him see that the fierce anger was all from the cat.

"I'll handle the woman. No one else will be going anywhere near her." Even as he stated it, he knew he meant it. He also knew it was a very bad idea for him to get personal about Ashe Bronte. He was going to blow it if he wasn't careful. One never got involved with or allowed feelings for a potential hit.

More and more, it looked as if Ashe was their enemy. He was responsible for the lives of his brother and Evangeline. He loved them both. He owed Fyodor. He wasn't throwing that all away for a woman he'd only just laid eyes on. Still, if she was going to die, she wasn't going to be tortured first for information.

"I want eyes on the messenger. Stay well back. No one take any chances. Jeremiah, you earned yourself a spot on the team. Kyanite and Rodion, I want you on the bakery. I don't care what Evangeline says or how she bribes you. I don't care if Fyodor gives you a direct order, you aren't going to fuck up and leave them even for a few minutes. If anything happens to either one of them, I will hold you personally responsible. I'm giving the job to the two of you because I trust you."

"Consider it done," Kyanite said.

Jeremiah frowned. "Wait a minute. The bakery was my old job. I know everything about it. I know the rooftops and alleyways. I know customers. I'm the best man for that job."

"You wanted out of it," Timur reminded him. He detested being questioned, and no other man under his command would be stupid enough to do so. "You wanted off Evangeline and the bakery because it wasn't exciting enough for you. You don't get to jump back and forth as it suits you. You don't keep your mouth closed, you'll be pulling kitchen duty instead of being part of the team watching the messenger."

Jeremiah's mouth closed. He even pressed his lips tightly together, which told Timur the kid knew he'd had his share of passes.

"Tell us what else, if anything, you found."

Jeremiah nodded. "When his leopard went for a run, I went through the garbage. There was pretty much nothing, but I did find partially burned papers. There wasn't a message I could read, but the fact that he'd taken the time to burn them in the first place bothered me. There were several pieces of paper that looked like correspondence."

Timur's heart began to pound. At last. Real evidence. "Did you think to bring those papers, burned or not?"

Jeremiah nodded. "Yeah, I thought you might like to see them."

Timur had always been curious. He liked to study and he liked chemicals. He also liked experimenting. He knew most people wrote on paper with fountain pens or ballpoint pens, sometimes gel pens. The charring of the paper hid the message from a white light illumination, but the original content was still there.

"I brought it with me," Jeremiah reiterated.

Timur let him see that he was pleased. "Nice, Jeremiah. Burned paper crumbles easily. Put it carefully on my desk in the other room."

Jeremiah nodded. "I tried reading it, but he made certain to burn the contents."

"We may still be able to recover something if the part with the message is still intact." He couldn't imagine being so lucky. Having the correspondence was a stroke of luck that couldn't be foreseen by either party. The messenger had no way of knowing Timur had spotted him. It had been instinct alone. Nothing had given the big man away.

"When are you going to talk to this woman?" Kyanite asked. "Do you at least want company so that if the messenger comes snooping around, we can warn you?"

Timur thought that over. He wanted to be alone with Ashe to give her a chance to come clean with him. It was possible Lazar was holding her family hostage unless she did as he said. Lazar would kill them anyway, but she wouldn't know that. He almost hoped it was something like that. If she came clean, he would spare her. He'd try to turn her to their side and offer her every opportunity to make amends for attempting to spy on them or even possibly trying to assassinate Fyodor or Evangeline.

He had made certain Fyodor knew to question Evangeline about her relationship, if any, with the woman. They looked as if they had worked together at some point, but if so, it was long before Evangeline had become Fyodor's wife. That made no sense. It would be too big of a leap to think Lazar knew Evangeline and Fyodor would meet and fall for each other.

He wanted to know everything there was to know about Evangeline's relationship with Ashe before he questioned the woman. Her life hung in the balance and he wanted to give her every opportunity he could to tell him why she was there.

He glanced at his watch for the millionth time that evening. It was late. Very late. The hours had slipped away while he plotted to send his men on a raid of a territory that belonged to a crime boss, Ulisse Mancini. He'd been running his counterfeit money with Emilio Bassini's weapons. They wanted to keep Emilio's business just steady, not thriving, and Ulisse was becoming such a problem that bosses in other states were beginning to worry about his greed.

Drake Donovan had begun to suspect Ulisse was the

man behind a large human trafficking ring and that he was in partnership with Lazar Amurov. If Ulisse had tied himself to Lazar, eventually he would be their biggest enemy. Timur needed to find out one way or the other. Fyodor and Mitya would both be threatened if that happened.

Timur had to take the plan to Fyodor for his approval before they could implement it, and he also wanted to know what Evangeline had told her husband. He left the others to go down the hall separating their quarters from the main house. It was huge. Fyodor had been given the estate by Siena Arnotto after her marriage. She'd given him not only the estate, but all of her grandfather's businesses other than the winery and vineyards, which she ran herself.

The house was an amazing mansion. Timur had seen some beautiful homes, but nothing he'd seen compared with the one deeded to his brother. It was two stories and had so many rooms, Timur thought his brother had better start filling it with children soon or it would start echoing in protest. The main room was enormous with a staircase that wound dramatically up to the second floor. Wood gleamed and banks of windows let in the sun or the starlit night, but also provided spectacular views.

He found Fyodor in his office, waiting. He was sipping scotch and had already poured a small amount into a crystal glass for his brother. "Everything all right? Jeremiah back?" He indicated the chair across from his wide desk.

Timur sank into the leather. "He's back. He followed the man I told you about, the one who gave me such a bad vibe." He picked up the glass and swirled the amber-colored liquid gently. "His name is Apostol Delov."

Fyodor closed his eyes and rested the crystal glass against his forehead for a moment. "So, Lazar finally found us."

"It appears that way." Timur took a sip of the scotch and felt the burn all the way down. He needed that. So, apparently, did his leopard. The cat stretched languidly. "You and I both know, no matter how much Evangeline protests,

Ashe's appearance at the same time is damning. Not only that, Fyodor, but the messenger is in a house one street over from Evangeline's house."

Fyodor's eyes sharpened. "Any idea when he rented it?"

Timur hadn't thought of that. "At least a month ago according to the electric bill Jeremiah brought back with him. That would leave Ashe off the hook." Unless . . . "Shit, if the messenger's job was to locate us and then she was brought in, she could be the assassin. When did she approach Evangeline?"

"Just yesterday." Fyodor shook his head. "I don't want this for her. Evangeline doesn't have the temperament to live like we do. Other women, maybe, but she only sees good in people and I don't want her to lose that. Damn it, Timur . . ."

"I'll do what I can to keep the damage to a minimum, but her safety as well as yours has to come first. You know that."

Fyodor nodded. "I talked to her about security, and this time I was tough on her. I even pointed out she could get someone killed. She listened and she's very sorry for putting either of us in this position. She also maintains that Ashe would never be here to hurt either of us."

"How can she know that?"

Fyodor shrugged. "I'm just relating to you what she told me. She also doesn't believe Ashe is leopard. She saw no sign of it in their previous relationship, and her cat isn't moody, so far, around Ashe. I wasn't near the woman at all, so I'm no help in that department. I walked through to my office and kept the door closed. I didn't want your attention divided by having to guard us both."

"Which I am very grateful for," Timur admitted. "It gave me time to study Ashe. I believe she *is* leopard. She's a little bit too fluid, too fast. She moves well, and there wasn't a single time when the two women were working that they accidentally bumped into each other behind that counter.

There was a time, right around four o'clock, when a large crowd came in and both were moving fast to take orders and filling them. Not one bump or spill."

"It's possible she is exactly what Evangeline thinks she is," Fyodor speculated.

Timur knew his brother wanted to protect his wife from what they were. From the things they had to do. From their past. All of it. He wanted the same thing for her. Evangeline was a good woman and he thought of her as a sister. The last thing he wanted to do was kill a friend of hers. Or tell her that friend had come to kill her just because of who she'd married.

"It's possible, Fyodor," he conceded, "but not probable. Who is she to Evangeline?" He wanted the bottom line. He needed to know what he was most likely going to have to do before he went to that house and confronted her.

"She says they met briefly a long time ago. Evangeline had gone up into the mountains and there was a coffee shop. She'd dreamt of owning a bakery and wanted experience. She also needed a job. She met Ashe while out hiking and Ashe told her the shop needed help, put in a good word for her and she was hired. That's where she got her experience as a barista."

"Was her name Ashe Bronte?"

Fyodor shook his head. "It was Ashe Mostafa. She told Evangeline she was in trouble and needed a place to stay and make some money. Ashe claimed she saw the articles about our marriage and speculation on whether or not Evangeline knew the truth about her husband." He rolled his eyes. "If Evangeline can read or listen to the news, she knows what everyone else knows."

"She knows the truth and she's accepted it, Fyodor. We're all in this together. The hell with others who make judgments without knowing."

"In any case, Ashe claims she saw the articles and came here hoping Evangeline would help her."

Timur downed the last of the scotch. "What else?"

"Evangeline lent her the house and told her she could work in the shop. She asked me to tell you that she needs this favor from us, to just back off and accept Ashe is no threat."

Timur raised an eyebrow at his brother.

Fyodor shook his head. "I didn't answer her. I've always told her the truth if she asks me questions. Make this quick, Timur. Kill her or clear her. But do it fast. Evangeline is going to champion this woman."

"Damn it." Timur heaved a sigh. He didn't want to hurt Evangeline any more than he wanted to kill Ashe.

"Evangeline was alone in the world for a long time. She climbed out of the mud—or the swamp might be a better way of putting it." Fyodor shook his head. "She doesn't have a lot of friends, and this woman means something to her. But if Ashe is setting Evangeline up, if she plans to hurt her in any way, I want it stopped. You understand me?"

Of course, he understood. Timur sipped the scotch. Preying on his sister-in-law was a very stupid thing to do. Targeting her was worse. He changed the subject and told his brother the plan to hit Ulisse's shipment in a couple of nights. His brother was highly intelligent and always tweaked the plans and made them much better. Timur wanted his input.

3

TIMUR had always liked Evangeline's house. It was small and comfortable, but very spacious. The front door opened into a small foyer, but that opened right into the living room, which was quite large, with high ceilings. That room went into a dining room and the kitchen. There weren't doors separating the spaces and one could talk back and forth from any room.

All the lights were out in the house and the heavier drapes were pulled, something Evangeline rarely did. She liked the night to come in through her windows. Fyodor had had to teach her that if she had lights on, people could see in when she couldn't see out. Drapes or no drapes, Timur could see in the dark. He had only to call on his leopard's vision.

The locks were good ones—and there were a lot of them. Too bad for the occupant that he had the keys. Even if he hadn't, he would have been able to get in. He was good at picking locks. More, he could take apart alarms if needed. His leopard's acute hearing allowed him to hear the faint hum some alarms gave off, warning him of their presence. Of course, he knew the code for Evangeline's alarm system.

Evangeline fit with them. She might be too compassionate, and she might think the best of everyone, but she fit. Timur knew she would back them with a ferocious fury if needed. There had to be something about this woman—beyond their brief friendship—that had her believing in her innocence. He hoped he believed just as strongly. He wanted that more than he'd wanted anything in a long time—for Ashe Bronte to be innocent.

The bedroom door was slightly ajar, and he opened it cautiously with one hand, staying clear just in case she was awake and had a weapon. The moment he touched the door and it moved inward, the overpowering scent in the room hit him and his leopard went wild. *Wild.* Insane. Crazy. He nearly fell to the floor as his body rippled and contorted, the cat desperate to claw his way out and take over their shared form.

Cursing, he kept a grip on the feral, snarling cat. His leopard was desperate, and he'd never felt the animal like that before. It was a new, puzzling experience and he took the time to breathe deeply and stay in control. He pressed his forehead to the wall and soothed his cat.

I get it. I understand. But we do things right. You don't want to blow this.

He didn't want to blow it. Ashe Bronte was theirs. She belonged to them. She definitely was leopard, and her emergence was very close, going by the powerful pheromones heavy in the air in the bedroom. Forcing the cat back, he once more went to the door, filling the frame. She writhed on the bed, her body restless and hot. She'd flung the covers off and was twisting first one way and then the other, a low moan escaping.

He resisted the need to moan as well. She was sexy without trying to be, and his body reacted. She wore a lacy racerback tank and some little lacy shorts, leaving her legs bare. Her hair was tamed by a thick braid, although with all her twisting and turning, hair was escaping. That was sexy as well.

She flipped onto her stomach with another soft moan. Timur was on her before he could think. Need consumed him. His leopard's fierce hunger for her. There was no other word for it. His cat had been starved, deprived, driven only by the need for blood, violence and killing. Now, something else took the place of that conditioned fury. Some*one* else. Ashe Bronte. And God help them both if she had come there to kill his brother.

He felt her stiffen the moment he stretched out on the bed, his body over top of hers, pinning her down. He reached under her pillow and withdrew the gun she had there. Her hand went to the left, and he caught her wrist as she found the knife she'd hidden.

"Don't. You know who I am and why I'm here. I'm not going to hurt you. Just breathe. This has to be done and then we can talk."

She turned her head to the side to look at him, her body relaxing when she recognized him fully. He kept his hand moving soothingly on her back, long caresses, careful not to touch her anywhere that might make her think he was going to harm her in any way.

"What has to be done?"

"Do you feel her?" He asked the question softly, his lips against her ear—the little shell of an ear he found fascinating and sexy. Who knew an ear could be either?

He had her top pushed off her back, up around her neck, and he took advantage, kissing his way up her spine to her right shoulder.

Silence met his question, but he hadn't expected her to admit she felt a living being inside of her. He wouldn't have in her place, but he knew she did. She'd become aware of her leopard.

"Does she talk to you? Does she feel him close?"

His teeth scraped back and forth over her shoulder. His leopard was rising. Moving through him triumphantly. He let it happen, let the leopard have his form. Fur burst through his skin and slid seductively over her. Soft. Caressing. The leopard licked her shoulder and then bit down and held her still, waiting. Just waiting.

Timur's heart beat as fast and as savagely as his leopard's. The cat held Ashe in place, keeping her still while they all waited. His leopard was patient, and that surprised him. Ashe had gone very still, her fists clenched tightly on the mattress, her eyes squeezed shut and her breath hitching. Her heart had gone crazy and it echoed through his mind. He should have warned her, assured her all was going to be fine, that his cat would never harm her. She was probably the only person in the world safe from his leopard.

Then he felt her. Sleek. Sexy. Purring. She rose in Ashe, moving up to meet his big male. The two leopards touched and then she was gone. Just like that, she'd accepted his cat's claim on her. The male slowly withdrew his teeth, licked at the spot several times and then subsided, allowing Timur to take his place.

He hadn't wholly shifted, only his head and shoulders, so the cat disappeared fast. She still refused to open her eyes, and he found himself smiling as he kissed the bite marks before rolling off and striding into the master bath. He knew where the first aid kit was. Evangeline was very predictable and had first aid kits in every bathroom.

Ashe sat up in the middle of the bed, legs pulled in, tailor fashion. Her gaze jumped to his face the moment he returned to the bedroom.

"What was that?" she demanded. "What did you do to me?"

He shrugged and opened the case. "That was all my cat, not me. You felt her. She accepted him."

She was quiet as he cleansed the wound with antiseptic and then put an antibacterial cream over the bite marks.

"Tell me your real name."

"I did tell you. It's Ashe Bronte."

Leopards could hear lies—most of the time. It was rare that they were fooled, and his leopard had never failed to hear a lie. She seemed to be telling the truth, but he already knew Bronte wasn't her last name.

"I accept that your name could be Ashe Bronte, but is Bronte your surname?" Because there was no record of Ashe Bronte that they could find that would fit with the woman sitting so still on the bed.

"No, but that isn't your business."

He let his breath out slowly. Again, that was the truth. Well, the fact that her last name wasn't Bronte. "Fyodor's security is my business. I take it very seriously, Ashe. I have to know everything there is to know about the people coming into his life."

"I'm not a threat to your brother. How could I be? What could I possibly do to him?"

Those amber eyes of hers fairly snapped and crackled with shocking intensity. Her leopard stared out at him and she was as furious as her human counterpart. That made the dominant in him flare to life faster than anything else could have. His leopard leapt toward the surface, showing himself through Timur's eyes. The two leopards stared at each other, unblinking.

"Stop." Ashe pressed her fingers to her eyes, covering them for a moment. When she took her hand away, the female leopard was gone. "I don't understand what's happening and you clearly do. Would you mind if we moved this inquisition to the living room?"

"Yes. You stay right where you are."

The living room was all glass. Anyone could see in if those drapes were open. He had the feeling she planned to do just that. In the bedroom, she was trapped. She was also more vulnerable. Both of them knew it. He had the psychological advantage as long as she sat on the bed dressed in her skimpy, lacy pajamas and nothing else. That made him a dick as a man, but a very good bodyguard for his brother.

Her chin went up. "My last name is Mostafa. I'm fairly certain that last name was made up, but I could be wrong. My parents were survivalists living up in the mountains. They didn't believe in walls. They lived free, off the grid, and raised me to do the same. I know they had my birth recorded because I do have a legitimate Social Security number. I try to stay off the grid as much as possible, but I got into some trouble and had to find a place to work and live under the radar. I read about Evangeline getting married to a man named Alonzo Massi, and I knew immediately I could go to her. I knew she wouldn't turn me away. Evangeline is . . . amazing. I know her husband changed his name, or took back his original one, but he has nothing to do with why I came. It's not like I have many friends."

Timur listened carefully for one note of deceit. He heard annoyance, anger that she had to give him anything at all on her, and hope that he would believe her. He didn't hear deceit . . . but . . . there was something, one note or two off. There were lies mixed with the truth. It was entirely possible a leopard couple had lived off the grid all their lives. Other than . . .

Pay attention, Temnyy, Timur said to his leopard. *Is she lying about the last name?*

No.

But she is lying.

She knows that her surname is correct.

His leopard was bored, but paying attention. This had to do with his mate's keeper. He was going to make certain she didn't give Timur any reason to kill her. Timur decided not to call her on whatever the deception had been for now, but the fact that she'd made one meant she might skate a lie alongside the truth another time.

"What happened to your parents?"

For a moment grief washed across her features. It was new. Close. They had died recently. She pulled back from the memory and shrugged, trying for casual. "Both are deceased."

He had known that just from an earlier conversation, but she hadn't told him exactly how they'd died. She was forcing him to drag the information from her. "How did they die?"

"Is that pertinent?"

That chin of hers was going to get her in trouble. He felt a throb start in the vicinity of his cock. He'd been doing a good job of keeping his body under control, but she brought out the worst in him.

"Anything I ask is pertinent, Ashe. You want to stay, you get cleared by me."

She was silent for a long time—long enough to make him worry, although he didn't allow that to show on his face. He'd grown up in a household where it was very necessary to hide all emotion, and it had become second nature.

"They were murdered, and I don't want to talk about it."

He heard the pain in her voice. He wanted to pull her into his arms and comfort her, but if he made a mistake and let his own needs, or any compassion, keep him from doing his job and he lost Fyodor or Evangeline, he wouldn't be able to live with himself.

"Ashe, we're going to talk about anything I say is needed. You arrived at a very bad time. It just happens to coincide with the arrival of an old enemy of the family. That enemy is out for blood. I can't take the chance that you have anything to do with him. Do you? This is your one opportunity to tell me everything. You get *one*. So talk to me now."

She rubbed her palms on her thighs, her eyes on his. She was mesmerizing. She could see him, the killer in him, and she hadn't flinched. She was utterly still with the exception of her hands moving up and down her thighs, calling his attention to her bare skin. That wasn't a good idea for either of them.

Ashe was a truly stunning woman. It wasn't just her physical body—and that was gorgeous—it was the way she held herself. The way she looked him straight in the eye. She couldn't cover fear, because he was leopard and could smell it, but she didn't flinch away. She didn't retreat. She sat very straight and looked at him. There was no panic, which meant she was thinking all the time. She held herself carefully, the daughter of survivalists, not giving anything away.

"I don't know what you want me to say. I would never harm Evangeline or Fyodor. Why would I? They've never done anything to me. I know he's reputed to be a crime boss, that he supposedly took over Arnotto's territory. I was never convinced that Antonio Arnotto was involved in the mafia. He was never convicted, and I believe he was investigated several times."

"How would you know that?"

She rolled her eyes, and his cock jerked. She made him want to yank her into his arms and kiss the sass out of her.

"I read. When you're alone a lot, you read. I happen to be fascinated by crime stories." Color tinged her face. "I write sometimes. You know. Stories. I like to write and I do research, studying crime and criminals. Arnotto was in the news a lot. More recently, his granddaughter, Siena, was in the news. I know Alonzo Massi took over the territory, but . . ." She trailed off, a little confused by the name change. She knew Alonzo's name had been changed.

"Fyodor Amurov and Alonzo Massi are the same person. Fyodor only recently went back to his name."

They were ready for their uncles to come after them. Coming out in the open was better than letting them think they were afraid of them. Lazar and Rolan would love nothing more than to think their nephews were cowering far from their homeland, living in fear of their retaliation. Fyodor had thrown down the gauntlet by taking back his name.

"Maybe I thought by coming here, I'd be safe, and I'd learn more and be able to write better. I don't know, I just felt it was the right thing to do. I can leave, Timur. I don't want Evangeline to think I came here to hurt her or her husband."

His heart clenched hard in his chest. She wasn't leaving. It was too late for that. His leopard had claimed her. He ignored her offer, but he also heard the mixture of lie with truth. It was difficult to hear, but something about her tone made him uneasy. "Tell me about your parents' murders. Who did it? Were they caught?"

She shook her head. Her fingers left her bare thigh and stroked her throat. He could see she wasn't aware of that defensive gesture, nor did she realize her hand trembled. The tip of her tongue moistened her full lower lip, ran all along the curve and disappeared. "I should have been there. I wasn't there, but I should have been."

He remained silent, but now she was rocking herself very gently. It took everything he had not to pull her into his arms. He understood why Evangeline had fallen under her spell. Ashe not only appeared innocent of any crime, she was compelling. Mesmerizing. She had a magnetism about her that pulled anyone near her right into her. He felt her emotions as if they were his own. Telling her she would have been killed along with her parents wasn't going to change how she felt.

"We weren't living together. My parents were very . . . private. I don't know the right way to put it. It was the two of them. They loved me, but they liked to be alone together. Maybe it was from living so long apart from the world. In any case, they encouraged me to go out on my own when I turned eighteen. I didn't go very far, but I loved having freedom. I checked in with them every week or so, or they found me and did the same. We were like that for a couple of years."

"So, you lived close to them. In a town?"

She nodded. "I got a job in a little café similar to the Small Sweet Shoppe, although it was more coffee than pastries. Hence my barista skills. That was where Evangeline and I worked together. Sometimes my shifts didn't give me much time off, and I was a little surprised my parents didn't come to see me after two weeks. We had never gone that long. The first two days I had off in a row, I went up to their cabin."

She dropped her hand, and he saw her swallow hard. Her small teeth bit into her lip and she shook her head. "They were in pieces. Tortured, it looked like. Whoever did it was sadistic. I could barely tell who they were."

She dropped her gaze from his, but not before he saw the sheen of tears. That hurt. An actual pain. He couldn't stop himself. He pulled her right into his arms and held her against him. She held herself stiff. Resistant. He almost released her but then her body melted into his. Her skin was hot, probably from the bout with her leopard's heat she'd wrestled with in her sleep.

She smelled good. Her hair. Her skin. He resisted tasting her and found he was a little resentful that his leopard had. He pulled her onto his lap and rocked her gently, trying to give her comfort when he knew there was none to be had. How could there be?

"Who could have done that to them?" She pulled back enough to look up at him. "It doesn't make sense. I knew they were leopard. I didn't think I was, because I didn't feel her. I hoped, of course, but my mother explained it wasn't always passed on. But I knew they were. Dad was a ferocious fighter. What could possibly defeat two leopards and then tear them to pieces like that?"

He had a bad feeling he knew. "Could they have seen something they shouldn't have? Did they talk to you about where they came from? Two leopards don't just appear out of nowhere. They had to have come from a lair."

Ashe all but crawled off his lap. He let her, because she didn't know she already belonged to him and he wasn't going to add to the mess she was already trying to comprehend. She swept back the tendrils of hair falling wildly around her face and once more took up her position in the middle of the bed.

"I don't know where they were from. Neither ever told me."

Her eyes hadn't quite met his and there was something in her voice . . . Not a lie exactly. A deception? He wasn't certain. "Did you ever see them in leopard form?"

She nodded. "Of course. Often."

"Describe what they looked like."

She smiled at the memory. "My father's leopard was interesting. That golden color was only along his spine, the rest of his coat was grayish-white in color with very widely spaced rosettes. I thought he was beautiful and unique."

She was describing an Arabian leopard. They were very rare. Their numbers had fallen below a hundred. Below fifty. Now, one had been killed.

"Your mother? What did she look like?"

"She was beautiful. Truly beautiful. Her coat was very thick and the ring around her rosettes was very thick. She was distinctive, even though she had a pale coat as well. Not like my father's but still not the gold color you think of when you describe a leopard."

He couldn't be certain without seeing her mother in leopard form, but it almost sounded like an Amur leopard. He was very familiar with the Amur leopard. He was one. He turned the information over and over in his mind. He had heard stories of an incident . . . "How old was your mother when she gave birth to you?"

"She was very young when she had me. A teenager. Barely sixteen."

He couldn't sit there on that bed. He got up quickly, all

flowing muscle, hot energy needing to go somewhere. Needing to do something. "Did your father keep a diary? A journal? Was there anything at all that might be a record of your parents meeting? Their life together?"

He talked too fast. Asked too many questions. She looked at him as if he'd grown two heads.

"Why? What are you thinking? Do you know who killed them?"

"I need more information." His eyes were on her face, and this time, he told his leopard very firmly to listen for any note of deception. "Why did you really come here? You read about Evangeline marrying. I know that is true, but you came here looking for answers about your parents, didn't you? You thought Fyodor might have those answers."

For the first time, her gaze slid completely from his. Just for a moment, but he caught it. There was the briefest of hesitations. "I did read about Evangeline getting married. I didn't have anyone else to turn to. I really don't have other friends, and I'm not trying to sound pathetic. It's the truth. I came here because I was afraid. As for answers, what would Fyodor know about my parents' deaths?"

She'd turned that around neatly, but he wasn't buying it. He paced across the room, sending her a scorching look. "You don't want to play games with me, baby. Not when I have to protect my family. You fucking tell me the truth. I want to know why you're here. Cut the bullshit and get to the facts."

"I have told you the facts."

He moved fast, a blur of speed. He had her down on the bed, his fingers wrapped around her throat while he loomed over top of her. He let her stare into his eyes. Flat. Cold. Glacier cold. Ice blue. Let her see the kills. So many. Too many. Let her see he was capable of ending her life right there. He let her feel it as well, his fingers easily cutting off all air so that she fought him instinctively, her body thrashing, her feet drumming, her fingers trying to pry his loose.

Only when he was certain she understood the rules did he let her go. She gasped. Wheezed. Fought to pull air into her burning lungs. He got up and got her a glass of water. When he returned she was sitting up slowly. She clearly considered throwing the water in his face, but when he stared her down, she took small sips to allow it to slide down her swollen throat.

She glared at him, but he could see he'd gotten his point across. He hated the fact that he couldn't disconnect with her. He had perfected the ability in his youth. It had been the only way to survive. Now, with Ashe, even knowing she was lying, he couldn't disassociate. He was disciplined enough to stay in control, to continue to give her that flat killer's look that kept her in line, but for the first time since he'd been a child with a father forcing him to hurt others, he felt what he was doing.

She cleared her throat, winced, and then glared some more.

He indicated the glass of water in her hand. "Drink some more. The cold will help."

She didn't argue. She drank. He leaned against the bureau, managing to look lazy and unsympathetic. It required all of his acting skills. He waited. He'd done enough interrogations to know when someone would crack. He'd scared her. He'd also pissed her off. She wasn't completely cowed, which would have been better for them both, but he liked the fact that she wasn't.

"My mother was a victim of human trafficking when she was just fifteen. At least, that was what was in her journal. I knew where she kept it. She was terrified of her father."

"From Russia?" The moment he heard the description of her mother's leopard, the thick, lighter-colored coat, it made sense. Some of the female children were auctioned off or sent to work for a man who ran the brothels for Lazar. He moved the women constantly so they would never make any friends.

"How did she come to be with your father?"

"He was from another country, but very wealthy. His father bought girls at an auction and he purchased my mother and gave her to his son for his birthday." She cleared her throat and then took another sip of water.

He was patient. In any interrogation it was important to read the one being interrogated. Every nuance. Every expression. He knew when to stay quiet and when to push. He didn't so much as raise an eyebrow.

"Her leopard rose and was claimed by my father's leopard. When my father realized that he couldn't ever marry her, or be with her on a permanent basis, that his father planned to give her to others and then return her to the man who'd sold her when he was finished with her, they ran. My father took enough money to survive for years if they were careful."

"They had to have been extremely careful to last, what? Twenty years?"

She nodded. "At least I thought they were careful."

She pressed the glass to her forehead as if it ached. He found himself staring at the marks on her throat. He wanted to mark her skin, but not like that. It didn't give him satisfaction to see his fingerprints on her.

She pulled the glass down and looked at him, sorrow in her eyes. "My father had been trying to stop the trafficking and the auctions. He had names and dates. He had even contacted some of the victims. He had someone talking to him from my mother's family, feeding him information, and then his source abruptly went silent."

"Who was this person?"

"My mother's sister."

He doubted it. Her mother's sister would have been trafficked right along with her, unless she was given to someone in marriage. Often, a lair would give a woman to a man in another lair so he could have children. Once she produced sons for him, he would kill her. That was the fate of the women in his world. Still, if that had happened, and Ashe's father had located her, most likely she was now dead and her husband had found some evidence of correspondence.

Was he really buying this? What kind of coincidence would it have to be to have the messenger show up right at the same time as Ashe? More, that he would find a place to rent just one street over from her? That was a lot to ask anyone to believe, let alone a suspicious man like him.

"I'm telling the truth."

"You didn't before."

"Everything I've told you is the truth. I just left off parts or twisted them to what I needed, but the truth was there."

"Because you know I'm leopard and can hear lies."

"Your leopard bit me. He called to my leopard. Why did he do that?"

"We'll get to that once we sort this out. I can't have you running around like a loose cannon when my brother's life could be in danger."

"Why would his life be in danger from me?" she demanded, but once again, just for a fraction of a second, her gaze slid from his.

"Do you believe he has something to do with human trafficking?"

Her mouth tightened. She didn't answer, but he didn't need her to. He shook his head. "Did you come here to kill him?"

"I would *never* kill an innocent man."

"Ashe, do you really think a woman like Evangeline, the woman you obviously respect, would be married to a man involved in trafficking?" He crossed his arms over his chest and regarded her levelly, daring her to say one unkind thing about Evangeline.

"She might not know."

"She's too intelligent for that. If he's involved, she would know. She wouldn't tolerate it, not for one second, and you know that. Gut level. Deep down. You know that about her."

She nodded because no one could be in Evangeline's company for two minutes and not recognize she wouldn't tolerate her husband being involved in something like human trafficking.

"He's still my only lead," she said. "If he isn't the one, maybe he can point me in the right direction. And it doesn't negate the fact that I needed a friend and a place to lie low."

He studied her face while the tension between them stretched to screaming. "Has it occurred to you that the reason your father died is because he didn't leave this alone? These men play for keeps."

"As do you." She coughed and took another sip of water.

He nodded. "I'm responsible for Fyodor and Evangeline. They have an enemy so cruel and so vicious, you could never conceive of him, not in your worst nightmare. I take that responsibility very seriously. It weighs heavy on me every time they are out of my sight. I walk a very fine line, giving my sister-in-law the things she needs to make her happy, and yet keeping her safe while she does them."

"Like her bakery."

He nodded. "She loves it, but she's very vulnerable there. Our enemies will always know when she has to get there and when she leaves. They will think nothing of killing others to get to her. Innocent people who've done nothing to them. They would bomb her bakery and think nothing of blowing up every store for a block."

"And you think I could be one of these people." She made it a statement.

He nodded. "It's possible. You carry weapons. You're leopard. You arrived at the same time one of our enemies sent a messenger. That's a big coincidence, Ashe."

"I'll leave." Her fingers went back to stroking her throat, a nervous gesture he knew she wasn't aware of. The action drew attention to the darkening marks there.

He didn't so much as blink and he breathed evenly, keeping the tension from showing in his body. His leopard was now prowling, suddenly very moody and bad-tempered. "If you left, I wouldn't have the ability to keep my eyes on you, now would I?"

She went back to glaring. "I can't win no matter what I offer to do. I told you the truth. My name really is Ashe Bronte Mostafa."

"And you know Mostafa is your true surname." He made it a statement.

Faint color slid up her neck to stain her face. She nodded. "Yes. I know that's my real name. My father didn't like us to use it. They both loved Brontë poems. I know Charlotte Brontë was famous for her novels, but she did write poetry. She, along with her sisters, wrote poems my parents particularly liked."

He particularly liked them as well. "What was their favorite?"

She raised her chin the slightest bit, as if she thought he was challenging her. "Charlotte Brontë's 'Life.' They often read that one to me."

He was familiar with it, but he wasn't going to tell her that. She had managed, in a very short period of time, to slip under his guard and get inside him. There was something very valiant about her. He straightened slowly, a thought coming to him. It was farfetched and completely ridiculous, but sometimes one had to consider the ridiculous.

"Did your father ever talk about the messenger? Or a messenger? Did you ever hear him use those words?"

She nodded. "Once, just after I moved out. I had gone to visit them, and they weren't staying in the cabin. I tracked them into the hills. I knew their favorite camping spots, so even when their tracks disappeared into water, I knew where I could find them. Dad said they'd be traveling in the mountains for a few months but staying relatively close just in case I needed them." She finished the water off and set the glass aside on the nightstand.

"Needed them for what?"

"He told me to look out for a man. A stranger. One calling himself Apostol. He said he was the messenger. I said messenger for what? Of what? He never answered me. He just looked at my mother and both shook their heads."

"He is the messenger of death," Timur supplied. "At least that's what his role is supposed to be. Most likely, he caught up with your parents."

"This messenger *killed* them? He tortured and then killed them?"

"I doubt if he did the actual killing. He found them, delivered the message so they would know they were living on borrowed time, and then the actual elimination team was brought in."

"Is that what you are?" She looked him straight in the eye. "Are you the elimination team? Is that why you're here?"

He didn't take his eyes from hers and, damn him to hell, he wasn't going to lie. "That's who I am right this minute, yes. I came here to find the truth, and if you were a threat to either Evangeline or Fyodor, damn straight I'd end you in a heartbeat." And go the rest of his life without a woman, because he knew she was the one and it had very little to do with his leopard driving him.

Her long lashes swept down and then back up. He found himself looking at her cat, and then the lashes did another sweep and he was looking at her. There was nothing there to suggest she found him as despicable as he expected.

"If I knew someone had threatened my parents, I would have killed them."

He hadn't expected acceptance. He found himself going still inside. Feeling hope. Trying to squash it down so he wouldn't be bitterly disappointed. He'd been disappointed all his life. He had learned not to want anything. To feel anything. He had known there would be no home for him. No loving family no matter if he dreamt of that. That dream had been destroyed before it could ever get off the ground.

First his father made certain his leopard was a killer by

beating him so severely and repeatedly that it forced the young cat to emerge in an effort to defend the boy. Then there were the training sessions, vicious ones, where men beat him with clubs to bring out his savage nature. His father drilled it into Timur that women were only to be used and then cast aside. He did that in a brutal way as well, wanting to harden his son. He raped and then beat women to death in front of him and then ended the lessons with the cruel murder of Timur's own mother.

"You make me believe there is good in the world after all," he said. Even giving her that felt like giving too much. She made him feel vulnerable when he couldn't afford to be. He was the one who kept everyone else safe. He couldn't afford to feel too much.

"I don't know why. I did come here under false pretenses. I'll tell Evangeline tomorrow."

He shook his head. "You're going to see this thing through. Until I know what's going on, I want you where I can see you at all times."

"What does that mean?"

"It means you have a roommate." He pulled out his phone and texted Fyodor first, because he knew his brother would be waiting to hear if there was any threat to Evangeline, or if he had to cushion the blow and tell her Ashe was dead. Then he sent a group text to Gorya, Kyanite and Rodion. They would have to keep a wall around Fyodor and Evangeline, whether or not his brother was agreeable.

Ashe drew back, shaking her head. "No way will you be sleeping in here with me."

"I didn't say I'd be sleeping in here." He had other ideas. Sleeping just wasn't one of them. "You know where the extra blankets are kept?"

She shook her head. "I'm not used to such a big place. This is huge."

It was very small in comparison to the mansion where Evangeline lived now. Timur thought the house was the perfect size. Other than the windows that gave him nightmares, he really liked the place.

"Do you know how to cook?"

"Why? Because I'm the girl?" she challenged. Sarcasm dripped from her voice.

"No, because I like to cook and if you don't, I can take over that duty."

Ashe sent him a faint smile. "If you forgive me that one, I'll forgive the choke-me-to-death one."

"I'm not certain the two can compare."

"I told you," she reiterated. "If someone wanted my family dead, I'd do whatever it took to protect them. My father was all about keeping us safe, so I do understand. I just don't want it happening again."

"Then don't ever lie to me like that." He edged toward the door. His body had just about all the abuse it could take. He wasn't used to his cock being so damned hard every fucking minute. He needed a little respite from her.

"Good night, Timur."

"Good night, Ashe. If you have to go wandering around in the middle of the night, make noise. You don't want me thinking you're sneaking up on me."

He found extra blankets in the linen closet and tossed a pillow and blanket on the couch. He had to think about why the messenger had arrived before she had. What was he doing there? He believed Ashe, her story about her parents, but there was more going on than met the eye. She was a good liar. He'd barely caught the tiny imperfections in her voice the few times he had. Something was just a little off and he needed to get to the bottom of it.

He told his leopard to guard him and then allowed himself to drift off. The nightmares came the way they always did, but this time, it was Ashe murdered in front of his eyes, not his mother.

4

FOUR o'clock in the morning came too soon. Ashe lay in the very comfortable bed and stared up at the ceiling. She hadn't expected to sleep, not with Timur in the house. He was sexy, gorgeous and dangerous as hell. Just the kind of man she was attracted to. She'd never had any sense when it came to men. Never. She knew better than to even go there. A woman could dream of men like him, but she didn't actually make that mistake. Not unless she wanted to pay a hefty price—which she most definitely did *not*.

She'd fallen asleep dreaming about it. It was the first time in a long while she'd felt safe enough to really fall asleep, not just dozing, but actually a deep, restful slumber. Well, as restful as a woman could be when she was totally perving on a man. Her dreams were mostly erotic. She didn't mind that so much, unless she moaned like an idiot and kept him awake. That was a very real possibility.

She sat up slowly, holding the sheet to her neck, as if the

thin material could somehow protect her. There was no protection. There was only common sense. She had to keep her distance from Timur if she wanted to come out of this alive. She'd told him the truth as much as she could. It was a matter of choosing the right words. As long as she kept that up, she'd be golden. He was suspicious, but then, what kind of a head of security would he be if he wasn't suspicious of everyone? He had to be.

She touched her throat and then stroked her fingers over the marks he'd put there. He'd scared her. Really scared her. At the same time, she'd been wildly exhilarated. That was her shameful secret. She liked danger. She liked dangerous men. She craved both. Still, there was the sane part of her that prevented her from making mistakes. Until now. She sat up straighter and circled her throat with her palm. Now she didn't know exactly what she was going to do.

She hadn't expected that Evangeline would be the same sweet girl she'd met in the mountains a couple of years earlier. She thought she would be a spoiled woman, putting on airs, threatening the world with her gangster husband. Instead, Ashe found her to be the same genuine spirit, compassionate, helpful and a very hard worker.

Evangeline could hire any number of people to work at her business, but she didn't. She did the baking and worked harder, even, than Ashe. There was nothing at all about Evangeline that suggested she considered herself entitled just because she'd come into money. She hadn't changed at all. Evangeline was sweet and very genuine. It was no wonder her husband and Timur were protective of her. Ashe felt a little protective as well.

She forced her body to move, to make it into the master bathroom. Hot water helped to wake her up. She had to decide what to do and she needed to make up her mind fast. She had brought danger to Evangeline. She'd had a completely different idea of who these people were. Criminals to be sure. But . . .

She turned her face up to the pouring water, letting it cascade over her and run down her body as she closed her eyes. Evangeline being so nice, being such a wonderful person, complicated things. They'd known each other such a short time and it had been a few years earlier, yet right away she'd given Ashe the use of her home. She'd offered immediately, without hesitation, once she'd made up her mind to help Ashe. Clearly she'd gotten in trouble with both her husband and the head of security, but she'd stood up to them for her. Who did that? If she was the wife of a terrible criminal, would she do that?

She washed her hair, contemplating that. What if Fyodor wasn't really a criminal after all? What if the couple didn't deserve hell knocking on their door? She pressed her forehead against the tile. *What have I done?* She'd set things in motion, and maybe she couldn't turn them around. If she couldn't, then she would have to confess to Timur and he would kill her for sure. Still, that would be better than setting up an innocent woman and her husband to possibly die.

She wrapped towels around her, winding one around her hair and the other around her body. She didn't have much in the way of clothes, but she hadn't planned on being there for very long. Now, she would have to leave even faster. Once she'd made up her mind, she felt better. She could lead trouble away from these people, just as she'd led it there in the first place. She just needed a good plan.

"Coffee's hot."

Timur stuck his head in the space between the bedroom door and the doorjamb. He'd obviously showered. He looked wide awake and very hot. Handsome. Sexy. Too much for her so early in the morning. Coffee sounded good, especially coffee she didn't have to make herself.

His gaze moved over her body and she just stood there like a sacrificial lamb, letting him look his fill. He took his time and there was genuine appreciation in his gaze. She kept her head up, trying not to notice that her nipples peaked and her sex fluttered under the intense scrutiny. She was susceptible as hell to him.

"Get a move on, woman. Breakfast is almost ready."

His head disappeared and she let out her breath, aware for the first time that she'd been holding it. There was something about those cold, cold eyes that set off sparks in her. Not just sparks. A timber fire. He found something deep inside her that had never been touched before and it ignited just for him.

She dressed slowly, afraid of spending too much time with him. She pulled on her tight tee, the one that was soft and thin and perfect, but clung to every curve. She'd never cared before, but now, her favorite shirt seemed a little too revealing and worse, it felt sensual on her skin. Sensual. A T-shirt. That was really his fault. Her favorite pair of jeans, faded to a near white, with a couple of genuine threadbare spots in them, felt as if the material caressed her skin as they slid up her legs and over her thighs and hips. That was just plain insane.

The door opened and Timur strode in. He didn't slow down, he just kept coming straight at her. Her breath caught in her throat. Her lungs seized. She opened her mouth, but nothing came out. He just dipped low, shoved his shoulder into her belly and lifted. Her head went down his back and she had to grab at the back of his shirt, clutching it in her fist.

"What the hell? I'm not a freakin' sack of potatoes." She all but yelped it. Sadly, her weird sense of humor kicked in and there was also a note of laughter in her voice. She doubted it mattered one way or the other to him. Laughter or anger, he was striding through the house, taking her into the kitchen to the little breakfast nook. She liked that nook: it was round and comfortable, windows surrounding it.

Timur set her on her feet beside the table and stepped back, fully expecting her to yell at him, or swing, one or the other. She did neither. She picked up her coffee mug and sipped. It was good coffee. The man not only cooked, but he actually made good coffee. She definitely couldn't set him up to die. Men with his talents were needed in the world. She sent him a sappy grin and slid onto the seat closest to the window without a word.

Timur went back to the stove and picked up a plate. "You a picky eater in the morning?"

She shook her head. She was grateful for anything. She just happened to be the worst cook in the world, especially in the morning, because she didn't want to do anything.

"Good." He returned with two plates. Steam came off the contents, declaring they were hot. He put one in front of her. He'd already set the table and had utensils waiting.

She picked up a fork and tried the concoction. It looked like an egg scramble of some sort with vegetables and maybe ham or sausage in it. Whatever it was, it was darn good. Suddenly, she was hungry. The smell of coffee had gone a long way to making her feel human, and the fact that she could actually drink a cup right away, as soon as she was up, was a miracle.

They ate in silence for the first few minutes. She put her fork down and picked up the coffee cup. "Thanks for this. It's really good." It had to be said. Manners were important.

"You're welcome. Are you grumpy in the morning?"

"Yep. Don't like to talk. Don't like to get up. Don't like to do anything but put the blankets over my head."

His slight grin was all about sex. Why she thought that, she had no idea. Maybe he looked at her like the Big Bad Wolf. She was no Little Red Riding Hood, but at the same time, her panties had gone damp and her sex clenched in a kind of warning. The lines carved into his face were purely sensual. Those cold blue eyes of his suddenly held a thousand secrets, all of which she wanted to know. She liked the way his tee stretched over his broad chest and all those delicious muscles were just waiting to ripple when he moved.

"You put the blankets over your head when I call you to breakfast, I'll be pulling you right out and bringing you in to eat, even if you don't have a stitch on."

Heat slid through her veins. Little fingers of desire danced up her thighs. Her clit pulsed with need. She wondered if a woman could have a spontaneous orgasm just from a few words from a man. If it was possible, she would have put her money on Timur as the man who could accomplish such a feat.

"I don't sleep in the nude." She gave him the information in her snippiest voice and forked another bite of his delicious concoction into her mouth. Spices burst on her tongue. It tasted good. She wondered what he would taste like. His skin. His mouth. He had a gorgeous mouth. She risked a look. She could fantasize over that mouth all day.

"That's going to change."

"What's going to change?" she asked absently, wishing he was nude and she could memorize his body with her tongue.

"Sleeping with clothes. I want you naked when you're sleeping with me."

He stated it so quietly, so perfectly matter-of-factly, that for a moment his declaration didn't register. She stared at him, her lashes fluttering because she couldn't quite believe her ears. Had he just said what she thought he had? She stole another look at his hard features. Yeah, he'd just said it.

"That isn't happening, although, I must say, the coffee was very welcome and this egg dish is amazing. But still, with regret, I have to decline your invitation." She forked more eggs into her mouth and feigned being calm while she chewed.

Who would pass up a chance to sleep with him? What kind of idiot was she? She was never going to have this kind of chemistry with another man. He didn't have to touch her, he just looked at her with that mixture of detachment and dark, dark desire. The kind of desire that set a woman's body on fire. She kept her eyes on his, not daring to look away.

A very slow smile barely curved his bottom lip, as if he didn't really know how to smile. His eyes remained as cold as ice. All that glacier blue. She could get trapped there if she wasn't careful. The need to see that ice melt was becoming far too strong in her, and gaining more momentum with each passing second they were together.

"It's happening."

His voice was low. A caress. The sound stroked over her skin like a velvet rub. She resisted the urge to squirm—to rub her thighs together. To scratch the itch that was beginning to throb between her legs. It was the best morning she'd ever had.

"Why would you think that?"

"Because I want you with every breath I take, and I always get what I want."

That was beautiful. Perfect. So what she needed to hear. She sighed with regret. "Not this time. I absolutely am not going to risk going to bed with you. You're not a man who has relationships. You're the kind of man who leaves. Fast. Do you even bother to buy a woman a meal, before or after?"

Keeping his eyes on hers, he shook his head slowly. A shiver of desire spiraled through her body. Why did she find him so sexy? Why was she so turned on, craving him like the worst possible drug?

"So, we're going to have sex, you're going to leave and I can get on with my life?" There was far too much speculation in her voice, because she might be able to handle that.

"I didn't say that."

"Well, say it," she challenged him. Maybe she was challenging herself. Would she take the chance? She didn't have an answer for that yet.

He took another sip of coffee and then set the mug on

the table. He leaned back in his chair, sprawling out, long legs spread out in front of him. He looked lazy and yet in complete control. Bastard. She was a mess. The least he could do was be a mess as well.

"I don't tell lies the way you do, Ashe, especially to myself. Finish your breakfast. I've got to get you to work so I can get to work."

She'd forgotten all about work, she was so wrapped up in him. She glanced at her watch, only to find her wrist was bare. She was barefoot as well. "What time is it?" She looked around the room to find the clock on the wall. "Already? I'm going to be late." She leapt up and ran for the bedroom—and for safety.

He knew she was lying. Of course, he knew. He was leopard. Her father had cautioned her that leopards heard lies. He'd coached her from the time she was a toddler in how to word sentences to minimize the risk. The more truth mixed in with the lie, the more it sounded like truth. He made her practice all the time. They'd lived off the grid, but they'd had a few friends, others who, like them, for whatever reason, lived a life away from society.

They'd gone without television, but he'd insisted on computers and all the modern technology. The very latest. Her father consumed newspapers, online and in every other form that he could get. Her mother helped him gather news and they would talk endlessly about it at every meal. Her father taught her how to fight, how to shoot, how to survive out in the wilderness. She could build her own gas mask a number of ways in just under fifteen minutes. He'd prepared her, telling her the day would come—and it had, she just hadn't been as prepared as her parents had thought she would be.

She had to leave. There was no other possible way to salvage this mess. She had to lead the enemy away from Evangeline—and Timur. He would try to protect her, but he couldn't possibly protect her, Evangeline and Fyodor. Everyone would lose. She had to come up with another way.

Maybe she could casually ask Evangeline who the worst criminal she knew was. Someone deserving of death. Someone strong enough to kill her enemy. Someone not Timur.

She pulled on her shoes, braided her hair and hurried into the foyer where she kept her car keys. Timur stood there, her keys dangling from his fingers. "You're riding with me." He closed his hand around the keys and slid them into his pocket.

"I might need to go somewhere." Like out of town. Far away. Her plan had gone to hell faster than she believed possible. It was like being on a runaway train. All because Evangeline was still that truly beautiful, compassionate person she remembered.

"I'll make sure you get to wherever it is you need to go. If no one else can take you, I will."

"That sounds more like a threat."

"You have a very good ear. Get in the fuckin' car, Ashe, and stop plotting. Whatever you planned to do isn't happening. I don't have the patience my brother does for bullshit, so if you're going to keep lying and keep plotting, do it when you're talking to him."

She glared at him, hands on her hips. "No one is asking you for your opinion—" She was cut off when he did that thing again, putting his shoulder to her belly and lifting. She found herself dangling upside down over his shoulder. This time he held her one-handed—the other came out with a gun.

Ashe gripped his shirt on either side of his waist, but she didn't distract him as they went out of the house down the walkway to his car. Even though it was still very dark out, she felt very exposed and knew he must as well, or he wouldn't have his gun out and ready. He was all business, moving quickly, but she felt the tension vibrating through him. His muscular body felt like that of a racehorse, ready to run as soon as the word was given.

He set her feet down on the curb on the passenger side

of the vehicle, his body pressing hers tightly against the car, shielding her from sight. "When I open the door, you get in, but stay low and put your seat belt on."

She didn't ask questions. If he saw something she didn't, because she'd been hanging upside down, there wasn't time to be discussing it. She'd ask questions later. She looked up at him and nodded. The moment her eyes met his, she knew she was in trouble. There was that whole dangerous, bad-boy thing she was so falling hard for right in front of her. Her body just melted. Right there in the middle of the danger zone, chemistry, hot and wild, very powerful, zinged between them.

He shifted position just slightly. His knee slid between her thighs, parting them so she found her pulsing sex pressed tightly along his hard thigh. It felt . . . delicious. She couldn't help the experimental rub. At once, a thousand sensations poured over and into her. His fist caught in her hair and yanked her head back.

That alone sent a shiver of need down her spine. Her sex clenched in desperate hunger. Her breasts swelled, aching painfully, and her nipples were so tight and hard she feared if she touched them they would shatter. Then his mouth was on hers, and her body went up in flames. That fast. She'd never felt chemistry like that in her life. No one had ever kissed her with such passion. Such ferocity. As if he owned her body and soul and she just let him.

She wanted him. Right there. On the spot. To hell with the neighbors. He was wearing too many clothes and she needed to feel his skin beneath her palms. She forgot about her vow to not let him touch her. Her decision to leave. Or possible danger. Everything was gone from her brain. There was only Timur and his mouth. That beautiful, brutal, savage mouth that fed her fire and burned her soul into ashes for his own consumption.

His hand slid under her tee, fingers spread wide to take in her bare skin. She was desperate for his touch on her breasts. She needed that as much as she needed her next breath. His mouth left hers to travel over her chin and down her throat, leaving behind a trail of fire. She caught her breath on a sob of pure need.

His hands cupped her breasts, pushing them up like offerings, and his mouth closed over her right one, through her shirt, sucking her deep into his mouth. The heat was scalding. So hot she was afraid of the burn, but she needed it, needed more.

"Undo your jeans."

She didn't hesitate. Not for a second. Her hands dropped to the waistband and she opened them, arching into his mouth, pressing her breast deeper. He pushed her shirt and bra up over her breasts and then there was nothing between his mouth and her soft mounds. Her cry was low, but she sounded shattered even to her own ears. She *felt* shattered. She had no idea chemistry could be like this.

"Push your jeans down, baby," he ordered.

She did, immediately, her hands shaking. She didn't want him to stop, his mouth felt so good, and he'd added his fingers and thumb, tugging and rolling, pinching so that streaks of fire ran straight to her clit.

"My trousers. Damn it, Ashe, hurry, just open them. Take my cock out."

She did as he commanded, her fingers fumbling a little, but she opened his trousers and managed to free his cock. It was long and particularly thick. Intimidating, but she didn't care. She needed him in her. She couldn't wait another second. Heat spread through her when his teeth nipped. He tested her readiness and then he bit down again and a fresh flood of liquid coated his fingers.

"Turn around. Hands on the door."

She spun around and then his hand was on the nape of her neck, pushing her head down while his shoe kicked her legs farther apart. He wasn't gentle or slow. He lodged the head of his cock in her entrance and then he slammed home, driving through her tight folds, so that her muscles gave way reluctantly, gripping and fighting, but allowing his invasion. He didn't stop until he was completely in her, all the way, the crown bumping her cervix.

The breath hissed out of him. "Fucking tight, woman, you're going to kill me."

She didn't have time for an answer. He began to move. Not slowly. Not gently. He took her hard, driving into her over and over, just the way she needed. Just the way she'd always dreamt her man would take her. Crazy wild. Ferocious need driving both of them. There was no time to catch her breath, no time to savor the experience. She didn't want to take the time to savor it. She wanted—no, *needed* this.

He hit every spot she had that drove her right up the wall. He seemed to know her body already, as if he'd taken her a thousand times and knew what to do, how to move. He had stamina and she went over the edge several times before she felt him swell even larger. His hands gripped her hips hard and he yanked her back into him, erupting like a hot volcano, her tight sheath draining every last drop from him.

She would have fallen if he hadn't held them both up. She pressed her forehead against the car, desperately trying to find air to breathe. She didn't want to turn around and face him just yet. She just wanted to let her body have its moment. She wanted him again—and again. How could anyone do this just once when it was like this? Every cell in her body sang. Was alive. Alert. Looking for him. No one else would ever do. But there was reality . . .

Men like Timur Amurov weren't into relationships. They didn't buy breakfast or dinner for the women they fucked. That's what had just happened between them. Sex. Pure and simple. Uncomplicated. Not just sex. Great sex. The best in the world.

Timur gently wiped between her legs with his tie. Despite the material feeling silky soft, it sent ripples through her entire body. He pulled up her jeans, and then fixed her bra and drew her shirt down before he turned her around. Ashe leaned her back against the car and watched as he calmly cleaned himself and then pulled up the zipper on his trousers.

"I guess this means we weren't in danger after all."

"No, we weren't, but I wasn't taking chances with your life walking out the door." His eyes, as cold as the bluest glacier, drifted over her face. "We get any hotter, Ashe, and we're going to spontaneously combust."

She let out her breath. "I need to go back in and change."

"No, you don't. I like knowing I'm still inside you."

"You don't believe in condoms?"

"You're on birth control, and I'm clean. I wanted to feel every fucking inch of you."

"How the hell do you know I'm on birth control?" she demanded.

"I saw them when I went through the house, looking for evidence that you weren't what you said. You take them regularly."

"You went through my private things?"

"It isn't like you have a ton of stuff, Ashe."

She folded her arms across her chest, still leaning against the car door, enjoying the burn between her legs. There was no question, Timur Amurov was hot. And now she knew what kind of a monster he had between his legs. More, he was still as dangerous as ever. Her blood was rushing through her veins, her chest rising and falling, her breasts aching, and she knew every step she took that day would remind her of him.

Ashe shook her head. "I still need a different T-shirt. You got this one wet."

"It will dry."

She looked around her, suddenly aware they were outside. It was dark enough, although light was filtering through and anyone could have seen. A neighbor could have looked right out a window. She hadn't even thought about that, or that an enemy could have shot the two of them. She had the feeling Timur *had* thought about it but just didn't give a damn, at least about the neighbors. The shooting . . . well . . . he probably would have had that under control. Most likely he wasn't as far gone as she'd been.

"It might dry by the time the customers come into the store, but Evangeline, my *boss*, is going to see." She'd see her in all her slutty glory. She didn't even care if her behavior had been terrible, the sex was that good, and if she had even a little bit of brains, she would repeat the experience as often as possible. But she didn't. She wasn't going to get caught up in something that would not end well for her.

She touched her tongue to her lip. She hadn't realized he'd bitten her there. It had been just a nip, but her lip was tender. "You know this can't happen again."

He caught her chin and tugged until she was looking him in the eye. "It's going to happen again. Many times. Just know that and stop overthinking. We have enough problems." He bent his head and brushed a kiss over her lips.

Her heart clenched hard. Butterflies took flight in her stomach. His mouth was gentle. That little caress spoke volumes, things she couldn't afford to hear or understand.

"Put your arms around me, Ashe."

She shook her head. He caught her close, one arm locking against her back, dragging her body right into his while his hand held her chin, forcing her to look up at him.

"Put your fucking arms around me. I'm kissing you."

"You can't. You know what will happen." But her arms slid around him. All that muscle. He was pure masculine heat. A statue carved of stone come to life. Cold as ice. Hot as the fires of hell. She was in *so* much trouble, but then, wasn't that why she'd come?

His mouth came down on hers, and her fingers dug into his shirt and caught skin. She needed an anchor, something solid to hold on to because she was spinning out of control that fast. He kissed like sin. He kissed his way straight through every guard until she was naked, vulnerable, her very soul exposed. Her body was his instantly, melting into his, soft and pliant, willing to do anything and everything he demanded.

Then he was setting her away from him, holding her at arm's length. "Holy hell, woman. Get in the fucking car."

Fighting for breath, she stared up at him. At those eyes of his—so cold they could freeze a person. Right now, the glacier was melted and blue flames stared back at her. She wasn't alone in feeling the whacked-out, combustible chemistry flaring so hot between them. Her gaze slid down his body and over his broad, muscular chest. He was fighting for air, just like she was. Her gaze dropped lower. His cock was as hard as a rock and demanding attention.

"Is that a smirk?"

Her gaze jumped back to his face. She pressed both lips together. "Maybe."

"Get in the car." He reached around her and yanked open the door, forcing her to move. She stepped back feeling very self-satisfied and then slid onto the leather seats. His car was very nice, built for speed. Built for comfort. "Bulletproof glass?"

"Absolutely. When my brother rides in this, I know he's safe."

"Why would anyone want him dead?"

He shut the door and walked around the hood. He paused for a moment and looked across the street and then said something. She knew he had because his lips moved. She was adept at reading lips but not from the angle where she was. He got in and started the engine immediately.

"Is everything all right?"

"Want you again. Now I'm going to have to wait for your break."

"You are not . . ." She glared at him. "We are not going to do anything on my break."

"I'm fucking you until we both can't breathe." He stated it like it was a fact.

She should argue with him. She really should. She should make it clear that they weren't going to keep going at it like bunnies, but she knew if he kissed her, if he touched her, she probably wouldn't be able to say no. She didn't seem to have a mind when he was around. She threaded her fingers together.

"Timur, I need to tell you something. It's important. You aren't going to like it."

"Say it then."

"I'm in a lot of trouble." She twisted her fingers together tighter. "I don't want to bring that trouble to Evangeline. I know you have it in your head that I should stay, but I'm telling you, I need to go. They'll hurt her. They might even take her. They'll use her to get to me."

There was silence and she couldn't stop herself from looking up at his face. He stared straight ahead, driving with ease. His hands were loose on the wheel, but very sure, just as they'd been sure on her body when he'd touched her. A muscle ticked in his jaw, but that was the only sign that he'd heard her—or that he cared that she had to leave.

She *wanted* to leave. She didn't want Evangeline in any danger, and more, Ashe knew it was imperative that she put as much distance as possible between Timur and her. Already her heart felt shaky around him, and her body . . . It didn't belong to her anymore.

"You're going to stay, Ashe." It was a declaration, nothing less.

The way he said it, the tone he used, got to her in places better left alone. Her heart jumped. Her breasts ached. If she'd been wearing a dress she might have hiked it up and given herself a little relief, right there in the car with him watching. That was what his voice did to her, and he wasn't even trying for that effect. What was she going to do?

"Are you listening to me? Even if you're considering that

we have great chemistry, this is your brother and his wife we're talking about."

"I'll talk to Fyodor," Timur said. "If he wants you gone, then we'll go together. We can lead your enemy away from the two of them."

For a long moment her breath caught in her throat as if a great lump had developed there and strained her airway. "You would come with me?"

He nodded.

She couldn't read his hard features. His eyes were back to ice-cold—that blue that was so beautiful but deadly. "Why?"

"You know why."

She didn't. For sex? He'd leave his job and go straight into danger for the sex? It was, admittedly, great sex, but he probably had it all the time. "Actually, Timur, I don't."

"You're leopard. So am I. My leopard claimed yours. He would never let you leave. Neither would I. If you go, we go together."

Comprehension dawned. How could she have been so stupid? She thought it was about her. About them. About the two of them together. Timur could care less about her. It was all about his leopard claiming hers. Her mother had talked to her about it. She had said when the leopard went into her first heat . . .

"Oh God." She covered her face with her hands. "This . . ." She flapped her hand between them. "This thing, the chemistry, it's about the leopards, not us, isn't it?"

"Did you feel your leopard come close? I didn't feel her. Neither did my male. She's resting up for the big day, or it's possible you missed it by a few days. No, Ashe, I believe that was just the two of us. When the leopards get involved, it's going to be unbelievable."

She rubbed at the denim over her thigh. There was no point in arguing with Timur; he'd made up his mind. She didn't have her car so that meant she'd have to wait until she got off her shift, unless Timur left the bakery for some reason. Fyodor had an office there, but Evangeline had told her sometimes he worked from home or had to see to other things. Timur supposedly always went with him. If that happened, she would leave fast. Until then, she'd play along. It was very clear she couldn't stand up to Timur.

He covered her hands with one of his. "It's going to be all right, Ashe. Don't be worried."

He didn't know what they were facing or who, and she did. She'd seen their work. She would never get that sight out of her mind. Not ever. She turned her head and stared out the window, her heart racing. She knew he heard; he was leopard and all his senses were extremely acute. He would hear. She didn't care. He could guess all he wanted, but he wouldn't know for certain what she was thinking—or planning.

She didn't wait for him to come around and open the door for her when he pulled into the alley and stopped just outside the back door. She leapt out almost before he turned off the engine. Unfortunately, her key to the door was on her car key ring and Timur had that in his pocket. He sauntered up and unlocked the door as if he didn't have a care in the world.

The lights were on and Evangeline was already there working. Ignoring Timur, Ashe hurried over to her boss. "I'm so sorry I'm late, Evangeline."

Evangeline's gaze drifted over her, clearly noting her disheveled clothes. Ashe blushed, remembering the wet spot on her T-shirt. She looked around for a full-sized apron and hastily tied one on.

Evangeline glanced past her to Timur. She shook her head. "Coffee's on, Timur. I still have some pastries in the oven. I'll fix your drink when I'm finished here."

"No worries," Timur said and went from the heat of the kitchen to the cool of the shop.

"I really am sorry," Ashe reiterated. "It won't happen again."

"He's a good man, Ashe," Evangeline said. "But scary dangerous. Be very sure you know what you're getting into."

"It was a one-time thing," Ashe assured. "Really. It just happened, but I'm not looking to start anything with him. He's not into relationships. He told me he doesn't buy breakfast or dinner for his women. Of course, it may have been said a little cruder than that."

"Sheesh. I ought to go out there and kick him or something."

That made Ashe smile because Evangeline probably would really do it. "It was worth it. Seriously. And I'm not looking for a relationship."

"What are you looking for?"

Ashe washed her hands and then pulled on tight gloves so she could begin putting the freshly baked pastries in their trays. "It isn't here," she said gently. "I thought it might be, but I'm going to have to go."

"Timur?"

Ashe shook her head. "Life, I guess. I can't seem to settle."

"What kind of trouble are you in?" Evangeline asked. She wasn't looking at Ashe, but at her oven as she slowly opened the door.

The fresh scent of cinnamon hung heavy in the air. Ashe inhaled. She loved the way the shop always smelled of freshly baked goods. "The bad kind. The kind that could get the people around me killed."

"Did you come here for help, or were you targeting my husband?"

The voice was very, very mild, but Ashe wasn't deceived. For the very first time she realized Evangeline would defend her man against any threat.

"Evangeline, please look at me," Ashe said.

The woman she respected so much turned her head,

not moving any other part of her body, hands still around the tray.

"I came here because I thought he was a criminal. I'm in trouble and I needed help. You're my only friend and you just happened to marry someone I thought might be able to help me. Don't worry, I told Timur I would leave. He said no, but I'm still going in spite of his orders. I hope you can forgive me."

"What kind of trouble?" Evangeline asked.

"The men after me are the real deal. They are criminals and will stop at nothing to get what they want."

"What is it they want?"

"Me dead."

5

ASHE was going to run. She had that same look on her face that Evangeline had when she'd tried running from Fyodor. That hadn't worked, and Timur wasn't about to let Ashe get away any more than Fyodor had allowed Evangeline to run. They were going to have to work things out, which meant whatever she was holding back, she was going to have to give him.

His phone buzzed. He glanced down. *He's on the move, heading straight toward Evangeline's home to put the mark on the door.*

His gut tightened. He glanced toward the kitchen as he texted back. *Pick him up. You know where to take him. Make certain he has his phone on him.*

If Ashe was in league with the messenger, then he was going to have to rethink his plan, but for the moment, he was going to believe she had nothing to do with Apostol Delov and that the messenger had been after her all along, not Evangeline. He caught up his jacket and went to stand in the doorway leading to the kitchen. He paused there for a moment, watching them work with a quiet efficiency that looked so smooth—as if they'd been at it for years.

"Got things to do this morning, Evangeline," he informed her.

Evangeline spun around, nearly knocking into Ashe, but Ashe moved, just like he knew she would, avoiding the collision easily. He liked the way she moved, so fluid, a sensual flow of muscle and bone, her skin glowing beneath the overhead lights. She was close to the emerging, the Han Vol Dan that would have her leopard insisting on shifting, insisting on coming out to meet her mate. He had to stay close to Ashe in the event that it happened.

Not yet, Temnyy, his leopard, claimed. The cat gave a lazy yawn. *Soon, but not yet.*

The male had mellowed considerably now that he'd claimed his mate. Ordinarily, he was at Timur night and day, demanding blood, hating everything that moved. He was bad-tempered and mean, but now, with his mate so close, he wasn't nearly as difficult. For that alone, Timur wanted to kiss his woman.

"Is something wrong? Fyodor?" Evangeline asked anxiously and pulled her cell from her back pocket.

"If something was wrong, *mladshaya sestra*, I would have told you straight up. I'm not the one always cushioning you. That would be my brother." He spoke the truth and saw the worry drain from her. Who knew truth could be such a distraction? He didn't want either of them thinking too much.

"Will Fyodor be coming in today?"

He shrugged. "You know we don't have set days we come here, and we never use the same routes. He changes his mind often, Evangeline, and that's a good thing. We don't want anyone getting a read on him. We're careful. As of this morning when I checked in with him and Gorya, he wasn't planning on it."

He glanced over his shoulder at the room behind him. It was empty of customers, but not for long. They would come in for Evangeline's pastries and coffee drinks. Some would come for the atmosphere. Others for the thrill of possibly rubbing shoulders with crime lords. The cops would come.

"I'll have two men in the shop and two on patrol." She didn't need to know about the man on the roof across the street, the one with a high-powered rifle. "Both of you stay inside."

Ashe's chin went up. He didn't give a damn whether she liked his orders or not. She'd just better follow them. He pinned her with an ice-cold gaze. "Don't think you're going to run off, Ashe. I don't have the time to go chasing you down, which I'd do, but then we'd have a reckoning you wouldn't like."

He saw all kinds of protest in her eyes. She was careful enough to keep them out of her expression, but she wanted to tell him to go to hell. She didn't. That meant only one thing. She thought she could lull him into a false sense of security.

"Evangeline, she's going to try to enlist your aid in helping her run off. She's my male's mate. He won't like it. You know what will happen if she takes off, so when she asks, you say no."

Evangeline looked from one to the other, and then she sighed. "I understand, Timur."

He stalked across the kitchen, straight toward Ashe. She backed up until she hit the far wall. He pinned her there, using his larger body and a hand on either side of her head. She dipped her head low so he could only see the top with all that thick hair gleaming like silk beneath the lights.

"Look at me."

She shook her head and put both palms on his chest as

if she could push him away from her, but she didn't try. "Go away. I mean it. We're not doing this."

"Look at me, Ashe." He kept his voice low. This close to her, his body reacted. Even his cat reacted, rising, purring, wanting to be even closer to his mate. How could either of them help it when her scent enveloped them?

"I can't."

"I'm not going anywhere without kissing you."

"You know what happens when you kiss me." She mumbled it, a small sigh of resignation in her voice.

"Do you know what happens when I don't kiss you?" He dipped his head and brushed little kisses into the silk of her hair. "My cat is a mean bastard. I'm just like him. You mellow us both out. You don't want me shoving commuters off the train, do you?"

Her laughter was sweet music and some of the tight knots in his gut unraveled at the sound. "Look at me, baby." He coaxed her rather than ordered her.

She tilted her head and those long lashes lifted so that he found himself drowning in her eyes. He took her mouth immediately, his tongue sweeping across her silken lips to demand entry. At once she gave it to him, as if she couldn't help herself. He took over, needing the fire she stored there, feeding on it, feeling the burn spread like a firestorm through his body.

It took discipline—and a few minutes—to raise his head enough to press his forehead tight against hers. "Don't leave, Ashe. Give me some time to sort through all of this. Just stay here with Evangeline where I know both of you are safe and let me do what I do best."

She was silent, struggling, like him, to catch her breath. He pulled her into his arms and held her. Close. Wanting to shelter her. Needing to know she was safe. She was already becoming something he knew he would never give up. Not because of his cat, but for himself. He'd never expected to have a woman. He'd never expected to feel the things he was feeling. He wanted to think it was all physical because the chemistry between them was so explosive, but he had to admit, if only to himself, that other emotions were suddenly overwhelming when he was close to her.

What was it about her that appealed to him? Her fight? Her abilities to shift gears, sliding from one skin to the other so easily? One moment she was all feminine power and the next she was a clawing cat, fighting her way out of a bad situation. Then she could be compassionate, genuinely worried about the problems she might have brought Evangeline, but she *had* brought those problems deliberately. He liked all of that in her. He needed a woman who could be ruthless and yet yield to him.

"Don't steal my heart, Timur," she whispered against his chest. "I know your type. You say all the right things and you do them—" She broke off and shook her head, once more looking up at him. "You're a dangerous man. Very scary. Evangeline and her husband might not be what I was looking for, but you're that man."

He wouldn't lie to her. "I am." He knew what she meant. He was exactly that man. He'd always be that man in order to keep his brother, Evangeline and now Ashe safe. He was the kind of man who could kiss his woman, laying his heart at her feet, and then go torture and kill an enemy to ensure those he loved survived another day.

"I don't want this life. I don't. It killed my parents. It will kill all of you, and I don't want to watch that happen."

"Don't run from me, Ashe," he cautioned again, something seizing hard in his chest. It was an actual pain and he had to resist rubbing his chest. "We'll work things out. Just stay here for right now. I need you to help protect Evangeline just in case the hit team slips through the ring of protection I have around her." He watched her face carefully and he could see by her expression she'd feared all along that she'd brought a team of killers down on Evangeline and Fyodor. She wasn't going to protest or act as if she didn't know what he was talking about. He could hear Evangeline working in the other room, putting pastries in the display cases. She needed Ashe's help and he was holding her up.

"You're just saying that."

"Give me your word."

She sighed. "Fine then. You have a few hours, but I can't stay all day. I need a head start. Running right now is my only option. This was the plan, leading him here and hoping your people would take care of him."

"He isn't the hit team. Apostol Delov is his name, and he is a messenger. He tracks and then fingers the prey, and the real killers come in and do the actual killing. It's always under the guise of justice. In this case, your parents had done something to bring down the wrath of someone powerful on them. That death sentence extends to you."

She shook her head. "How do you know so much about it?"

"I'm part of that world. I was born into it. I will die in it. I never had the chance to get out."

She held his gaze steadily. "But you wanted out."

"Of course, I wanted out."

"Then let's run together, Timur. I'll drop my vengeance plan and you drop whatever it is you're planning and let's go. Together. I'll go with you right now. We'll run so far they'll never find us and we can live free, away from this kind of thing."

The temptation was strong, but he could hear Evangeline moving around in the next room, trying to give them privacy. His brother's innocent woman. Even if he could abandon Fyodor to his fate, he couldn't leave Evangeline.

"What of her?" He nodded toward the shop room. "You brought this down on her, but you would expect me to leave her to whatever fate happens?"

"No, they'll follow us. That's why I'm leaving. He'll follow me. It's me he wants, not Evangeline or Fyodor."

"You led our worst enemy straight to our front door, Ashe. Believe me, if he's sent word to his master, they will forget all about you and concentrate on killing Fyodor, his woman, me, Gorya and our other cousins. We committed unforgivable crimes against our family and they want us to pay for those sins."

Her face went very pale. "What are you talking about? I led him here because I thought, when he made his move, Evangeline's husband would kill him. Why would he suddenly switch his interests? You're wrong, Timur. You have to be wrong."

She was pleading for him to be wrong, but he knew he wasn't. "Apostol Delov isn't the real name of a real person. He is 'the messenger.' My uncle Lazar Amurov has a very bad sense of humor. He wants his victims to know they are living on borrowed time, so he sends a man who calls himself Apostol Delov to his prey. That man marks the door of the house they live in. This morning, he was on his way to mark your door, the door of Evangeline's house."

"See?" She grabbed hold of that eagerly. "He was after me, not Evangeline."

"He knows who we are. He will have sent word. We left Russia under very bad circumstances, and the rewards for our whereabouts are hefty. Lazar has been looking for us for a long time."

"I'm sorry. I'm so sorry."

"Don't feel too guilty, we made certain we were prepared before we came out of hiding and Fyodor took back the family name."

"What can I do?"

She didn't question whether or not he told the truth; she heard it in his voice. He was grateful she didn't ask him questions he didn't want to answer. He stepped back, away from the warmth of her body.

"You can stay right here so I don't have to worry on more than one front. Give me your word."

"I'll stay."

There was the strange little twist to those two words that

made him think she wasn't telling him the exact truth. She wasn't exactly lying, but she wasn't telling him everything. He didn't have time to puzzle it out.

"I mean it, Ashe. I won't be happy if you run and I have to go after you."

She shrugged. "I don't live my entire life with the idea that everything I do should make you happy."

It was difficult to keep every expression off his face, but he managed. "Well, work on it, baby. It will make life easier all the way around for both of us."

She laughed again. It wasn't her real, full-blown laugh, but it was there all the same. She shook her head and stepped away from the wall. "You're ridiculous. I'd better get to work or I'll get fired and then I won't have a choice."

He stared down at her for a long time, trying to read the truth in those two little words she'd given him. The twisted ones. *I'll stay.* How could they be both truth and lie? He stalked to the doorway of the kitchen. "No matter what Ashe does, don't fire her until I get back, Evangeline."

She pushed past him to grab another tray of pastries. "Do you plan on doing something that will get you fired, Ashe? Because I really need the help. Today is always one of my busiest days."

"I hadn't planned on it," Ashe said.

He heard the ring of truth, glared at her, just to make certain she knew he meant business, and he hurried out. I'm on my way, he texted Kyanite.

Did you contact Fyodor?

He didn't want his brother anywhere near this mess. And it was a mess. By claiming Ashe, he'd made it even messier. Still, Fyodor needed to know what was going on. He called his brother's number—the one nearly impossible to trace. They used short bursts and always talked in code.

"Yeah?"

He heard the worry in his brother's voice. He knew Timur

wouldn't be calling on that phone unless they didn't want cops—or anyone else—to overhear.

"Heading to visit an old friend. Want to come along?"

"Busy."

"Message me if you can get away later to join us."

There was a short silence. "I can probably get away. I'll put work off."

"There's no need. I'll ask him to come around tonight."

"That sounds good."

They both hung up. The conversation was seconds only, but it told Fyodor that the messenger had arrived and Timur was going to interrogate him. They didn't want Fyodor to be followed to the old building where they brought in the occasional prisoner they needed information from. Timur knew a million ways to extract information. He'd grown up learning from the best. His father and two uncles enjoyed their work and they'd made certain to teach their sons everything they knew.

He pulled on his gloves and slid into his car. There was rarely a tail on him. The cops were much more interested in his brother. Sometimes they had someone watching Evangeline's bakery, but more likely they just went in for the pastries and coffee. Nevertheless, he took evasive action, maneuvering through streets, changing lanes and turning abruptly. He went down two long alleys and made a circle of the outskirts of the city before finally reaching his destination.

He pulled the car under cover. They never parked on the streets. The warehouses had been part of the business Fyodor inherited when he took on the mantle of Antonio Arnotto. There were two auto body garages, one tire shop and a towing company, all strictly legitimate. The cops had investigated often and still sniffed around, but they weren't going to find anything.

Timur parked in the parking garage that ran overhead,

the length of the building. The only cameras were the ones that would tell him if they had unexpected visitors. He took the elevator to the ground floor and then stepped off. He turned right, and then went through a door that led to a hallway between the shops. Six steps in, he unlocked another door and stepped through. A retinal scan got him into the elevator that took him down another story.

Kyanite and Rodion waited for him. They sat calmly playing cards while their prisoner wriggled and thrashed at the end of a rope. He could barely touch the cement floor with his toes. There wasn't a mark on him anywhere that Timur could see. The two men he relied most heavily on—other than Gorya, who was with Fyodor—could always be counted on.

When he walked in, they put down their cards and rose to their feet. Apostol froze, his gaze on Timur's face. Timur didn't deign to look at him. He jerked his chin toward the cards. "Who's ahead?"

"Kye, because he cheats."

Kyanite laughed. "I am, because he doesn't pay attention to what's been played."

"That's true," Rodion admitted. "I never understood why you like this game."

"Because we get your money," Kyanite said, shoving his shoulder into the other man.

Timur wandered over to Apostol. The man eyed him the same way a mouse might a cobra. He didn't take his gaze from Timur. His mouth opened and closed and then he shook his head repeatedly so hard, Timur was certain if he didn't stop, he'd snap his own neck. The distinct smell of fresh urine permeated the room.

Apostol Delov was a strong man who kept himself in shape. He had skills in tracking, in investigative work, and he was very good at protecting himself. It didn't look as if Kyanite or Rodion had touched him, but he was already terrified. They'd done their job well.

"I see my reputation precedes me," Timur observed, keeping his voice pitched very low. He glanced at Kyanite, who immediately handed him the messenger's phone. It was already queued to the pertinent material. Send the team. I am on my way to mark the door.

A separate text followed. Is the reward still good for the whereabouts of your nephews?

Yes. Very worried about them.

Timur smiled down, without one iota of humor, at the damning message already sent to his uncle. No doubt there would be two hit teams on the way. He might have even hired some of the *bratya* that were already in the States. They'd known it was coming, they'd just hoped for more time. Fyodor had taken back his rightful name, no longer hiding under the guise of Alonzo Massi, an Italian. They had talked it over and determined it was better to know Lazar was coming after them then to wonder when he would stumble across their trail and come at them unawares.

"Tell me about the woman, Delov." It was an order.

The man didn't make a sound. His eyes were wild and his heart beat out of control.

"You can die hard or you can just die. It's up to you." Timur sounded bored.

"You can't kill me. I'm just the messenger. That's the rules. You can't kill the messenger," Apostol stuttered.

"We don't live by the rules," Timur said. "Lazar knew if you were taken, you would be killed. Why do you think he chose the lowest leopards in the lair for his messengers? He expected you to be caught. I don't mind taking you apart. I grew up learning those skills. You get used to it. My old man was a master at it. It's your choice."

Deliberately, Timur shrugged, but he didn't take his eyes from his prey. He let Delov see his cat, that murderous leopard who wanted to tear the prisoner from limb to limb. This was the man who had chased their mate and would have marked her for death, although he hadn't succeeded in marking the door, nor had he sent the address. Kyanite and Rodion had gotten to him first.

"Tell me about her. Why does Lazar want this woman?"

For a moment, it looked as if the prisoner would try to hold out, but when Timur took a step toward him, he changed his mind.

"Her mother was sold at auction to a very wealthy man in Greece. He bought her for his son, just to play with for a time. She was supposed to be given back when the boy was tired of her. She would have come to Lazar's lair. Lazar had promised her to his lieutenant. The two kids ran off. Lazar vowed to find her and kill both of them." Apostol stumbled over the explanation he gave it up so fast.

"How did he find them?"

Ashe told Timur her family had lived off the grid, and yet, in spite of that, Apostol had been sent after them, along with a hit team.

A sob escaped, hastily choked back. "The girl, Raisa was her name, wanted to find her sister and help her get out before Lazar ordered her killed. The sister, I think her name was Sarafina, was the wife of Lazar's lieutenant, given to him because they'd lost the other. Raisa got in touch with Sarafina and her husband found out. They talked about exposing the trafficking pipeline."

Stupidity. Ashe's mother hadn't known the first thing about survival in their world. Her husband had been more cautious, but he should never have allowed his wife to communicate with her sister.

"More information, Delov." He kept his voice very low, seemingly non-threatening, knowing from a thousand experiences that a low tone would be taken as a threat.

"They had a secret means of talking to each other, a kind of code, but Sarafina's husband found her diary and tortured her until she told him what it was and how to decipher it. She's dead now. He beat her to death as a testament of his loyalty to the lair and its leaders."

"And then Lazar sent you straight to the United States to find them?"

"I need a cigarette. Please. Let me have a cigarette."

"I don't allow my men to smoke, nor do I," Timur said, wishing he did smoke. His leopard would never have stood for it. "You'll have to do without. Answer the question."

"Yes, yes. He sent me. I found them and marked their whereabouts for the team. The team missed the daughter."

"You mean *you* missed the daughter."

"Raisa never mentioned her daughter to Sarafina." There was a whine in the voice. "That wasn't my fault."

"And you made certain Lazar knew it wasn't your fault, didn't you?" Timur asked, his voice much gentler than before. "You told him about the girl yourself."

"Yes. I can't be held accountable if no one knew about her," Apostol insisted.

"No, only accountable because you all but signed her death warrant by giving her up to Lazar. She wasn't on his radar and could have gone her entire life without having a gun aimed at her, but you trained it right on her."

"No. Yes. No. But you see, I had to. If he found out . . ." Delov squeezed his eyes shut but then couldn't take the silence stretching out and had to open them again. "I'm just the messenger. I don't kill anyone."

"Of course, you do. You bring the hit squad right to the door of Lazar's victims. First a girl who had been sold into slavery at what age? Fifteen? Sixteen? Younger?"

"Fifteen." Tears tracked down the messenger's face.

This was a man who was dangerous. Scary. In spite of what Timur had said about Lazar choosing the lowest leopards, it wasn't the truth. This man hunted, and he had to be able to defend himself over and over, on his own. What did that make Timur, if Apostol was so terrified now? Timur didn't want to think too much about that.

Timur might have relented if he thought for one moment that Apostol Delov was crying for that young, frightened girl sold to strangers for their pleasure, but he knew better. He knew the messenger cried for himself. He despised the man. Ashe could have been free and clear if the man had just kept his mouth shut. Her mother had been careful not to allow one hint of her existence in her coded correspondence with her sister.

"You gave the daughter up to save your own skin," Timur mused, slowly circling the bound body. "What did you tell Lazar about her?"

"That she was running. Only that she was running. I followed her. It wasn't easy. She's very good, but she's attractive, and people remember attractive women."

Timur knew that was true. He would have noticed her if she'd been in a crowd. "Do you know who she belongs to, Apostol? Me. My leopard. You know the reputation of our leopards. They want blood for the least infraction. They demand it. Right now, he's raking at me, trying to claw his way out to get to you."

He still spoke in a low voice as he completed the circle and ended up standing in front of the messenger. "You are the direct cause of the hit out on my woman. And then, as if that wasn't a big enough insult to me, you were really greedy, weren't you?"

Apostol nodded over and over, sobs escaping. He couldn't take his eyes from Timur, mesmerized by him, terrified of him, still hopeful that he would relent and pardon his sins.

"You sold out Fyodor and Evangeline for money, didn't you? You sold out Gorya and me." He indicated Kyanite and Rodion. "The others who were loyal to us. You traded our lives for money, Delov."

"I didn't tell him where you were. I just asked about the reward. I just *asked*. Someone else was going to see you. One of the members of the hit squad. They would have seen you."

"That excuses you?"

Apostol grabbed at that, clearly not hearing it was a question. "Yes. Yes. It isn't my fault. I needed the money to get out from under him. Someone was going to get it. Why not me? I needed it more than anyone. I *deserved* it more."

"Tell me about the team coming for Ashe. When do you expect them and where are they staying?"

"They came in through Miami. I supplied their weapons. It's standard for me to do that," Apostol said hastily. "I have to do it, it's part of my job."

"How many are here to get my woman?" He said it deliberately to remind Apostol of his sins against Timur.

"Three. Three came in."

"Where did you get the weapons you provided them, and how did you arrange to deliver them?"

"I contact the local supplier, get the weapons and then leave them in the motel for the hit team."

"Who was the supplier?"

"A man Lazar does business with."

Timur stared at him until the messenger let out a wail.

"Trafficking business. He brings the girls in from Russia and other places Lazar's people get them and in return, the man here, Ulisse Mancini, ships girls from here back to Russia."

"Mancini's territory is Houston, but he does a lot of business with a man by the name of Emilio Bassini. Are Mancini and Bassini both doing business with Lazar?"

"Mancini is the name I hear all the time."

"Did the other hit teams come in through Houston?" Deliberately he made it plural. He had the feeling the second hit team was already close. The texts were from several days earlier, time enough for Lazar to get his men positioned in the States.

Apostol nodded several times. "Mancini's men met them at the airport and hooked them up with a car. I left their weapons in the motel."

"Name of motel."

Apostol shuddered and then his body began to contort, his leopard staring through his eyes. The messenger's fear finally pushed the animal out. Timur waited until the leopard had fully shifted and then he shot him fast and mercifully. There was no point in prolonging the death of the hapless creature. Apostol had held back his leopard as long as he possibly could, but in the end, the animal had overcome his will and emerged to protect his human counterpart.

"He has to be burned," Timur said. "Ashes scattered as usual."

"No problem, Timur," Kyanite said. "Are you going after the hit squad?"

He nodded. "I have no choice. They're here to kill Ashe, and she belongs to me. In any case, we'd better prepare for an all-out war. I think the second team may have arrived as well. I'll send word to Fyodor. We need a meeting with the others. If we're bringing them all to town, we'd best have Lazar's team—or teams—shut down before that."

"This woman, Ashe, is she really yours? Your leopard's mate?" Rodion asked.

Timur knew the man, like him, had lost all hope of such a thing happening. The fact that Fyodor had found Evangeline, and now Timur had found Ashe, gave them back that hope. "My leopard claimed her. Like what happens when we're close to Evangeline, he calms when he's close to Ashe. It gives me a respite from his continual clawing. He's always out for blood."

"Mine too," Rodion admitted. "Sometimes I'm afraid to go to sleep at night. He wants to kill everything and everybody."

"That's what we get raising our leopards on violence," Timur said. He looked at the sad proof suspended in the air by the ropes. The leopard's fur was thin and lackluster. The messenger hadn't allowed him out in a long while. Most likely, Apostol knew, at one time, the leopard was the stronger of the two of them and should he have allowed him out, he wouldn't be able to shift back into his human form.

Abruptly, Timur turned. He needed to get back to his

brother and discuss everything the messenger had told him. He also needed to make a formal claim on Ashe and then inform the other bosses in their closest circle that they needed a meet. He and Fyodor would have to decide who they would trust and who they would avoid giving the information to.

"It seems odd that Lazar would spend so much time looking for your woman's mother," Rodion said. "She wasn't related to him. She wasn't going to be given to him. He had a wife. Why was she really that important to him?"

"I don't know," Timur admitted. "But Delov was telling the truth as he knew it. Lazar sent him to first find Ashe's mother and father and then to finish the job by finding Ashe. Finding us was a coincidence. He thought he was about to cash in on the ultimate prize."

"Lazar would have killed him before he paid one penny of that money to him," Kyanite said.

"Absolutely. Delov should have known that too," Rodion added.

"He didn't want to believe it." With a sigh, Timur turned away. "Get back to the bakery as soon as possible. I don't like that we don't know the exact whereabouts of that squad. A standard team would be three men, especially if they're really only after Ashe. Keep your eyes open, and remember, if they get Evangeline, we're all dead men anyway. Fyodor will lose his fucking mind."

"Pretty sure the same will happen to you if they get Ashe," Rodion said with a small grin that didn't, in any way, light his eyes. "It won't happen, Timur."

Timur nodded, a short jerk of his chin the only answer when his heart clenched painfully. These two men had come with him when he'd fled the lair. When his father, Patva, had murdered his mother in front of Timur and Gorya, both of them had tried to stop him, but Patva was a huge, powerful man with a mean, vicious leopard. Only Fyodor had been able to best him.

Fyodor not only ripped him to pieces, but he went after every male in the lair loyal to Patva. In spite of their injuries, Gorya and Timur had tried to aid him. Although Rodion and Kyanite hadn't been present during Patva's attack or Fyodor's subsequent destruction of the lair, they'd both been Timur's boyhood friends. And despite the fact that they had powerful and violent fathers of their own, they hadn't hesitated to follow Timur and Fyodor when they'd fled Russia. That kind of loyalty could never be bought. Fear couldn't buy that loyalty. Timur was reminded of that every time he saw the two men. They weren't related by blood, but they were brothers all the same.

Timur controlled his impatience to get back to the bakery. He had a duty to his brother and he had to trust Kyanite and Rodion to safeguard the two women along with the others assigned to their protection. He drove as sedately as possible. They couldn't do much about their cars moving through the city being caught on traffic cameras so it was important to always have a reason to be where the cars could be traced. In this case, he made certain to talk to one of the garage owners about their lease that was coming due. The conversation was brief, but he had said he would be looking around at some of the other spaces they still had open. He was seen doing just that.

Fyodor was not so patient. He didn't like being at the helm and was still getting used to the mantle of authority sitting on his shoulders. He had grown up as a soldier and then enforcer, and he didn't like to have others guarding him. He particularly didn't like anything that kept him away from Evangeline.

He threw open the door before Timur could even reach for the doorknob. "Everything, Timur, and fast."

That was Fyodor, no fucking around. Timur looked past him to see Gorya shaking his head, annoyed that Fyodor had broken protocol and opened the door, possibly exposing himself to a sniper's shot.

Timur sighed. "You can't do this bullshit every time you're worried about Evangeline, Fyodor. I can't be in two places at one time. You want me interrogating a prisoner, then you have to cooperate with Gorya or Kye or Rodion." He gestured to the man standing just to Fyodor's left. "Or Vitaly. If someone shoots you, Evangeline is going to be a widow."

"No one's going to shoot me. You've got so many patrols roaming these grounds, we can't keep any other animals around," Fyodor said. "Tell us."

Timur gave him all the information he'd gotten from the messenger. "I've got his phone. We should be able to go through the texts and find out the motel where the team is staying. We need the information immediately, Vitaly. Everything you can get. I want names, if possible, the address, when they got into town, what weapons they have."

Vitaly took the phone. "You got it."

Fyodor reached for his phone. The first call was to his cousin Mitya. Mitya had nearly died protecting both Fyodor and Evangeline. He had been voted in to take over a crime lord's territory. Patrizio Amodeo had put out the hit on Evangeline, and now Mitya was wearing Amodeo's ring and commanding his men. Mitya was Lazar's son, and Sevastyan was Rolan's son. Sevastyan was responsible for Mitya's protection now. More than anything, Lazar and Rolan wanted the two dead. They had to be warned.

He set up a meeting with Drake Donovan and all of their trusted allies, promising first that they would deal with the hit squad. They couldn't have those men sneaking behind their backs while they readied themselves for war. They also needed the women safe, and that meant Evangeline would have to turn her beloved bakery over to someone else for a time. Timur made it abundantly clear that Ashe would be going with Evangeline. Fyodor protested.

"You said yourself you can't tell what's the truth. She led them straight here."

"She's my leopard's mate," Timur argued patiently when he didn't feel patient at all. "She's mine, Fyodor. Mine. She'll be your sister-in-law, so shut the fuck up and deal with it."

"We may all end up dead with a viper right in the heart of our nest," Fyodor groused, but he didn't protest again.

Still, Timur knew that meant Fyodor would be questioning Ashe himself and it probably wouldn't be pretty. He'd stick close just in case. His brother was very protective of Evangeline and Timur couldn't blame him.

"I've got everything we need to get these fuckers," Vitaly said.

6

THERE was a certain smell to law enforcement, as if they rubbed shoulders during their morning meetings or all inhaled the same closed-in air. Maybe it was just a look about them in spite of their plain clothes. Ashe didn't know exactly, but her father had taught her at an early age to be observant and to use every sense she had. She'd inhaled the scent of officers and smelled that same faint scent on plainclothesmen. Now, she was certain, there was a convention for undercover cops being held right in the bakery.

Evangeline obviously knew a few of them and she handled them exactly as she did every other customer. She smiled and chatted with them while she worked as fast and efficiently as ever. She seemed to pick up names fast and she retained them. By the afternoon, Ashe was certain Evangeline could charm the birds out of the trees. She certainly had the policemen enamored of her.

There was one called Jeff Meyers who flirted outrageously with Evangeline. Ashe studied him while she drew a shot for his drink. He wasn't joking like some of the others. He definitely had a thing for her boss. While Jeff flirted with Evangeline, his partner, Ray Harding, tried doing the same with her.

Ashe had been programmed at an early age by her father to be careful around any law enforcement. She'd never understood why, but it made her leery. Right now, with so many on- and off-duty police in the bakery, she was on edge. She exchanged a quick, concerned glance with Evangeline. What were they all doing there? They knew Fyodor had an office there, but if they were watching the bakery, they would have known he wasn't there.

Evangeline shrugged, telling Ashe that customers were just that and it was good for business. Even if Fyodor came in, he hadn't done anything to warrant an arrest. But what about Timur? Anxiety gripped her. She was fairly certain Timur did a *lot* of things to warrant his arrest. He might be doing something right that very minute and every one of the police officers knew about it. She didn't because she never carried a cell phone.

Deliberately, she bumped her hip against Evangeline's in passing. When her boss turned to look at her, she mouthed, *"Text Timur. Make certain he's all right."*

Evangeline nodded, and kept working as though they hadn't consulted at all. She drew three more drinks and sold fifteen pastries, all to one table, before she pushed open the door to the kitchen to get another tray out. Ashe saw her pull her phone from her pocket.

She smiled at Ray, who was hovering. "Another? Are you certain? You're getting double shots. You'll be unable to fall asleep if you keep it up," she warned. Then she could have groaned aloud when she saw his inevitable grin at her choice of words.

"You come out with me tonight and I can show you why

sleeping is overrated," he said, leaning one elbow on the counter.

Deep inside, she felt that alien being, her cat, stretch languidly. It was really weird knowing she was a shifter, like her mother and father, that all along a leopard had been dormant inside her. She'd dreamt of having her own leopard after her parents had shown her theirs. She'd wanted one, but now, she was very aware the mood of the leopard could affect her own mood.

"I'm thinking that's as cheesy as hell, Mr. Harding." She flashed him a look from under her lashes, all too aware several of the cops in the room were listening. She leaned closer, as if she was being conspiratorial. "What's with the sudden show of the boys in blue? Not that I'm complaining, you all make me feel very safe, but we've never had this many in at one time."

Ray leaned one hip against the counter and turned to survey the room. "We took a vote this week and this bakery won, hands down, as the best in San Antonio. Everyone wanted to try Evangeline's pastries."

He wasn't a good liar. The fact that he was lying made her more anxious than ever. Why were they there? She smiled at him as she took his money. Cash. She was meticulous about giving him his change. She had a sudden nightmare vision of being hauled off by several cops for stealing pennies from Ray.

"Call me Ray, not Mr. Harding. Mr. Harding is far too formal for a beautiful woman to be calling me. You're making me feel old."

"You're a customer, and Evangeline told me to address all customers by their surnames if they give it to me. You gave it to me."

"Clearly a mistake," he said.

She knew he waited for her to acknowledge his given name, but she pretended to be busy straightening pastries in the case.

He sauntered away, trying to look casual. Timur always looked casually powerful, a look Ray hadn't learned to pull off yet. She nearly groaned as she took the next order. She had it bad for Timur already and she hadn't been around him all that much. She must really have a thing for dangerous men.

The bell over the door sounded and she suppressed a little sigh as she glanced up. They hadn't had a break during the morning and now the afternoon crowd showed no sign of slowing. Two men came in and her heart sank. They had every sign of being leopard with their stocky, fighter builds. They wore business suits, a dead giveaway as far as she was concerned. The bakery got its share of the business crowd, but the suits didn't go with the toughness neither man could quite conceal.

Directly behind the two men were Kyanite and Rodion. She recognized them from being in the bakery the day before. Evangeline had pointed them out as Fyodor's security. That made her even more anxious. She didn't want Fyodor anywhere near his wife's Small Sweet Shoppe, not with two men she suspected were there to kill her and a room full of police officers.

Her heart jumped and then began to pound. Kyanite flashed a grin at her and stepped around the two men who appeared to be reading the chalkboard menu. Now he was in front of them and Rodion was behind them.

"Twenty-ounce latte," he said and mouthed the words, *"Just breathe. This is under control."*

What was under control? How did Evangeline do it? She was busy with a customer, laughing, acting like she didn't notice the potential war developing. Ashe forced air through her lungs. If she was contemplating, even for a moment, being a gangster's moll, she wasn't going to get far applying for the job. When the question came about how she did when cops and hit men were in the same room, she was going to flunk big-time.

Then her leopard was there, rolling around like a kitten, purring loudly so that Ashe couldn't fail to feel the stroking caresses along the insides of her body. That friction created a blossoming need that struck fast and ferociously, adding to her anxiety. Had Timur been there, she would have dragged him to the ladies' room by his ridiculous tie and had her way with him. Multiple times. Because, seriously, with the monster need so urgent, painfully throbbing between her legs, she was certain once wouldn't be enough to put out the fire.

It came on so fast, she could barely think. Pressure built, coiling like a spring, winding tighter and tighter until she was sure the tension in her would snap. Every step she took, her jeans rubbed along her clit, sending shooting sparks through her bloodstream and inflaming her more.

"Take a break," Evangeline said. "I've got this."

Hot color rushed up Ashe's neck and into her face. Even Evangeline knew that she was exhibiting the signs of heat in her cat. Where the hell was Timur when she needed him? Evangeline looked at her with sympathy, but Kyanite and Rodion, along with the two hit men, stared at her with fixed fascination and more than a little lust.

Abruptly, she turned and hurried into the privacy of the very warm kitchen. She had never wished for a cell phone. Her father had told her those were too easy to track, even the ones supposedly untraceable could be traced. She believed her father. He'd been a genius in a lot of ways. He'd built their own generator and could take apart and put together a computer. He didn't seem such a genius now when she wanted to call Timur and tell him to run over. As in *run*. Fast.

Her body felt on fire. Scorching hot. Desperate for relief. She paced and breathed deeply, trying to rid herself of the hormones raging through her bloodstream. Something moved beneath her skin and her entire body itched, the wave slipping through her at an alarming rate, slowing and then beginning over again.

Her breasts felt swollen and achy. Her nipples were twin burning peaks. Her clit pounded with hot blood, but deep in her core intensity raged, a fiery passionate storm she couldn't control. She needed sex desperately. Timur's kind of sex. Hot and brutal. Wild. She wanted him to be so desperate for her that the moment he saw her, he would throw her up against the wall and get down to a savage pace that would quench the need pouring through her.

The broom closet door slowly opened. The movement was so stealthy, she might not have noticed but for her leopard, who was on alert. She wanted a mate near. She was rubbing and calling out, using her very potent pheromones to signal her closeness to her time. She wanted her mate close. Any motion, no matter how small, attracted her attention.

Ashe backed up, getting around the work island to put distance between the closet and her. She could try to hide, but the pheromones were easily read by a male leopard. If the hit team—and she was identifying the men as such—was the distraction so another member could slip inside and kill her, her going into heat had only aided them. She looked around quickly for a weapon. Evangeline had spilled milk earlier and had mopped it up. The mop lay against the far wall, its handle a long, thick wooden cylinder, the only thing she could see that might work. She made her way to it while the door continued to open.

As her fingers settled around the long handle, a man in a blue shirt burst out from behind the door. She swung the mop with all her strength at his head. It was the last thing he was prepared for. A knife dropped from nerveless fingers as she connected with his head, knocking him backward so that his body hit the closet door, slamming it closed. He seemed to bounce, and she hit him again.

Ashe had no idea if the background music playing would drown out the sound of the slamming closet door, but she kept her lips pressed tightly together to keep from making a sound. The man drew a gun from his boot and started to lift it. She struck, slashing down on his arm with the thick wooden pole.

"Bitch," he snarled, as the gun went flying.

"Kyanite!" She wasn't too proud to call for help, especially when blue shirt caught the mop handle and yanked. "Kyanite! I need your help."

The man ripped the pole out of her hands and she leapt toward the far corner where the gun had landed. Now, he was in possession of the longer reach and he swung it at her head with lethal force.

Kyanite leapt into the air from the doorway, driving at his opponent's chest with both feet. He took him all the way down to the floor. They landed in a rolling tangle of arms and legs. She stood there, holding her breath, legs apart, hands up and aiming straight at the assassin's head. The problem was, her target kept moving, and she couldn't fire and take the chance of hitting Kyanite. Nor did she want to fire, not with a roomful of cops just beyond the kitchen door.

"I knocked over the mop bucket, Evangeline," she called. "Sorry. We're cleaning it up."

Both men could shift easily, both partially and wholly, and did so, raking claws down chests and bellies to try to eviscerate or slice each other's heart. Blood sprayed across Evangeline's clean floor, marring the black and white tiles and the lower doors of the oak cabinets. Then Rodion was there. She knew he must have heard the fighting, which meant any other leopard in the room heard as well. She didn't care if that tipped off the entire police force; she didn't want Kyanite to die because of her.

She turned the music up and stuck her head through the door. "Sorry, Evangeline, Kyanite slipped in the water and hit the sound bar. He keeps falling into the island and he's sent all the dishes crashing down. Don't worry, I'll get it clean." She deliberately let herself sound desperate, so that she was believable. She looked only at Evangeline while she spoke and then she closed the door again.

Rodion timed his entry into the fight, looking at his partner. Something passed between them—she caught just a glimpse of expression and eye movement. Kyanite shifted again, and using two claws, ripped his opponent open, at the same time turning the man's body so that his head was close to Rodion.

Ashe was certain the assassin never saw death coming. Rodion caught the man's head in his very strong hands and wrenched. Slowly, the assailant's body relaxed and then he lay dead on the floor, all life drained out of him. It seemed to be such a gradual process, that dying. His body went first and then she saw the life leave his eyes. Her stomach lurched.

It was Kyanite who took the gun from her hands. She slowly sank to the floor, adrenaline coursing through her veins, and she realized her leopard was going crazy in an effort to protect her.

She'd practiced for this moment and she'd blown it. Completely. "I'm sorry, Kyanite, I didn't have a clear shot." She hadn't moved around the fighting either, as she should have, but she'd been mesmerized by the horrific battle between the two leopards. They'd fought as humans and as cats. Sometimes half and half. "I'm afraid I didn't do very well my first time out."

"You did fine," Kyanite objected. "More than fine. The other two have taken off. They'll know soon enough that their friend didn't make it out of here alive, nor did he get to you." He turned his head to glare at his partner. "What the fuck took you so long? One shot or yell, and every cop in that room would be back here and we'd be tied up with bullshit questions for hours."

Rodion had the grace to look embarrassed. "Honestly? I thought, at first, she called you back here to . . . um . . . help her. You know. As in help. I was trying to figure out how to cover your back when Timur found out."

"Are you kidding me?" Kyanite snapped. "Do you think I'm the kind of man who would poach on a brother's territory?"

Could this get any more humiliating? First, they all felt the effects of her leopard's heat. Now, they were discussing her as if she wasn't a real person at all. They'd designated her Timur's property, and that meant Kyanite wouldn't cross that line with her.

"Commendable." She forced her body to move when it didn't want to cooperate. "I'm not Timur's woman, or his mate, or whatever you think I am to him, and that isn't an invitation to either of you."

Rodion nudged Kyanite. "There's that little flash of temper we were warned about."

Fury burned through her, an aftermath of her leopard's rising heat. She needed an outlet for her scattered emotions. "Who told you I had a temper?"

Kyanite grinned at her. "Wash up, *malen'kiy smerch.*"

She narrowed her eyes on him. "What did you just call me?"

"It means 'little tornado,'" Rodion said helpfully.

Kyanite kept grinning, completely unrepentant. "That's what Timur calls you."

"Not to my face, he doesn't," Ashe said. "That's because he's a very smart man. It's a good thing you have the gun in your possession, otherwise it might accidentally go off." She turned away from them with an indignant sniff. Her leopard had settled, and Evangeline would want a break.

"Ashe, you might want to wash up," Rodion pointed out again.

She hurried to the bathroom to clean up. Evangeline couldn't hold the line with policemen everywhere, not alone anyway. Since she considered this her mess to clean up, she needed to step up her game and give Evangeline whatever she needed.

"Kye?" She shortened his name because it was so much

easier. She came out of the bathroom drying off her hands. Trying not to look at the dead body they were rolling up in a large tarp, she forced air through her lungs. "Do you think they came for me? Or for Evangeline? I don't want her to get hurt."

"What matters right now is that neither of you were harmed. We've got a roomful of cops, honey, and it seems to me there's a reason they've come."

The door swung inward and Evangeline stuck her head through the opening. "You about ready, Ashe? It's quieting down and I could use a break." She looked tired. Flushed. So un-Evangeline-like. She took a step into the room and staggered.

Ashe leapt over the island work table and landed beside her, circling her waist with one arm and taking her weight. "What's wrong?" Had the hit team managed to get off a shot before they left the bakery? A poisoned dart, maybe? That would be silent enough. "Did you feel a sting? Like a wasp bite?" If by drawing the hit team to Evangeline's door her friend was harmed or even worse, she would never forgive herself.

"Shit, Evangeline," Rodion snapped, coming up on her other side. "What's wrong?"

"I just feel a little faint. I'm too warm all of a sudden. I didn't eat breakfast, and I think maybe my sugar is low." Evangeline sounded like she always did, very matter-of-fact. She didn't seem bothered by her weakness. "Go out there and make sure our local police don't get any ideas about visiting our kitchen. And, Kye, you can stay and explain to me what's going on while Rodion sticks with Ashe."

Now she sounded like the wife of a powerful man like Fyodor. She gave orders and clearly expected everyone to follow them. She hadn't freaked out over the dead body, and she'd chosen Kyanite to stay behind because it was going to take some doing to clean him up.

"He's going to need first aid," Ashe said.

"No worries. At this point, I should apply for med school," Evangeline quipped, but she sank into the chair Ashe and Rodion took her to. "Who is he?"

Kyanite was going through the assassin's pockets. "I don't recognize him, but then, I didn't meet too many of Lazar's soldiers. He appears to have come from Lazar's lair." He came up with a wallet. "ID's a fake. It says he's from Bulgaria. He's definitely leopard, and he was fast and strong. He nearly tore my guts out." He pulled a pack of cigarettes out of the man's shirt pocket. "These are Russian. He gave up his identity, but couldn't give up his smokes. That figures. He has three weapons on him."

"How did he get into the kitchen when there are men patrolling and more on the roof?" Evangeline demanded.

"They're leopard, Evangeline, just like we are," Kyanite said softly. He pressed his fingers to his forehead. "We'll go through this again and again until we figure out how he got in here. We'll dam up the holes."

He looked up at Ashe. "You'd better get out there, honey, before someone gets suspicious. A break is one thing, but both of you back here talking to us—no one is going to buy that—not even if you admitted to dishes breaking. Not if they come in often and know how Evangeline is about her business."

Ashe pushed the swinging door outward but looked back toward Evangeline. "I think you're all a little crazy," she said, overly loud, and laughed. Even to her own ears, her laughter sounded a little hollow, but it was the best she could do.

She took a step toward the display cases and counter when her shoe caught her eye. She'd washed up, but she hadn't cleaned her shoes. Drops of blood were splattered across the toe. She glanced toward Rodion, who had followed her out, and then deliberately looked down at her shoe.

"Wait, Ashe, your shoe's untied." He dropped down to

his knee, at the same time reaching for the damp cloth that hung near the espresso machine. He wiped the drops of blood, putting a little strength into it to make certain he removed the stains.

"Thanks. I have a bad habit of sitting around with my bare feet up." She dared to look around the bakery. The crowd of policemen hadn't thinned out. She went to the counter to take orders. Thankfully, no one was angry because they'd left the counter unattended for a few minutes. "Who's next?"

Ray was at the front of the line. "You should put in a deli, Ashe."

She didn't like the way he said her name, as if he thought it was fake. Timur had thought it was as well. She liked her name. It was unusual and had been given to her by her deceased parents. That made it extra special.

"If we did that, we'd be a deli, not a bakery. Most of our customers like our pastries and desserts, Mr. Harding."

"Call me Ray. Did you break all the dishes? It sounded like it."

"It felt like it, cleaning up the mess. I tripped over a mop and then Kye did the same."

He leaned his elbow onto the counter and studied her face. "I'd like us to be friends. At least call me Ray instead of mister. Will you do that?"

"I can do that," Ashe said. "If you stop asking me out. I can't go out with you because I'm already in a relationship with someone." She wanted to roll her eyes as the lie slipped out of her mouth. The last thing a man like Timur would want, no matter what he said, was a relationship. He might think his male leopard claiming her female leopard meant they'd be together, but sooner or later he'd be bored. Still, if it stopped the nonsense Ray Harding was handing out, then she was all for calling the whacked-out, crazy-on-fire, astonishing sex a relationship.

Ray stood up straight, annoyance flashing across his

face. Somewhere a red flag went off in Ashe's mind. Ray seemed easygoing enough until things didn't go his way. Men like him didn't always make the best boyfriends or partners. She set his cup in front of him, punched in the amount for his drink and held out her hand for his card.

"Just who are you in a relationship with?" Ray demanded, sounding like a jealous lover.

"Timur Amurov," she answered and turned the iPad around so he could leave a tip if he wanted and sign the line.

"Are you fucking kidding me? This is like history repeating itself." He signed and then raised his voice. "Did you hear that?" He partially turned toward the others sitting at the various tables. "Timur fucking Amurov. She's just like Evangeline. She likes things rough." He caught her wrist when she would have turned away. "I can give it to you rough," he hissed, his voice low so his friends couldn't hear.

Before Rodion could react, Jeff was there, very gently removing her arm from his partner's viselike grip. She raised her lashes to take a good look at Jeff's face. He knew exactly what Ray was like and didn't care for it. Jeff might flirt with Evangeline, knowing she was married, but the attraction was genuine. She was pretty certain he was a straight-up good cop, not one who would take a bribe.

"Ray can get enthusiastic when he likes a woman," Jeff said with an easy smile. "That looked like he gripped you a little hard."

She rubbed at the sting around her wrist. "It's fine, but I don't like being manhandled."

"You could have fooled me," Ray snapped. "Timur? You'd better get used to getting roughed up if you're dating him."

"Please go away." She wiggled her fingers in a shooing motion toward the door. "Jeff, take him away before I make a formal complaint against him." She said it loud enough that the other cops in the room turned around and one stood up, presumably the man in charge.

"You aren't going to be seeing too much of your friend

once he shows his face here," Ray snarled and shook off Jeff's hand.

The older man who had stood came up to the counter and gestured toward the door. Ray nodded abruptly and then went out, the older man following him.

"Is Timur in some kind of trouble?" she asked.

"I'm sorry you had to hear that," Jeff said. "We just want to question him. A tip came in, and we have to follow every lead. We would very much prefer if you didn't get in touch with him regarding this matter."

She shrugged. "I don't own a cell phone."

His eyebrows shot up. "How could you not own a cell phone? Are you living with him? A woman should at least have a phone if she's going to be on her own."

"That sounded just a little bit sexist. Why wouldn't she be on her own without a phone?" Out of the corner of her eye she caught sight of Rodion. His hand was down by his side and he was texting with one thumb, presumably sharing that half the police department waited in the bakery for Timur's return. She was sure Evangeline had already informed both Timur and Fyodor and Kyanite had as well.

"I'm not trying to be sexist," Jeff objected. "I'm just saying a woman alone can be considered prey for certain types of criminals."

"Like your partner?"

"Ray has a chip on his shoulder regarding the Amurov family. Crispin, another one of our friends, disappeared. There was evidence that Crispin was a dirty cop, but Ray believes it was manufactured. He also believes Crispin was killed by either Fyodor Amurov or Timur. Of course, at that time, Fyodor was living under the alias Alonzo Massi."

There was a distinct accusation in that. She tilted her chin at him. "What do you believe?"

He sighed. "I believe Crispin was dirty and got in over his head. I wanted to believe it was Fyodor because Evangeline—" He broke off and then tried again to be more tactful. "She's a good woman. I hated to see her mixed up with a man I know is a criminal. I can't prove it, Ashe, but in my gut, I know it. A cop has to have good instincts, and mine have saved me a few times."

"Did your instincts tell you that your friend Crispin was a dirty cop?"

He sighed and then shook his head. "No, they didn't. I suppose I wasn't listening because I didn't want to know. It's hard when it's your friend."

She could understand that. Rodion had slipped his phone back into his pocket and was once more reading a book. He lifted his hand, and she rolled her eyes. "That's my cue to bring his majesty more coffee."

"And those cinnamon cookies," Rodion added, without looking up.

She made a face, and Jeff laughed. "Since Evangeline started this bakery, those apple-cinnamon cookies of hers have become so popular she has to make triple the batch she used to."

"They are good," Ashe conceded. "I find myself sneaking one every now and then." She made Rodion his espresso and put three cookies on a plate to take them to his table. "I'm not a waitress," she hissed at him.

He grinned at her, unrepentant. "I was afraid the boss would walk in and catch you giving that cop an eyeful."

She narrowed her gaze on him. "I wasn't giving him an eyeful of anything." Nevertheless, she looked down at her shirt to make certain she was covered up.

He laughed at her. "You're so easy, Ashe. You're going to have to be faster than that to keep from being the target every time we want a laugh."

She flicked him behind his ear with her index finger just the way her mother had often done to her when she was behaving in a manner her mother didn't find acceptable. She made her way through the tables back to the counter, where she felt safer. She cast several anxious glances at her shoes, praying Rodion had gotten all the blood spatter off. Since no one had called her to stop so they could examine damning evidence, she thought she might be out of the woods.

Evangeline joined her to serve the evening crowd, and just as the last of them left the store, the black town car pulled to the curb and the room went electric in anticipation. Evangeline looked up and smiled as Timur came through the door, glanced around and then moved all the way inside. Ignoring the cops spreading out in the room, he went straight to Ashe, reached over the counter and caught her shirt in his fist. He pulled her toward him.

She wanted to tell him so many things. Warn him. His gaze dropped to her mouth and he settled his lips there as if coming home. It felt like coming home and going straight for the bedroom to Ashe. The moment his mouth was on hers, the rest of the world and all the danger in it dropped away. She was blind and deaf to anything or anyone but Timur. She wanted to press her body tightly against his, preferably without a single stitch between them.

The moment he touched her, she went up in flames. He reached out with both hands and lifted her across the counter, still kissing her, his tongue singeing her soul, branding her, scoring so deeply she knew she would never get him out of her bones. When he lifted his head and smiled down at her, once she was able to see straight again, she noted that his eyes were blue flames.

For a moment Ashe was elated. She wasn't alone in her terrible need of him. And then she looked around. The police officers she'd been serving coffee and pastries to were all on their feet in a semicircle around Timur and her, weapons drawn. He'd known. Timur had known the cops were waiting for him because the others had let him know. He'd deliberately come in and kissed her, making them think his entire attention had been on her—making her think that.

He slowly lowered her feet to the floor. "Gentlemen. I'm

armed. I have a concealed weapons permit in my wallet along with my ID in my left pocket. The gun is in a holster on my left as well."

She hadn't even felt the weapon. She tried hard to get her breathing under control. It had been a crazy day. While she'd been serving police officers, Kyanite had been taking a dead body out the back, wrapped in a tarp, or more likely because he knew eyes were on the bakery, he'd hidden it somewhere inside. She shivered.

"It's going to be okay, Ashe," Timur murmured, his voice gentle.

She hated him for that tone. He sounded like she meant something to him other than a cover he was using. Damn it all, why did she have sex with him? Now he had it in his head that he could use her for anything he needed, including distracting cops. No matter what he said to her, she had to keep disbelieving, because if he was being deceptive, her heart would shatter.

"I've called our attorney," Evangeline said.

"You're not under arrest," the older gentleman said while Jeff stripped the gun from the holster and patted Timur down. He was thorough about it. "We need to detain you in order to ask you a few questions."

"You brought an army to do that? If you'd phoned ahead, I would have met you at the police station," Timur said. He sounded calm. Reasonable. As if he wasn't in the least worried.

"I'm Detective Wayne." The older man indicated one of the empty chairs at the largest table where he'd been sitting. "Please take a seat. I don't think we need handcuffs, although I want Jeff to read you your rights, just so you're aware anything you say can be used against you."

"Why so many?" Timur asked.

"We thought your brother would be with you, and we expected some resistance," Wayne admitted. "He usually comes for Evangeline."

Ashe heard the lie in his voice and it took everything she had not to call him on it.

"Do you need to question him as well?" Timur asked. "We can call him and get him down here, or better yet, so you don't taint Evangeline's business, we could meet you at the police station. That would have been much more polite. You didn't need to fuck with her or Ashe to ask me questions."

Ashe couldn't believe how calm he sounded. His heartbeat was pure steadiness. She could hear it. The detective's heart beat far faster and harder than Timur's.

"Ashe, can you get the door and lock it?" Evangeline asked. "I don't want my customers to be afraid to walk into my bakery." She glared at Wayne. "You and your men have lost your privileges. Sheesh. Whatever you think Timur's done wasn't worth ruining my business."

"It's a threat, Evangeline," Timur said. "Scare tactics. If I don't cooperate, you lose everything. Isn't that the way this works?" He directed his query to the detective.

Ashe hadn't thought of that. It hadn't occurred to her that Evangeline's business might be hurt by the police officer's actions. It was no wonder Timur had come at the end of business hours. He'd made certain to drag the wait out until Evangeline could close her doors and most of her customers would never witness the police questioning Timur so publicly.

"Of course not," Wayne denied.

Jeff read Timur his rights, and then asked Timur if he understood them.

"Do you know Emilio Bassini?" Wayne asked.

Ashe didn't know the man, but she recognized the name. Before, when she'd researched for the stories she wanted to write, she'd studied as many of the reputed crime bosses as possible. Emilio Bassini's name had come up often.

"Yes, of course. He comes here to the bakery, and sometimes my family does business with him," Timur said readily.

Ashe winced. Her inclination was to tell him not to say

a word until the attorney was present. Evangeline seemed to have him on speed dial. There was a reason for that.

"What is the nature of your business with him?"

Timur shrugged. "You'd have to ask Fyodor." He leaned back in the chair, sprawling his legs casually in front of him. He looked deceptively lazy—a leopard pretending to doze, but in reality, ready to kill. "It has something to do with one of the tire shops, I think."

Ashe leaned against the counter, but Evangeline tugged at her arm and indicated the few remaining pastries. Together they began putting everything away. Evangeline baked fresh every morning so the last of the baked goods were put in a bag to take to the shelter. Ashe began cleaning their espresso machine while Evangeline wiped the display cases down. She caught up the remaining pot of coffee and whisked it into the kitchen to pour the contents down the drain, glaring at Jeff when he tried to get another cup.

Timur answered the questions Wayne put to him in vague terms. When the Arnotto lawyer showed up, he asked a lot of his own questions. He seemed to know all about the business between the Amurov family and Bassini. Ashe tried to listen in on everything, but there didn't seem a specific reason for the questions. As far as she could tell, Emilio Bassini was in the best of health and whatever business the Amurov family had done with him seemed to be legitimate and aboveboard.

"I don't get it," Ashe whispered to Evangeline as she rinsed dishes and put them in the dishwasher. "Why the big show?"

"I think they're after the books."

"What books?"

"My books," Evangeline said. "They can't conceive that Fyodor runs legal businesses. He works as a manager for Siena Arnotto and her various businesses. They have subpoenaed the books of nearly all the businesses he runs, both for her and for our family. When they couldn't find anything, they began going after the books for all the Amurov businesses. They didn't find anything there either. This place was mine before I married Fyodor. I don't think they believe it could have made so much money so fast without us doing something like money laundering or selling drugs, along with the pastries. Or maybe a few guns, I could hide them in the cannoli."

Ashe couldn't help but laugh, even though she detected a little bitterness. "I'm sorry, but the visual on that was good."

Evangeline's answering smile was slow in coming. "This is bullshit. They really are trying to ruin my business."

"More like blackmail you into cooperation." Ashe pulled open the door to the walk-in freezer carefully. Her stomach dropped. Sure enough, there was a rolled tarp under the shelves. She closed the door quickly and dropped the chain lock into place.

"It's not like I can tell them anything," Evangeline said. "But I am getting sick of the harassment. I thought some of them were actually my friends."

Ashe frowned. "You know that's not possible, right? Those men out there are after your family, and just like the ones who went after mine, they'll stop at nothing to tear all of you apart. I don't think it makes much difference which side of the law you're on if someone is out to get you, but you can't really be friends with anyone trying to hurt your family." She couldn't keep the sorrow out of her voice. "If I had been there, I would have fought to save my parents, but I wasn't. They liked to be alone together and I was in the way. I knew that. I even accepted it, but that doesn't change the fact that I would have lied, cheated, stolen or killed to save them."

Evangeline put her arms around Ashe and hugged her tightly. "I'm so sorry about your family, Ashe. I'm glad you had them for the time you did. Fyodor, Timur and Gorya are my family now and I feel that way about them. The next time a cop comes in, I'm spitting in his drink."

"Can you bake one batch of those apple-cinnamon cookies with something to make them very sick?" Ashe asked.

"Not really, but they so deserve it."

"Especially Jeff. He pretends to care about me and then he pulls something like this. And what was that with his partner? With Ray? Rodion group texted all of us that he said some things and grabbed your arm too hard." She reached for Ashe's wrist, gently turning it over.

"Group texted who?" Ashe asked suspiciously. She was beginning to feel as though she was the only one not in the loop and needed a cell phone.

Evangeline shrugged. "All of us. Fyodor, Kyanite, Gorya, Timur. Even Mitya and Sevastyan. You don't know them but they're cousins. They're my family too."

"So of course, they had to know."

"Of course."

7

ASHE was far too quiet. Timur had heard from Kyanite the moment the hit men had walked into the bakery and Ashe's leopard rose. And before that even, when all the cops were drifting into Evangeline's place of business, a deliberate show of strength. It had cost him to stay away, to wait until the end of the day for Evangeline, so her customers would never see the threat the police made against her. Against them. Their family.

They had that now. It had been a very long, uphill battle for them, but Evangeline had brought them all together as a family. He had his brother and Gorya. He had Mitya and Sevastyan, his cousins. And now, although she was going to try to fight him, to run from him, he had his woman.

He hadn't been far from her. He'd known better. She was in heat and he didn't want to take chances. The moment the two men in their business suits had left the bakery and all but run for their vehicle, Timur was after them. He had been silently following with three others. The men had gone, not back to the motel, but to Evangeline's old residence where Ashe was staying. That had been their last mistake.

He hadn't had time to extract information from them before he killed them. Their leopards had leapt forward to fight. His big male had defeated one, and the other had been killed by one of the leopards Drake Donovan had sent them. Logan Shields had been in the Borneo rain forest, working with the teams there. Timur was learning to trust Drake's men.

He glanced sideways at Ashe. She stared out the window of the car, not looking at him, her hands folded neatly in her lap. Unfortunately for her, he was extremely good at reading body language, every little sign a person might give to allow him to better figure out what they were thinking. She wasn't considering white dresses and roses. Or family. She was angry or hurt. One of the two emotions, and neither was good. He'd take anger over hurt. He didn't know what to do with hurt.

"Are you going to talk to me?"

She looked up at him. Their eyes met and he saw hurt, not anger. Damn it all. What the hell was he supposed to do with that? She blinked and he found himself looking directly at her leopard. Her leopard wasn't hurt; she was angry. Very. The amber eyes had gone a deep golden with darker rings around them. Her leopard had risen to protect her from him—from hurt that he'd inadvertently caused. It had gone deep, he could see that.

Timur reached out and covered her hands with one of his own as he easily steered the car toward her house. "Talk to me, Ashe. I want to know what you're thinking."

She didn't pull away from him, and he almost wished she had. It would have been better than her sitting there so meekly. There wasn't anything meek about Ashe, so he wasn't buying her performance. But the hurt was real. Her leopard's anger was real.

"I'm not thinking about anything."

As lies went, that was a whopper. His leopard flagged that immediately. He took his eyes off the road long enough to look at her again. "Baby, I'd rather you not say anything than have you lying to me. Whatever this is, we can make it right."

She took a deep breath, and he braced himself. The storm was about to break. He considered that a good thing.

"I don't want you staying at the house with me. I know you think I'm in danger, and I'll take precautions, but it's too hard to have you there."

"Hard to have me there?" he echoed. "You mean you used me for sex and now you want me to go away."

She scowled at him. "How many women have you used for sex and then made go away? You don't get to judge me. And you don't get to be sarcastic. You know you've done just that a hundred times, probably more. We're not in a relationship. We had sex in the street. Great sex, but still, it was just sex."

"My leopard claimed your leopard." He turned onto the quiet little cul-de-sac where the house was located. He really liked the house. Mansions weren't his thing. He thought his brother's home was extremely cool, and right for Fyodor, but this much smaller house suited him. He pulled into the driveway and hit the remote that opened the two-car garage. Her car was already parked on one side and he liked that. He liked that his car made up the second part of the garage. Hers was a shit car, and really banged up. It had so many dings and dents in it, he wondered how it could actually be on the road.

She shrugged. "Your leopard will be fine. He's been fine the last few years, and he'll be okay until some other woman comes along."

"You know better than that. Your parents shared information with you. You know that a leopard shifter mates with his only. You're my only."

"That's bullshit and you know it. I'm not your only. I just look at you and know you're one of those men who go through women like they're candy and leave a trail of broken hearts behind."

He turned off the engine. "Their hearts can't be broken if I have one-night stands, Ashe. We have sex and we walk away."

"No woman walks away from the kind of sex we had, Timur. You broke hearts."

It was an accusation. He couldn't defend his position, because she told the truth. He had broken hearts, but he hadn't meant to. On the other hand, he did have to set her straight on one issue. "We had off-the-charts, amazing sex together, Ashe. It wasn't all me. It was a combination of the two of us. I've never had that with another woman."

That meant something to her. Her eyes went soft and there was a flash of awareness. Then she was pushing the heavy car door open and sliding off the seat. He followed. She wasn't kicking him out that easily. He glanced down at his watch.

After Temnyy, Timur's leopard, and Logan's leopard had defeated the other two men who had been after his woman, Jeremiah, who'd been assigned to watch the motel, announced the arrival of another group of men. There were six of them. He had Logan take the phones of the dead men to Vitaly and he'd gotten past their codes as usual. Their phones had blown up with messages to regroup back at the hotel, that their original mission was terminated, and it was imperative they break off immediately. Too bad they hadn't gotten that message before he'd killed them.

"You aren't going to persuade me," Ashe said, resolution in her voice.

He followed her right into the house. "I'm not going to try to persuade you. There's no need." And there wasn't, not as far as he was concerned. The decision had been made the moment he'd set eyes on her. The moment he'd inhaled and taken the scent of her deep into his lungs. He'd deepened that promise by tasting her mouth. The commitment had been made right then, at that moment, when his mouth came down on hers. That was long before his cock was involved. His resolve was permanent.

She looked at him over her shoulder, her long, feathery lashes capturing his attention. He liked those little details about her. The way she moved. The sound of her voice. Those little glances she gave him as if just looking at him hurt. "Why do I not believe you?"

"I think you do believe me, *malen'kiy smerch*, but you're afraid. You haven't ever been around a large family like ours and you're just feeling a little out of your depth. I'll get you through it. You were taught to run in any situation that scared you, and that's your go-to, baby. You want to run because you know everything I say is the truth, not a lie, and that is terrifying to you."

He could see by her expression he'd hit the nail on the head. He was going to have to be vigilant and counter any of her arguments, because she was going to have a lot of them. He wrapped his arm around her waist and locked her to him, her back to his front. His mouth found the sweet little spot between her neck and shoulder, the one that made her shiver and moan. The one he knew drove her wild. He spent a little time there and then kissed his way over her delicate jaw to the edge of her mouth.

"You're mine, Ashe. Your body knows it, no matter how hard your head tries to fight." His hand wrapped around her throat, thumb pressing into her chin so she faced him enough that he could take her mouth.

Both of them caught fire that fast. Kissing her was like a terrible storm, completely out of control. He turned her in his arms and lifted her, his mouth still on hers. Flames licked over his skin, and electricity seemed to arc between them. Her mouth was pure heat, not sweet, not spice, but a fiery cinnamon that left him craving more every time he took his mouth from hers.

He carried her through the house straight to the bedroom, feeding off her, devouring her, kissing her again and again, until her body seemed a part of his own. He caught at the hem of her shirt and pulled it over her head, ruthlessly ripped her bra away so her breasts spilled out into his hands. He kissed his way down her throat to the two soft mounds.

She was . . . exquisite. Perfection. All that soft skin. Her breathy moans. The way her hips bucked and moved so restlessly. He wanted her clothes gone. If he had his way she'd be waiting for him at home every night, naked, her skin glowing under candlelight. He didn't need food when he had her to devour.

There was a strange roaring in his head, thunder in his ears, hot blood rushing through his veins. He wanted a slow seduction, but he knew he was too far gone to give that to her. At least not the first time he had her in the bed. He kept his mouth on her breast, his tongue and teeth working her nipple while he pulled strongly with his mouth, and his hands dropped to her jeans.

Her hands were already there, desperate to get them off her. He liked her desperate for him. He didn't want to be alone in his urgent need. He had to release her breast so he could get to her shoes, but he took her hands and used them to knead both soft mounds.

"Work your nipples, baby. The way I do." He *loved* seeing her hands on her body. It was sexy to him, and the look on her face, the flushed skin, all of it together had him as hard as a rock. He tossed her shoes aside and then dragged down her jeans and panties, leaving her bare to him as he tossed her on the bed.

Her breath was coming in ragged gasps, the sound driving his body further into a frenzy of need. He yanked her thighs apart and put his mouth right where he needed it to be. Her cry shattered what little control he'd been hanging on to. His tongue plunged deep, finding hot liquid. She tasted like honey and cinnamon. She was exquisite, like a fine hot cider. He couldn't get enough of her and he drove her up fast, using his teeth on her clit and his fingers to stretch her tight sheath.

Her hips went wild so he had to clamp her down tightly, locking her in place so he could have his way with her. He savored the explosion when he took her over the edge, her body giving him more, so that he devoured her like a feast, taking her right back up.

Now, her breathing changed to gasping hitches. The roaring in his ears grew until it was thunder rolling while lightning forked through his body and struck at his cock. He felt huge. Full. Throbbing and burning. He opened his trousers and the relief was tremendous. Circling his thick erection with one hand, he lifted his head enough to wipe his face on her thighs. Her hips bucked, and he knew how she felt. He needed her just as much.

Then he was kneeling between her legs, the broad crown nearly swallowed by her body. Watching his thick cock disappear into her was so sensual he could barely breathe. Her body stretched around his, straining to accommodate his size. He couldn't look away from that beauty.

"You're so fucking beautiful, Ashe. This is. You. Me. The two of us together. Tell me this isn't what you want."

Her head thrashed back and forth, her eyes dazed yet excited. He waited, breathing deeply, until she focused on him. "Tell me what you feel right now."

"Burning. You're so big. It's like my body is saying you can't possibly and at the same time, you can't stop. I won't make it if you stop." She didn't hesitate to tell him. She didn't pretend she wasn't as desperate for him as he was for her. "You have to move, Timur. Right now. I need you to move."

"You going to run the minute you get the chance?" Holding still was so difficult. Only half his cock was in her, and looking down on that was amazing. Sensual. So damned sexy he thought he might really blow it and explode.

"Yes. God, yes. You would try to rule me."

"That's what you're afraid of?" He slid another inch into that slick, liquid heat. She bathed him in a fiery honey. So good. He counted her heartbeats right through his cock.

"Yes."

Because she told the truth, he rewarded her with another inch. His entire body screamed at him that he needed more. He needed all of him buried deep. He needed to be moving, not slow, not savoring, but hard and fast until that ultimate explosion came.

"I *will* rule you, Ashe," he admitted. "I'll tell you what to do and you'll give me that snippy look you have and tell *me* what to do. It's going to be the best of the best. And we'll have this, any time, day or night. How would you ever do without my cock buried in you just like this?" He took himself home, plowing through those tight folds, her muscles gripping at him, creating an unbelievable friction.

He caught her hips, holding her still while he plunged in and out of her. Her little gasps and the way she gripped his cock like a vise nearly had him losing control immediately. He breathed deeply, holding back, wanting to keep this time for as long as possible. Her fingers slid down the front of her, right to their joining, brushing his cock every time he withdrew. Each touch sent fire burning down his spine.

His fingers dug into her hips. Her nails bit deeply into his shoulders. Her breath hitched again. Her lips parted. The moment they did, he had a vision of his cock sliding between them, of that beautiful bow stretched around him. The image sent a firestorm burning out of control through his entire body and he slammed into her. Deep. Hard. Over and over, riding her as if there was no tomorrow.

Her body clamped down hard on his. Her muscles felt

like strong fingers milking his cock. There was no stopping the eruption. It blasted out of him, a frenzied storm that sent his seed rocketing into her, splashing against the walls of her sheath, mixing with her hot honey, coating them both in their combined sex. He felt brutal. He felt savage. He felt like a primitive, possessive male staking his claim.

"I want you forever. Not for fifteen minutes. Not for an hour. Not for a day. It has to be forever." He collapsed over top of her, keeping his hips wedged between her thighs, his cock buried deep, feeling every aftershock, every ripple, bathing in the hot combination of the two of them. "Do you really think I would let you go after this?"

"It's sex, Timur," she whispered, circling his neck with her arms.

"Fuck, baby, no one has this kind of sex. You don't throw something like this away."

"It will go away eventually. Then what? What will we have then?"

"I'll be eighty and still want you, woman. Why do you keep wanting to run from me?" He bit down hard on her shoulder, deliberately leaving his mark.

Ashe yelped and tried to pull away. He didn't allow it, easily holding her still. "You'd better get over this phase fast, because we're too good together to call this just sex."

"I don't know you at all."

"You're beginning to know me. You know me enough to be a little afraid of me."

"That's not a good thing. Why do you say that like it's a good thing?"

"Because you know we need to talk things out. I respond to talking. You run, and you know I'll come after you." He felt the little shiver that went through her body.

The problem was that female leopards liked to lead their males around for a few days. Sometimes a week or more. They would get amorous, rubbing their bodies enticingly along trees, leaving their alluring scent on everything in an effort to draw in the male. Once he responded, she rebuffed him, cuffing him with her claws, snarling and lashing out. He thought of his woman that way, just as moody and as demanding as her leopard. She had no intentions of committing to him. He knew that was fear.

He even understood why. Her parents had raised her off the grid. They'd kept to themselves, excluding her. The love they'd showed her was teaching her to survive in any situation. They'd taught her not to trust anyone and to get out if she was uncomfortable. She'd told Evangeline quite a bit about her parents. While they'd clearly loved each other, they'd been no more than children when they had Ashe. They had no idea how to be parents, not any more than his parents had.

"I would, Ashe," he reiterated. "I would come after you. And if I found another man with you, I can tell you, without hesitation, there would be no holding my leopard back."

Her fingers moved through his hair, the nails feeling good on his scalp. For just one moment they were both at peace, their hearts beating the same rhythm. He let himself relax into her. He was always careful to keep himself strong, disciplined and in complete control because his leopard was so dangerous. With Ashe, he had the luxury of completely letting go.

He'd poured himself into her. Emptied himself. He was able to let go of his past, forget his horrendous childhood for a short period of time. She'd done that for him. She thought it was just sex, but he was far more experienced than she was. Maybe she really didn't or couldn't recognize that what they had was different and completely out of the norm.

"I won't be a prisoner for you, Timur. I came here with the thought that I could use one criminal against another. I thought you and your brother were powerful, dangerous men who could wreak some sort of revenge for me. All I did was lead trouble to your doorstep. While I'm very sorry about that, I have no intention of selling my soul to make up for it." Her fingers closed around his hair in a tight fist. "I'm worth more than that."

He lifted his head to look down at her face. At the beauty that belonged to him. He planned on making her happy, not keeping her prisoner, but he was a man of few words. He'd always preferred to let his actions speak for him. He framed her face with his hands and kissed her. Kissing melted her. Kissing made her catch fire. Kissing stopped her from thinking about running from him.

He spent time, savoring every moment, every exchanged breath. The flames. The fire. The storm that kissing her generated in his body. He never moved from between her legs, locked inside her, the sweet haven of her body. The longer he kissed her, the more his body responded. The more hers did. He felt a fresh flood of liquid heat surround his cock. The bite of her muscles, the almost languid way his mind slipped down that road of craving.

He threaded his fingers through hers and lifted her arms above her head as his hips began a slow grind. This was no fast and hard ride; this one was a slow burn that built and built. He didn't try to hurry it. He wanted slow. He wanted to feel every inch of her and let her feel what he was trying to tell her with his body. He might not get the words she needed to hear out, but he was good at action, good with his body.

Her fingers tightened around his. She murmured his name. He lifted his head to look into her eyes. That might have been a mistake on his part. She might not be feeling overwhelmed by the way the two of them were coming together, but he certainly was. His heart contracted in his chest at what he saw there. She wanted him. She wanted him to be hers. Triumph burst through him. She might think she wanted to run, but he was her choice.

Her lashes fanned her cheeks as his body couldn't stop moving just a little harder and faster. Her breath caught in her throat and then he felt the rise and fall of her chest beneath his. That drew his attention to her breasts. The soft mounds were pressed tightly against him, the small hairs of his chest rubbing over her nipples.

"Stay with me, Ashe," he whispered enticingly. "Take a chance on me."

She stared into his eyes for a long time, searching for something, but he wasn't certain what that was. Reassurance? What man could give that kind of reassurance to his woman when they had the role he had?

"Come away with me," she countered. "Leave this all behind."

He closed his eyes and began to pick up the pace, his body insisting on moving faster and harder. He couldn't have stopped himself if he wanted to. "Stay with me, baby," he repeated.

"You'll live this way forever. Outside the law. You saw those cops today, Timur. They aren't going to stop. Evangeline is innocent. They know she hasn't committed a crime. They *know* that, but still, they harassed her. They deliberately questioned you in her shop. Had you not stayed away, they would have done so in her busiest hour, on purpose."

The sorrow in her voice tugged at his heart. She wanted to stay with him, but she was still planning on going. He knew he couldn't let her go. His leopard was too cruel, too savage. Just having the small respites he'd been given when he was close to Ashe had been miracles.

"Ashe," he began and then broke off.

He moved his body, using it to tell her he was capable of being gentle. Kind. That he would be the best man possible for her. He'd seen the changes in Fyodor. They were men who appreciated their women. They knew what life without them was like. It was hell for them and hell on their women.

"I don't always have to be rough." He liked rough, but he could live with this—with gentle. He took his time with her, making sure to build her need slowly this time.

"You're not too rough." She pressed a kiss to his throat. "I like the way you do rough."

He kissed her throat. Pressed more up her chin. "What can I do to persuade you to stay voluntarily?"

Another shiver went through her body. He understood. He'd made that implication on purpose. He would have her, one way or the other. If she meant no, he didn't know what he would do, but he was very well versed in reading people and body language. She wanted him just as desperately as he wanted her. She was just very, very scared.

He felt his cock swell, pushing at the sensitive tissue, those tight muscles that didn't want to give way to him, to surrender to him, the way she didn't want to surrender. Too bad, she didn't know it was too late. She was his. His leopard had claimed hers. There was nowhere she could go that he wouldn't find her. And he'd go after her no matter how many times she ran.

"Catch up, baby," he whispered.

"I'm there."

Her orgasm was surprisingly strong, when they were going slow and taking it easy, almost lazily. The aftermath, her body clamping down, wringing every last drop from him, was equally as strong. Little mini-earthquakes rocked them both.

She waited for him to roll off her and for their breathing to get back under control. He stretched out beside her, hands behind his head, legs sprawled wide, one over hers, pinning her down so she couldn't escape. He stared up at the ceiling.

"I want a family someday, Timur. I need that. It was always my parents and then me separate from them. I grew up knowing they wished they didn't have me. They loved me, but they still wanted to be alone. I think they honestly regretted having me."

She turned her body toward him and he felt the impact of her eyes.

"Don't get me wrong, they loved me. I felt their love every day. They were good to me. It was just that, I never fit into their partnership. It was too strong and too exclusive. I want my own family. A man who loves me the way my father loved my mother, but more, so that love includes the children I want. Not just a single one, I want my firstborn to have siblings. I need that, Timur."

"I can give you children, Ashe." He spoke quietly, directing his statement to the ceiling.

"I'm sure you can, but what would we be bringing them into? Sooner or later, the cops are going to catch you at something and you'll be incarcerated, if not dead. They'll never allow you or your family to live in peace."

"You have a point," he agreed, because she did. She spoke the truth. "It's too late for me. Fyodor has no choice, and that means neither do I. I have no choice, and that means neither do you. We're leopard, baby. You. Me. It isn't just the two of us. We have to consider them. *You* have to consider them."

He felt her entire body tense. He rolled to his side and splayed his fingers across her belly. "My seed's in you. It's not even dry yet. You screamed for me. It was my name you called. Your leopard rose to allow my leopard's claim."

"But—" she started her protest.

He shut it down. "Nothing else matters. The rest, we can work on, we can work things out. Those are irrevocable facts. You're mine. I'm yours. Exclusively. We have different rules in our society than humans do. Your parents had to have taught you that."

"In a *lair.* The rules apply to living in a lair."

"You know better or you wouldn't sound so desperate." He cupped the side of her face, his thumb stroking a caress across her cheek. "No one will ever need you more than I do, Ashe. And no man will ever work harder to make certain you're happy. I can promise those two things."

A small frown slid across her face, but when he raised an

eyebrow, she just shook her head. He pressed his thumb to her lips. "One of us needs to know how to talk. I'm good with a gun, I think you should take up talking."

Her lips curved under the pad of his thumb. They felt soft. Her breath was warm on his skin. It was painful how easily she got to him. He had been around other women longer, never a lover, but other women, and none of them got under his skin the way she had.

"I'm good with a gun."

She made him want to laugh. Somehow the world was a better place just because she was in it. She told the truth, even when it wasn't easy for her, once she realized Evangeline had no part in their sins. The amusement faded as he thought about his sister-in-law.

"She's an angel. Evangeline. We realized she was most likely an angel sent down to help us since we all lived in hell," he admitted aloud, because his mind had gone there.

"Why do you say that?"

"Don't you think so too?" he challenged.

She was silent for so long he didn't think she'd answer, but in the end, she sighed and nodded, her hair sweeping his chest. "Yes. She let me back into her life immediately. She gave me a job and a home all because she knew I was in trouble."

Her gaze drifted over his face. "Why do you think she is?"

He rolled over to stare up at the ceiling again. "I don't like thinking too much about my childhood, let alone talking about it. None of us do. Not my brother and not my cousins. Our leopards are killers. They hate every moment of their existence and are always out for blood. That means we're at war with a part of ourselves at all times. We put bars on the windows and have metal bars across the doors so when we sleep, if they get loose, they can't get out to hurt anyone."

He glanced at her. She was propped up on one elbow,

her amber-colored eyes wide, those long lashes framing them making them seem even bigger. Her lips were slightly parted as if she might protest, but she remained silent. There was shock and compassion in her expression and one hand slid over his chest, her palm seeking and then finding the beat of his heart.

He felt those fingers, her palm, the way she touched him, branding him so that her touch sank beneath skin and found its way to bone. Her name was written there. Ashe. His woman. It didn't matter so much what happened in the future, or what came before, he had this moment with her. This peace. He let himself feel everything. He let the tension drain out of his body. Felt the calmness of this leopard. That was a victory he would savor for the rest of his life. His leopard content to just lie still, waiting for another stroke of her fingers.

She looked particularly beautiful with her hair tumbling around her face and over one breast. He liked knowing a part of him was still inside her. Looking at her lips just made him want to kiss them, and kissing seemed to lead to out-of-control behavior by both of them.

"Tell me more, Timur."

Those fingers fucking *owned* him, moving up his body to his lips. Sliding over them with soft little pads. Stroking caresses, she didn't even seem to notice when her touch was making his head explode and his body throb with pure need. Every one of those reactions told him he was alive. On fire. Headed in the right direction. Toward something big. Something that would save him.

Did she feel the same way? His gaze moved over her face. Possessive. Still a little unsure. What was he giving her, after all? A whole lot of bad. The trouble coming for him—and for his brother and cousins—was far worse than she could imagine—and it was coming for her because Lazar believed she had to pay for the sins of her parents. He knew the cruelty of leopards and shifters gone rogue. Gone bad. Out for blood. That was all he could ever offer her. He'd tried to get out, and now he was in so deep he didn't even know how to tell her.

"Timur."

Her voice wrapped around his heart. It was insane to feel this way about her so fast, an overwhelming sense of rightness. Of need. More than those things; bigger. He hadn't known it was possible for him to feel so much. He understood Fyodor's desire to give Evangeline whatever she wanted. It wasn't as if they could offer safety. Or even a decent reputation.

"Don't stop talking. Tell me what your leopard is doing right at this minute."

How could a man resist his woman's voice when she pitched it low like that? When she lay unashamed, naked and vulnerable to him? He just knew he wasn't that man. "My leopard is very content, the way he always is when we're close to you. I could fall asleep, just as I did on the couch last night, with no worry about bars on the windows or across the door. I think it was the first real sleep I've had in a few years."

"I'm glad then. That I was the one to give that to you."

"He knows he has his mate close and he's patient. He says she's close, but not quite ready for him. He likes to stay near you." He wrapped her hair around his finger because the temptation to touch her was too strong. "I know you want to run from me, Ashe, and frankly, I don't blame you."

"It isn't that I *want* to run, so much as I know this situation isn't good. You know it isn't, Timur, and I have to look out for myself. Being with you would be like jumping on a fast-moving train with no way off."

He couldn't prevent the wince. She'd scored with that observation. Once on his train, she was right, there was no getting off. She couldn't know the reasons, not yet, or the extent of just how bad it really was. Still, how could he let her go? His leopard would be completely uncontrollable.

He stayed silent, because there wasn't much he could say to that.

He could plead his case, and hope she would listen, but in the end, what was he going to do? Let her run? Leave his brother at the worst possible time? He probably wouldn't survive the coming war and he wouldn't want to. Not without Ashe.

Where the hell had that come from? He couldn't survive without her? He'd just laid eyes on her. He knew it didn't matter. She was his one. His only. She was the woman who calmed his leopard and offered him a place of comfort. Of peace. He'd caught a glimpse of paradise. What man would let that go when he'd never had a fucking decent thing in his life?

"Don't run, Ashe. I'd find you. Wherever you went, I'd find you."

"Don't try to scare me, Timur. I don't take threats very well."

"Then don't fuckin' consider it a threat. Consider it a fact of life." He sat up and shoved at the hair falling on his forehead. He thought idly that he needed a haircut, but he liked the way her fingers smoothed it back.

"You would truly be hell to live with," she snapped, sitting up as well.

She looked around for her clothes and then slid off the bed to go to a drawer. She pulled a T-shirt from it and dragged it over her curves. Hiding her body from him. Taking that away. Still, he couldn't help but feel as if he deserved it. He watched her stalk to the bathroom, tension in every line of her body. Perversely, that just made him want her all over again.

He put his feet flat on the floor and snagged his phone out of his trousers where he'd left it. "Fyodor," he said as soon as his brother answered. "Am I a psychopath?"

"Yes," Fyodor answered without hesitation. "So am I."

"What the fuck does that even mean?"

"I looked it up a while back," Fyodor explained. "Said we exhibit abnormal or violent social behavior. I think that fits us."

Timur put his head down and drew in deep breaths. He couldn't say he didn't exhibit violent behavior—not with the crimes he'd committed.

"The definition also included the description aggressive and/or unstable," Fyodor went on helpfully.

"What the hell did you offer Evangeline to stay?" he demanded. "Tell me one decent thing you give her, and don't include sex in that, Fyodor, because we both know that's all about you, not her."

"Is it all about you when you have sex with Ashe?" his brother countered.

What was he supposed to say to that? Hell, when he was in her, he couldn't even think straight. Someone could walk in and put a bullet in his head and he wouldn't be able to stop. He'd have to be dead first. Was that all about him? Was it? He hoped he wasn't that selfish. He knew he wasn't. It was important to him to give her as many orgasms as possible. More, he wanted her to feel cared for every time he touched her. Sex wasn't all about him. With Ashe, it never would be.

"What about your leopard?" Fyodor asked.

"He's crazy about her. Her leopard is taking her sweet time to rise, but she's close." Was this relationship about his leopard? He knew better. He couldn't keep his eyes or his hands off the woman, and her leopard wasn't even trying to seduce his. In fact, at times she was eerily quiet.

The bathroom door opened and Ashe stood in the doorway, leaning one slim hip against the frame. "You're not a psychopath, Timur, and if I made you think that, I didn't mean to." She heaved a small sigh and jerked her chin toward his phone. "Is that your brother?"

He nodded.

She walked over to him and took the phone from his

hand. "He's not a psychopath. I've seen the results of one, and that isn't either one of you." She hit end and handed him back his phone. "That's why I can't stay, Timur. Not because you're not the man who will always be someone I want to see. It's because you're not a man insane enough to take on the bastards who killed my parents."

He wrapped his arm around her waist and buried his face against her stomach, pressing into her, laughter coming up from somewhere deep. Regret. Self-loathing. He held her tightly, knowing he was damned either way.

Her fingers were in his hair immediately, stroking those small caresses he found he was beginning to live for. It made no sense that she could take over his life so fast, and yet she had. He forced air through his lungs and looked up at her.

"Baby, you have to know the truth before you make your decision. I'm *exactly* that man. The one they send to fuck up others. Or to kill them. I made my first kill at eight years old and, believe me, that was two years too late. My father despised me because I didn't want to kill people. He beat me until I couldn't stand up, until he could force my leopard out of my control so he could have his leopard deliver a beating to him that was so severe, at times I thought they'd broken his back. I learned to be that killer, Ashe, the one you're looking for."

She stepped back and then knelt between his legs, her hands framing his face. "You're not that man, Timur."

Her voice, so gentle, turned his heart over. He met her eyes, wanting her to see the real him, not the fantasy she had in her head.

"Only you could look into my eyes and tell me something like that," he said. "I am. I know what I am and I know how I got to be this person. Had I had a chance, I might have been different. God knows, I wanted to be different. You get fed violence and blood your entire life, and it shapes you into something dark and ugly."

"Timur, you're breaking my heart. Do you really believe that of yourself? They tortured my parents. They murdered them for no real reason."

"I torture and kill when I have to."

"Why would anyone have to?"

"To protect the people he loves."

"The men torturing and killing my parents did so not because my parents were a threat to anyone they loved, but simply because someone ordered it. If Fyodor asked you to kill innocent people, would you do it?"

"Fyodor would never ask such a thing of me. He's a good man, Ashe."

"He has to be or he wouldn't have Evangeline."

She leaned into him and brushed kisses over his eyelids and then his nose. Her lips felt cool on his skin. Her touch had his heart stuttering in his chest. She could twist his insides into little knots just by smiling at him. Add in her touch, and then her kisses, and he was lost.

"I don't know what's true or not, Ashe, only that I want to be with you. I'll try to be a better man for you, the one that I might have been before my father decided to twist me into something ugly."

Her mouth touched the corner of his and then pressed against his lips. He opened for her and her tongue swept inside. At once the temperature in the room went up several degrees. His mouth moved, following wherever she led. It didn't take long before he took over. He cursed himself for that trait, always having to be the one in control, but that was his nature. He kissed her thoroughly, hoping she understood what he was trying to convey.

When he lifted his head to look down at her, those amber eyes stared back at him solemnly. She wasn't giving him promises and he appreciated that she didn't try to lie to him.

"I don't want you to have to be the man your father forced on you. Find your own way, Timur, and the heck with him."

"He's dead. I don't worry about what he thinks or feels. I have uncles who want us dead, but that isn't my biggest worry. I have a woman, stubborn as hell, and I would prefer her to tell me straight up she was staying, but she can't do that right now. So until she can, I'm going to be a little out of whack."

She burst out laughing. "What does that even mean?"

"It means we're shelving this conversation until I make you dinner. You have to be starving."

8

ASHE perched on a high-backed barstool in her kitchen to watch Timur work. He was silent while he chopped vegetables, but he worked with a calm efficiency that told her he was very comfortable in a kitchen. She loved watching him. It was strange to feel as if she'd always known him. Already, she wasn't certain she could leave even if she really wanted to. She felt at peace when she was close to him.

He wore a pair of gray sweatpants with a black racing stripe down each leg. He'd pulled on a black tee that stretched across his chest, one tight enough that she reaped the benefits, watching his muscles ripple with every movement.

"What was your mother like, Timur?" The moment she asked the question, she knew it was a mistake.

Timur stiffened and seemed to concentrate even more on chopping up the vegetables. "She was fragile. She knew my father was going to murder her one day. All the women in the lair knew their husbands would kill them."

"Why didn't they run?"

His dark lashes flicked up and she found herself staring into his ice-blue eyes. "They knew they couldn't go far enough. They'd have been run to the ground."

"Maybe, but at least they would have had a chance. Why didn't they ban together and fight back? If I thought you were going to kill me eventually . . ."

"After you gave me sons."

She narrowed her eyes at him, although it was a waste. He was back to chopping vegetables and tossing them into a wok where small pieces of steak had already been seared. She loved watching him when he cooked. He seemed to relax more. "Okay, *especially* after I gave you sons. I'd wait until you were asleep, and then I'd shoot you. I wouldn't miss either. If I used a silencer, I could go around to all the other houses and shoot my friends' husbands."

A slow smile curved the hard edges of his mouth and her heart nearly stopped beating. He was gorgeous when he smiled.

"Bloodthirsty little thing. I'm keeping all weapons out of your reach. Of course, I have no intention of doing in my woman, even though I'm more than certain you're going to piss me off royally very often."

She took a snap pea and waved it at him. "Where did these groceries come from?"

"The store." He grinned down at the last of the vegetables, scooping them up and tossing them neatly into the wok.

"I don't own a wok either."

"No, this is mine. I looked at your pots and pans, baby, and I can assure you, they're all shit. Completely. I have liberated them."

"What does that mean?" She didn't really care what it meant, she had no interest in pots and pans. It was just that she wanted to keep him talking. She loved to hear the sound of his voice, especially in this mood, where there was near-laughter in him. He was so adorable standing there, slathering butter on sourdough bread, his hair falling in his face making him look younger. Then there were those eyelashes. So dark, like his hair.

"I threw them out and I sent Jeremiah to the grocery store. I threatened to beat him to a bloody pulp if he forgot one thing on my list or if he deviated in any way. I double-checked the groceries, and he got everything I asked for."

"Now you have perfect strangers bringing groceries into my house."

"You were working. So was I, and believe me, there is nothing perfect about Jeremiah. We needed a little help and Jeremiah needs a little guidance. He's too enthusiastic and has very little patience. I don't want the kid to get in over his head before he's ready. Pulling him off main assignments to do a few errands bugs the hell out of him, but it keeps him from getting too bored and screwing up."

"I see. By letting him come into my home, without my permission, by the way, you're saving this kid's life." His reasoning eluded her, but she wasn't going to get too worked up because one of his men brought them food. "And the clothes you're wearing? Where did they come from?"

He shrugged, his wide shoulders rolling, drawing attention to his very muscular chest. "Packed a duffel bag before I left my brother's house. I told you I was going to stay with you."

"You are so pushy, Timur. What if I don't want you staying here?"

He put the bread in the oven, and then tossed the vegetables around in the wok before looking at the rice cooker. "Doesn't matter. I'm keeping you safe."

"You just want sex."

Those blue eyes went from ice to flame. Fingers of desire crept down her spine. She couldn't help her reaction to the intensity of that look.

"All the time. In fact, come over here." He pointed to a spot right in front of him.

There was the counter between them, but she knew she wasn't safe, not when he had that look in his eyes. "We're talking."

"You talk. I've got other plans." He pointed to the spot again.

"You're making me very nervous. What kind of plans?"

"Baby, I'm not asking. I want you to walk around the counter and come right over here to me. Since when did you decide you were a little chicken?"

Since he got that look on his face, but she wasn't going to tell him that out loud. She slipped off the barstool, not really understanding why, but she was helpless to do anything but obey him. Excitement had her blood rushing through her veins and her heart beating wildly. That was it. All of it. He made her feel alive. Every second she was with him, no matter the emotion, she felt intensely alive.

Ashe moved around the center island and stood right in front of him, so close she had to tilt her head to look up at him.

"You wearing panties?"

"Of course, I am." The tone of his voice had her heart thudding even harder. Her sex clenched and those panties were instantly damp.

"You shouldn't be. Once we're home, you don't need them, Ashe." He held out his hand, palm up.

"We're in the kitchen, and I'm all about hygiene," she protested. But even though she was protesting, her thumbs looped in her lacy little boy shorts and she peeled them off, wadded them up and put them in his palm. Now she was just in her old T-shirt.

He stuffed the panties into his pocket and caught her

around the waist, lifting her right onto the very edge of the counter. Her heart went into overdrive.

"I'm hungry, baby, and looking for a snack before dinner. Don't have a lot of time, so this will have to do, right here. And I claimed the fucking kitchen after one look at those poor excuses for pots and pans you had. That means I get to make up the rules in here, not you."

One hand pressed on her belly, urging her to lie back. She complied, watching his face, watching those blue flames darken with lust. The look on his face, those sensual lines carved deep, sent a fresh wave of hot liquid slicking her sheath in readiness. He caught her thighs and pulled them apart, lifting her legs over his shoulders. Then he just paused and looked at her. There. Breathing warm air over her. Just staring, as if in wonder.

"You're so fucking beautiful, Ashe."

She tried not to squirm. "I'm glad you think so."

"I've never had this. Not a single moment like this one. Thank you for giving it to me."

She didn't know what that meant. She couldn't imagine any woman turning him down. He was so sexual. Intense. He focused completely and solely on her. He gave her all the things a woman would feel, heady pleasure rushing over her, when she was with him. Each time he touched her, their connection seemed to grow. Had it only been about their leopards, she knew she never would have entertained the idea of staying with him. Or trying in a relationship she knew would be challenging.

Timur was a difficult man. He would want to boss her. Rule her. She wasn't that type of woman—or at least she didn't think she was. She liked figuring things out for herself—mostly. She had to admit, she felt safe when Timur was close, and she hadn't had that luxury in a long while. She couldn't imagine what it would be like to be him. To have a mistreated leopard that was out for blood and demanded it day and night.

"Timur." She whispered his name. Knowing she shouldn't. Unable to help herself. She waited until his blue eyes lifted to hers. "You're not a psychopath, nor are you what your father tried to shape you into. You're . . . extraordinary."

She thought he was. He gave up everything for his brother. He didn't leave, he couldn't leave Fyodor and Evangeline to their fates. He felt responsible for them and he sacrificed for them, so they could have a life together. Did they know? Did they even care?

Something flickered in the depths of his eyes. Something amazing and scary. Sensual and vulnerable. An emotion she couldn't recognize because it was so fleeting and then he shut it down. He leaned forward and pressed a kiss between her legs. Her stomach somersaulted.

One hand slid to her belly, fingers splayed wide, pressing down. The other slipped up her thigh while his mouth closed around her clit. He suckled and then his tongue plunged deep. Immediately his thumb and fingers began a rhythmic flicking. There was no getting away from the building intensity. It was hard and fast. It both stung and sent streaks of fire ricocheting through her core.

She heard her soft cry, felt his hair bunched in her fists. She wanted to watch him, see that dark lust and the lines of sensual hunger carved deep that drove him on and on, but the world had narrowed to that of just sensation. Her eyesight seemed to fade as did her hearing so there was only feeling. She felt beyond sensitive so that she could hardly take what he was doing.

Her first orgasm hit like a freight train, rippling through her with a force that shook her, but he didn't slow down. He didn't stop or decrease the way he was using his mouth and teeth and tongue. His fingers slid into her, massaged and stroked. The second orgasm had her crying out, trying to find a purchase with her heels to back away from the relentless pressure. Over and over he flicked and pinched. He stroked and caressed. He stabbed deep and licked. There was no way to combat those things and her body coiled tighter and tighter.

Ashe was afraid she would pass out. Her lungs felt raw and burned with the need for air. She never wanted him to stop, yet he had to if she was going to survive. She found herself resisting the urge to fight him, and then the tsunami was there, sweeping her up into a vortex of pleasure, sending her careening over the edge.

She screamed, loud enough, she was certain, for the neighbors to hear. He lifted his head just enough to wipe his face on either thigh, the shadow of bristles dragging across the sensitive skin there, sending another strong aftershock that caused a shudder to run through her body.

Ashe lay on the counter, staring up at the ceiling, her body limp and pliant, fighting for air that refused to come.

Timur pressed a kiss into her belly button and carefully lowered her legs. He went to the sink and washed his face and hands before turning back to her. "Are you all right? Do you need help?" There was amusement in his voice.

She didn't care how much enjoyment she was giving him, lying there, making a spectacle of herself. Her body was alive. Humming. Every cell sparking so that if felt as if electricity ran through her veins and spilled over to every organ. She could just stay right where she was and not care about anything.

She closed her eyes. "I'm perfectly fine, thank you very much."

His soft laughter tempted her to open her eyes, but she didn't. Instead, she threaded her fingers behind the nape of her neck and listened to the sounds he made as he moved around the kitchen. A drawer opening. Water running. His footsteps. It all blended together and was comforting. Then a warm cloth was between her legs. That felt soothing and caring and deserved at least a peek through her lashes.

His expression was intense and focused completely on

her. Her heart lurched. She could get used to that attention. She'd had a happy enough childhood. Her mother was barely sixteen when she had her and for whatever reasons, she'd remained a little distant from Ashe. Her father had been the main caregiver, of both of them really. Of her mother mostly.

"My mom was beautiful," she murmured aloud. "She really loved my father. She would look at him with this one expression, as if he was her entire world. It made me envious. I wanted her to look at me like that." And now Timur was looking at her with that focused intensity, that look that said she was everything to him when they'd only known each other a couple of days. But it was there. Undeniably. And she liked it far too much.

"He had to be her world, baby," Timur said softly and pulled her into a sitting position. "He saved her from being the wife of a man like my father, a man who would have beaten her. Abused her. Forced her to have children, all the while taunting her that she was nothing and someday he would end her life. She knew what the lairs were like. Any male shifter in the lairs was expected to take a wife and then kill her to prove his loyalty. Your father saved her from being passed around to his father's friends before she suffered that fate."

"What was I to my mother then?" She pushed at the hair tumbling around her face. The thick strands annoyed her, mostly because she needed to be annoyed rather than feel the way she had as a child—unwanted by her mother.

"She probably was terrified that if she had a female child rather than a male, eventually, her husband would get rid of her. That was ingrained in them. Every female child in our lair knew what her fate was going to be. There was no way out for them."

"She was disappointed I was a girl?" That hurt. She'd known it, but it still hurt. Hearing him confirm it was almost devastating.

He lifted her off the counter and held her until she got her legs to work. She stepped away as quickly as possible. She could be naked in front of him and that didn't bother her. She could have wild sex with him, and she wasn't embarrassed. But she didn't want to feel this kind of vulnerability. To keep him from seeing her expression, she went to the cupboard where her dishes were stored.

"I don't think it was disappointment, Ashe," he said as he lifted the lid on the wok. "I think your mother loved you very much. She wanted your father to teach you how to survive. They held themselves away from society or anywhere that might put your life in danger. She also wanted her sister safe, yet she didn't try to go rescue her. She didn't ask your father to rescue her. She stayed here with you to make certain you survived, and no one could get to you. That's love. I know love when I see someone like you. Your parents gave you that."

Ashe was silent, turning over and over what he'd said. She tried to remember her mother picking her up. Had she? It had always been her father's voice she'd heard telling her to push herself harder. That she needed to learn to swim faster. To run farther. To shoot with expert precision. He used to yell at her that there was no reason to waste a bullet. It had to hit precisely where she aimed it.

Her mother had been there with them. Her father never went anywhere without her mother close to him. What had her mother been doing while father and daughter trained? Ashe set the table as she thought about it. Yes, she'd been there, wringing her hands and occasionally objecting that her father was being too harsh with her. He hadn't stopped or listened to her. In fact, now that she replayed those scenes in her head, she saw her father send her mother a quick, quelling scowl.

"She catered to him. She did everything he told her to do," she mused aloud.

"Probably. She was a terrified child when he saved her

life. They came to a foreign land. It was his money they lived on. She might have loved him, but she didn't feel equal with him. How could she? She adored him. Doted on him. Wanted to please him."

Her mother had been like that with her father to the point that Ashe had felt pushed aside. She hated feeling as if she was being a huge baby when she'd had a really good childhood and Timur's childhood had been pure hell. She poured water into tall glasses and then sank down into her favorite chair at the small table where the built-in alcove was. The little breakfast nook was round, the small circular outcropping coming out of the kitchen, creating a space that was intimate. She liked it but had added heavy drapes. She liked looking outside during the day, but in the evening, she felt vulnerable with the lights on.

"I love this house," she murmured as he put the bowls of rice and stir-fry on the table.

"I do too," he said. "I've asked Evangeline if she'd sell it to me a couple of times. She's thinking about it."

She glared at him. "Don't you dare buy my house out from under me."

"You can't have it both ways, *malen'kiy smerch.* You're either running or you're staying."

She shrugged and helped herself to the rice. "You're always saying you're going to catch up with me, so either way, I need my house." She scooped a healthy portion of the stir-fry onto the rice. It smelled wonderful. He'd cooked that morning. If that food was anything to go by, he was an awesome chef, and she didn't plan to waste her opportunity to eat something good.

She felt his eyes on her, but she refused to look up. Truthfully, she had no idea what she was going to do with Timur. "I'm not like my mother, you know. Even if I did stay, I wouldn't dote on you. Or adore you." She couldn't help sneaking a peek at him to see how he took that declaration.

"Yes, you would. You'd also argue with me about anything and everything. That will more than balance out your adoration of me."

She gave an inelegant snort of derision. "You wish."

"I don't wish for the crap you're going to give me," he denied, pushing the basket of bread toward her. "But the rest of it, yeah, I'm looking forward to it."

"This is too fast. Don't ask me to make decisions when I know I've got the ones who murdered my parents on my trail. I would have brought them straight to Fyodor in the hopes that he would have gotten rid of them for me."

"How well did you actually know Evangeline before coming here?"

She ducked her head, cursing under her breath. He had a right to know. She'd brought trouble with her. "We met at a little café up in the mountains where I worked as a barista. She was camping for a while in the hills there and she was alone. We naturally gravitated toward each other. Our first encounter was actually at a creek where she was washing up. We got talking and I found out she needed a job. They needed help at the café, so I told her to apply and I'd put in a good word for her."

She glanced up to find his gaze fixed on her face. The cold one. Ice-blue. Glaciers of blue. A little shiver went down her spine. He was wholly focused on her, but this time, it wasn't sexual, or at all friendly. This time, he wasn't asking because he was interested so much as because he was looking out for his sister-in-law.

Ashe couldn't help the way her heart beat faster. Danger. Why did she find herself running right toward it all the time? What was it about adrenaline that made her such an addict? She wanted to feel this way, exhilarated, alive and not quite safe. It was playing with fire, and she knew better.

"Ashe," he prompted.

She deliberately shrugged and forked more stir-fry into her mouth. "This is good. You're a really good cook, and I could get used to coming home from work and watching you put together meals. There's something magical and mesmerizing, watching you take a few ingredients and put them together to make something to eat this good." She flashed a small smile at him. Coaxing that look off his face. "Maybe I'll even learn to do the chopping for you."

She nearly got a smile from him, but the ice didn't melt from his eyes. She knew it wasn't going to be that easy, and she was glad. She didn't want easy. She wouldn't respect easy. Timur wasn't a man she could push around. She should have known it because Fyodor was a force to be reckoned with and Timur didn't allow his brother to push him around.

"You can drop the sweet act, baby. You were talking about your relationship with Evangeline. I need to know everything."

Ashe gave an exaggerated sigh, but she was secretly happy he was pushing her to answer. "There isn't much to tell. We were both alone and we gravitated toward each other. She was from Louisiana, and I was from the Appalachian Mountains. We spent time together, but I was careful not to tell her my secrets, and she didn't tell me hers. We were both aware we weren't sharing important things, but it didn't matter. We both understood we couldn't."

She shrugged again and took another bite. The meal really was delicious. She kept her eyes on his face, which was laughable, because he gave nothing away. It was as if he wore a mask and whatever went on behind it wasn't for the world—or her—to see. And she wanted to. She wanted to be that woman, the one who knew him inside and out. He was offering that to her, or at least he was offering her . . . what? What was it really? Sex? The sex was better than good, but what else did he offer?

"Don't," he ordered softly.

She raised an eyebrow. "Don't what? Worry that if I stayed I'd never have any more of you than I do right this minute? Of course, I'm going to worry about that. We barely know each other. You've expressed fear that you're a psychopath. You've threatened to find me if I run. These are not things conducive to making me want to stay with you."

"I was hoping the food would help."

For a moment they stared at each other, and then Timur laughed. The sound was unexpected, and it struck at her, piercing her heart as surely as if he'd thrown a spear. His face lit up and the blue flames in his eyes danced. The sight took her breath away. She could listen to that sound for the rest of her life. She knew it was hers. His laughter was for her. She held that to her. She'd dreamt of having a man of her own and he was always dangerous and brooding. He presented a mask of indifference to the rest of the world, but for her—and their future children—he would be different. He would share fun and laughter. Just like this moment.

"The food helps," she admitted when his smile had faded.

"Tell me more about Evangeline and you."

"There isn't much more to tell. She left after a few weeks. I could tell she was restless and wanted to go back to wherever it was that made her feel safe. I know that feeling. I sometimes can't breathe because I feel so exposed." She looked around the room at the heavy drapes she'd added to the house.

"No one is going to get to you. I'm with you now, Ashe, and that means they'll have to walk through me to get to you. That won't be so easy."

"Why? You know, just by being here, I'm a threat to Evangeline and your brother."

"Because you're mine."

He said it so simply. So positively, as if he didn't have a doubt in the world. She shook her head. "Honey, sex doesn't solve every problem, and we'd have major ones."

His eyebrows shot up and his fork paused halfway to his mouth. "Why do you think that?"

She laughed. "Because you're you and you think an order is meant to be obeyed. And I'm me. I think an order should be ignored."

"You'll get over that."

The way he said it, so simply, so smugly and complacently, as if there was no other conclusion, made her want to laugh again with sheer happiness. He was made for her. Custom-made. But what was the old saying? Be careful what you wish for. Still, she loved that he was so in control. That he had so much confidence in himself and his ability to command her.

"Maybe, if you're worth it, Timur, but most men aren't."

"I was born to be with you, Ashe. I have no doubts at all about that. You're the one who needs to catch up. Try the garlic bread and tell me how you came to be here."

She had been trying to resist the garlic bread, although it smelled wonderful and more, it looked fabulous, calling to her repeatedly. She had curves. Lots of them, and she knew bread was one of her weaknesses. She gave in and took a warm piece from the basket.

"Evangeline was my savior. I read about her marrying Fyodor. Of course, at the time, the papers used the name he was living under, but it didn't matter. He was a member of the mafia. At least the speculation was there. I was looking for a dangerous man and that was what I needed. I knew whoever was after my parents had found me and I led them right here, hoping Evangeline's husband was fierce enough to protect her and kill them. I wanted them dead."

She looked him in the eye when she declared it. She meant every word and if that meant she was a bad person and was going straight to hell, then so be it. She was ready to accept those consequences. She was even willing to accept that Timur might be playing her in order to better find out why she was there and that meant he might pull out his gun and shoot her. He hadn't seen the carnage left behind, the bodies of the only two people she loved in the world, so ravaged and mangled that she had barely been able to identify them. "I want them dead," she repeated.

"They'll die," he said.

She heard the promise in his voice and let out her breath. He was strong enough. He was that man—the one she'd dreamt of. "I'll help in any way I can."

"Then give me your word that you'll stay so I'm not worried that you're going to take off while I'm looking the other way."

She was inexplicably proud of him for taking advantage, so much so that she couldn't stop the grin. "Nice. Take advantage."

"Always."

"I'm going to remember that."

He shrugged and took a drink of water, washing the sourdough bread down. "As long as you're staying, I'm okay with that. Tell me more about Evangeline and you."

"Honestly, Timur, there isn't that much to tell. I went to the bakery and she recognized me right away. I told her I was in trouble, and I was very honest with her, that someone had killed my parents and they were after me. I needed work and a place to stay. She gave me both. All the utilities here at this house are in her name. Evangeline is the most generous person I've ever met. She didn't even hesitate. Not for a moment."

Ashe flicked him a quick look from under her lashes. "She did warn me about you."

Timur looked a little smug over that. "She warned you about me, not Fyodor?"

Ashe nodded almost reluctantly.

Timur looked extremely superior and arrogant over that. "Because that little minx has him wrapped around her finger. He does everything she asks. I wouldn't be surprised if she tells him which suit to wear in the morning."

"I think that's sweet," Ashe said, just to watch his eyes change color.

"Don't think you're going to get to do the same, *malen'kiy smerch*, because I can assure you, it won't happen."

She was up for the challenge. "I am not a little tornado," she insisted.

"That's exactly what you are. You wreak havoc wherever you go."

She laughed because it was a fair assessment of her. "I suppose you're right." There was no sense in denying it. "My father used to say that all the time. He said my grandfather would have liked me."

"The grandfather who bought your mother from a human trafficker and planned to pass her around to his friends when his son had no more use for her? That grandfather?"

She nodded. "I didn't say he thought I would like or forgive his father, but he talked of him often and I know he missed him."

"Did he ever speak of his mother?"

She shook her head. "Not once. I never once heard her mentioned and when I asked about her, he said she'd died long before he could remember her."

"It is possible the lairs there were also extremely violent, as the ones in my homeland," Timur said, "but from what you tell me, your father wasn't a violent man. I believe, no matter what, that your mother was his true mate. He stumbled across her by accident. He would never be violent toward her. Others? Who knows?"

She put down her fork and rubbed her thighs with her palms, back and forth, a gesture that often soothed her. Lately that horrible itch that engulfed her body would come at unexpected times and she rubbed her skin in the hopes of soothing it. Now, she knew that was her leopard pushing close to the surface, rising again and again before the emergence.

"I never saw my father violent, but he did tell my mother about some of the men in his lair. The ones who didn't have a wife, and some who did, waited for new girls to be bought and passed around. The things my mother told me sickened me. She didn't want me to ever go looking for my grandfather, no matter how much my father hero-worshiped him."

Timur's eyes went cold again. The blue flames flickered beneath the glacier, giving the blue a deeper color. His eyes fascinated her. Sometimes she thought she was catching glimpses of his soul. Ice or fire. Those were her choices and she wanted them both.

"Did your father encourage you to seek out your grandfather?"

She hesitated. She always protected her parents, preserving their memories and talking about everything good. She felt she'd already put her mother in a bad light, which was wrong. Her mother had been loving, just a little hesitant and distant, but always loving and kind. There had been good times with her, where they'd both laughed and celebrated being women.

Her relationship with her father had been more complicated. He'd been a strict taskmaster. He'd forced her to run every day, no matter how bad she'd felt. He'd insisted she learn to handle weapons, and he'd been harsh with her. He'd used a rubber knife and raised welts all over her body when he'd slashed or struck her with it, to show her that she would have been cut that many times before she'd disarmed him. He'd been the one to teach her to swim and dive. To do everything.

He'd been fun as well. He'd made her laugh and sometimes, he made her feel like a princess with her knight guarding her castle. She'd loved him for those times. He'd been a perfect mix of love and danger. Of harshness for necessity, tempered with love. She understood that he'd had to be harsh in order to ensure her safety—to make certain his wild child obeyed him.

"It was the only time I ever heard them fight. My mother rarely contradicted my father, in fact I would say never. She would beg him to go easier on me, but she didn't tell him to stop and when he wasn't easier, she didn't argue her point. She went along with everything he said. He was talking about his father and how he was wealthy, and he would one day love to see his grandchild. He told me I would be welcome in my grandfather's lair, that he was still alive and wanted to get to know me."

"Your mother wasn't happy about that."

Ashe shook her head. "Absolutely not. She told me under no circumstances should I go there and that I should forget all about him.

"My father was furious with her and told her I would be welcome. She reminded him that his father *bought* girls—young girls—and used them before returning them to the lairs to die." She looked down at her hands, ashamed of her father and horrified by his furious outburst at her mother. "My father said that his father only bought castaways, little whores, not good women."

There was silence, and she couldn't bring herself to look at his face. "My mother struck him. Hard. Right in the face and she left. I just stood there, and I remember crying. Crying for her. Crying for knowing my father had called her a whore. Later she told me that females in her lair were treated as less than human, with no rights. Some were killed at birth because the fathers wanted no part of them. She had been sold to my grandfather, but she'd done nothing wrong and she said even if she had, it was no excuse for any man to treat a woman that way."

"She wanted you to know that."

Ashe nodded, grateful he could understand. "My father was horrified the moment the words came out of his mouth, I could see that, but it was too late. He'd said them. He followed after her and they were gone for days. When they came back, he stuck close to her and no one smiled much. I left a couple of weeks later when I turned eighteen."

"I think your mother was right. Staying away from your grandfather sounds like a good plan. Evangeline had a grandfather who many classified as a monster, but then, they'd never met my father or his brothers." He gestured toward her with his fork. "Finish your food, baby."

"I've been eating," she pointed out. "Your plate is nearly full."

"Because I took a second helping. In any case, I have plans for you."

His voice made her heart jump, and a delicious curl of heat danced down her spine. Deep inside, her sex clenched and she felt a rush of delight go through her veins.

"Plans?" She tilted her head and looked at him, speculation and interest in her gaze.

"I want you under the table, on your knees, your mouth around my cock."

"I see." She drew the two words out, but now heat had turned to fire. "When?"

"As soon as you're finished with your meal. I intend to be the dessert."

She ran the tip of her tongue around her lips. "Since you put it that way . . ." She slipped off her chair.

"Wait."

Her heart beat faster. She loved the way he talked. The accent. The command. More, she loved the blue eyes darkening, all the ice melting, leaving those twin blue flames licking at her skin. She didn't move a muscle.

"Take off your shirt and then drop down right there and crawl around to me." As he spoke, he turned his chair slightly to an angle, so she would no longer be under the table. He widened his legs to accommodate her.

She reached for the hem of her T-shirt and pulled it over her head. She took her time folding the material, liking the way he looked at her naked body. She had breasts, high and firm, with hard little nipples, already in tight peaks just because he was using that voice of his. After placing her shirt on the chair, she went down to her hands and knees.

The moment she did, she felt her leopard wake—and she woke with a vengeance.

Her body went from feeling sensuous to feeling on fire. Blazing hot. She let the feeling consume her. Every cell in her body had come alive with want. With need. With an all-consuming hunger for Timur. His gaze burned through her skin to brand her bones. She wanted him. Not just because he had those blue flames for eyes, or he was so scorching hot and gorgeous, but because he was danger and intrigue and he could cook.

She crawled between his thighs and knelt up, deliberately brushing her swaying breasts against the material of his sweats. The friction felt amazing. He didn't wait for her to slide his sweats over his hips, he did so, pulling his heavy erection out for her.

Her heart pounded as her eyes met his. She found her legs were shaking and she was glad she was on her knees because she might have fallen. For the first time in her life, she was giving herself to someone. Letting him see her, because he looked at her with his complete focus and saw her. Not through her, he actually saw her and what coming like this to him meant to her. It wasn't a game lovers played. This was about something deep inside her answering his call. This was about her leopard answering his male's call.

His cock was in his hand, a hard, thick shaft of pure steel, forged into beautiful artwork. Her breath caught in her throat. She loved the way he looked and marveled at how big he could get. There was no way all that was fitting in her mouth. When he was in her body, he stretched her ability to accommodate him. Still, her mouth watered, and she couldn't help leaning into him, lifting her face toward him.

His hand was unexpectedly gentle as he touched her forehead, a small caress before he settled his palm at the back of her head. She felt his fingers, very slowly, pull her hair into his fist. The small bite of pain deepened the desire already beginning to rage through her body.

"Open your mouth for me, Ashe."

She did. Instantly. Wanting him. Wanting what he was offering. Her pulse pounded through her clit and her hungry body clenched emptily. She felt herself trembling.

"Are you afraid?" For the first time his voice was strained.

She kept her gaze fixed on his cock, on the mesmerizing rhythm of his hand as it pumped up and then slid down. She shook her head. "Only that I might not please you. I want to give you the same kind of pleasure that you gave me but you're . . . intimidating." It was the only word she could settle on. He was. And she wanted him as far gone as he'd made her. Mindless and out of control. She wanted him to feel the emotion she was experiencing just offering herself to him.

He cupped one breast, his thumb gliding over her nipple. "You will not do anything but please me, Ashe. You did as I asked. You're giving me you. What more could I possibly want?"

He slid the wet, slick head of his cock across her lips. It was warm. Firm. Like velvet. She opened her mouth and took him in, showing him without words that she was very serious in her veneration, in her complete devotion to the art of devouring her dessert.

9

TIMUR extracted himself from the naked woman sprawled over top of him. He'd worn her out finally, after hours of taking her, showing her various ways a man could take a woman. She'd never once balked, or protested, or even hesitated. She'd said yes to everything, and he'd wrung a number of cataclysmic orgasms out of her, allowing very little rest in between.

Once, she'd been drifting off to sleep and his body had gone into overdrive, his cock so hard he was afraid it might break. He knew part of it was she was close to the emergence and her hormones and pheromones were riding the two of them. He didn't care what it was, only that when he took her, driving hard, rougher than he intended, she hadn't stopped him. She'd pushed back every bit as hard. Every bit as rough.

She liked to play, and when they were done, she liked to be close. He found he did too. He wanted her on top of him or under him. He wanted to feel every inch of her body covering him like a blanket. Her soft breasts, her sweet pussy, her arms and all that hair brushing his skin every time she moved. He needed the contact in the same way he needed air to breathe. When he'd put her there and told her not to move, she'd cooperated, just as she had when he was inside her.

The vibration from his phone had alerted him to the fact that the hit team was on the move. He didn't want them anywhere near Ashe, but his crew couldn't take them at the motel. It was little better than a flophouse, one that prostitutes frequented, bringing their johns. That made for too many witnesses. They had set a trap, but the team had to actually take the bait. In this case, it appeared they had.

Timur would never use Fyodor or Evangeline to draw out an experienced hit team. He wouldn't want Ashe to know he had already killed the two men he suspected had killed her parents or that if it wasn't them specifically, this newer team had to be the ones. She would want to be a part of taking them down, and he wasn't risking her. Kyanite had texted the members of the new hit team via the cell phones they found on the dead bodies.

It was impossible to know for certain who had sent them, or which lair they came from, because they had no real identifying marks on them or papers. No one had recognized them. Still, Timur surmised that they had been sent from Lazar. In any case, it didn't matter very much, not when they were there to kill the people he loved.

He dressed, and then picked up the can of spray Drake Donovan had given him. The spray had been developed by, of all things, a female shifter who owned a perfume factory. She grew her own flowers and hybrids. This particular combination covered all scents of a leopard's passing. He stopped in mid-spray. Why hadn't any of the security guards smelled the hit team? Not one single person, Ashe included, mentioned scenting them. So where had their scent been?

Very slowly, Timur put down the can of spray. It wasn't something one could purchase. It wasn't for sale. Only a handful of men knew of its existence. So why hadn't anyone smelled the leopards before they'd gotten so close to Ashe?

He put a knee to the bed, hating to wake her. She deserved to sleep. He knew she was scheduled to work in the early morning hours and that was only a couple of hours away. He wanted to be back by then, but if not, he'd have guards escort her to the bakery. If not the shop, they'd be going to his brother's estate where he knew she would be safe.

"Baby, wake up for me."

A small frown flitted across her face, but her lashes lifted. She blinked sleepily, and he found himself looking into her drowsy eyes. His heart clenched and he couldn't help but push back the strands of hair that had come loose from her thick braid during one of their wild sex romps.

"When you were attacked in the bakery, did you smell him? Did your leopard?"

Her frown deepened, making his cock jerk hard. It didn't take much when she was around. He was beginning to think he was insatiable when it came to Ashe.

"No. That's weird, isn't it?"

His heart jumped. "Get up right now, Ashe. Get dressed."

The urgency to his tone was nothing compared to what he was feeling. He swore under his breath as he caught up his phone to warn the others. Don't rely on smell. They can disguise their scent. That's how they got to Ashe's parents. They didn't see the hit team coming because there was no way to identify them. Look inside the motel room.

Ashe hadn't argued with him. She leapt out of bed and caught at her clothes, dragging on a pair of jeans and a T-shirt.

"Pack a bag. Hurry, baby. Fast. You've got two minutes to get whatever you think you need."

She pulled a bag from the closet. "This is my 'go' bag. I've got everything in it to run."

He was going to remember that. He caught her arm and gestured toward the door leading to the main part of the house while he looked at a text from the crew outside the residence.

Sorry, in the wind. They're in the wind.

It was what he expected to hear, but he still wanted to put a fist through the wall. He should have gone with his first gut instinct—taken Ashe to Fyodor's estate and made certain she was safe.

We're coming out. Check rooftops and the trees.

Ashe was close to the front door. He made a sound and she halted, turning her head to look at him over her shoulder.

"I'm armed," she acknowledged. "Two guns and a knife."

"Most likely you won't need them, *malen'kiy smerch*, but if you do, don't hesitate and go for a kill." He caught her shirt and pulled her up to her toes, looking down into her eyes so she knew he meant business. Inside, he was as cold as ice. A fucking freezer. He would kill in a heartbeat for her and never look back. "Do you understand me?"

"Yes, Timur. I won't hesitate, and it will definitely be a kill shot. I don't want them getting back up and coming at either one of us."

He realized she was more apt to protect him than herself. He was staying close. He brushed a kiss over her forehead and released her. "Give me another minute. The boys will be waiting for us outside. They're clearing the area and the car again, just to be safe."

He texted Gorya. Get Fyodor and Evangeline to the safe room. He's going to protest, and you don't take any shit off him. Get him in there even if you have to knock the son of a bitch over the head. He might get mad, but I'll come after you if anything happens to either one of them so don't let him give you any crap.

Consider it done.

Timur didn't envy his cousin the job of taking Fyodor, a man of action, to the safe room to wait it out with Evangeline, although having Evangeline there was an advantage. Fyodor would do anything to protect her. Timur knew that feeling now, the unreasonable fear that had him gripped by the balls. He had to protect Ashe at any cost to anyone or to himself. That was all that mattered to him right then.

"You stay tucked in close to me, Ashe. Don't touch my arm, but stay right into my body."

She nodded and drew her weapon, just as he drew his.

"Stay in sync with me. I'll keep my steps shorter." He was significantly taller than she was. "I'm not going to be looking at you, baby, so it's up to you to stay tucked into my side." He had pulled on his long trench coat. He had multiple weapons in it. It also gave him the advantage of having a garment that would flow around her as they moved together so if a sniper was taking aim at her, he would lose her with every step.

"Coming out." He spoke into the small radio.

The front door was pulled open and Ashe stepped into Kyanite's protection until Timur got through the doorway and closed the heavy oak door behind him. He moved forward, and then Ashe was between Kyanite and Timur, walking fast toward the car that was parked right out front. It was already turned toward the street, and the engine was on, with Rodion at the wheel.

They made it to the car, Ashe tucked in close to his body. She didn't brush his arm, but he could feel her body against his with every step. She was silent and steady, setting a fast pace so they reached the vehicle quickly.

Kyanite and Timur swept the rooftops again, checking to make certain there was no sniper sitting up high waiting to get his shot. They were using Timur's car, which was armor-plated for Fyodor and had bulletproof glass. That didn't make them safe from every weapon, but certainly the majority.

Timur slid into the seat beside Ashe and took her hand. Kyanite slipped up front and Rodion immediately put the car in motion. The entire sequence hadn't taken them more than a minute. Timur exhaled and brought her hand to his face. "How would they get hold of the spray that removes all odors so our cats can't smell them?" He pulled out his phone again and texted his brother. Talk to Drake. He has to investigate this slip. We need a meeting immediately. If we can't get all the players together, we need the ones who know about that scent-blocker.

He rubbed the palm of Ashe's hand back and forth across the dark stubble on his face while he waited for Fyodor's reply. Texted Drake. He doesn't know. Hasn't heard any rumors. It would have had to have been sold on the black market if it was going to the Russians. He's contacting Sasha in Miami. If it was offered, it had to go through him.

Timur disagreed. He'd met Sasha, and the man was pretty straightforward about joining them. He wasn't going to fuck it up for a can of spray. That would mean he'd sold them out, and Sasha was more vulnerable than anyone right then with the exception of . . . Emilio Bassini. They should have killed the fucker when they were cleaning closets. Damn.

Does Bassini have ties to anyone in New Orleans?

Don't have a clue, I've asked Drake. He's leader of a lair there. He'll know that information.

Check to see if Ulisse Mancini or Fredo Lombardo have ties there. He included the other crime bosses with close territories. Do they ever do business with anyone from that region? Anything, any tie at all, no matter how remote.

He waited impatiently and found himself biting down on the pads of Ashe's fingers. She jumped but didn't pull her hand from his. Maybe, without thinking, he'd bitten down a little too hard. He stroked his tongue over the marks and then kissed her.

His phone lit up. *Both Mancini and Lombardo had business ties to Rafe Cordeau.*

Recently, Rafe Cordeau had been killed and his body burned so no one would ever find him. Joshua Tregre had taken over his territory. Joshua was one of them. He would never sell them out. Timur glanced up to see where they were, how close to Fyodor's estate. It was located out of San Antonio and up in the hill country. Even driving fast, it would take a few more minutes to get there.

Timur wanted to move Evangeline's bakery closer to the estate. She was flown in each morning by helicopter, but that didn't help when they needed to travel fast and they didn't have access to one.

Is Tregre doing business with either of them?

Both. Not a lot. They wanted in on the opium business that was being run through the perfume sales a while back. That side of the business was shut down.

Timur wanted to bellow with rage. What the fuck was wrong with his brother that he hadn't imparted any of this information to him? *You didn't think to tell me this?*

Drake shut that down, so no, I didn't.

This is the same perfume business where the scent-blocker comes from? His head was about to explode. He was head of security for Fyodor. What he knew, Sevastyan knew, and Sevastyan was head of security for Mitya. They were all at risk. What the hell was wrong with everyone?

Who owns the perfume factory?

A woman by the name of Charisse Mercier, along with her brother, Armande. They were cleared of all charges.

Who the fuck was guilty? It was like pulling teeth to get information. Important information that could save lives. He was punching Drake Donovan in the face the next time he saw the man. Everything should have been disclosed at their last meeting, rather than because Drake took care of it without mentioning it.

Joshua Tregre's uncles. The opium was put in boxes by Charisse's mother and the two uncles took it out to buyers by boat at night in the swamp. The mother was some piece of work. A serial killer. That's how they found out about the opium.

Timur closed his eyes and rubbed his temples. Immediately, Ashe was on her knees on the seat beside him, her fingers digging into his neck, massaging the tension out of him. She was strong, pushing through the knots to ease them out. It was heaven, but more importantly, no one, not even his mother, had ever noticed when he was in any kind of discomfort.

"Thanks, baby, but you need to wear your seat belt. If for any reason we have to take off fast, I don't want you hurt." He didn't want her to stop with the neck massage either. Her hands were amazing.

"I'm a leopard. I have great balance," she reminded. "Whatever you're reading on your phone is making you tense and angry. Stop reading it until we're at your brother's place."

He found himself smiling instead of wanting to rake his claws over the leather seats. "My brother has always played things close to his chest. Now he's out there, exposed, and he can't afford to do that, but he still wants to be the soldier instead of the man at the helm. He's going to get killed doing that."

Timur leaned into Ashe and brushed his mouth over hers. The moment his lips touched hers, he felt a strange rolling in the region of his heart. *"Moy malen'kiy smerch,"* he murmured. "Sit down and put that seat belt on."

She continued to kneel up on the seat beside him, her amber-colored eyes looking into his. He felt that look right down to his soul. Something twisted in his chest. Hard. Broke open. He wrapped his arms around her and pulled her down onto his lap. Then he was kissing her. He knew better than to kiss her in public, even in the back seat of his car, not when anyone was around. Kissing Ashe was like lighting a stick of dynamite. The two of them went up in flames.

He forgot where he was and what he was supposed to be doing. The world fell away until there was only his woman and her incredible mouth. The fire roaring between them. The electricity arcing from one to the other. His body reacted the way it always did, going hard and making urgent demands.

Her mouth was as hot as hell, the firestorm raging out of control that fast. It was a beautiful, terrible thing, to fall so far, so fast. His hand tightened in her hair.

"We need to get a privacy screen for the car." She whispered the words against his ear. "Imagine how I could make all that tension disappear right out of you if we had that screen." Her mischievous smile went right through his cock.

He knew she felt that part of him straining against his trousers, reaching for her. "I couldn't care less if they were here watching."

"Sadly for you, I do." Her grin went wider, and her eyes danced. She slipped off his lap and reached for the seat belt. "Safety first and all that."

"I will retaliate," he warned.

"I'm looking forward to it."

He realized she'd distracted him from the continual reports on his phone. The anger was gone, replaced by a much more enjoyable sensation. He glanced down at his phone.

I've sent word to Drake to have Joshua look discreetly into his two uncles as well as Charisse and her brother, Armande. If he missed something and they're doing business with either Emilio or Ulisse, we could be in trouble. Fyodor had sent the text.

Someone sold us out, Timur texted back. *Either one of them wants you gone.* Emilio wanted Evangeline and had been very upset when she'd chosen Fyodor. Ulisse just wanted to expand his territory. He was looking for power. There was always Lombardo to worry about as well. Hell, they had to worry about everyone.

Is Mitya on alert? If this is Lazar's hit team, they will go after him first.

Timur wasn't certain he agreed with Fyodor's assessment. He'd had a lot of time to think about it. It was up to him to prepare for their uncles' retaliation. Lazar would want to deliver the killing blow to the son he believed betrayed him and the code of the lair *bratya*. He might want to personally kill his nephews as well, but regardless, Mitya would be Lazar's own target. He didn't bother to explain his reasoning to Fyodor. What did it matter who was right and who was wrong? The hit squad was knocking on their door and had the help of a powerful scent-blocker.

Mitya has been kept apprised of the situation.

"A mile out, boss," Rodion said.

"Do we have a tail?"

"Not that I've seen. I took evasive action, just to be certain, but I didn't spot anyone remotely looking as if they were tailing us."

Timur threaded his fingers through Ashe's. He wanted their world to be different, but he'd made his choice and there was no going back. "I'm not offering you a safe environment."

"I got that."

Her little smile twisted his insides, but he wanted her to know he was serious. "My leopard claimed yours, Ashe. He isn't going to let her go. We both know that. I don't want to let you go. Me. Not my leopard. You're the first thing I've ever wanted for myself. You're the first time I've ever thought maybe I could have some kind of life. I don't want you to go, not for my leopard or yours, but for me."

He kept his voice low. There was no privacy, not when two leopards sat in the front seat with acute hearing. He would have much rather they heard her blowing him than him spilling his private emotions to her, but it had to be said and who knew if he was ever going to get another opportunity.

Her fingers tightened around his. Her gaze drifted over his face, and everywhere her eyes touched seemed to burn her name deeper into him. He turned away from her, looking out the window, needing to breathe air that didn't have her scent in it, that didn't bring her into his lungs. She was stamped into his bones and wrapped around his heart. He needed to be Timur, the man with no emotions. The man capable of great cruelties should they be necessary—and he feared they would be.

The car came to a halt and beside him, Ashe removed her seat belt just as he removed his. Now, more than ever, he felt danger surround them. He'd always had that sense, that radar. He'd known the exact moment his father had made up his mind to kill his mother. Timur had used his leopard to make the run, trying to get home before it was too late. Gorya had run with him, neither exchanging so much as a sound, but both had known. Timur knew now.

"They're out there, Kyanite. Rodion, get as close to the front door as possible. I don't give a damn about the landscaping. Take it right up to the door. They're going to hit us the moment the doors open. Rodion, get out on the passenger side and into the house. There will be a moment we're vulnerable. One moment. I'm texting Vitaly to open the door, but to stay under cover."

"Got it," Rodion said as he maneuvered the car across the lawn and over the walkway. He positioned the car within feet of the door.

Timur pushed send on the text to Vitaly and then, the moment the front door opened, he shoved the car door open as well. When he bailed out from the car, he dragged Ashe across the seat and jerked her out of the vehicle and under his shoulder. They ran the few steps to the safety of the house.

Something heavy hit Timur and drove him to the ground. He felt the slash of claws and shifted, tearing at his clothes as he did so, shoving his woman as far as possible. Ashe rolled away from him toward the open door, taking his trench coat with her. His shirt ripped as his roped muscles changed to accommodate the cat's size and ferocity. His had always been a large leopard. They rolled, two leopards in a tangle of cloth as his jeans tore but his shoes remained intact.

He ripped at the leopard's belly with a killer's claws. His leopard had grown up in an environment of blood and hatred. Finding his mate hadn't changed those things, nor would it ever. The leopard challenging him broke away, sides heaving. Timur's cat had managed to score his assailant with savage claws while Timur's own wounds were less severe, the loose skin and thick Amur fur protecting him.

His last sight of Ashe had been of Vitaly's hand wrapped around her arm, dragging her inside. If he survived, Timur made a mental note, he'd buy the bodyguard a good bottle of scotch. He deserved it. Timur shifted only two limbs, giving himself hands so he could untie his shoes and get them off. The entire time he was unlacing his shoes, his leopard watched his opponent through hate-filled eyes.

They were a team, leopard and man. They were in perfect sync when it came to fighting. Timur wanted to win as quickly and as viciously as possible. His leopard held that same desire. Both had serious combat skills and were experienced. Timur's brain worked fast, cataloging every weakness the other cat had. Obviously, the animal didn't like to get hurt. It was used to leaping down from a high place and ending a battle quickly with a bite to the neck. The assassin was no Amur leopard, with his golden fur and lazy battle technique.

The moment Timur had felt the cat's weight on his back, driving him to the ground, he'd shifted his head and neck and turned just enough so the attacker hadn't severed his spinal cord. His male got to his feet. He was a big leopard, mostly dark with golden rings around the rosettes pressed into his fur. Timur called him Temnyy because of the darker color. The name meant dark one. He had the beautiful thick fur of the Amur leopard and was every bit as savage as any predator out there.

Timur kept him in fighting shape. They trained daily. His entire security force trained. Weapons. Hand-to-hand combat. They ran scenarios all the time. Their leopards fought and kept battle-ready. That kept the human shifter on his toes, fighting for control to take it back from his leopard when his leopard went into a blood frenzy.

If his male could have smiled, he would have. The lazy leopard facing him, used to his way of killing, had no real chance. He leapt into the air. His opponent jumped a fraction of a second after him. Temnyy, using his flexible spine, turned slightly to avoid claws and raked savagely down the exposed belly and genitals of the other cat. The leopard screamed as it went down on all four feet.

Temnyy was relentless, ripping and tearing at the cat as he landed beside it. His teeth tore into the throat, while his claws raked at the sides and belly. He didn't break away as was expected. Often cats would fight and then pull back to take a breather. Timur didn't believe in taking breathers. Oftentimes the win went to who was in the best condition. He was determined that his leopard would always be in prime shape.

That inner warning system blaring at him had Timur commanding Temnyy to leap away. As he did so, a second cat joined the first. This one was snarling and taunting, deliberately trying to draw Temnyy away from the injured leopard.

A bullet hit the doorframe just inches from the Amur leopard, sending splinters of wood flying in all directions. The boom of a gun answered from somewhere on the roof, and Timur knew Gorya was up there. He was the best marksman they had. He seemed to have an uncanny knack for knowing exactly where an opposing sniper would secrete himself. It was Gorya who often saved the day, taking out their enemies from a distance.

Temnyy attacked, uncaring of bullets, wanting to kill the leopard trying to drag itself away. He used the downed leopard as a springboard, hitting him so heavily on his back the snap was audible. He leapt from the now-dying leopard to the fresh one. For some insane reason, the newcomer hadn't expected Temnyy to attack. The big cat landed on him, teeth driving deep, stiletto claws raking for a purchase in the thick fur. The cat howled and shook, trying to dislodge Temnyy.

Move. Timur issued the command in a hard voice.

Temnyy obeyed, leaping off and to one side. A shot rang out, followed by a second one. The bullet tore into the siding of the house, right where Temnyy's head had been. This time, he was certain Gorya had scored a hit on the sniper. The two shots had nearly been simultaneous.

Temnyy's opponent whirled around and flung himself at Timur's leopard. His lips were drawn back in a snarl of rage. The eyes were focused and deadly. Ears were down, lying flat on the head. Temnyy met him belly to belly, raking and clawing so that fur went in all directions.

Rodion's leopard tumbled past them, rolling away from his opponent and then was on his feet, rushing the cat that had attacked him. Timur could hear the sounds of Kyanite doing battle with another leopard as well. It seemed as though Lazar had sent an army of leopards after them.

The leopard facing Timur scored a lucky rake across Temnyy's face, tearing open skin so that blood poured out. That seemed to excite the cat and he drove at Temnyy, trying to take him off his feet by driving hard into his side. Temnyy waited, acting as if he was disoriented, and then at the last moment was in the air, whirling around and taking out his opponent's hindquarters. He broke its back deliberately, so the leopard screamed with pain and the knowledge that he was helpless.

Timur didn't want to wait for Temnyy to deliver the killing bite. He urged his leopard to hurry, not gloat. Temnyy's female was in the house unprotected, he pointed out, even though he knew several of his security people were with her. That did the trick. Temnyy stopped his pacing and fake attacks, rushed the downed leopard and delivered the killing bite.

Timur immediately took over, forcing the leopard to shift, rubbing at the blood pouring from the rake mark across his forehead and temple. The cat's claw had barely missed his eyes.

"Check the house. Check the house," Timur snapped as he caught the jeans someone tossed him. "They have a scent-blocker. That was staged. They wanted to kill me, but they needed the door open and they got it. When the first one jumped on me, and all eyes were there, another could have slipped inside via a window somewhere."

"No way could they have slipped in through the door, boss," Kyanite said, dragging on his jeans. There was blood on his chest and dripping down one arm. "I blocked the door. I made certain nothing got in this way."

"Then check every other entry and the windows as well. They had an entry point and they're in this house. I know they are. I can feel them." He dragged his own jeans on but didn't bother to secure them. Instead, he strode through the great room toward the master bedroom where he knew Fyodor was safe inside the panic room. He could live in that room for weeks if need be. They had food and water and a bathroom. "Where's Ashe?"

"I'm here." She stepped out of the drapes and then, instead of coming straight to him, turned to Kyanite. "I need a first aid kit. We have to stop that bleeding." She looked past him to Rodion. "All three of you are a mess."

"There's no time," Timur said. He yanked her to him,

relieved that she was alive and no one—human or cat—had touched her. "Get moving, baby." He turned his attention to his men. "There's more of them in this house. Find them. Be careful. They have a plan."

"They can't know the layout of the house," Kyanite said. "We barely know it."

"Timur." Ashe was firm. "It isn't going to do you any good if that blood gets into your eyes and obscures your vision. There's a bathroom right here, let me look under the sink."

He gripped her upper arm hard but detoured with her into the bathroom. "Evangeline had her brother visit not too long ago. What the hell was his name? It was Cajun. Ambroise. He was here. She took him on the tour of the house. Wasn't her father here as well? I wasn't here that day."

Ashe pulled a first aid kit from under the sink, opened it and pressed a cold cloth to the long rake mark. She closed it with several butterfly bandages and then nodded. "You're good. Where to?"

She was all business in a war zone. Timur loved her all the more for that. "Kye, they're in the house. They're concealing themselves. I feel them here. Tell all the men to be watchful and ready to shift instantly. No shoes. Get them off." His shoes had slowed him down and if his attacker had had more actual fighting experience, then he could have been in trouble. "Stay right behind me, Ashe. We're heading to the safe room."

"That's what they want you to do," Ashe said as she fell into step behind him.

"What?" Timur whipped around to face her. "What did you say?"

"She showed her brother around the house, but she wouldn't have told him about the safe room. Even if she had, she wouldn't have shown it to him. Evangeline was very leery when she talked to me about her family. Even if they reconciled, I don't think she'd trust them all that much. She's sweet, Timur, but she remembers and she's careful."

Timur knew those things about his sister-in-law, about her being careful, but he hadn't taken the time to find out about her family. What did he know? She had two older brothers—Ambroise and Christophe. Her grandfather, Buford Tregre, had been a monster, and her father had taken her out to the swamp to hide her existence from the man. She'd grown up mostly alone, certainly not close to her family.

Her father and uncle had been involved in the sale of opium, although both denied they knew much about the business. As far as he knew, Ambroise and Christophe weren't involved at all. But someone was, and that someone had access to a scent-blocker that tied back to Evangeline's family.

Timur stood in the center of the room, away from the walls and any place a leopard might conceal itself before an attack. He stared down into Ashe's upturned face. She was right. Their enemy might know the layout of the house, but they wouldn't know about the safe room. They wouldn't know where Fyodor and Evangeline were hidden. He'd been about to lead their enemy straight to his brother's hideout.

"I need somewhere safe to stash you."

"I need to stay with you," Ashe argued. "I'm not going to play the crazy heroine, Timur. I'm quite fine leaving all fighting up to you."

He thought it over. He would much rather have her under his wing than somewhere in the house where he couldn't see if she was safe or not. The leopards could smell them. Worse, her female was throwing off some strong pheromones. Every male leopard for miles would know she was in heat and he'd . . .

"I can't believe I'm about to say this, but is there any

chance you can get your female to react in some way to what is going on?"

Her long lashes fluttered and then comprehension dawned. He half expected her to be angry that he might use her that way, but she grinned at him, the mischievous one that turned his insides to mush.

"Bring your male close to the surface."

He cupped the side of her face, needing to touch her. Right there, in the middle of a potential war zone, he found himself falling deeper under her spell. He reached for his big male. *Come close and call to your mate.*

At once Temnyy climbed toward the surface, pushing at his muscles and skin. The familiar itch moved over him like a wave. Then Temnyy was there, staring out of his eyes to look at the woman who carried his mate.

Ashe smiled at him. "There you are. I see you." Deliberately she stepped closer and laid her hand on Timur's chest, right over his heart.

At once the leopard scented the potent female as she rose in Ashe toward her mate. She was coquettish, rubbing along the walls of her prison, but Timur could see her, those darker rings spreading through the amber of Ashe's eyes. Her scent permeated the room. All those pheromones telling every male leopard she was in heat. Ready. Or close to ready. His big male was fighting him for control, and Timur remained steadfast in his authority. The last thing he needed was for his leopard to be in command.

He heard the cough of a leopard and it sounded as if it was coming from behind them, from the room off to their left. The door was open and then he caught a glimpse of the leopard's head as it poked around the door in an attempt to catch a sighting of the alluring female.

Another leopard sounded off, his voice distinctly different from the cough produced by the one closer. The second leopard sounded as if he was sawing through a log with his harsher roar. Timur's leopard went wild. No other leopard could claim his territory or his mate. Timur stripped his jeans off and shifted, embracing the change fast.

The one thing Drake had insisted on was practicing shifting fast. They practiced all the time, and the change swept over and through him in no more than a fraction of a second. Temnyy sprang past Ashe and charged the leopard coming at him from the next room. The two cats met in the air, raking at each other's belly and genitals. The sound of their panting was loud in the room.

They hit the floor and rolled over and over. Ashe climbed up on a chair, her back to the wall, her gun in her hand, but with the two cats tangled together and rolling as one, it was impossible to get off a shot. Temnyy's thick coat was much darker than the other leopard's, and Timur recognized immediately that this was no Amur leopard. A second leopard, not from Lazar's lair. Where was he getting his recruits?

Temnyy didn't care what kind of leopard he was fighting, only that this one had come into his territory and had the audacity to challenge for his female. Her scent permeated the room and filled both cats with the need to triumph over the other.

A sawing roar announced the arrival of the second leopard enemy. Temnyy had the first cat pinned down, but aside from the occasional rake of claws, Temnyy couldn't move without allowing the other up. He sank his teeth deeper, trying to suffocate the other leopard. All the while, his hate-filled eyes remained on the new intruder.

The golden leopard entered the room slowly, his manner stealthy. He ignored Temnyy and the other cat where they lay on the floor, a good distance from Ashe. Timur wanted to yell a warning to her, but if he opened his mouth, he would release the leopard before it had been killed. It wasn't out of the fight yet and it was a very strong cat. He couldn't call out to the others to come, they would be fighting their own leopards and their instincts would tell them to keep their cats as far from Ashe as possible.

They were also systematically searching the house, and that took numbers and time. A leopard generally went for high places, but if they couldn't be scented, one had to rely on sight, and they were good at blending in.

Timur watched as the leopard took another step closer to Ashe. He was going to have to force Temnyy to release the cat from his bite if the newcomer charged her.

10

COME on, baby, you're going to have to tell me what to do, Ashe whispered to her leopard. *You've got everyone hot and bothered.*

Her leopard pushed closer to the surface and the burst of fire caught Ashe off guard. Even the touch of material against her skin hurt. She couldn't stand the tightness of her jeans. She wanted to squirm, to push her fingers inside her jeans and try to alleviate the terrible hunger that rose like fire between her legs.

Both hands dropped to her zipper, and it was only then that she realized she had the gun in her fist. Immediately she lifted it and took careful aim at the newcomer. The leopard watched her with a narrowed, very focused gaze. It took a step toward her. She squeezed the trigger just as it leapt to one side and then changed direction, coming at her at an angle.

She turned toward the cat but realized it had put Timur

and the other leopard in her line of fire. If she missed . . . It was too late. The leopard hit her hard in the side, so hard she fell from the chair, hitting the back wall. Its teeth closed around her wrist and she dropped the weapon reflexively.

Come out. She'd never shifted. She didn't even know if she could, but she ripped her T-shirt over her head one-handed and then tore at her jeans. *Godiva, come on, come out now. I can't defend against this horrible thing.* Even as she pushed her jeans down, the large male leopard's breath blasted her face with hot air as it looked into her eyes. She knew Godiva was looking back at him because she was seeing through heat bands.

She threw her shoes at the cat, both hitting him squarely in the face, first one and then the other. He roared his displeasure and swiped at her with a claw. It barely connected, spreading pain across her bare thigh, as the long nails ripped open her skin.

That was the last catalyst for her leopard to emerge. She felt her muscles contort. A familiar itch slid over her skin in a long wave that sickened her. She could feel her bones move and she heard them crack and pop. For a moment she thought to scream, terrified now that it was happening. It wasn't a fast takeover by any means. It felt as if the entire process was happening in slow motion. She felt everything.

She resisted, although she didn't want to, and Godiva immediately backed off. *No, no, come out. I need you to take us over,* she assured and forced air through her burning lungs.

The extra breath allowed her to still her mind and keep panic at bay. She wanted this. She was born for it. She was a shifter and a shifter embraced the change. She'd seen her mother and father shift. She'd watched Timur only minutes earlier. She could do it.

This time, as Godiva rose, Ashe reached for her. She needed her leopard. She had been told she would still be there, a breathing, living, *thinking* Ashe. She wouldn't survive a leopard attack, but the chances of the leopard killing Godiva were very slim. His instincts would take over and no matter what his human directed him to do, the cat's natural drive would prevail. At least, that was her hope.

She found herself on her hands and knees, only her hands were curved and had thick fur. Her arms had white, very thick fur with black rosettes widely spaced apart. She was smaller than the males in the room, but no less alluring to them. She flipped her tail and rubbed her head along the wall and furniture, spreading her scent everywhere. She warned the male pursuing her off with a snarl and a swipe of her paw.

He instinctively backed off, just as Ashe hoped. Godiva sensed more males in the house and wanted them to pursue her as well, but Ashe held her to the room where Temnyy was once again in a full-out battle to kill the other leopard. He'd released the animal to go to her aid, but the leopard had leapt on his back and dragged him down by his hindquarters. He'd sunk his teeth at the back of Temnyy's neck, far too close to the spine.

Godiva, once she saw the trouble her mate was in, rushed the large male holding him. She slammed right into his side, knocking him over and off Timur's leopard. Temnyy was on the cat immediately, delivering a killing bite. The newcomer saw his chance while the female was focused on Temnyy and the other leopard. He was on Godiva, flipping her to the ground, his teeth closing on her shoulder in a holding bite, his larger body blanketing hers.

Godiva struggled, keeping her tail curled down tightly against her body. They rolled, and then he had her again, the teeth causing such pain she could barely function. They'd landed close to the gun. Ashe stretched one front leg toward the weapon, risking the newcomer's attack on her female. One stiletto nail managed to catch in the trigger. She pulled the gun toward her, shifted and turned, all in one movement. The barrel was in the cat's mouth and she pulled the trigger, firing off several rounds rapidly.

The male collapsed over top of her, blood spraying everywhere. She shoved the heavy animal away with a mixture of revulsion and adrenaline. A hand slid over hers and Timur was there, gently removing the weapon.

"You were brilliant, Ashe," he soothed. "Absolutely brilliant. Come on, baby, let's get into the bathroom and clean you up."

She didn't look at the leopard she'd all but destroyed, or the other one Timur had killed. She didn't look down at her hands or naked chest. She felt blood running down her skin. She just let him lead her into a smaller bathroom where there was a tiled shower. He turned on the water and indicated for her to step in. Ashe had never loved water as much as she did in that moment. She closed her eyes and turned her face up to the spray.

"I'll be right back, baby. I'm going to get your clothes."

She would have walked around naked, uncaring who saw her as long as she didn't have to wear anything bloody, but she wasn't going to say that to him. She wasn't going to say anything until she'd removed the blood.

Thank you, Godiva, she whispered. *You saved us both. You were so brave.*

He saw me. The one who is called Temnyy. There was smugness in Godiva's voice. *He knows the others want me.*

Ashe found herself wanting to smile in spite of everything. *You little hussy. I can't believe that's what you're thinking about. I killed one, and Temnyy killed the other.*

We killed one and Temnyy killed the other, but there are more.

Ashe went still, her eyes flying open. *More? In the house? How many more?*

Several. Godiva was complacent about it while Ashe was panicking.

Ashe thought quickly, trying to figure out how she could put the question to her leopard without confusing her. *You know all the men who work with Timur. Not counting their leopards, are there others in the house that are strangers to us?*

That was a long concept for her cat. She had always communicated with her in the hope she had a leopard, although those communications had been one-sided until recently when her leopard had begun her heat cycle that corresponded with Ashe's.

Three. One is very close to us. Two are a distance away. They started to come to us when I emerged, but there were too many between us.

How can you know that? Can you smell them? Why wouldn't the scent-blocker work on the female as it did the males? That made no sense.

No. It isn't that.

Godiva gave no more information. Ashe scrubbed fast and then stepped out of the shower, finding a towel and quickly drying off. She smeared an antibiotic cream on the shallow rake marks on her thigh, her eyes on the door.

Timur wasn't back, and that worried her. He wasn't a man to leave his woman alone too long in a dangerous situation. Her gaze dropped to the gun on the sink where Timur had put it. There were droplets of blood on it.

She wrapped the towel securely around her and then picked up the gun and went to look for her man. She padded barefoot down the hall and immediately heard voices.

"Take me to him or you're dead and so is your little play toy. Of course, before she dies, we're going to have fun with her."

She peeked into the room. A naked man stood with a gun pointed at Timur's head. She didn't want to chance a shot. If she missed the kill shot, he would certainly pull the trigger and even if she didn't miss, he might still pull the trigger in reflex. So no shooting him.

She leaned against the wall, just beside the door, and took off her towel. She put it just in front of the gun in her hand, as if she was walking in, drying herself off. If he turned toward her, just for a moment, she would take the shot. If not, hopefully her naked body would make the man react the way the leopard had. She only needed a split second of distraction. Timur would do the rest.

She took a deep breath and stepped fully into the doorway. "Timur . . ." She allowed her voice to trail off.

The gunman turned toward her just slightly, his gaze taking in her naked body. She froze, trying to look stunned that Timur wasn't alone.

Timur spun, slamming his palm into the barrel of the gun, so that it went straight up. He locked the arm and wrist so it would be impossible for the gunman to fire. Timur stripped the gun from him and stepped back.

Ashe didn't hesitate or call out. She simply took aim and shot the gunman. Three times. She couldn't stop pulling the trigger until she'd gotten off those other two shots. The sound was loud and she hadn't missed. Timur had also fired, using the man's own weapon. He only fired once but he didn't miss either. The gunman crumpled to the floor.

"Godiva says there are at least two others in the house," Ashe announced as if she hadn't just killed another human being.

Timur nodded. "Kye and Rodion are on them. The others are sweeping the house room by room." He indicated her clothes.

They were too near the dead man and the bodies of the two leopards, but she refused to act horrified in front of Timur. She forced her reluctant body to move, delicately skirting around the pools of blood.

"This isn't going to be easy to clean," she pointed out as she picked up her jeans and T-shirt. It was obvious that Timur had gotten to them first and inspected them for bloodstains. They were still partially folded. She slipped into them.

"You did good, Ashe," he praised.

"Why are they here? Why so many? Do you think my

grandfather sent all these men after me? That would be just plain ridiculous."

He shook his head. He'd been caught by the gunman as he'd been pulling on his jeans, and now he did them the rest of the way up. "No, babe. These men were sent specifically after my brother and me. Gorya, Mitya and Sevastyan are at risk as well. They probably have orders to kill Kyanite and Rodion too. The two outside, I have no idea where they came from, but these in the house are from our lair in Russia, Ashe. Anyone coming with us, or helping to hide our trail from my uncles, will be on that hit list."

"I brought them right to your door," Ashe said. She'd done that and she was ashamed. Evangeline had been a friend, one of the few she'd ever had. They hadn't shared much about their lives, but they'd had fun that summer and the friendship meant something to her.

When she'd first arrived, and told Evangeline she was in trouble, Evangeline hadn't hesitated at all. She hadn't betrayed Ashe's confidence or turned her back on her, she'd given Ashe everything needed to survive. A home with no ties back to her. A job without paper. She'd even done so without first consulting the security force.

He shrugged. "They were bound to find us anyway. Fyodor's picture has been plastered all over the place. He changed his name back to Fyodor Amurov. It was a matter of time. We planned to draw them out so we didn't have to be looking over our shoulders for all time." He wrapped his arm around her. "Baby, I've told you this several times. You need to get past feeling guilty. We expected them to come."

Ashe wasn't certain she could get past the guilt, especially if any of them got hurt. "Have the others found any more of them?"

Timur nodded. "Kyanite killed one. Rodion and he have the other one locked up. He's raging and trying to scare them with his killer leopard, but he knows me. At least according to what Rodion and Kye say, this one is from our lair and probably was supposed to have done the identifying for sure." He indicated a fallen leopard.

"It's been a few years, hasn't it?"

He nodded. "But we have the Amurov features. Same as Lazar. He'll know if he's seen us before."

"What are you going to do with him?"

Timur's cold eyes held no emotion. She wasn't looking at his leopard, this was all man. That ice in his veins was really there. He could go so quickly into that state that it shook her a little and scared her even more.

"I'll question him and then kill him." He toed one of the dead leopards. "They came looking for us, Ashe. We stayed out of our homeland, but they came looking."

"I'm not disturbed by you having to kill him, Timur," she admitted. "I came here with the idea of getting help to find those who murdered my parents. I didn't want to take them alive and turn them over to the police. My parents were shifters, and we don't go outside our world for justice. I understand that it has to be different than human law."

"What disturbs you then? Because I saw that little shiver that went down your spine."

That was impossible because she was facing him. Still, she didn't argue with him. "You go so easily from looking at me with warmth to that ice-cold place. If you're angry with me, or something happens between us . . ." She trailed off.

She didn't want to put the words out there, to acknowledge that it was even a possibility. She didn't think he was a psychopath. She thought his father had been one. Maybe not born. Maybe made, but his father had tried to shape him into the same thing. In her opinion, he hadn't succeeded.

Timur remained silent, so she decided to ask her question—the one she'd been turning over and over in her mind. "Did your father ever talk to you about his mother's death?"

Timur nodded slowly, his eyes never shifting away from her face. "Often."

"Did he try to save her?"

"No."

The coldness in his voice made her shiver again and remember that they were talking about his grandmother.

"He helped. He took great delight in telling us that he helped and that's what was expected of us when the time came. He wanted grown men like his brothers. He wanted Lazar's admiration. That was important to him. Apparently, Lazar delivered the killing blow to his mother."

She couldn't decide what disturbed her the most. It could have been his lack of emotion when he told her, but more likely it was simply that he'd been raised by such a cruel, despicable man.

"There's your answer, Timur. Your father was the psychopath, not you. You knew what they did was wrong and you tried to fight against them. You were young, and he had all the fighting experience and power."

Timur shook his head. "Don't think I didn't have training, Ashe. I had it constantly and I used it, just not quite as effectively as my father. I fought him. Gorya fought him. If it hadn't been for Fyodor, we'd both be dead. My father wanted us to stop, to admit that what he did was the right thing, but we wouldn't. Either of us. I hated that man for killing my mother. I hated him with every breath I drew and I still do even though he's dead now."

He held out his hand to her as he glanced down at his phone. "The house is secure. Let's go check in with Fyodor and Evangeline."

Before she could respond, he glanced at his phone again. "They're coming out. We'll meet them in the sitting room. He doesn't want Evangeline staring at the dead bodies. I'm sorry, *malen'kiy smerch*. I should have thought of that and gotten you out of here."

Ashe wasn't about to say it was all right. She couldn't stand looking at the mangled body of the one leopard Temnyy had killed, or the one with most of his head blown off that she'd killed. And then there was the naked man . . .

His fingers circled her wrist and he tugged until she followed him into the next room. He closed the door on the scent of blood. Ashe moved across the room. She liked the sitting room with its cozy fireplace and informal chairs. It looked less like an elegant showroom and more like an actual lived-in home.

"It's nice in here."

"It is."

The way he looked at her, his blue gaze wholly focused on her, was a bit disconcerting. He always saw too much, and right then she was feeling extremely vulnerable.

"Ashe, how did your female know there were other males in the house? Was she able to smell them?"

"No, I asked her that question. I was a little shocked that she knew, but then thought maybe the scent-blocker didn't work on females. She indicated otherwise, but then she didn't elaborate. Obviously, I have a connection with her, but I don't always know how to ask questions to make her understand what I need from her."

"Ask her again, Ashe. We need to know."

Ashe wandered around the room, mainly to put a little distance between her female and Temnyy. She could feel her female's attraction to the big cat and didn't want the leopard's hormones raging, not when Fyodor and Evangeline would be there any moment, presumably with bodyguards close.

Godiva, how did you know the others were here?

The silence stretched for so long Ashe was afraid she wouldn't answer. Eventually the little female gave the impression of stretching. *I sense them with my whiskers. My fur. They rub against furniture or walk on the floor and the scent isn't there, but that doesn't mean I cannot feel their passing. They aren't ghosts. They leave behind a trail.*

Elated, Ashe swung back to Timur. "She says they aren't ghosts and they leave behind a trail. If she can sense them, even with the scent-blocker, we should all be able to do so, especially the leopards."

She couldn't help the excitement in her voice. "We're relying on our normal senses because we're programmed that way, but from having a leopard, I know there are other senses we haven't yet tapped into. Their fur and whiskers act like radar for them, telling them something's close and what it is. Our hair does the same because we're shifters, right? So, if other leopards touch anything or even walk on the floors, they have to leave something of their passing. That's just the way it is."

He nodded slowly and went to the small table where a decanter of scotch sat with four glasses. He poured himself a small drink and sipped at the amber liquid. "She has something there. It's a way to track them when they think they're invisible. I'll give that some thought."

She liked the way he gave weight to Godiva's remark. It wasn't as if her female had given him a lot to go on. There was nothing all that specific, but Ashe knew she was telling her the strict truth as she saw it.

The door opened and Fyodor came through, followed by Evangeline. Ashe could see Evangeline was doing her best to get around her husband, but his hold on her was very secure and there was no way for his wife to break free. When he had assured himself that Timur and Ashe were alone in the room, Fyodor released Evangeline. She rushed to Ashe and hugged her tightly.

"I saw what happened, Ashe. We were watching on the monitors. I'm so sorry, that must have been terrible for you."

"I hate to say this, but it was easier shooting the man than the leopard," she admitted, grateful to get the truth off her chest. "Leopards are so beautiful, and although Godiva didn't want him to harm us, she thought him magnificent."

Timur nearly dropped his glass of scotch. "Magnificent? Temnyy is already royally pissed at her, I can't imagine what he'll think about that."

"He wouldn't think anything if you didn't have a big mouth," she pointed out.

"Why Godiva?" Fyodor asked.

Ashe tried not to squirm. She'd just called her cat "baby" for a long while, when she didn't know her and the leopard wouldn't respond. She tried to coax her to come out and visit, especially when she was lonely, but that hadn't happened. Then, the first blazing hot, urgent need for a man hit. It was wild and uncomfortable, and Ashe had stripped naked and tried to alleviate the terrible burn that refused to stop.

She shrugged, rather than tell on herself. *She* had been Lady Godiva, running around nude, because she couldn't stand material against her skin while trying to figure out how to put out a fire that was only partially hers. She felt Timur's eyes on her and tried not to look at him. When she did, those blue flames were back. He knew. He might not know exact details, but he knew. Godiva, the little hussy, had probably ratted her out and told Temnyy.

"You did good, Ashe," Fyodor said. "I didn't expect you to be such a good shot or have such quick reflexes. I thought that leopard had you."

Ashe shook her head. "I wasn't about to let him have my female. She might have enticed him there, but she didn't want him and she wasn't ready." She couldn't help the indignation in her voice.

Timur smiled at Ashe and then switched his attention to his brother. "They got that scent-blocker from someone." His gaze flicked to Evangeline. "And they knew the layout of the house, with the exception of the safe room. They'd never been here before, and yet they knew." He was careful. Fyodor was very protective when it came to Evangeline and wouldn't want any accusations made against her family, especially if she was trying to reconcile with them.

Fyodor didn't respond. That could be good or bad, but Timur continued. "I'm head of security and if I'm going to protect *both* of you, I need to know everything going on in this house. Fyodor, you know that. You can't tie my hands like you have."

Both women turned toward the men. Evangeline sank into one of the deep chairs. "It's my fault, not his, Timur."

Timur shook his head. "No, Evangeline, it isn't. Fyodor knows what it means to protect others. If he wants to stay alive and wants me to keep you alive as well, I have to know everything, down to the smallest detail. There can't be secrets."

Evangeline's eyes met Fyodor's. Fyodor nodded. "He's right, baby. I've tied his hands and so have you. It has to stop. Now, more than ever, we have to be careful. Once I received your texts, Timur, I realized we were under more threats than one."

Timur nodded. "That's very clear."

"Not to me," Ashe said. "I knew I was being followed when I came here . . ."

"Apostol Delov is a messenger. He was hired by Lazar to find your parents," Fyodor said. He looked at his brother. "I haven't had a chance to tell you yet, but Drake got back to me and said that a war is brewing between Ashe's grandfather and Lazar. Her grandfather is really upset that his son, and only heir, was murdered and that a hit team was sent after his granddaughter. Apparently, he had agreed to the killing of his daughter-in-law, who stole his son from him, but not her husband or daughter. Lazar apologized and blamed the team in the field, but the apology wasn't accepted."

"From now on, have Drake include me in all communication," Timur ordered, half expecting his brother to give him trouble.

"Yes, of course, it's already done. A meeting has been set up for three days from now. It was the soonest everyone could get here," Fyodor said. "It also gives Drake more time to tap into his sources to find out if more opium is being shipped out with perfume orders. We need to know if the factory is being used again in spite of the fact that it was shut down. We also need to know whether or not an alternate route has been set up."

"Do you think my uncles are involved?" Evangeline asked.

Timur saw his woman put her hand over Evangeline's to comfort her. "It's possible, even probable that one or both might be. Has either of them been to this house?" He had to ask, and he didn't look at Fyodor as he did. He knew, because his men communicated with him, that her father had been there.

Pain slid into Evangeline's expression. Not just pain. Sorrow. That got him in the gut, but Timur had to know everything. He was responsible for her, Fyodor and Ashe. As far as he was concerned, he was responsible for all of his men as well. Quite a few of them had abandoned the lairs and followed him to the United States. That made them his responsibility.

Evangeline's chin went up. She didn't break easily. She was a strong woman and she'd faced adversity head-on. Timur not only adored her, he was proud of her toughness.

"My father and Uncle Gilbert came with my brother, Ambroise. Uncle Gilbert and my father stayed in the poolroom while I visited with my brother," she said. "If someone betrayed me, it was Ambroise. We weren't raised together. I barely saw him when I was a child. I'd hoped he would become part of my family here."

"Did you show him the house?"

She nodded. "He asked for a tour and I didn't think anything of it. Lots of visitors ask for a tour."

His eyebrow shot up. "*Lots* of visitors? Who comes here, and why the fuck don't I know about it?"

Evangeline winced. Ashe glared at him, and Fyodor spun around and took a step toward him as if he might actually swing at him.

"The women. You know. Saria, Drake's wife, came one

day with him. They brought their son. Siena, Elijah's wife, came with the triplets. I had Jake's wife here one day when he was talking business with Fyodor. You were here at all times when they were. Emma, Jake's wife, brought all three of her children. Catarina came with Eli and their son. He was here the same day as Elijah to talk with Fyodor."

"Who else?"

"Jeff asked for a tour, but I told him not under any circumstances." She tapped the arm of the chair with nervous fingers.

"What the fuck was he doing here?" Fyodor demanded. "And when did he show up?"

"You and Timur were out, and he wanted to talk. He's actually very sweet, Fyodor. He didn't ask a single question about you. He wanted someone to bounce things off of, and we get along very well."

"Your husband doesn't get along with him and I don't want you alone with him in this house or anywhere else for that matter." Fyodor all but hissed the words. Cold. Like a snake. Timur knew that tone. It wasn't a good one. If Jeff didn't leave Evangeline alone, he was going to disappear one day.

"I was hardly alone with him, honey," Evangeline said. "I made certain Gorya stayed in the room with us every minute. He was across the room, but he's leopard, he could hear every word said."

"And why wouldn't my cousin report to me or Timur, the head of security, that a cop had come to visit you?" Fyodor asked, his voice even colder.

"He did, and so did I," Evangeline said. "We both referred to him as the detective. You asked if he was questioning about anything specific and I said no. So did Gorya. Gorya said he had no idea why he came and I did as well, because neither of us did."

"Don't give me that load of crap," Fyodor snapped. "If you'd said Jeff Meyers, I would have known exactly who he was and you know it."

Evangeline shrugged. "I'm not getting a good man killed because you're jealous."

Fyodor turned away from her, his eyes on Timur's face. Timur nodded without hesitation. He would be paying the cop a visit and, one way or another, the matter would be closed.

"Let's get back on track, Evangeline," Timur said smoothly. He didn't glance at Ashe because he had the feeling she saw the look that passed between his brother and him. "Who else came to visit recently that I might not know about?"

"Charisse Mercier is a friend of mine from when I was a teen. I was very alone, and Saria introduced us one day. After that, she would come to see me, and she brought books and food. She's one of the few friends I have. She was in San Antonio on business and she came with her brother, Armande. That was about three weeks ago. You were visiting Mitya, and Gorya was on Fyodor when he went to see someone." She waved her hand at him dismissively. "Vitaly was here and he watched very closely."

"Was it an arranged visit?" Timur dug deeper, not liking all the suspects. He could dismiss Saria and Drake, Eli and his wife, Elijah and his wife; they were all allies. He knew Jake Bannaconni was also an ally. That gave him Charisse and Armande Mercier, Jeff—but he was a good cop and it was absurd to consider him—and Ambroise Tregre, Evangeline's brother.

"No, as I said, she had business in San Antonio and she came to see me."

"With her brother."

"Yes, they often travel together. They're good people, Timur."

"Good people tend to drop friendships when they believe their friend is married to a gangster," Timur pointed out. "That goes with the territory."

"Not my friends. I only have four, aside from the women

I've recently met through Fyodor. Those four friends—Saria, Charisse, Bijou and Ashe—have stayed loyal to me. Bijou, by the way, is married to a cop. They came to visit as well, but you know that because you and Fyodor were both here."

That was true. He'd discounted them because Remy, a detective, was Drake's brother-in-law and a good man. They had ties to the swamp, but he couldn't see Remy or his wife, Bijou, a very famous singer, being involved with the sale and distribution of opium.

"Then your brother Ambroise came to visit."

Evangeline nodded. "It was the first time I'd seen him in two years. He said he wanted the chance to get to know me. He hated that he'd gone along with our father and pretended I was dead. He sounded very sincere and I couldn't detect any lies. Although, Timur, I wanted him to be telling the truth, so maybe I didn't listen as well as I should have."

"What does he do?"

"He works for Charisse's company right now, designing their labels. He's very artistic and has paintings hung in galleries. He said he likes his job. He did tell me that Christophe wanted to come but couldn't because he was busy that day. He asked me to invite them both for dinner one night so they could meet Fyodor and you and maybe Christophe could get a job with you."

Timur sighed. He hated crushing Evangeline's dream of her family becoming closer to her. He also had to protect her—even from herself. She might hate him after, but he would know she was safe. He risked a look at Ashe, hoping this exchange, where he was interrogating his sister-in-law, hadn't made her want to run even more. She sent him a look from under her heavy lashes, but he couldn't interpret it. She also wasn't a woman to keep quiet if she believed someone was out of line—even him—and she remained quiet.

"Does Ambroise have a good memory?"

Evangeline ducked her head, and he knew he wasn't going to like her answer. "He didn't need to. He sketched pictures to show Christophe," she said. "He showed a couple of quick sketches to me. He'd drawn them on a Post-it note I had by the coffee table and the drawing was extremely accurate. I love the house and was proud of it," she added in a little rush.

"Of course, you are," Ashe said. "I would be. No one is going to blame you for showing off your home, least of all Timur, right?" She looked up at him expectantly.

"I think that's natural, Evangeline," he forced himself to agree. Mostly he thought their women should be locked up somewhere safe where no one could ever get to them. Bars on all windows and doors seemed reasonable.

"Charisse has nothing whatsoever to do with opium and neither does Armande." Evangeline rubbed her temples. "My head is killing me. I know Charisse wouldn't do this. Ambroise, I hope wouldn't, but I don't know. Honestly, if he's anything like my uncle or father, he might. Charisse and Armande were heartbroken over what their mother had done, using their factory to distribute drugs, so they monitored it very closely. I just don't see how . . ." She trailed off, pressing a hand to her mouth as if she couldn't say another word.

Fyodor went to her immediately. "I think we're done for a while, Timur. Evangeline needs a break. She's been sick quite a bit lately. She can't seem to keep any food down."

"The cleaners are taking care of the house," Timur said. "Gorya is overseeing that right now. Kyanite and Rodion are both here. Vitaly is here. I've got men patrolling the grounds. You should be safe. I need to take Ashe somewhere private but still stay close. Her leopard could emerge at any time, and I don't want Temnyy to have to fight off half my men and possibly kill them in order to keep his mate."

"Take the guesthouse," Fyodor said instantly. "It's a distance from the main house, and you can instruct the men to keep their leopards away when patrolling that side of the property. For once, they can patrol as humans, not cats."

"They aren't going to like that," Timur said. He turned his brother's solution over and over in his mind. While doing so, his gaze fell on his sister-in-law. She looked abnormally pale and she'd definitely lost a few pounds. Concern washed through him. "Evangeline, have you seen the doc?" He looked at his brother for the answer, even when he put the question to her.

Fyodor shrugged. "I made her go last week."

"And?"

Fyodor and Evangeline exchanged a long look. Timur waited, his heart racing. They couldn't lose her. She centered them all. Even Mitya gravitated toward her and Mitya seemed to be a lost cause.

"I'm pregnant," Evangeline said after a long pause.

Elation swept through him and he found himself smiling like an idiot. "That's good, that's good, isn't it?" Somewhere along the line it occurred to him that neither his brother nor Evangeline seemed happy.

"I have some complications," she admitted. "That's why we weren't telling anyone."

"Should you be in bed?" Now Timur was back to looking at his brother. Fyodor might be wrapped around her finger, but her health and safety were everything to him and he wouldn't hesitate to use whatever means it took to make his woman stay in bed if the doctor ordered it.

Evangeline shook her head. "Not yet. Mostly, I'm just sick all the time. I've already lost fifteen pounds and I've been dehydrated several times." She shrugged. "Other women have the same problem, Timur, I'm not unique."

"What causes it? Or is it normal?" Timur asked.

Fyodor scowled at the thought that some illness dared to come to Evangeline. "It's normal to be nauseous, and have sickness in a pregnancy, but this is more than that. There are several causes. In this case, it's a multiple pregnancy.

That's why Siena was visiting. To talk to Evangeline about what it's going to be like."

Timur leaned down and pressed a kiss against Evangeline's cheek. "You need anything at all, you tell me."

She nodded. "Thanks, Timur. I'm sorry I've been difficult over security. I find myself irritable and annoyed over everything."

"Stop giving me days off," Ashe said. "I can handle the bakery for you."

Evangeline nodded and waved them off. "Go and be together. Once you get pregnant all you'll see is the inside of a toilet bowl."

11

ASHE woke toward morning, her skin burning hot. She'd gone to sleep naked, tangled with Timur. He'd been a gentle lover the first time, something she wasn't certain she could handle from him yet. When they had wild, uninhibited sex, she felt more in control of her emotions. Not her body—he was in complete control of that—but she could pretend to herself that she had time to make up her mind about him.

She knew herself very well. If Timur turned that ice-cold, compartmentalized demeanor loose on her, becoming violent or emotionally abusive, she knew she wouldn't tolerate it, not for one moment. If the attack was physical, not only would she fight back, but she was mean enough to wait until he was asleep and beat the crap out of him and then get out. She wasn't certain she was the best match for him.

Her skin hurt with just the sheet touching it, so sensitive she wanted to cry in alarm. Very carefully she tried to extract herself, afraid of waking Timur, wanting to know what she was facing first. She had so many questions and felt so much uncertainty. She genuinely liked Timur. She liked being with him. He had that edge she needed, and yet was sweet to her.

He loved Evangeline and the emotion was wholly genuine. That should have told him right there that he wasn't even close to being the psychopath he thought himself. He wasn't selfish. His every thought seemed to be for the protection of others.

Ashe suppressed a groan and covered her face with her hands in an effort to block out her thoughts. Was she trying to give herself reasons to stay with him? He needed her more than any other man ever would, that much she was certain of. She wanted to be needed. He focused completely on her, which was a good thing, except that she didn't want their relationship to be like her parents'—she wanted children, and her husband had to love them as fiercely and as protectively as she did.

"What is it, *malen'kiy smerch*?" Timur's voice was soft, tender even.

She felt that tone right through her heart, as if he'd pierced her with an arrow. He shifted positions, turning toward her, propping his head up with one hand so he could look down at her. His eyes glowed in the dark of the room, telling her his cat was close. Of course, Temnyy would rise, looking for his female.

She tried not to flinch at the thought. Timur's arm slid around her waist, locking her to him, but she felt the difference in his hold. He was more protective than sexual.

"You're burning up, Ashe."

"I know." Her hair felt too heavy for her head. Her skin felt as if it had shrunk and was far too small for her. Her mouth ached, as if her teeth were stretching the limits of her jaw. As hot as her body was, there was no comparison to what was happening between her legs or in her deepest core. There was no doubt in her mind that Godiva would be emerging soon.

"I'm afraid, Timur." She might as well admit it.

"You've shifted before, Ashe. It gets easier every time. Your body remembers, and your mind becomes more accepting. You know you, the human being, is still there. You're strong, you'll be in control of her. She needs to know she can count on you. When you let your leopard free, she has to be able to count on you to keep her from doing anything that will get her killed or harmed."

She had to try very hard not to rub her body with her palms. Her skin hurt. Burned. Felt as if she might die if she didn't touch herself—or worse—beg him to touch her. "If I let her out and your male claims her for his mate, it will be impossible to get out of this relationship. You know that, Timur. Don't you?" She hoped she was wrong, that she hadn't run out of time, but it felt that way.

Ashe had to move. She couldn't stop herself from rubbing along the sheet and over his body. The chemicals under her skin were driving her insane with need. She wanted to claw her way over top of Timur. Her hips slid along the sheets, legs sprawled apart, so her hand could creep down her belly to curl inside of her with the hope of putting out the fire—or at least stalling it.

Timur stroked his hand over the curve of her buttocks. "Baby." His voice was so gentle it turned her heart over. "He's already claimed her. You know that. The leopards are fine. You just have to let yourself catch up. Tell me what your worst fear is."

"That you'll change your mind and become abusive. Men do that. Some men," she qualified. "You're capable of violence, Timur. You are. There's no denying that."

"Not toward a woman." He bent his head and kissed her hip, his hair sliding over her burning skin, adding fuel to the fire spinning out of control inside her.

She lifted her lashes, so he was looking her directly in the eye. "Some women take it, Timur. They do for whatever their reasons may be. I'm not one of those."

"Did you think I wasn't aware of that, Ashe?" He stroked a caress from her hip to her thigh, leaving behind a blazing trail of fire. "I see you, the real you. You aren't hidden from me. It's my job to assess people's nature quickly, size them up and assess the threat. I'm damned good at my job, that's why Fyodor relies on me. It isn't because I'm his brother."

She knew Fyodor hadn't hired Timur because he was his brother. Just in the short time she'd been around them, she could see Fyodor relinquishing more and more of his power to his brother. He was doing so because Timur had earned his trust and respect.

There was a strange roaring in her ears making it hard to hear. Her hips moved of their own accord, restless and wantonly hungry for him. His fingers drove her to distraction, stroking her skin so there were trails of flames licking over her thigh and hip.

"Timur." His name came out breathless. Fearful. She had expected to handle this moment with grace because she knew what was coming. She knew what to expect. Her mother had talked to her about it. Hearing it, thinking about it and feeling it were very different things.

He rolled her under him, his hips wedging between her thighs, spreading her legs wide and leaving her feeling very vulnerable. He caught both her hands in his and brought her arms up over her head, stretching her under him.

"I know you're scared, Ashe. Keep looking into my eyes. I'll get you through this, I promise. No one is ever going to love you, or need you, the way I do." He transferred both of her wrists into one hand and then slid his fingers along the inside of her thigh.

Ashe thought she might die from wanting him. At the same time, she was terrified of the consequences of her actions. She couldn't help but move into him, her body no longer under her own control. Something much larger had taken over. A force as big as nature commanded her and she was helpless under its onslaught.

His fingers were right there. So close. Stroking flames over her thighs. That wasn't where the true fire was. Didn't he know that? On the other hand, she knew she would never leave him if they did this. If their leopards were allowed to mate, which would happen as soon as they were finished, she couldn't take Godiva from Temnyy. That would be . . . cruel.

"Look at me, Ashe."

Even his whispers held command. She hadn't realized she'd lowered her lashes to prevent herself from falling into him, which she did every time she looked him in the eye. Very slowly, with great reluctance, she lifted her lashes. She knew what she would find. Those eyes of his. Ever changing. Eyes that no longer reminded her of glaciers, but of fires burning so hot the flames had gone blue.

She fell, just as she knew she would. She was trapped there, right in the center of those blue flames. There was no getting out. And did she even want to? Where else could she find such perfection? Danger and yet sweetness? She needed both. Usually they didn't go hand in hand. Usually danger was bad, very bad.

"Please," she whispered back, the fever burning so strong she thought she might die.

"I'm here."

She felt him pressing against her entrance. That broad, velvet head, so wide she felt she couldn't possibly take him inside, yet every cell in her body demanded she do just that. She needed him. At the touch of his cock against her, the need rose until she was practically sobbing.

"Timur, it feels as if I'm going insane." She made her confession in a rush.

"I've got you, baby. Just keep looking at me."

He was pushing into her, a slow, steady invasion that

forced her tight muscles to yield. Just the touch of him, that thick shaft and broad head, sent her careening over the edge, straight into madness. Her nails dug into his shoulders. Her heart pounded so loudly she could hear the way her blood drummed along with her heartbeat.

"It burns."

"I know. I know, sweetheart, but it's a good burn. You like the way this burns."

Of course, she did. She knew that, yet why was she so worried? Why couldn't she just enjoy what was happening between them? He moved deeper in her and flames lashed over her skin and seemed to swallow her whole. She screamed as sensations poured over her.

He gripped her hips in his large hands and lifted her, driving down savagely. It felt . . . wonderful. "More," she demanded, uncaring what he might think.

He moved in her, fast and hard, plunging deep, over and over until the breath was coming out of her in ragged pants and she was streaking her nails down his shoulders and back in an effort to find something to anchor herself to when she was flying too high.

She never wanted him to stop, and he seemed more than willing to oblige her. He kept her on the edge for so long she was afraid she might really lose her mind, but then when he tipped her over, it was worse, her body rippling with contractions, with waves of such intense pleasure, it was both ecstasy and hell. Opposites, yet so close together. She had both sensations at once and it didn't matter. She needed more.

Then he was pouring himself into her. She felt the lash of that heat, the swelling of his shaft as it pushed against her tender muscles, demanding she surrender completely. *Completely.* Staring into those blue flames, she did, letting herself fall, flinging herself right over the edge of the cliff, praying he'd catch her before she hit the earth below.

The fall was unlike anything she'd faced in the past. She

floated, her body on fire, feeling so good she couldn't do anything but experience it. Still, the fire refused to be put out, and she found herself in tears.

"It won't stop," she whispered, burying her face in his neck.

"We're just starting," he assured. "I've heard this can be brutal on women. I'm right here, Ashe. I'm not going anywhere." He pulled out of her, and she cried out as his heavy erection dragged over her sensitive clit. It hurt. It felt good. She needed more. He rolled off her, and with one arm around her waist, took her to the edge of the bed and positioned her easily, bending her over, so that her feet, on the floor, were spread apart, and her head was on the mattress.

"Hurry," she whispered again, jamming her fist into her mouth.

The need was building and building, a wild, feral urgency that left her breathless and terrified. It had to go away. It had to be assuaged. There was only Timur in her world in that moment. Timur was her only hope.

She felt the broad head of his erection push into her and she pushed back, desperation setting in. His hands smoothed over her buttocks and down her thighs, creating the sensation of flames licking over her skin. Deep inside, she responded to that feeling, that brutal need. It was as if she was made for anything Timur could do to her.

Then he was riding her hard and she couldn't think. His hands were everywhere, heightening the sensations pouring over and into her. Her breath came in those raggedly insane pants that meant she couldn't find her voice, but it didn't matter. Everything he did, everywhere he touched or rubbed, or smacked, it was everything she needed.

Every hard jolt set her nipples rubbing along the sheet, the friction feeling like a fire in her breasts. Her nipples seemed to have a connection, a line straight to her clit. He was manipulating that little bud as well, flicking with his fingers, patting it hard, tugging and rolling so that crazy waves of heat rushed back and forth between her breasts and her sex.

Then she was sobbing as her body took over, the hardest orgasm she'd ever had rolling through her like thunder. Like a firestorm. "The tornado" he called her. It was huge and so strong it shook her and him as well. She heard his husky cry as if in the distance.

"You're so hot, Ashe, and you're milking me dry. Taking everything." He collapsed over her even as her muscles continued to grip at him, dragging everything he had out of him.

He held her for a few minutes while they both fought to catch their breath. They didn't have that kind of time. Ashe felt her female pushing hard for the surface, desperate, now that she was on such fire too. Her own body immediately felt the urgency again, the fire so hot and strong she buried her face in the sheets and wept. She couldn't do this. It was flying too high. Singeing as the fire only got hotter. It was brutal. Terrible. Wonderful. Truly frightening.

"Timur . . ." Her voice held despair.

"I'm here, baby. I'm not going anywhere. She needs out. You have to let her out."

"I hurt already. I don't see how."

"Slide to the floor and call to her. She's close because Temnyy is right on the surface. Look at my arms, Ashe." He held them out on either side of her.

She'd been concentrating on the heavy erection inside of her. She made herself concentrate on lifting her head enough to look at his arms. They were contorting. Something clearly moved beneath the surface, demanding to get out.

"I'm pulling out of you now, and it's going to sting a little." He was careful, sliding his cock out of her.

She felt the sharp pain, almost as if the tip of a tack had dragged across the walls of her sheath and then over her clit. She heard herself cry out and then she was empty, and he was rolling away from her, going to the floor beside the bed.

She spun off the bed, onto the floor, her muscles contorting. Where before, it hurt and she'd been terrified, now every sensation was sexual. She was practically writhing on the floor, rubbing her body along the bed and crawling toward Timur on her hands and knees. She felt that need inside her building and building until it was so raw and urgent she was on him, her mouth trailing up his thigh, tongue licking at him, stroking demands of him all the way to his cock.

She saw her arms and legs change, felt thick fur slide over her skin, and when she turned her attention back to Timur, he was all leopard. For a moment, her heart nearly stopped. Those eyes were on her, a killer blue, lost in a sea of black rosettes, but staring at her with the focused, unblinking gaze of a pure predator.

He was beautiful and all hers. Godiva brushed along his side, rubbing her fur along his. He answered by rubbing his muzzle all over hers and then his chin down her body. Timur had left the window open and Temnyy turned and padded toward it, looking back at Godiva.

The thought of freedom was too hard to resist. Godiva was interested in enticing her mate, while Ashe was mostly interested in running. Fast. Hard. Long. Wearing herself out. She was exhausted and yet she wasn't. She needed more, and she wanted Godiva to have her turn with Temnyy. Maybe, just maybe, that would help.

Godiva landed on the ground outside and lifted her head to scent the world around her. Ahead and just a little to the right were the vineyards. Acres of grapes. To the left was the grove of trees Antonio Arnotto's family had planted. Antonio had added to that thick paradise for leopards. Branches formed unique highways for the leopards to travel from tree to tree without ever touching the ground.

Temnyy didn't take to those tempting branches. He

chose to run along the ground. Godiva followed him into the coolness under the canopies of the trees. Once in the darker and more protected area, Temnyy paused to allow her to take the lead, which she did without hesitation. She had never been there before and took her time exploring. She also claimed every inch of the territory she could find.

Another female had been there before her. She didn't like that and scent-marked over her offending smell. Godiva made certain that Temnyy knew another male had also claimed this territory. He reacted as expected, roaring his rage and promising death to any challenger. Godiva had to be satisfied knowing he would fight for the privilege of having her as his mate.

She ran a few steps toward the small stream that rushed on a winding course through the grove and then she crouched, inviting Temnyy close. The moment he came near, she was up, slapping at leaves and sending them at him in a whirling eddy of debris. She ran toward the stream, ignoring the large fenced-in tea garden where her rival female's scent was strongest.

The night was dazzling seen through a leopard's eyes and smelled through the cat's olfactory senses. The moon appeared to be much brighter, the stars like diamonds shining overhead. Moonbeams danced across fallen leaves and spotlighted the cicadas holding their nightly concert.

In spite of the beauty surrounding her, Godiva's attention was mainly on Temnyy as he paced alongside or just behind her. He lifted his head continually and sent out sawing challenges to any other male in the vicinity. He rubbed his scent over Godiva's, making certain that any cat coming across their trail would know she belonged to him.

Godiva pranced and preened and occasionally crouched seductively in front of Temnyy. He was alert but very cautious when he came close. Each time he approached, she let him get closer before she snarled and swiped her paw.

Deep in the leopard's body, Ashe felt the gathering heat

and knew her female was close. She had to get her to see that she needed to accept her mate. In doing so, she would be sealing her own fate. Once the two leopards had mated, there would be no tearing them apart. Her mother had made her very aware of that. Her mother's leopard was her father's leopard's true mate. They had found each other in another life cycle and recognized each other.

Staring at Temnyy's rugged, handsome fighting form, Ashe recognized that sometime, a long time ago, she had seen him at least once before. He had a beautiful coat, thick and light, with amazing dark rosettes. She loved the way he looked and remembered the feel of his fur beneath her fingers. From where, she couldn't remember, but she knew she was familiar with his coat.

Why do you lead him on this way when you know you're ready?

You are not. Her female didn't sound her usual complacent self. She was suffering, needing her mate, just as Ashe had needed Timur.

Just those three words told Ashe the bond between shifter and cat was stronger than anything else—even the primal drive to mate. Her leopard suffered because she feared Ashe wasn't in sync with her.

I am. I will handle my relationship with Timur. I want him just the way you want Temnyy. I have reservations, but that doesn't mean we can't overcome them. Have fun with your mate, Godiva. I want you to.

Ashe found she did want her female to feel as satisfied and happy as she had with Timur. He'd taken care of her. That first time with him, staring into her eyes, had been intense, but even the second time when her back was to him and his hands were everywhere as he pounded into her, she'd felt his caring. He'd made certain to take care of her.

She let go of her female as the cat crouched once more. This time Temnyy was on Godiva, teeth biting down on her shoulder to hold her in place, his body blanketing hers as he took her. Ashe gave them privacy, keeping her distance through the long night. The cats went at it every fifteen minutes or so, and then they would stretch out beside each other panting before repeating their mating. The sex was rough and yet very affectionate.

Ashe found Temnyy guiding Godiva back toward the guesthouse when the first light began streaking through the darkness. Godiva stumbled a few times and lay down. Temnyy allowed her to rest and then nudged her to get her moving. By the time they made it to the porch, Godiva didn't want to get up again.

Timur shifted back to his human body and opened the door. "Shift, Ashe."

She was too tired and probably wouldn't have obeyed him, but he used that voice on her, the one that everyone obeyed. She used her last ounce of strength and shifted back to her human form, collapsing on the porch.

Timur leaned down and lifted her into his arms, cradling her against his chest. "Bath for you, baby, and then you can sleep."

She circled his neck with one arm, uncaring what he decreed. She was going to sleep, and there wasn't much he could do about it. She dozed on his lap as he sat on the edge of the very large tub. The sound of running water was soothing and reminded her and Godiva of the babbling of the stream.

"Okay, Ashe, we're good. I'm putting you in the water."

She answered by tightening her grip on him. She was aware of everything around her as if from a distance, she was that tired. Her body was sore, every single muscle, but the rawness between her legs felt delicious and sensual, not that she wanted to move.

He laughed softly against her ear, his breath warm. "Fine, I'll get in with you. I just hope the bath salts Evangeline stocks this house with aren't perfumed."

He already knew the salts were scented. The fragrance

was lavender. He lowered them both into the very hot water. She hissed a little as the water climbed up her body, touching sore places and encompassing her until it was over her breasts. He kept her on his lap, his arm around her, a bar under her breasts.

She found herself smiling. "I like being alone with you," she admitted. "You're very different."

He nuzzled the top of her head. "I can afford to be different when we're alone."

She understood that. She knew she was just as careful with others as he was. She could be open with him about her parents, where she wouldn't be with someone else. "How often is that going to happen?"

"Our leopards mating?"

She shook her head. "Us. That was wild. Crazy. Crazy wild. I don't know if I'm ever going to walk straight again."

She heard the rumble of laughter in his chest. "It's going to be that way often, Ashe. Especially over the next five to seven days."

She turned her head to look up at him, half hoping he was joking and the other part of her hoping he wasn't. "Really?"

He nodded. "She'll be in heat for the next few days, and that affects us. Both of us. My male was insane with need. I could barely hold him in check."

Ashe rubbed her chin on his arm. "I have to admit that I liked it, although I was very worried a couple of times before we could be alone together. The hunger was growing to the point that I didn't think I could control myself."

"You don't need to be in control," he pointed out. "We're leopards. You can be as wild as you want, Ashe. I'll look after you."

She laughed softly and kept her eyes closed, loving the feeling of drifting while the hot water lapped at her skin. The sensation was mildly erotic and yet soothing at the same time.

"You wouldn't say that if you knew I was thinking of yanking down your trousers and sucking you dry right in the middle of one of the annoying attacks on your family."

His cock stirred. Just hearing her talk that way made him hard. The visual was even hotter. He pressed his mouth to the side of her neck. His tongue caught the tiny drops of sensual sweat before he did a little sucking of his own, leaving his mark there. He knew his prints were all over her body.

"I'd still say it. You want to blow me anywhere, anytime, have at it, woman."

She turned her head up slightly to look up at him. He really did have the most beautiful eyes she'd ever seen in a man. "I'm going to hold you to that, crazy man."

"You do that. I carry a gun. Anyone in your way, distracting you from your goal, just point them out, *malen'kiy smerch*. I will gladly shoot them."

"Over a blow job?" She couldn't help but laugh.

He gave her a mock frown. "Is there a better reason?"

"I guess not. If we do this, Timur, really do this, where would we live?"

The smile faded from his face, leaving his features bleak and cold. "I will always guard my brother and Evangeline."

"I'm well aware of that. I meant, where would our home be? As in house?"

"Would you want to continue working at the bakery with Evangeline?"

She closed her eyes again and rubbed the back of her head along his chest. "If we could pick up the shop space next door, we could actually expand the drinks part of the shop. If I was able to purchase the machines and other equipment needed, maybe Evangeline would go in halves with me. If not, then I'd want to figure out a place, not in competition with hers, where I could have my own little shop. But I don't bake, so I'd have to get all my baked goods from her."

"I would make certain Evangeline sees this is good for you both to own the bakery together. She has never liked doing the drinks and it would free her to do more baked goods. For me, this is a winning situation. I'd have you both where I can see you, and Fyodor won't have to move offices yet again. I've introduced quite a few new security measures at the bakery, especially these last couple of days."

"Why these last couple of days?"

"Evangeline hired you without talking to me. That can't happen, Ashe."

"I know, Timur. I'm sorry. That's my fault."

"No, you don't get to take that one on. Evangeline knows the score. Fyodor doesn't tell her everything, but she knows enough that she should follow all the security measures."

"More importantly, an enemy slipped past all my guards and managed to get into the kitchen. That's not acceptable."

He kissed the spot between her neck and shoulder. She loved the sensation sizzling over her pulse and streaking under her skin straight to her nipples and then ricocheting to her clit. The feeling wasn't so overwhelming and intense that she had to put out the fire, it was a slower burn that intensified as it spread.

"Are you going to tell me everything?"

She felt him stiffen beneath her, but his arms never relented. He held her to him. He sighed and rubbed his chin over the top of her head again.

"That depends on you, Ashe. I'm not chancing losing you. You want to know something, be very, very certain you really do, because I'm not going to lie to you. If I have to kill someone and you ask, I'm going to tell you I did it and why. You don't have to agree with my decision, but you have to live with it. I get information for Fyodor and the others. I'm that man. It isn't always done politely. I don't like it and you don't have to like it either, but you still have to live with it. That means, baby, don't ask me if you don't want to hear that shit. And when I tell you I won't go into details, you back off, do you understand me? You back the hell off and never ask me again."

She shivered a little and wrapped her arms around her own waist. Just the sound of his voice indicated danger. "If I feel I have to know something, Timur, I'm going to ask. That's the way I am. I can't be anyone different any more than you can."

His teeth bit down on her shoulder. Held for a moment and then slowly put pressure until she felt that bite go through her like a lightning strike. "You don't need to know *how* I do something ever, Ashe, just that I do it. Can we at least agree on that?"

Ashe thought about it, all the while rubbing her chin back and forth on his arm.

"I've told you what I do. I'm an enforcer. When we need information, I don't just kill an enemy outright. I do whatever it takes to make them talk—and they always talk. I don't kill indiscriminately, nor do I like the things I'm forced to do at times."

She knew that was all he was going to tell her, and it wasn't anything she didn't already suspect. He'd all but said that to her when he talked about the men who had murdered her parents. He'd been taught to take apart human beings from a very young age.

"I shouldn't be able to live with that, Timur. What does that say about me?"

"That you are leopard and you have already seen the worst our people can do. Shifters can't live under the same laws as humans, Ashe, it would never work. Our cats our moody and vicious and if one goes wrong, we have no choice but to put it down. Humans have problems understanding that because they are doing their best to evolve to a higher plane."

Ashe didn't point out that she thought it wasn't working. She pressed her lips to his arm, up high, near his shoulder. "I can live with it, but you tell me the truth when I ask you anything. You have to give me your word."

"I will, baby, but not details," he reiterated.

Another shiver went through her. What was she getting herself into? "I don't want to be any part of running drugs. Or human trafficking. I don't, Timur. That's important to me."

"None of our people are involved in either of those things. We do our best to shut that shit down, Ashe, but we can't always. It's a lucrative business, and we would tip our hand if we concentrated too much in one place. The cops are always after us, always looking at us and will do whatever it takes to bust us."

"That's their job," she pointed out.

"I know." He was silent for a moment and then he pulled the plug. "I'm getting you in bed. Don't want you falling asleep on me before we have the rest of this conversation."

He lifted her out of the tub and put her feet on the thick mat. She took the towel and dried her body. No way would she fall asleep before Timur told her the rest. She knew they were in very dangerous territory now. The more she knew, the more she realized there was no chance of going back. If she was aware of any detail of Fyodor's work, she was a threat. It was that simple. Timur removed threats. She was either with them or against them.

She turned her head to look at him standing beside her, wiping down his body with efficient movement. He had the roped muscles of the leopard. He was taller than a lot of shifters, but it was those blue eyes that really set him apart. Few leopards had them.

Ashe made her way to the bed and flung herself facedown on the sheets. The fabric was cool on the heat of her skin and felt wonderful against her naked body and her nipples that had been on fire since Godiva had gone into her heat. The mattress dipped under Timur's weight. He stretched out on his side and propped his head up with one hand while the other went to her bottom, stroking caresses over the curve of her buttocks.

"You can't get rid of all crime, Ashe, it just doesn't work that way. You cut off one head and another, twice as powerful, takes its place. I finally had to come to that conclusion. I tried dumping businesses my uncle and grandfather built up. Very big alliances, pipelines around the world. I thought I could get away from all of it, but I couldn't. Drake Donovan offered me a way, not out of the business, but to keep the worst of the bosses from succeeding at the worst of the crimes."

She turned her head toward him, her gaze steady on his face, needing to see his expression, to read what he was saying along with hearing it. "How did he do that, Timur?"

"We have slowly been eliminating the worst of the bosses and replacing them with our own people. We keep the pipelines open and have alliances with those not in our organization. Only a few men are with us now, but we hope to recruit more. We've all gotten to that place where we know there will always be crime, but we can make certain it stays in the underbelly and doesn't spread out to regular citizens."

"But all of you still run drugs and guns? Human trafficking?"

He shook his head. "We have no choice but to work with other crime bosses who do those things. We don't move human beings ever, but we do find the lines to cut them off and that often means working with those who do. We go after the heads of those lairs or territories participating. If we're not involved, we don't get the information. We make certain we're hit as well, so no one can point a finger at us. We're good at manufacturing evidence and pointing the finger at the worst of them. Jake Bannaconni goes after the companies they use to launder dirty money. He takes them apart systematically. That puts him right in the middle of the firing squad."

His fingers became more insistent, spreading warmth through her body. He leaned down and nipped her left cheek. The sting sent an arrow of desire piercing her sheath so that she felt the empty clench. She was sore after their wild sex, and yet she wanted him all over again just with that little bite.

She rubbed her chest against the sheets, letting fire spread through her nipples to her breasts and then down her belly to her groin. His fingers slid over the curve of her cheek and he nudged her legs wider apart.

"That's a little scary, Timur. The cops will think you're dirty . . ."

"We are dirty." He nuzzled between her legs. She spread them wider still and lifted when he pushed a pillow under her belly.

"But if you're found out, the other crime bosses will go after you. You can't possibly think you can control all the crime in the world." Her breath came in pants as his mouth slid over her. She might not be able to take his cock, but this was paradise. She pushed back against his mouth, needing more. He obliged, and she closed her eyes as his tongue and teeth started ravishing her.

It was a long time and two orgasms later before he spoke again. He wiped his face on her thighs and then turned her over, an easy maneuver when she was boneless. He pulled the pillow out from under her, straddled her and moved up her body until his legs were on either side of her chest.

"We *are* going to try to control it all, baby, we just need the right recruits." He scooted closer, until his knees were on either side of her head. One hand circled his cock and he smiled down at her as he slowly stroked it. "All that talk of a blow job has me wanting to see just how much of me you can take."

She wet her lips in anticipation.

He pressed the large velvety head to her lips until she opened for him.

Then her lips were stretched around him, and he was moving in and out of her mouth. Slowly at first. One hand controlled his cock while the other slid around her throat. She felt him going deeper with each stroke. His eyes burned through hers, welding them together. She relaxed for him, wanting to give him the kind of pleasure he gave her.

Twice, when she thought she might not be able to breathe, and she reached for the base of his cock, he shook his head and caught her hands. "Over your head, baby. I'm not going to let anything happen to you. Trust me to take care of you."

It was impossible to do more than stroke his shaft with her tongue as he slid into her mouth. She kept her hands where he said, and watched his face, his eyes. He went deeper still, and she felt him swell, cutting off her air. She stared into his eyes, trusting him just as he'd asked. Then he was stroking her throat gently as he came in great rocketing jets. It was hot and salty and sexy as hell. She loved it.

When he was finished, he stayed still, waiting. Almost instinctively, like the leopard in her demanded, she licked him clean, claiming every drop that was the essence of her man.

12

TIMUR woke the moment Ashe moved. He'd had her a dozen times and yet the moment he opened his eyes, even before, when he simply became aware, his body reacted. He knew they had to slow down, but he'd never been so hungry for a woman in his life. He watched as she padded out of the room on bare feet. She was naked, and his marks were all over her skin. He knew he was a dick, but he couldn't help but like seeing them there.

He stretched when he heard the shower go on. His fist circled his cock, remembering the way he'd sat on her chest. Just thinking about the feel of her fighting for air, lips stretched around his girth, while he'd pushed impossibly deeper in her mouth got him hard. All the while, her eyes had stayed locked with his. Tears had swum, her throat had convulsed, and it had sent jagged lightning pulsing through his cock. It had been the sexiest thing ever, and he knew he'd never forget that moment when he'd erupted down her throat and pleasure had all but consumed him.

Lazily he replayed the images over and over in his head. She hadn't stopped him when he'd gotten a little out of control, his hips pushing deeper. He knew he should handle her with more care and each time he thought about touching her, it was always with reverence. Then he actually touched her and it was like he went mad. Completely, utterly mad.

His fist tightened, and he began to move his hand faster and faster. He felt his balls grow tight, his cock jerked and pulsed. He closed his eyes and imagined her mouth around him. He loved the way she sucked him. The way her tongue danced up and down his shaft, and she moaned, the vibrations driving him wild. His seed erupted, spurting like a geyser into the air and falling like white rain over his hand and down his cock.

He knew the moment she entered the bedroom. She stood in the doorway looking beautiful, her hair wet. Little droplets clung to her body and ran between her breasts. Two dripped from her nipples and more ran straight down her belly to the vee at the junction of her legs.

"Come here, baby." His voice was a little hoarse. Very husky. Sensual from the way he had given himself pleasure.

"I'm all clean and feel refreshed. She's subsided, and I don't want to wake her."

"I didn't ask for a rundown of what was going on with you, now did I? In fact, Ashe, I took care of myself, which clearly isn't my favorite thing, to give you a break." He didn't move his fingers from around his cock.

"And you're grumpy about it too," she pointed out.

"Get the fuck over here."

"Because you ask so nicely."

He opened his mouth to add to his sins when she took her first step toward him. When she did, her breasts swayed temptingly.

"Why are you so grumpy, Timur?" She came across the

room to stand at the foot of the bed, looking down at him. "I thought you'd wake up all sweet and loving."

"I woke up as hard as a fucking rock and you weren't here with me," he groused.

She laughed, and the sound was tantalizing. He didn't understand how musical notes could stroke a man's skin and dance along his thighs. He didn't understand how the notes could be an arrow that pierced his heart. She owned him. He'd thought to own her, but there was never a question that it was the other way around.

He couldn't tell her that, so he acted like a dick. A fucking asshole. That was sure to earn him points. "I'm sticky as hell, baby. I need you to clean me up."

He expected her to tell him to go to hell. To order him into the shower. To, maybe, if he was really lucky, get a warm washcloth. Instead, she put one knee on the bed, reached with her hand and began a slow, sensuous crawl to him. He'd never seen anything sexier than the way her breasts swayed with every movement of her arms and legs. Her nipples looked hard and drops of water glistened on her skin. She looked like the leopard she was.

"Keep your hands to yourself," she warned. "I'm as sore as hell, and if you wake her and I go into heat again, I might be tempted to rake your face off with my claws."

Why did he find even her threats sexy? He put his free hand behind his head and kept the fingers of his other hand wrapped around his suddenly thick cock. Heart pounding, he watched her ease down on the bed. Her hair trailed over his thighs. He nearly jumped but held himself very still.

Her tongue touched the back of his hand. A touch only. It was velvet soft and made his heart pound through his cock. He could feel that beat in the fingers of his hand. His breath left his lungs in a wild rush. She was like an angel sent from heaven to make him remember there were good things in the world. He was suddenly glad he was leopard and so was his woman. Oral fixations were normal for them, and he truly wouldn't mind if his woman began an oral fixation with his body.

Her tongue lapped gently at the back of his hand, slowly removing the sticky essence, the volcano that his body produced, over and over, for her. She licked the back of his hand clean and then took his cock from him and gently laid it across his thigh, so she could pull his index finger into her mouth. She sucked it as if it was his cock, her tongue sliding up and down and curling around it.

He forgot how to breathe. It was a simple enough function, one every person in the world knew how to do, but he couldn't remember how to take a breath. How to get the air into his lungs after it had all rushed out.

Her mouth pulled his middle finger deep, her tongue flicking and licking, dancing up and down, and then she was sucking hard again. His cock felt so heavy he wanted to reach for it all over again, but he held himself still, watching her face. There was beauty there. So much of it.

She looked as if her entire concentration was on what she was doing, just as she had in the early morning hours when she'd taken his cock into her mouth. She'd focused on it completely, looking as if she was worshiping it with her mouth and tongue. Now, it was his hand.

Ashe didn't leave one speck behind. Not one. He knew because he checked the moment she released his hand and reached for his shaft. She cradled it lovingly in her hands. She was just as thorough there, her tongue lapping at him gently, until not only his cock, but his balls were thoroughly clean, and he thought he might burst with his need of her.

His heart actually ached. His eyes even burned. He felt her love. She might not know she felt love for him, but it was there in the way she touched him. In every velvet stroke of her tongue. No one, nothing, had prepared him for the overwhelming emotions that rose in him for her. He knew he didn't deserve her, he would never deserve her, and he didn't understand how he'd gotten so lucky. He also knew if, after having her, even for such a short while, he lost her, he wouldn't survive it. None of his emotions had anything to do with his leopard.

"I'm sorry I left you unattended, Timur. I'm really quite sore this morning and I was afraid if we . . ." She trailed off and looked up at him over the broad head of his cock.

She looked miserable and that stopped the wild beating of his heart. He cupped the side of her face, his thumb sliding over her cheek and lower lip. "I want to wake up to your mouth on me, baby, but never at the expense of your body. If you hurt, we abstain. It's that simple. Don't apologize to me, not after what you just did for me."

She leaned over him again and kissed the pearl drops leaking from the wide head before rolling over and stretching. Her body was a miracle of softness to him. He could see and feel the firm muscles beneath the surface, but that surface was amazing. "Still, I should have told you, honey. I didn't, I just tried sneaking away."

He splayed his fingers in the middle of her belly, taking in as much territory as possible. "You're never going to get away with sneaking, no matter what, Ashe, so you may as well just start off by communicating with me."

She turned her head to look at him. Her lashes curled at the ends and they were thick and long, so feathery he wanted to touch them. Instead, he leaned over her and brushed a kiss over each eye just to watch them flutter.

"You do know you're bossy, right?"

He laughed as he subsided back on the bed. He was bossy, and he'd probably get a lot worse the more time they spent together. He was already thinking of her safety and how best to keep her out of the public eye where his enemies might discover they could hurt him through her. Yeah, he was going to get worse.

"I do know," he admitted, a little too much complacency in his voice.

She narrowed her eyes at him. "Don't say it like you're

all proud of that fact. I'm not a woman who takes to bossy men."

"You take to me," he pointed out. "You like it."

She shrugged. "Maybe a little. But that doesn't mean you're getting away with anything. I'll still make up my own mind about what I want to do."

"You do that, baby. Make up your own mind about what you want to do. That doesn't mean you're going to be doing it."

She rolled her eyes and turned over onto her stomach again, her eyes meeting his. Now there was laughter there. "I'm not listening to you."

He smacked her ass. Not hard. Just a little teasing, playful smack that left an intriguing red handprint on her left cheek. He liked it. He bent his head again and pressed a kiss into the middle of the palm print.

"Ouch." She glared at him. "I'd repay you in kind, but I'm too hungry, Timur. You need to feed me to keep my strength up. Evangeline gave me a couple of days off, so I wouldn't have all the security guards and their leopards going crazy."

He liked that there was laughter back in her voice. "That's a good thing, because I wouldn't like it if I had to cut out their hearts."

"You're so bloodthirsty."

He laughed and sat all the way up, putting his feet on the floor. He had a few sore muscles himself. "Pancakes?"

Her eyes lit up. "Absolutely." She was up and off the bed. "I'll go brush my teeth and join you in the kitchen. I can do prep work." She was already heading toward the bathroom again. She glanced at him over her shoulder. "I told Evangeline that when I went back to work, I could handle the shop for a few days on my own to give her some time off."

His first thought was a resounding no. He kept his mouth shut. Evangeline looked as if she needed a few days off, and the reason she'd hired Ashe in the first place was because she needed her. Ashe had the experience, and he'd seen her in action. She was fast. He wouldn't make up his mind until he'd taken the time to interrogate their prisoner, and he wouldn't do that for a day or two. He wanted the hit man to have time to stress over his situation. To really think about what it meant to be taken to a place no one knew about. A place that was soundproof and far below the house where he'd come to kill the occupants.

The man had been stripped, so there was no chance of his having a pill to kill himself while he waited for Timur to decide the time was right to ask a few questions. Timur had found the more time given, the easier the interrogation. Imagination was a huge tool in his favor, and right now, he couldn't leave Ashe. Her female was in heat and that meant his woman needed him as much as her female leopard needed his male.

He padded on bare feet to the guest bathroom and quickly showered. He found her in the kitchen making coffee. His woman made really good coffee. She looked good as well, dressed in a long flowy dress. It was a midnight blue. She turned away from the coffeepot and sent him a smile that raised his temperature by several degrees. Clearly, she wasn't wearing a bra, and her breasts pushed at the tight confines of the dress's bodice.

"I thought I'd make you some coffee to get you going, Timur. They have everything in this guesthouse. Even an espresso machine, and it's a good one. Guests aren't going to want to leave."

"Would you rather live here, or in the house you're staying in?"

He wanted Evangeline's house. He'd wanted it since the first moment he'd been in it. He'd broken in late at night when she was asleep. That was before he'd met her. Before he'd ever been to the bakery. He knew his brother was completely enamored with Evangeline and as his brother's head of security, he'd investigated her.

Evangeline's house was perfect. There were the wide-open spaces he needed. He liked that he could be working in the kitchen and yet see all the way through to the living room. He didn't need big, the way Fyodor did. He liked that the house was more intimate. He liked the location, the neighborhood with the huge park and rolling hills stretching out behind it. He could run Temnyy nightly and not put anyone in jeopardy.

If Ashe preferred this guesthouse, he would accept that. He would be happy anywhere she was, and the estate had massive amounts of property to run his leopard. More, he'd be close to Fyodor at all times and that would mean less time spent away from his woman.

Ashe perched on a barstool and watched him get the ingredients he needed to make her breakfast. He enjoyed spending time with her. He really liked the way she watched his every movement, as if he intrigued her the same way she did him.

"Evangeline's house is awesome," she said. "The minute I walked in, I knew it was perfect. I understood why she bought it. She told me it took all her spare money, money she really needed for her shop, but she couldn't resist it."

"Was she sad about moving?" He began mixing the batter, his gaze on her face. He liked watching the different expressions that flitted across her face when she talked.

"No, not at all. She told me she loves it here. Fyodor let her take over his home and decorate it any way she wanted. She likes going room by room and changing things to suit her style. She has lots of rooms to play in."

"And her house?"

Ashe leaned across the bar to wipe flour from his chest where some had dropped when he'd stirred the batter. "She said she'd been considering putting it up for sale right before I showed up, so my guess is, that's what she's going to do."

"If you like it enough, we could ask her to sell it to us," Timur ventured, watching her face carefully.

Her eyes widened, and she sat up straighter. "I love the house, Timur, you know I do, but isn't that moving a little too fast? We can't just decide to buy a house."

He indicated the coffeepot with his chin while he worked. "Why not? Our leopards are committed, so are we. You're not going anywhere. We both know that. If Evangeline is willing, let's get the house while we can."

"You're a distance from work."

He shrugged. "There's a large yard, and the garage roof is large enough to land a helicopter on it. We can see about getting permission to keep one there."

"You can fly a helicopter?" She paused in the act of pouring him a cup of coffee.

"Yes. I have my license here. I learned in Russia, in the military. The skill has come in handy at times."

She poured him coffee and brought it to the bar. "Do you think Evangeline would sell us the house?"

His heart jumped in his chest. She wanted the house. He heard it in her voice. "Yes. I'm her brother-in-law, and most likely she'd sell it to me anyway, just to get me out from under her feet. It's close to her bakery and she worries about that all the time. She loves that little shop."

"I could start inquiries about renting or buying the shop next to hers. I just need to find out who owns the space."

"Fyodor does. Well," he hesitated. "We do. Gorya, Fyodor and me. The three of us. We have a business together and the business owns the entire block of buildings. Evangeline was getting shaken down . . ."

"Shaken down?" She sipped at her coffee, a question in her eyes.

"That territory is actually Emilio Bassini's. He demands protection money from every storeowner in his territory. When his men came in to collect from Evangeline, Fyodor happened to be there. He shut that shit down and then went to Emilio to offer the money to purchase the buildings. Emilio struck up a deal with him. With us. I don't think he wanted war and at the time, Fyodor was still a soldier for Arnotto. It was months before he ever admitted to himself or anyone else that he cared about Evangeline."

"This is fascinating. Even then he was crazy about her."

"Enough so that when he took over for Arnotto, we all told him he couldn't go back to her bakery. That was the one place anyone looking to kill him would know he'd be. I think the world knew, at that point, that he had fallen for Evangeline. Certainly, if Emilio knew it, and he wanted to get rid of Fyodor, what better place to hit him? We changed our routes every day. His security was tight, but if he insisted on visiting that bakery, his enemies had only to wait for him to show up. And still he went."

He put three pancakes on a plate in front of her. She had the butter and syrup already out.

"These look so good. Thanks, Timur. I really will take some cooking lessons. I know I could cook if I had an interest in it, and I don't want you to have to do it every night." She scrunched up her nose when she made the offer.

"I don't mind, but I won't be home every night. When I'm working late, you could go with me and visit Evangeline and eat there." Getting her in that habit would be good. Timur didn't look at her when he made the suggestion, not wanting her to see that he was going to maneuver her into doing what he wanted no matter what. "Especially now, she could probably use a friend. I don't like that she looks so fragile." He wasn't lying about that. Evangeline was very special to him. He knew Ashe could hear it in his voice. And the worry.

Ashe nodded her head. "That's a good idea. Even if she's really tired, I could at least be in the house and read or something. I'm a huge book reader. I love stories."

"Your favorite?"

"Anything Sherlock Holmes or like it," she answered readily. "Mysteries, but they have to have romance in them.

Even an action movie has to have at least a touch of romance or it's not going to be a favorite."

"I see a theme," he teased.

She flashed him a smile that nearly stopped his heart. "Happy endings or I'm not a fan," she agreed. "What do you like to read?"

"My favorite was always Aleksandr Pushkin. I like classics, but of course Tolstoy and Pushkin. I consider Pushkin to be the founder of Russian literature. We had many arguments in my classes over this."

"A little romance as well," she said.

He shrugged his shoulders. "I would never admit that, not even to you."

She threw her head back and laughed. "Of course not, because you're so tough. You worry about Evangeline, and yet you're a tough guy."

He wasn't about to admit that yes, he did worry about his sister-in-law, but he had ulterior motives when it came to making certain his woman was visiting her when he was there working.

Ashe's entire face lit up when she laughed. That laughter did something to his insides, turning him to mush, so he thought some of the ice that had frozen all emotions so many years earlier had melted and allowed her in deeper.

"Eat, woman. You need to keep up your strength. Your leopard is going to rise again soon and she's going to be very demanding of us."

She made a face at him. "She's a little hussy. Thank you for the care last night, the soaking in the tub really helped. I can't imagine what I'd be feeling like now if you hadn't done that. As it is, I didn't put on any panties because I thought exposure to the air would help heal me."

He groaned. "Baby. Really? You're going to tell me right now you aren't wearing any panties and then in the next breath tell me you have to heal?"

Her grin turned mischievous and he knew she'd done so deliberately to tease him. She licked the syrup off her fork. "Yep. That's exactly what I'm telling you. Not a stitch on under this dress. And you were delicious this morning. Shame on me for missing my opportunity to wake you up properly."

"Now my fuckin' cock is as hard as a rock again." He glared at her.

She threw her head back and laughed again. The sound filled the room and his heart with joy. He hadn't considered that having a woman could be fun. She made the simplest things exciting and amusing. He already couldn't imagine his life without her. From the moment he opened his eyes, he'd looked forward to the day.

His phone vibrated, and he took it out of his pocket and glanced down at the text. "Cops are back asking questions. Fyodor would like us over there, you for Evangeline and me to answer questions."

"About what?"

He shrugged. "It's always something. You're going to have to get used to a little bit of harassment. He's called our lawyer just to be on the safe side. Come on, we've got to go. Get your shoes."

"I'll stay here and do dishes. I don't feel like getting dressed."

"You're going to have to come with me. You don't need to get dressed, just get your shoes. You look beautiful."

"What if the little hussy suddenly makes an appearance?" She sounded nervous.

"They aren't leopard. They won't be able to tell and, in any case, they won't be there that long. Let's go see what they want." She was coming with him, even if he had to carry her, but he waited patiently, hoping she would come to the conclusion he wanted.

She heaved an exaggerated sigh. "Fine. But if she comes out and gets all amorous with cops, that's on you, not me."

"I won't hold you accountable." He might kill a few cops, but he wouldn't blame her.

They walked over to the main house, which was a good distance away. He held her hand, feeling a little bit of a fool, but liking the way it felt in his larger one. It was a new experience for him and one he savored. He'd pulled on a tight tee and loose drawstring pants. His loafers he could kick off immediately if he needed to shift.

Ashe wore her long dress and a pair of sandals. He liked that she wasn't in the least bit shy about her lack of underwear. She seemed utterly unaware of it, while he was aware with every single step he took.

When they entered the house, Gorya nodded toward the sitting room. It was the one place Fyodor consistently took guests, especially the police. They could easily contain anyone in that cozy little room. The walls had secrets. And catching an enemy in a crossfire was extremely easy. The lighting threw more shadows than light. Timur walked in with Ashe and chose the two chairs Fyodor had left in the darkest area of the room for him.

Jeff and Ray were there, along with two other cops, one in uniform. The fact that the other man wasn't in uniform meant he was at least a detective. Timur was introduced and found out the newcomer's name was Anton Lipin. The uniform cop was Finn Moran, an Irishman through and through.

Timur studied Lipin. Definitely Russian, or at least of Russian descent. The man stayed in the shadows as much as possible and that marked him, as far as Timur was concerned. He watched him closely, while keeping the others in his line of vision.

"What can I do for you, gentlemen?" Timur asked as he drew Ashe down onto his lap. She immediately pulled up her legs beneath the long skirt of her dress. "You've come at a very bad time. I've only got a couple of days off and I had planned on enjoying them with my fiancée."

Every eye went to Ashe, first on her face, then dropped to her bare hand and then back to her face in speculation. She squirmed a little, her bottom rubbing over his groin. Instantly, his cock reacted, growing hard and long beneath her. She shivered visibly but stopped moving when his hand pulled a blanket from the opposite chair and spread it over top of her.

"Are you cold?" Timur was all solicitation, but he knew she wasn't cold. He knew it was his reaction to her innocent squirming that sent that little shiver down her spine.

"I'm good now," she said and leaned back into him, putting her head on his shoulder.

The action thrust her breasts forward and he slid his hand beneath the long skirt of her dress to splay his fingers over her belly. The tips brushed the undersides of her breasts. His cock jerked in response. He kept his features blank.

"Again, what can I do for you, gentlemen?" He looked to Jeff, who usually led the others.

"We were called to a motel this morning when several of the rooms were found abandoned." It was Moran who answered.

Timur found that utterly astonishing, but he kept his mask in place. Why would the uniformed officer be the spokesperson? He stayed silent, waiting for an explanation as to why they were there.

"The motel charges by the day and rents are paid one day at a time. The rule to be out is very strict. Money changes hands by ten A.M. or the tenant must leave. There were six rooms rented and not one paid. No one was in their rooms and it looked as if they hadn't spent the night there. More, all security cameras were on the blitz. The ones in the parking lot and above the door of each of those rooms along with the cameras installed on either side of the rooms."

Timur drummed his fingers against the arm of the chair as if becoming impatient. With his other hand, he began to rub along the underside of Ashe's breasts with the tips of his fingers. She was achingly soft right there. He loved the way she felt. She didn't move a muscle, nor did she try to stop him.

"Get to the point, because I don't see where this is going."

"The point is this." Moran leaned closer. "Clothes were still in the room, as if they were coming back. In the suit pocket of one of them was this address. Written on that paper was Fyodor Amurov, Gorya Amurov and Timur Amurov. There was a second address. I believe your cousin Mitya resides there. His name and his brother's, Sevastyan, were also written there. There were other names as well. The names of men you employ and some in your cousin's employment."

Timur shrugged. "First, Sevastyan isn't Mitya's brother. They're cousins, although quite close. And I'm not certain where you're going with this. Was there a threat made against us? Against my brother or cousin?" He slid his fingers down to her belly and dipped them in her little belly button. He wished his fingers were his tongue.

"They are here from Russia."

Timur frowned. "I still don't understand. We haven't been in Russia for many years." That was strictly the truth. "What does that mean? I don't understand."

"We were hoping you would tell us what that meant."

What it meant was Jeremiah had fucked up again. His job had been to erase all threads between the men who would never be returning to those rooms and the Amurov family. Clearly, he'd dealt with the cameras, but he'd left behind an important piece of paper. That left the burning question: Had he missed anything else?

"I have no idea. Who are these men?" He looked to his brother. "Did you have visitors I wasn't aware of while I was out?"

Fyodor shook his head. "No. It was very quiet yesterday."

Timur stroked the pads of his fingers down Ashe's soft

skin and settled them just on top of her mound. "What are the names of these men? Perhaps we know them from our homeland."

Finn Moran indicated Fyodor. "He's got the names."

Fyodor passed a piece of paper to Timur. "I didn't recognize any of them. Do you?"

Timur pretended to study them. His entire attention was on Ashe's body. She was warm and soft and more than anything, he wanted to hold her close and spend time kissing her. Exploring her mouth. Learning every erogenous spot she had on her body. He knew he wasn't the best man in the world, but for her, he would try to be, within the context of who and what he was. He wanted her happy above all else.

He nuzzled her shoulder and pressed his mouth to the nape of her neck, kissing her there. Her heavy fall of hair had been pulled up into a ponytail, leaving her neck bare. He liked the little shudder that went through her body when he put his lips to her skin.

"I'm sorry. I don't know any of these men. Having said that, it doesn't mean that I've never run across them before. It just means that I can't recall them."

Jeff seemed restless. He stood up and moved around the room, hands in his pockets, but his gaze was on the knickknacks and artwork Evangeline had placed in the sitting room—as if it might all be stolen. Timur found himself resenting the cops, and the fact that they seemed to think they could show up at any time and interrupt their day.

"Are you looking for something in particular?"

Jeff turned his head, his gaze on Ashe. "I was just wondering how you do it. Your brother with Evangeline, and now you've got her." He jerked his chin toward Ashe.

Timur instantly went on alert. Jeff might be the most annoying man in the world, but he was always respectful.

"Jeff," Ray said, standing, as if that might deter his partner. "It's not worth it."

Jeff shook his head, holding up his hand to stop whatever Ray was about to say. "They're good women. Both of them. You know that, don't you?"

Timur pulled his hand free of Ashe's skirt, the blanket and the warmth of her skin. "I'm very aware of that, yes." He kept his gaze steady on Jeff.

"They could get killed living with you."

For the first time, Timur allowed himself to look at Jeff as a human being, rather than an enemy out to get them. "We have protection in place," he supplied quietly. "You know I carry a weapon, as does every man on my security force. The women come first at all times."

"Even before your brother?" Jeff jerked his thumb toward Fyodor, his voice bitter.

"Evangeline and Ashe are always first," Fyodor answered. "These men from that motel. Do you believe they are somehow a threat to our women?" There was a rumble of menace in his voice.

Timur sat up straighter. Did Jeff know the missing men were hit men?

"We found several other cameras in cafés and stores across the street from the motel with photographs of the men. Two were recognized as hit men. Interpol is sending what they have on them. We're searching for them now, but they haven't returned to the cars they rented. We did trace them to this man . . ." It was again Finn Moran who spoke. He passed a photograph to Timur. "Do you recognize him?"

It was Apostol Delov. Timur nodded slowly. "He's known in our world as the messenger. Apostol Delov isn't his real name. He isn't the only one using that identity, but they're all from the same family. They're the trackers. They're hired to hunt down a particular person and when they find them, they send for the hit team."

"He's renting a house just one block over from Evangeline's home," Jeff said.

"*This* is Evangeline's home," Fyodor said. "She's my wife. She lives here with me and she's protected."

"He meant," Ray said, glaring at his partner, "to say that he's staying one block from the house your wife owns and where Ashe is living now. That's an awful big coincidence."

The stranger, Anton Lipin, stood up and wandered over to Jeff as if to calm him, or to show solidarity. He was a big man, his size dwarfing Jeff just a little. He leaned against the fireplace, running one hand along the mantel, giving the impression of a man very much at ease.

"Delov was identified as the man who originally rented the rooms and was there on at least two occasions with these other men," Moran continued.

"Ashe," Ray said, ignoring Timur's instant scowl. "Do you know any of these men?"

Ashe had looked at the photographs when Timur had. "I've got a fairly good memory and I think this man was in the bakery a couple of times." She pointed to the picture Fyodor was handing back to the uniformed policemen. "He didn't cause any trouble. He just got coffee and a pastry. I didn't see any of the others, at least that I can recall."

The photographs through the café's security cameras were grainy. Even if later it could be proved that one or more of the men had been in the bakery, she could always claim the pictures weren't clear.

"Is there a reason a hit might be taken out on you?" Ray asked.

Ashe sank deeper into Timur's body. She shook her head, one hand going defensively to her throat. "No. I mean, what could I have done to someone to make them pay to have me killed?" She looked at Timur as if he might have the answer.

He could see she was very nervous. He leaned forward and took her mouth. Beneath his, her lips trembled, but she didn't hold back. She gave herself to him. He wrapped his arms around her. "Is it necessary to scare the crap out of her? She's safe here."

"She doesn't live here," Ray pointed out. "You all live

here. She lives in Evangeline's house, the house one block from the one Delov is renting."

"Pick him up and ask him what the fuck he's doing here," Fyodor snapped.

"He's missing too. All of them have disappeared. They could be anywhere," Jeff said.

"And now they won't go near the motel again, or Delov's rented house," Timur pointed out. He sighed. "I guess I should thank you for the warning, but it always seems that every time any of you come around, you bring trouble with you."

"The trouble was already here," Jeff said. "Where is Evangeline?"

Timur glanced at his brother. Fyodor wouldn't have much more patience when it came to Jeff's lovesick infatuation.

"She's feeling under the weather," Ashe said, unexpectedly. "The flu's going around big-time and being in the shop, we get exposed to everything. I told her I'd hold down the fort for the next couple of days for her."

"*Not*," Fyodor said, "that it's any of your business."

Jeff didn't answer him. He just shook his head, jammed his hands in his pockets and looked into the fireplace. Anton Lipin awkwardly patted his shoulder.

"I think we're finished here," the uniformed officer said.

Timur studied his face. He looked to be about forty. Tough. The others clearly respected him. The stranger in street clothes hadn't said one word. He'd nodded when he was introduced, but that was about it. Timur took another look at him. His features were definitely Russian. His name certainly could have been. Was there a reason he didn't speak? It stood to reason they might bring in an expert on Russian mobsters.

The cops stood as soon as the uniformed officer made his statement. Timur set Ashe aside so he could stand with his brother.

"Thank you for the warning," Fyodor said.

Timur deliberately went up to Anton Lipin and held out his hand. There was the briefest of hesitations and then Anton took his hand and shook it. Timur smiled at him. "I really appreciate you coming to warn us. Have you been to the bakery yet?" He was certain the cop hadn't. He would have recognized the policeman.

"No." The briefest of answers.

"You'll have to come in. Evangeline is an amazing baker."

The man just nodded. He might not be from Russia, but if not, his parents were. Timur would stake his life on that.

13

TIMUR closed the door on the cops and turned to face his brother, his finger to his lips. He mouthed, *"House bugged."*

"I despise that arrogant prick Jeff," Fyodor said aloud. "He's after my wife."

"She's in love with *you*," Timur said. He pulled out his phone and texted Gorya to bring equipment to find any bugs the cops might have left in the house.

Fyodor caught his arm and pointed toward the kitchen. The police hadn't been there. Still, Timur didn't like it. He went to the door of the sitting room, put his finger to his lips again and then indicated for Ashe to come to him.

He circled her shoulders with one arm. "Check on Evangeline, baby. Make certain she's resting."

"She needs to drink plenty of water," Fyodor added. "She gets snippy if I tell her to drink it, but if you do, she'll be good about it."

Ashe sent him a reassuring smile. "No worries. Where is she?"

"She's in the master bedroom right now. She's up, resting on the lounge, reading, but I know she'll want your company and I want her down as much as possible," Fyodor said.

Ashe went up on her toes to brush a kiss along Timur's jaw. "I'm on it, Fyodor, don't worry about a thing."

Timur and Fyodor watched her walk down the hall and then both went in the opposite direction to the kitchen. Just to be certain whatever bug the cops had placed wasn't capable of hearing them, he flipped the switch on the audio jammer. They had them in every room throughout the house and switching one on in one room would activate them in every room. The jammer emitted a random masking sound that desensitized microphones. That would render them unable to record.

"Did you place Lipin? He's got to be their Russian expert. He was the one who had to tell them about Apostol Delov."

Fyodor shook his head. "I've never seen him before. I didn't get it at first. I was too busy wanting to rip Jeff's head off."

"Jeff was their distraction. He never would have behaved that way in front of a superior officer if it wasn't planned." Timur had studied Jeff Meyers for a while, assessing the threat to his brother. Jeff was a cop through and through, a man with principles. He'd acted totally out of character.

"Moran?"

Timur nodded. "He was in charge. They were fishing. Lipin must have already identified the hit squad for them. They have their names. Damn that kid for leaving anything behind. I told him to be thorough. To double-check every pocket. To wear gloves. To make certain he wasn't caught on camera." He paced away from his brother and halfway across the great room. It was a large room and still, his leopard didn't ease up. Something wasn't right.

"I don't like any of this, Fyodor," he admitted. "They dressed their boss up in a uniform and brought an expert with them. What are the odds the expert showed up? Have Drake find out everything he can about this man. Is he local? I doubt that. Is he a Fed? Interpol? That seems more likely."

Fyodor already had his phone out and was texting Drake. "We'll get replies fast."

"He's dirty," Timur said. "He's in Lazar's pocket."

Fyodor spun around. "Why do you think that?"

"I just have a gut feeling. My gut hasn't been wrong yet. He didn't want to shake my hand. I put it out there deliberately and tried to make him talk. He didn't want to speak and he didn't want to touch me."

"Cops think we're dirty, and we are. We have been our entire lives. He might be a good cop with an aversion to the *bratya*."

Timur shook his head. "No, not like this. I was unclean to him. A traitor. He also wore gloves. My guess?" He looked at the tattoos on his fingers, the ones proclaiming he was part of a lair, part of something big. The *bratya*. "I think he's wearing Lazar's tattoos."

"The Feds or Interpol would know."

"Not if he says he was a cop in Russia and went undercover. That's what I'd do," Timur declared.

He glanced down at his phone. "Gorya found three bugs. One in the seat where the bastard was sitting. One on the mantel and one on the lamp in the front room, just by the door."

"Have him go over it again. Then do every room."

"Do you want him to destroy them?"

"Hell yes. We're not going to pretend we didn't suspect them. Fucking cops come to our home, pretend to be concerned for our women and then take the opportunity to leave behind bugs. How would they even get permission for that?" Fyodor was on his phone, texting Gorya again. "On second thought, let's keep them in evidence. We can turn them over to our lawyer."

"He was supposed to be here," Timur snapped.

"He got stopped by a cop. Cop said he cruised through a stop sign. It turned into some kind of huge thing."

"Fuckin' cops," Timur said. "I actually felt sorry for Jeff. I know he genuinely cares for Evangeline. Ray is an asshole. He acts like he already owned Ashe and she owed him, but Jeff is an upfront kind of man."

"No one upfront tries to steal another man's wife. I've got to tell Evangeline that we have to be careful. If they were given a warrant to bug the house, he could come by for a visit and try it."

"We sweep every day, and when I asked Gorya about Jeff's visit," Timur said, seeing his brother was getting worked up at the thought of the cop using Evangeline, "he told me he swept immediately after the man left."

Fyodor looked as if he wanted to hit something. Timur couldn't blame him. "Are you certain you got every single one of Lazar's squad?"

"I have no way of knowing that, but we have to find out who gave them the layout of your home, Fyodor. That means we need to talk to Evangeline's brother. He visited her and she gave him a tour of the house. Her father and uncle were inside the house. Who knows whether or not she gave them a tour as well? Women do that shit and don't think anything of it. Someone wants to see their home and they show it off."

Fyodor swore under his breath. "She said they were playing pool. Damn it, Timur, this is going to break her heart. If her brother is guilty . . ."

"I'll kill him quietly and he'll just disappear."

"She'll know."

"She won't know. She might suspect, but she won't know and she won't want to know."

"It will change your relationship with her, because she'll

know," Fyodor insisted. "She's smart. She thinks things through."

"Better my relationship with her than yours." Timur sighed and pushed his hand through his hair, wishing his woman was close. Right then, knowing he might have to kill Evangeline's brother to protect the ones he loved, he needed the comfort of her body.

Fyodor swore again. "I'll message him to come to the house."

Timur nodded. "Do it for dinner. Tonight. My leopard is getting anxious. He wants his mate. I've got to take care of things on the home front and then we'll join you."

"Evangeline might not be up to it."

"Her brother doesn't need to know that until he's here. She doesn't need to know he's coming if she's too ill. The point is to catch him off guard. I'll talk to him, not you."

Fyodor looked around, his fist doubled, as if he might hit the wall. "Evangeline's had enough of all of this, and your woman is just beginning to get to know us. We're going to have to put both of them under guard and keep them close. When do you think you'll interrogate the prisoner? Maybe he'll shed some light on this mess. And don't forget to ask about our new cop—Anton Lipin. It will be interesting to see what our hit man has to say about him."

"He probably runs the squad."

"It's a distinct possibility. Any man who would come into my home like that, if he is dirty or runs the hit teams for Lazar, has balls of steel."

Timur was inclined to agree with his brother. "What are your thoughts on Evangeline's family? Would they betray her? Sell her out for their own gain?"

"Her father and uncle distributed opium, although to this day, they say their father got them into it and they couldn't get out."

"They blame everyone but themselves," Timur said.

"That's right. They have never taken responsibility for

what they did. Evangeline's father refuses to admit in any way that he should have stood up to his father so his daughter could have an actual home, not live in the swamp, mostly alone."

"The boys were kids, but they knew she was all alone out in that swamp," Timur pointed out. "They knew, and they didn't do anything to help her."

Fyodor nodded. "That's right." He glanced in the direction of the bedroom. "I hate that I can't just wipe all that out for her."

"She wouldn't want you to. She's strong, Fyodor. Those early days are why she can live with you. With us. With what we do. We've got to keep Drake apprised. He's leader of that fucked-up lair he inherited. Evangeline's family falls to him."

Fyodor nodded. "Good call. I should have been on that all along." He glanced again toward the master bedroom. "What about Ashe? You're certain she's yours? Not just your leopard's, but yours?"

"She's mine." He said it firmly. Irrevocably. "She can't make up her mind whether or not to run. She's leaning toward trying, but she has it in her head she has a choice."

"It's best to let her think that, Timur."

"I got that impression." Timur moved through the house on silent feet, making certain everything was in place. Leopards were cunning, stealthy creatures, capable of going into a house, choosing a target and then dragging the body out right under the noses of anyone else in the house. They were never seen. The last thing he wanted was for one of the hit squad to still be in the house, waiting, scent-blocker hiding them.

Timur didn't trust everything to his leopard. He used his leopard senses, but he also used his brain. He spent a great deal of time working out strategies for making his brother's home and vehicles safe. He changed routes regularly, and he especially covered the bakery and Fyodor's office there.

The cops, as enemies, were a new twist. He didn't mind

playing cat and mouse with them, but when he thought one or more might be on Lazar's payroll, that changed things significantly. A dirty cop had powers a hit man might not have. A cop could get in and out of places using his badge. He could persuade others to help him and could hide behind that badge. If Lipin was dirty, Timur needed to know and he needed to take him out quietly and very fast.

"I'm not going to let her go, Fyodor, even if she wants to try to run. I can't. My life has been so fucked-up and it will continue to be—" Timur broke off and shook his head. What was there to say? What could he say?

"I'm sorry. I didn't want this for you," Fyodor said immediately.

Timur shrugged. "It's my choice. I'm suited to the work. I hate to admit that, but I am. Our father broke something in me and it can't be fixed. I didn't think anything could overcome it, but Ashe seems to be able to. When I'm with her, I feel. Not just feel—the intensity is like nothing I ever imagined. I can't have that and then let it go, not when I thought I'd never have anything or anyone for myself."

Fyodor sighed. "We put a lot on our women."

The two moved down the hall toward the master bedroom. The hallway was wide enough for them to walk side by side, even with their broad shoulders.

"Do you think Lipin was looking for signs that his hit squad had been here?"

Timur shrugged again. "We're already thinking he's a dirty cop and head of Lazar's hit team. I'm not sure of anything yet, Fyodor, but I'll find out. I'll step up the interrogation of the prisoner, but the more time he has to think about how cut off he is from the rest of the world, the more information I'll extract quicker." He didn't like to think what he would have to do if the man wasn't going to give him information easily.

Fyodor sighed again. "I hate this life for you. When we were kids, I thought maybe I could get you out."

"This is my choice, it always has been," Timur said. "What else could I do?"

Soft laughter slid from beneath the door of the bedroom. He put his hand on the heavy wood and absorbed those notes. They were real, the genuine thing. Laughter tugged at his heartstrings. Gave him a joy he hadn't known he could feel. To hear both women, Evangeline and Ashe, laughing together made his world right. Made everything he had to do worth it.

He pushed open the door and stepped back to allow his brother through first. Evangeline was on the bed, back against several pillows, her legs stretched out in front of her. Ashe had pulled a chair to the side of the bed and was sitting with her legs in the air, nearly upside down, bunching the material of her dress around her hips to preserve a semblance of modesty.

"I shouldn't ask, but what are you doing?" Whatever explanation his woman had wasn't going to erase the sight of her, head hanging off the side, hair a wild mess, feet waving in the air.

Both women turned their heads toward the door and then burst out laughing again. Ashe righted herself, dragging the hem of the dress she wore to her ankles. "Hi. I didn't expect you so soon."

Her cheeks were bright red. Timur went straight to her, tipped back her chin to study her face and then bent his head and brushed her mouth gently with his. "I can see that. Was there a particular reason you were upside down?"

She snuck a quick peek at Evangeline and then both women were laughing again. "If I told you, you'd think we were a little crazy."

"I know you're both a little crazy," he pointed out. He couldn't help smiling. Just looking at her made him happy, but when she was like this, flushed, smiling, mischievous, her eyes bright and especially when she was sharing some private joke with Evangeline, his world was right. Perfectly right.

"There was this woman we both worked with," Ashe said. "At the little café."

"She thought she was a perfect little sexpot," Evangeline added. "She was certain every man who came into the café wanted her."

"They kinda did," Ashe said.

Evangeline nodded. "That's true. Because she wore these little skirts. Tiny skirts."

"*Teeny*-tiny," Ashe reiterated. "Micro-mini. If I tried to wear something like that . . ." She trailed off.

Evangeline laughed. "We had a miniskirt day, in honor of her. Her name was Sophie, and she squealed a lot when men were around. So that meant she squealed all the time. She flipped her hair . . ."

Both women provided a demonstration, flipping their hair this way and that. Both erupted into giggles.

"She liked to bend over a lot," Ashe added. "As in all the time. She dropped things just so she could bend over."

She stood up and faced away from Timur. She bent over, straight-legged, hiked up her skirt, giving him a good view of her bare bottom and her sweet little pussy. His cock jerked hard when she smiled at him from between her legs. "Like this. And she didn't wear panties."

"She said it was a complete waste of money and time," Evangeline explained. "Money, because men tore panties off, and time because it was one more article of clothing to get off when she was in a hurry. She didn't have a lot of time during her breaks or lunch and she took men into the backroom often."

"It sounds as if she led a colorful life."

Fyodor skirted around the end of the bed and came up on the other side so he could perch next to his wife. He leaned down and brushed a kiss to the corner of her mouth. "I see you were in here resting."

"I was entertaining her," Ashe said. "With colorful tales of our past."

Timur sank into the chair she had vacated when she came to her feet. He tugged at her until she sank down onto his lap. He liked her there. She wasn't yet comfortable with being on his lap, his cock pressed tight to her bottom, but she was getting there. In fact, she wiggled. The friction sent a jolt, much like a lightning bolt running through him.

Her skin was hot. Too hot. The skirt had ridden up to her thighs. He tugged up the back so her bare bottom rested on him, only the thin material of his trousers separating them. He scraped his teeth over her neck and she shivered.

"We're going to have to go, Evangeline," Timur said. "But we'll be back tonight for dinner." Ashe's fingers were driving him mad where she stroked the pads of her fingers against the bare skin on his neck.

His male roared and pushed against the human frame trapping him as he sensed his mate close. Timur nipped Ashe with strong teeth, just on her chin. Her entire body shuddered. They'd almost left it until too late. The female's rise was fast this time, not unexpected, but fast.

He set her on the floor and stood, waving at his brother and sister-in-law as he tugged on Ashe's hand. "I'm sorry, *malen'kiy smerch*, I should have been paying more attention."

"It's not your fault." She dismissed his crime immediately, defending him when he knew there was no defense. She had to be his priority when she was in heat like this. One never neglected one's mate, and he had no intention of ever neglecting Ashe.

He used his longer legs to take wider strides, so she was practically running, but it gave her female something else to concentrate on for a few minutes. He wanted to put as much distance as possible between them and the house. Cursing himself for not taking better care of her, he kept his gaze fixed on the guesthouse, which was a good distance away.

"You're muttering."

The soft laughter in her voice stroked sensual awareness right through his body. She sounded happy. She also sounded in need. Hungry for him. That took his body to an entirely different place.

"I should have been paying attention to you. I'm your damn mate and I neglected you," he reiterated. Every muscle was tight. Aching now. What was her body like? Her skin glowed with heat, need pouring off her in pheromones.

"I'm not certain I can make it back to the house," Ashe admitted, stopping. When he turned toward her to scoop her up, she wound her arms around his neck, going up on her toes to kiss him over and over.

He lost himself in her mouth, in the way he did the moment he touched her. His cock hurt like a son of a bitch, so hard he was afraid any movement would make him shatter. He slid his arms down the curve of her spine, kissing her, his mouth demanding. The roaring in his ears increased.

With her arms circling his neck, the skirt had ridden up and his hands bunched the material until he found her bare bottom. He caught at her perfect cheeks, fingers digging deep, claiming her. He walked her backward toward the small garden at the side of the house. Flowers climbed archways and ran along a short white fence. He barely noticed his surroundings. He could only feel flames licking over his skin and fire burning hot in his belly.

He did his best to be gentle, but needs were riding him hard. His needs, hers. He tasted her hunger. Tasted the taste that would always be his. Only his. She was practically purring as he devoured her mouth and stroked her tongue with his. He wanted to crawl inside her, share her skin, share her body, put his marks on her so it was clear to every other male in the vicinity that she belonged to him.

He needed rough. He wanted to be gentle. He needed to own her. He wanted her to feel his love for her. Her hand crept down and slid over his hard length, stroked, and then gripped.

"I want to feel you in my mouth," she whispered. "I love how heavy you are. How you feel like velvet and steel at the same time. I like the way you stretch my lips so wide. It makes me know how you're going to stretch me deep inside."

Her soft voice nearly was the end of his strength. Just when he was certain there was no way to love her more, she did something like that. She made him feel as if he was everything to her. He'd never been everything to anyone. Not even that first day he was born. He knew, because his male had been aware. His mother had felt not love, but trepidation, fear that her husband would choose that time to kill her now that she'd given him more than one son.

Ashe looked up at him with pleading eyes. Her hands slipped inside his drawstring pants and found him hot and ready. Her thumb slid over the crown, smearing the drops of his need before she fisted him.

"What is it you want, baby?" He whispered the question, needing to hear her say it one more time. Wanting her to look at him while she asked.

"I want your cock in my mouth." There was no hesitation.

"That's good, because I need your mouth on me, baby," he whispered against her lips. "I'm going to break in half if I take another step."

She kissed her way down his throat while she pushed at the material of his shirt, wanting it off his skin so she could get to him. He reached with one hand and whipped it over his head, slinging it somewhere. Anywhere. Out of the corner of his eye, he saw it float down to the short white fence where vines grew and settle there.

Her hands caught at the waistband of his pants and she took them down to his ankles. He kicked them away. "Take the dress off, Ashe," he said, desperate to see her body.

She didn't take her gaze from his. Both hands went to the hem and she pulled the dress from her body, leaving her completely bare to him. Her skin gleamed, a rosy color, flushed with need, the ritual heat on her.

He cupped her breasts in his palms and ran his thumbs over her nipples. Strumming. Watching her reaction. Her breath caught in her throat. He changed the rhythm and then pinched and tugged. She gasped. Her eyes glazed a bit. Her mouth opened.

"Need you on your knees, Ashe," he said. He wasn't certain he was capable of handling this. She was so beautiful. He kept tugging on her nipples, his gaze glued to her face, needing her reaction the way he needed air.

She knelt immediately, still looking up at him, almost in adoration. He circled the base of his cock with one hand. "Put your hands behind your back." He could barely breathe. He couldn't see anything but his woman kneeling there in front of him, surrounded by flowers and curling vines, completely naked, her skin glowing with need.

Ashe obeyed him, putting both hands behind her, threading her fingers together. His heart tripped as the action thrust her breasts toward him. He stepped closer and rubbed the sensitive head of his cock over her lips. She parted them for him and he fed it to her, one slow inch at a time, watching with a kind of wonder how his girth stretched her lips. How she struggled to take him. She didn't pull back or hesitate, not even when he was certain she would choke. She just kept her eyes on his, and there was trust there. Complete trust.

Timur had no idea how he'd earned that from her, but by some miracle she'd given that to him. He moved in her. Gently. Carefully. It was difficult with his entire body shaking and his seed boiling. Every cell in his body urged him to go faster. To bury himself deep in the silken heat of her mouth.

"I need you to suck harder." He gave the command through gritted teeth. He could barely talk, barely manage a voice instead of an animalistic growl. He felt like an animal, need consuming him, driving out sanity, every thinking part of him.

He threw his head back when her mouth tightened and he felt that suction gripping him, the friction as he drove deeper. He watched her struggle to relax for him, to let him go deeper, cutting off her airway for longer moments. Never once did she let go of her hands or pull away from him. She didn't break eye contact either.

He'd never seen anything more sensuous than his woman with her eyes watering and her lips stretched around his girth. His cock disappearing and her throat working. He didn't want it to end, that ecstasy when she gave up every semblance of control to bring him pleasure. He felt the burn starting somewhere in his toes. The tingling up the back of his spine, like the tips of flames, licking at him. The burn in his belly, the roaring in his ears and the brutal tightness in his balls as they drew up, covered, he was certain, in flames.

He caught her hair in a tight grip and thrust deep, feeling her open at his demand, feeling nothing now but the terrible burst of raw fire that turned fast into a raging storm. It roiled in his gut and groin, and then there was that one moment where he teetered on the edge staring down into her eyes. So beautiful. So perfect. Giving him this when he did nothing to deserve it. Giving him everything. Then the volcano erupted, long jerking spurts he was helpless to stop.

His hand went to her throat to feel her swallowing. That added to the pleasure, to the force of his explosive eruption. He tightened his hold in her hair as he withdrew and held himself there, waiting just out of her present reach. She leaned into him and did what he silently demanded, her tongue lapping at him gently. His entire body shuddered with pleasure as she took every drop of his essence into her. She took her time and was very thorough. By the time she was finished, he was hard again.

He used his grip on her hair to pull her into a standing position. He indicated the small fence and she turned and faced away from him, her hands gripping the top rail. He kicked her legs wider and wider until he could see her sweet pussy gleaming at him. She was so ready for him, pink and swollen and nearly crying in her need. He didn't wait. Didn't hesitate. He caught both hips and drove into her.

Fire streaked up his legs and centered in his groin. She was scorching hot, surrounding him with silken flames. It was heaven and hell combined. He plunged into her again and again, hard driving strokes, his powerful hands pulling her back to meet him. He could hear her ragged breath as he drove air from her lungs with the force of each surge.

He wanted to be gentle, but the grip of her heat wouldn't allow it for either of them. She needed to be sated, and wild and rough was their only recourse. "This is love, Ashe." He whispered it over her head. Stroked one hand down her back in a caress before gripping her hip again. "This is love for you the only way I know how to show it to you." Giving her what she needed. She gave him everything, and he would burn for her always. Burn until there was nothing left of him.

She pushed back hard, impaling herself as he drove through those soft folds. Then she was keening, wailing, calling out her orgasm to the world. He felt her body clamp down on his and couldn't stop the storm in his body from erupting into her. He didn't want to stop it. He let the force of his own orgasm match hers and yelled her name as he blasted his seed into her.

Timur wrapped his arms around her waist and buried his face in the nape of her neck. "Someday, Ashe, I'm going to make love to you so gently, you won't know who you're in bed with," he promised. "I'm going to worship your body the way you worship mine. Don't think I don't know or appreciate what you do for me, because I do."

He would never have said the words to her face. He wasn't there yet. No one else knew about the poetry he wrote, tucked away in a secret diary he feared an enemy might find someday. A killer with a poet's heart. How had that happened? He vowed his woman would get that side of him someday, but not yet. His feelings for her were too new, too overwhelming. He had to find a way to reconcile the killer with the lover and poet.

His body gave another shudder and then he began to withdraw. He heard her little cry of pain as he did so. The leopards were so close, pushing on each of them for freedom. He didn't like being out of her body. Away from her. Alone in his own skin once more. Still, he stroked another caress down her back.

"Shift for me, baby. I want to see your leopard. She's beautiful. My male says she's the most beautiful leopard that he's ever seen. He says she's unusual."

He knew his woman would want her female appreciated. He watched her body contort, the fur sliding through to cover her skin. She was a shade faster. He would work on that with her when she wasn't in heat. The faster they could shift, the safer they were. She stood in front of him, her little body compact, fur very thick, like that of an Amur leopard, but the coloring was different, shades of platinum and gold running through a darker fur. The rosettes were ringed with the two colors and he'd never seen that before. His male was right. She was beautiful, her fur different, and therefore she was more at risk for an enemy to want her pelt.

He shifted quickly, letting his male out. Instantly Temnyy scented the air and grimaced at the smell of several male leopards in close proximity. He nudged his mate, shouldering her, pushing her to run for the grove of trees. She swiped at him with one paw, not at all enamored of his bossy ways. She could scent the other males as easily as he could and knew that in her present state, she would create chaos. They would fight for her. Adore her. Vie to be her mate.

Temnyy turned and raked his teeth down her side. She jumped and went in the direction he pushed her, right toward the grove. It was large and shaded due to the heavy canopy above them. The branches on the trees were thick and twisted one into another to create an arboreal highway aboveground.

Beneath the trees, the vegetation was more scarce because sunlight had a difficult time getting through the canopy. Still, there were bushes and a little stream that ran through the small forest the Arnotto family had created so many years earlier. Godiva ran to the stream and played in it, cooling her paws and then rolling so that the cold water bathed her side where Temnyy had raked her. She snarled at him, letting him know she wasn't happy with him.

Temnyy moved closer to nuzzle her muzzle with his own, and then he lapped at her side with his tongue, taking the sting away. They ran together, side by side, Godiva learning the forest area, mapping it out in her mind so she would know it well if there was danger. Several times she stopped to mark the trees with her alluring scent. The moment she did, Temnyy marked over the top to warn the others away from what was his.

She rolled in the dry leaves and playfully swatted some at him. He watched over her, her antics telling him she wasn't quite ready for him. They ran another distance and then she began rubbing along his side and pushing her muzzle into his neck. He licked her. She was receptive to his display of affection, rolling over for him and then coming to a crouch.

Temnyy was on her immediately, his teeth holding her in place, and then he began their hours of mating. Every fifteen minutes he took her roughly, again and again. His teeth held her, biting deep, and his barbed penis scraped her as he withdrew, causing pain. Still, she crouched for him, her heat driving her to the mating ritual.

It was evening before Timur pushed his leopard to return to the guesthouse. The two leopards entered panting, sides heaving, tongues rolling, Godiva clearly exhausted. Timur shifted first and immediately went to run a hot bath for her, throwing in soothing salts to help ease any bruising.

Godiva padded after him and lay on the cool tile, her eyes closed as he filled the deep tub for her. Everything in the Arnotto estate had been designed for the comfort of shifters and their leopards.

"All right, baby, shift for me," he whispered, running his hand through her soft fur.

Godiva lifted her head and looked at him. He could see his woman there, behind those exotic, beautiful eyes. The strange light amber with the darker rings around them, eyes that seemed to see into his soul. He hoped not. His soul was black with sins.

"Come on, baby, or I'll have to put you in the water just the way you are." It wasn't much of a threat. Leopards liked water. They could swim and often did. Some had achieved the skill to catch prey in water.

Godiva gave a little sniff of disdain and then her body contorted. He winced when he saw the rake mark along Ashe's satiny skin. It was a long red streak that went from her hip, over her ribs, to just below her arm. It appeared more of a scrape than anything else and it wasn't deep, but it reminded him that any mark on Godiva was a mark on Ashe.

She was on her hands and knees, and looked so exhausted he wanted to gather her into his arms and put her to bed. They had a dinner with Evangeline's family to get through, probably another wild mating session and then he had to go to work. Hopefully, she would be so exhausted she would sleep and wouldn't even know he was gone.

"What's wrong, Timur?"

Her voice was husky. He willed his cock to behave. It was so close to her mouth. To those lips. To keep from doing anything he might be ashamed of later, he lifted her into his arms and stepped into the bathtub.

"I don't like Temnyy raking Godiva with his teeth."

"She was being a hussy." Ashe turned her head into his chest.

Her breath was warm against his skin. He felt the tip of

her tongue touch his flat nipple. Unsurprisingly, he was sensitive, and he felt as though an electric wire ran from nipple to his cock.

"Were you okay with everything that happened this afternoon?" He kissed the top of her head. "You have to tell me when you don't like something."

"You mean when I had your cock down my throat?" She looked up at him.

She was a fucking temptress. How could she say that and look at him so innocently? His cock was going to be out of control, and she was more exhausted than she knew. One of them had to be sane. He put her down, off his lap so she couldn't feel his reaction to her deliberate phrasing.

"That's exactly what I mean."

"I loved it. I loved being outside surrounded by nature, vines and flowers. Feeling the sun on my skin. It was very intoxicating."

"I was so out of control I couldn't wait long enough to get you inside," he confessed.

"I was so out of control I didn't care," she admitted. Her eyes met his. "You'd already warned everyone away. I saw you texting just before we left Evangeline and Fyodor."

He nodded. "I was afraid we'd left it too late. Your female goes from zero to a full-out burn in seconds." He leaned closer and smiled at her. "Before you protest, I love that about her. I like not knowing when we're going to have to make a run for it. Believe me, baby, it will keep me on my toes, checking for closets or alleyways."

She laughed softly. "I love being with you, Timur. You're so unexpected."

"Will that be enough for you when I'm ordering you around?"

She shrugged. "That all depends. I don't mind your orders if they're for my protection or someone else's. I love that about you. I love that you'll watch over our children and your family with that fierce side of you. I won't love it if you start thinking you can control my everyday life. I will always be me. Always, Timur. If you really are in love with me, then you'll realize controlling me would ruin everything we have, or could potentially have."

There was truth in what she was saying and he hoped he would always have the wisdom to know when to back off from trying to control his environment.

14

TIMUR was head of security for Fyodor, but he was also his brother. Tonight, with Ashe at his side, he was Fyodor's brother—seemingly. He dressed accordingly, but the clothes he chose were easily gotten rid of, should he have need. He would be walking a fine line, convincing Ashe and Evangeline he had the night off and was simply enjoying a meal and getting to know Evangeline's family.

Evangeline had been with them long enough to know they were suspicious of her brother, so tonight he had to convince her all suspicion had been allayed and she could relax, her family was out of danger. He knew Ashe was exhausted and she didn't want to go, she even suggested that maybe resting up for the next round with Godiva's heat would be a good idea, but he needed her there as a distraction.

The truth was, he detested using her that way, but he had to put Evangeline's fears to rest as well as put her family members at ease. He was not an easy man and he knew it. He made others uncomfortable. He didn't fit in at dinner parties. He didn't know all the right forks to use and he didn't care to know. Fyodor could handle all those things. Still, Timur dressed with care. He would do whatever it took to make certain his loved ones were safe, even if that meant deceiving them, and it was never easy to mislead a leopard.

Ashe walked in looking as if she had just stepped off the cover of a magazine. He couldn't believe how beautiful she was. Her hair fell in a waterfall around her face, tumbling down her back, thick and shiny. She had the kind of hair that begged a man to run his fingers through it. Her makeup looked nonexistent, when he knew she had spent some time getting it just right. It emphasized her large, exotic eyes, drawing attention to the dramatic sweep of her lashes and the unusual color of her irises.

Her lips were painted a darker mauve, accentuating the beautiful bow. His heart beat a little faster as she walked in. She wore blue jeans. He knew she didn't have much in the way of clothes, and they'd only brought a small overnight bag, so she only had a couple of items of clothing to choose from, but with Ashe, it didn't matter. The jeans hugged her in all the right places and the dusky-rose-colored top clung to her curves.

"You look beautiful." He breathed the words, shocked that he could actually speak.

"I don't have much in the way of clothes for a dress-up dinner party. I wore the only dress I have earlier and it's really more of a cover-up, not a dress. Evangeline assured me that this would be all right to wear." She ran her hands nervously down her thighs. "What's her family like?"

There it was, the beginning of a careful mixture of truth and deceit. Leopards heard lies. More than ever he had to choose every word.

"I don't know. Evangeline wasn't raised around her

brothers, so she barely knows them. They've been pushing for a closer relationship and I think she wants to explore that."

"Why wasn't she raised with them?"

Timur took another breath and let it out. He was on much safer ground. "Her grandfather was a predator. He liked to abuse women, all women, especially family members. When Evangeline was born, he was told she died immediately. They took her to a cabin they had prepared in the swamp. As she got older she was left there alone, more and more."

Ashe narrowed her eyes at him. "They left a child alone in the swamp?" Disbelief edged her voice.

He nearly laughed. The truth was unbelievable, and that was a good thing for him. He nodded. "They left her there to fend for herself. She got very good at looking out for herself and in the end, she wanted away from all of them."

Ashe shook her head. "And now they want a relationship with her? Why? Because she has something they want?"

"I don't know the answer to that, baby. I hope it's because they really want to get to know her and they're sorry they didn't have that chance when they were children. Remember, her brothers were just kids. They didn't make the decisions and more importantly, we don't know what they were told about Evangeline. Most likely, they were told she died. If their grandfather questioned them, they had to sound believable."

Timur hoped that was the case. He wanted Evangeline to have a family. He knew it was important to her.

"Where were her parents in all this?"

"Her mother is dead. The father is the one who had her living in the swamp. Supposedly, his brother, her uncle Gilbert, knew and helped bring her food and books."

She shook her head. "I would have put a knife through my father's throat before I allowed my child to live alone like that. What a crock."

He burst out laughing. "I'm beginning to realize you're a bloodthirsty little thing."

She tilted her chin at him. "I came here for revenge, remember? Someone took apart my parents and I wanted them to pay."

Timur couldn't help but think about the man waiting for him downstairs in a room few knew about. "They'll pay, Ashe," he assured.

She reached up to brush at the lapels of the sports jacket he wore over a T-shirt. "You look very handsome, although I think you're bound to scare her brothers just a little bit."

He hoped not. He hoped he lulled them into a false sense of security. He caught her chin in his fingers. "If I kiss you, am I going to ruin the work of art you created? Your lips look very kissable."

"It's supposed to stay on until I use a makeup remover. I think that highly unlikely, but we should definitely check it out."

"I'm all for experiments," he murmured and lowered his head.

Her lips were cool and firm, but the moment he touched them with his, the taste, so unique to his woman, burst on his tongue. He had tasted her in his mouth so many times throughout the day, fixating on it, needing more, hungry for just that one flavor—the one that was all Ashe.

He locked his arm around her back and kissed her as if there was no tomorrow. For him, there might not be. He deepened the kiss, needing to take control of her, to let her know she belonged to him. Everything he demanded, she gave to him willingly. He didn't have to fight her, she just surrendered to him.

"I love you." He whispered the truth. He'd never once told another human being that, because, other than his brother and Gorya, and now Evangeline, he hadn't felt that kind of deep, overwhelming affection and trust for another human being. The love he had for Ashe was different. All-consuming. He needed her. She completed him in some way.

Her eyes searched his and then she smiled. "Funny thing, Timur. I don't even know how you did it in so short a time, but I find myself loving you right back."

He wrapped his arm around her and studied her face, waiting for his heart to settle. "I think your lipstick stayed in spite of my best efforts."

Her eyebrows shot up. "That was your best effort? I don't know, Timur. You're slipping. This afternoon was by far better."

"Really? I'll have to try that again."

"Please do."

Everything was fun with her. This time he took his time and made an art out of kissing her. The trouble with kissing Ashe was he never wanted to stop. His body went up in flames and he lost his ability to actually breathe—so much so that he stole her air. Kissing Ashe was insidious. He kissed her once and had to kiss her over and over. He craved her taste and the way her lips felt under his. He needed her body melting into his. Kissing Ashe was dangerous.

This time when he lifted his head, she sagged against him, letting him take her weight. "Do we have to go to this dinner party?" He murmured the question against her forehead.

Her lashes fluttered, and he kissed both of her eyes because he couldn't help himself. That was how little control he had when he was with her.

"You said we did," Ashe pointed out, but she didn't say it with conviction.

He laughed and set her on her feet. "Fyodor asked us as a special favor. Well," he hedged when he knew the ring of truth wasn't there for her to hear, "he didn't exactly ask. He told me I had to be there." That was the strict truth. "You were optional." That was also the truth. "But I knew Evangeline might need to have someone on her side there."

Again, that was true. It was all a matter of twisting the truth to suit his needs. He needed Ashe to believe Evangeline needed her presence there. He cleared his throat. "I want you there because these things are a pain in the neck for me." That was extremely close to the truth.

Ashe was his woman, and she had more compassion in her little finger than he did in his entire body. Of course, she was going to rally, no matter how exhausted she was. "If I start to fall asleep at the table, just pinch me or something."

He grinned at her wickedly. "I'll make the evening very exciting for you if you like."

"Don't you dare do anything to rouse my leopard, or me, for that matter. I'm going to admit to you, I'm very sore. I don't know how Evangeline or other women do this. Having sex is becoming painful."

"Fucking barbs," he said under his breath, but he meant it. It wasn't like they were there all the time. Not on him, anyway. During a heat, he had them and knew his counterpart, Temnyy, had them as well. The more aroused Timur was, the more hormones Ashe had, the more the barbs were triggered.

Most of the time, their women would barely, if at all, feel pain when they withdrew, but for some reason, Ashe's wealth of hormones triggered the animal in him every time. All the bath salts in the world weren't going to help.

"You know she's going to rise again soon, don't you?"

She nodded and took the hand he held out to her. "I know. It's all right. I'll be so hot for you I won't feel anything but good. You always make it amazing for me."

"And then after, you're so tired you can't move."

She flashed her mischievous grin, the one that made him as hard as a rock. "Gets me out of all the cooking and household chores."

He'd been doing both and happily. He found himself smiling at her for no reason other than she was the best thing that had ever happened to him. They walked through the moonlight to the main house, hand in hand again. He had placed his leopards close to the house and also at the outermost positions just in case Evangeline's family was part of a larger conspiracy. Sadly, he was fairly certain that was the case.

His human soldiers were patrolling through the middle sections. They were good men, loyal to Fyodor. Fyodor took care of his soldiers, having been one for many years. They made good money and were given all kinds of extra perks. It was the new age of criminal, with health benefits and retirement built in.

"You have a frown on your face."

He forced himself to smile at her, when he wanted to shred Evangeline's family. One, or more of them, had betrayed her. Ulisse Mancini was hungry for more territory and power. The other crime bosses had cut him off at the knees, but he still found a way around them. He used Emilio Bassini's international pipeline to move his counterfeit money with Emilio's weapons. Now, Timur knew, that wasn't the only thing moved. He trafficked young girls, sending them to Russia, to Lazar. Lazar distributed the girls throughout Europe and sent Ulisse European girls.

One or more of Evangeline's family was in Ulisse's pay. It was the only answer. The one member who had been, for certain, given a tour of the house was her brother Ambroise. That didn't condemn him entirely. Her father and uncle had been to the house as well.

"I'm not a dinner party kind of man, Ashe. I never will be."

Her fingers tightened in his. "Don't worry, honey. I'm good at this kind of thing. I just chat about nothing. It works every time. I'll get you through it."

He believed she could get away with chatting about nothing. Her voice was melodic and anyone listening would want to hear more. She was cute, adorable and gorgeous.

He kissed her fingers and then pulled open the door to the kitchen. He'd chosen to enter the house that way in order to make certain his security force was standing by. He wanted them at every door. He wanted patrols through the house checking windows. He wanted to know every time a guest visited a restroom exactly how much time it took and if they deviated from their destination to look into other rooms. After they were seated back at the table, the rooms they'd been in had to be searched for bugs and to ensure nothing had been left open to allow a hit man to get inside.

He nodded to young Jeremiah, the bane of his life. Of course, Gorya would put him in the kitchen where he could make the fewest mistakes. With his hand on Ashe's back, he moved through the large room quickly to get to the dining room. The table was set for eight, Evangeline's four family members, and Fyodor, Evangeline, Ashe and him. He had made certain to tell Fyodor to put him across from her family.

Evangeline had done so. He could see the little name tags above each place setting. She'd used the more formal china, the set he knew she never used. His heart contracted. She was making the dinner as nice as she could for her family. She wanted things to work out between them. If it was possible, he wanted to make certain she never knew that one of them had betrayed her.

They went through the dining room to the great room. Instantly, Temnyy went crazy. He recognized the visitors were leopard, and that meant four males were there when his female was in heat. Temnyy didn't like many people, so adding these four to the mix at such a bad time wasn't the best of ideas.

Evangeline looked up when they entered and relief immediately came over her face. "Timur. Ashe. I'm so glad you could make it." She waved them over to be introduced.

Ambroise Tregre was tall and sinewy. He might have the roped muscles of a shifter, but if he did, they were well hidden. He wore a sports jacket over an emerald tee, tucked into dark jeans. He looked classy. His clothes screamed of money, just the opposite of his brother.

Christophe Tregre had just returned from a seven-month stay in Borneo with Drake's friends. He was fit, his muscles moving not so subtly beneath the thin, stretched dark-colored tee he wore with his fitted jeans. He could be considered a good-looking man, although next to his brother's handsome face, some might call him too rough-looking. His hands showed hard work, where Ambroise's were soft with perfectly manicured nails.

In contrast to the two younger men, Evangeline's father, Beau Tregre, had lines in his face and showed his age. Few leopards could tolerate much alcohol, but the man looked like he had, at some time in his past, drunk a great deal. His hair was gray and he hadn't bothered to clean up the way his sons had. He wore bibbed overalls that were stained with oil. At least they were clean and didn't reek of the swamp.

Her uncle, Gilbert Tregre, was a little shorter than Beau and his face was a road map. His lips were thin, and he avoided Timur's eyes when they were introduced. Like his brother, he had the signs of an obvious drinker. He looked like a man beaten down by life, or one looking for revenge. Timur couldn't quite make up his mind.

They made small talk until they were called into the dining room. Timur was seated straight across from Evangeline's father and Christophe. Ambroise sat beside his brother with his uncle on his other side. That put Evangeline's two brothers between their father and uncle. The two older men barely looked at each other.

Timur was certain they were at odds, so why would both come? Why pretend they weren't? What had caused the rift between them? When everyone was served and eating, his woman kept up her part, chatting away, laughing softly at Christophe's replies until Timur wanted to shake her, but she was the one keeping the conversation going.

He hadn't expected to feel pure, black jealousy. Temnyy raged, scraping cruelly at him, wanting the strangers gone. The cat wasn't alone. Christophe had concentrated completely on Ashe, as if no one else existed. Evangeline's father mumbled a few replies to his daughter's questions, but for the most part, neither of the two older men had much to say. Both of them seemed focused on Ashe as well. Timur couldn't blame them. She was in heat, and they couldn't fail to scent the pheromones or see the glow on her skin. Their leopards had to be raging.

"Ambroise? That's true? You draw?" Ashe asked.

Timur immediately tuned in on the conversation.

"He doesn't just draw," Christophe declared. "He's a master at it. Anything he sees he can make beautiful. He sketched this room for me, in fact the entire house. I couldn't get here when he came to visit you, and he told me he'd make certain I saw every detail. He drew every room and I don't think there was one detail missing right down to the ornate hat rack in the hall."

Timur didn't look at his brother. He didn't speak. Evangeline would know immediately if he did. He mentally nudged Ashe, hoping she would say something to continue the conversation.

"I make mistakes," Ambroise said, color flushing his skin.

"What does that drawing get you? I told you to get rid of those pencils of yours and get a real job," his uncle sneered. "Always prancing around thinking you're better than us. Next thing you know, you'll get yourself a sugar mama so you can feed off the money tit just like your sister did."

"You've had enough to drink, Gilbert," Beau said. "If you can't be polite to my children, you'll have to leave."

"Didn't want to come in the first place," Gilbert muttered and stood up, his chair crashing over backward. He didn't bother to right it. "Don't have a way back home so I'll wait in the car."

Timur glanced at Gorya, who stood in the shadows. Gorya's nod was imperceptible. He slipped out of the room, tailing after Evangeline's uncle, who staggered a little. As he stumbled out, he pulled a little flask from his pocket and took a drink.

"I'm sorry about your uncle, honey," Beau said. "He's gotten very resentful, and all he does is drink these days. Drake sent your cousin Axel to Borneo and he stayed there, workin' with Drake's friends. Gilbert hasn't been the same. He'll sleep it off in the car and feel the fool for making a scene."

"It's all right," Evangeline said immediately, dismissing the entire incident.

Timur didn't dismiss it so easily. He leaned toward Ambroise. "You were telling us about your sketching. Do you sell your work?" He poured genuine interest into his voice. He was interested, just not for the reasons it appeared.

Ashe beamed at him. Evangeline smiled gratefully. Ambroise squirmed a little and then glanced at his father.

Christophe wasn't so shy. "He's sold several. In fact, he had a showin' the other night and it was a huge success. You should get somethin' he's done and put it in your home, Evangeline. His drawings are beautiful, and eventually they're going to be worth a fortune. I've been tellin' him to quit his job and sketch full-time."

"The sketches of my home aren't up for sale, are they?" Evangeline asked.

"No, of course not," Ambroise said hastily. He stirred cream into his coffee. "You need privacy, and it would be a security risk. Christophe made that very clear to me. The drawings were just for him. There was a discrepancy I couldn't quite account for, and I like talking things over with Christophe because he . . ." He trailed off, waving his hand in the air as if that gesture finished his sentence.

"He what?" Ashe encouraged.

Ambroise looked more uncomfortable than ever. He

squirmed on the chair, his face flushed with embarrassment. "When I bring him a math equation, he doesn't act like I'm a total lunatic."

"Eccentric," Christophe corrected.

Timur's phone vibrated. He pulled it out and glanced at the screen beneath the table. The text was from Gorya. Evidently, Evangeline's uncle was wandering around outside the house. Timur discreetly texted back to allow the man enough rope to hang himself.

"What was the discrepancy?" Evangeline persisted.

Ambroise shrugged and looked once more to his brother, as if the man would bail him out of the awkward conversation.

"The measurements were off in each of the rooms with the outside of the house. In other words, sister, you either have the thickest walls known to mankind, or you have secret passageways in your home." Christophe smirked. "You can't hide much from a mathematician artist like Ambroise."

Evangeline slipped her hand into Fyodor's and glanced at Timur. He kept his face blank as he chewed the filet mignon the chef had broiled to perfection. He was uncertain how best to handle the situation. Anything he said would tip off Evangeline to the fact that he was going to interrogate her brothers and father and definitely her snake of an uncle, who wasn't in the least bit drunk.

"Ambroise, what wonderful gifts you've been given," Ashe said, her eyes soft. Her features showed nothing but appreciation. "I can't wait to visit the gallery where you're showing some of your work. Evangeline, we'll have to go. Maybe you wouldn't mind showing us around," she added.

Ambroise sent her a shy smile. "I'd like that actually. I especially wanted Evangeline to see my sketches of the swamp. Some of them are really good, but others, I'm just missing some little detail. It keeps me up at night thinking about it. Charisse and Armande took me out around their property, and Armande even walked through the swamp with me, but I just can't get it right."

"It?" Evangeline said. "What are you looking for?"

He frowned and put down his fork. "I draw the trees and brush and even the moss with no problem, but when it comes to the water, it's never right. *Never.*" Frustration edged his voice.

Timur had to believe Ambroise's irritation was genuine. He didn't even seem to be tasting the food, which was more than excellent. Beau and Christophe had no trouble eating everything put before them.

"It's probably because the water changes all the time," Evangeline said. "From one moment to the next. Wind, leaves, wildlife, snakes, birds, all of it touches the surface and changes the look. More than once I've seen what looks like diamonds glittering on the surface. Other times, that same area gleamed like glass. Another time it was a mirror, reflecting everything around it."

Ambroise started to stand, but Christophe waved him back to his chair. "Sit and eat. You can sketch later."

"But she's right. The things she's saying, those are the details I need . . ." Eagerness edged his voice.

"You never forget a thing," Christophe said. "Never. You'll remember if Evangeline hiccups." He grinned at his sister. "You look good, *belle soeur.* I wanted to make certain you were well taken care of, and I see that you are. You look happy." He sat back, his gaze going to Fyodor. "I'm looking for a job."

Evangeline frowned and shook her head, looking up at her husband. He curled his fingers around the nape of her neck. "What position were you thinking?"

"Security. I've worked in Borneo, and Drake's been working with me as well. I've brought a résumé, but hoped you'd give me consideration because I'm family."

Evangeline looked as if she might faint she went so pale. Timur knew she didn't like Gorya or him working as bodyguards for Fyodor. She certainly didn't want her brother taking that same position. Timur didn't like anyone being a question mark.

"Timur is head of my security detail here on the estate," Fyodor said easily. "He can interview you later and we'll see what we have available."

"You're not working with your father?" Evangeline sounded desperate.

"He's *our* father," Christophe reminded, but his voice was gentle. "He works for Charisse and Armande at their perfume company. It isn't my idea of work. I enjoyed getting out of the swamp but I need a place that—" He broke off, looking at Ashe. Clearly, he meant where his leopard could run. "I want to see more of you, Evangeline. This is a chance for me."

Ashe moved, suddenly uncomfortable, squirming in her seat and then trying to cover the movement by dropping her spoon. She reached down to pick it up from the floor and when she did, she looked a little desperately at Timur. He cursed under his breath. He couldn't be distracted. Temnyy leapt for the surface, at the first hint that his mate had woken.

"I suppose Timur interviewing you would be okay," Evangeline ventured, clearly not liking the idea.

"I've heard you're making quite a name for yourself with your bakery," Beau said, leaning back in his chair as a maid came in and removed plates. He kept his gaze fixed on his daughter. "I've been thinkin' of ways I could help you, make up for your childhood."

Timur kept his features blank. He didn't make the mistake of looking at Fyodor. There was something off in Beau's tone. He had the feeling they were about to hear the real reason Beau Tregre was sitting at his daughter's table.

"You could ship all over the country. Why keep your baked goods just here? You get a website, and people order from you. I'm used to packin' boxes. I've been doin' it for years for Charisse and Armande. You'd do three times the business you're doin' now, maybe more."

There it was. The real reason they were there. Timur hated being right. Out of the corner of his eye, he saw Fyodor lean into Evangeline, brushing his mouth along her neck.

Ashe put her hand on Timur's thigh and squeezed tight, her fingers digging deep into his muscle, feeling desperate. Her body was throwing off so much heat he felt as if he was sitting next to a furnace. A leopard didn't leave his mate in a world of hurt. When she was in heat, his first priority had to be her. Timur had never felt so torn in his life. He needed to hear what Beau had to say, and he needed to leave.

He bent his head to Ashe, and pressed his mouth tight to her ear. "Can you hang on, baby?"

She swallowed hard but, with her eyes steady on his, she nodded. His heart stuttered. He had the most fantastic woman imaginable. She didn't know what exactly was going on, but she knew it was important. Her fingers dug into his thigh even deeper beneath the tablecloth. He put his palm over her hand and pressed in an effort to reassure her.

"*Pere.*" Christophe sounded as if he was choosing his words carefully. "We talked about this. We agreed it wasn't a good idea, remember?"

"*You* and Ambroise agreed it wasn't a good idea, but here you are, askin' your sister for a job and you don' want your old man to get in on the action. What I'm offerin' would be big."

Before Evangeline could shut down the conversation, Timur leaned toward her father. "What exactly would you do?"

Beau grinned at him, relaxing now that he had his moment to explain. "We could pattern the website right after the Mercier site. Ambroise can put the site together for us, can't you, boy?" He pinned his son with a steely gaze.

Ambroise shook his head, but looked at his older brother, not his father.

Before Christophe could speak, Beau continued. "The orders go up, they pay with credit cards and then either Gilbert or I pack the boxes every day. One will pack here and the other in New Orleans. We don' want to leave the Merciers in the lurch. When we start makin' enough money here, we can turn the perfume business over to someone else."

"You do realize that would mean Evangeline would have to work three or four times as hard as she does now," Fyodor said in a quiet voice. That voice tipped off everyone in the room to the fact that he was the boss and no one would do a damn thing without his permission.

Timur felt Ashe shiver and realized Fyodor had never pulled rank on her. She only saw him as Evangeline's husband and his brother. Now, he looked every inch the predator he was. He was the big shark in the room, not Evangeline's father. He pressed her hand down harder on his thigh and surrounded it with his fingers, caging it in. She had his protection. She'd committed to him and that made her family. Fyodor's family as well. She needed to know that.

There was an awkward silence. Beau tapped his fingers on the table. He didn't look at Fyodor, but kept his gaze fixed on his daughter's face, as if he could will her to do whatever he wanted. Before she could speak, Fyodor leaned back in his chair and took Evangeline's hand, raising her fingertips to his mouth.

"My wife is pregnant, Beau, with twins. You're going to be a grandfather." He looked from one brother to another. "You're going to be uncles."

Timur hadn't taken his eyes from Beau. His heart sank at the ugly expression that flitted across that heavily lined face. Everyone thought him weak. Beau had been supposedly trapped by his father into a criminal business and then threatened so he was afraid to quit. Timur didn't believe it for a moment. This man was evil. The way he looked at his sons, the way he looked at Evangeline, there was no love there. He was out for himself.

"That's wonderful," Beau murmured. He poured enough sincerity into his voice that it was believable to everyone but Timur. His gaze flicked over Ashe. There was speculation there, and something else Timur didn't like. Temnyy slammed his body hard against the confines that held him. He really didn't like the way Beau looked at Ashe.

Timur wasn't certain if anyone else caught the expression on Evangeline's father's face. He shifted his gaze just enough to look at the man's two sons. Ambroise stared into his coffee cup, carefully avoiding his father's eyes. Christophe still looked angry, but he managed a quick smile in his sister's direction.

"Twins? You don't believe in doing anything the easy way, do you, *belle soeur*? Are you feeling all right?"

Evangeline shook her head. "I'm pretty sick most of the time."

"How are you getting the bakin' done?"

"So far, I've managed, but Ashe is working with me now. I'm hoping if I run into trouble, she'll be able to keep the bakery open."

Beau beamed. "That's good thinkin', Evangeline. Always have a backup plan when it comes to business. Your friend can help you bake even when you expand the business."

Now it had gone from her father suggesting she expand, to him acting as though it was a done deal. Timur still was uncertain about Christophe and Ambroise. Ambroise had sketched the entire layout of Fyodor's house for his brother, and mentioned that the measurements of the rooms were off. Christophe had guessed correctly that there were secret passageways built into the mansion. He had also just gotten Evangeline to admit that Ashe helped her with the baking.

The entire family was suspect as far as he was concerned. He was getting regular updates on the uncle, who had abandoned his drunken persona and was walking around the house, probably looking for weak points in security. The leopards watched him, but stayed out of sight. He had to smell them, but he also had no way of knowing the last time the leopards had been present in the yard.

"It will be good to build our own family empire," Beau said. "I've never liked working for Charisse and Armande."

"I thought they were easy to work for," Christophe said. "They have good benefits, the best in the region. They give out bonuses at the end of the year . . ."

"They make the money. Hand over fist, they make the money," Beau corrected. "It isn't about the work environment, it's about the fact that we work from sunup until sundown for someone else. Evangeline knows what I mean, don't you, girl? It's better to have your own business and control the flow of the money."

"Do you think having money is that important?" Ashe asked.

The older man turned his gaze on her. His leopard had to be acting up. All the males had to be. The pheromones coming off Ashe were potent. Her skin glowed. She looked absolutely beautiful sitting there. Timur had all he could do to keep his features blank when Beau looked at her so speculatively. It wasn't all his leopard either. Beau didn't like women. He clearly had the drive of the leopard, but he didn't like it.

"Of course, it's very important. You'll learn that as you get older."

"Are you worried about retirement?" Timur asked, mostly to get the man's attention off of Ashe. That look made his skin crawl, and he couldn't imagine what it made Ashe feel like. Threatened, most likely, because that was what it felt like to him.

Beau nodded. "That's somethin' everyone has to look at when they hit my age. I put some away, but not near enough. Gilbert and I have been tryin' to figure out how to make more money fast before we hang it up." He turned his gaze back on his daughter. "I did my share of fishin' and huntin' to keep you kids fed. I'm willin' to do the work, gettin' Ambroise to set up the website and then fillin' the orders. Don' think that's askin' too much in return for what I did when you were young."

"What did you do, Beau?" Fyodor asked. "Because my understanding is you put your daughter out in the swamp and left her there."

Beau narrowed his eyes, glaring at Evangeline. "Is that what you told him? I saved you, girl. I saved you from your grandfather. He was a mean, vicious killer and he liked to get his hands on females. Age didn't matter to him."

"What did your wife think of him?" Timur asked, turning the attention back to him.

"My wife?" Beau sat up straight, alarm skittering over his face and then, there it was, for just that few seconds, distaste, rage even. Then he had control and he looked sorrowful. Very sad. "She was afraid of him. She begged me to hide Evangeline from the old man. I did as she asked, although it was difficult to leave a child under those circumstances."

Ashe leaned into Timur, and he knew he had to get her out of there. She'd done as he'd asked and held out for as long as she possibly could. "I hate to break up the dinner party, particularly before dessert, but we have to go. It was nice to meet all of you. Ambroise, I'd definitely like to see your work. Perhaps we'll have an opportunity to talk later. And, Christophe, leave your résumé and make certain your number is on it. I'll call you in the next day or so and set up an interview. Beau, it was very nice to finally get to meet you."

Timur rose and drew Ashe up as well, pulling her to his side, tucking her beneath his shoulder. He wrapped his arm around her, trying to shelter her, to keep Beau and the others from seeing her distress.

She waved toward Fyodor and Evangeline. Timur hated to leave his brother and sister-in-law alone with her family, but he knew they would both understand. He'd already texted the guards and Rodion and Kyanite had slipped into the room, each standing by a door. Beau couldn't fail to notice them, but he didn't say anything. Christophe had glanced up as they came in and then looked over to Timur, but he hadn't said anything either. Ambroise appeared not to notice, but Timur wasn't buying it. The man saw every detail and was able to sketch from memory. He would definitely notice two men entering the dining room at his sister's dinner party.

Timur shook his head as he ushered Ashe out. Intrigue wasn't his specialty. He didn't like games or pretense. He got to the truth in a much more direct way, one that assured him he knew who was selling them out and who was loyal.

15

"I CAN'T stand my clothes on one more minute," Ashe whispered.

Timur couldn't stand his either. His cock was raging. His leopard was raging. The grounds were crawling with leopards, all male. The last thing he needed was to turn a female in heat loose in the middle of so many. There was also a large human security force moving through the grounds. One glimpse of a leopard and panic would ensue.

"We have to get to the house, baby. You can do it." He poured confidence into his voice, when he wasn't feeling it. He'd waited too long. He'd gotten more information, but it was all speculation, not fact. His conclusions might be based on experience, but he still didn't have enough in the way of proof to eliminate any threat to Fyodor or Evangeline.

Ashe made a small sound of distress and began to move away from him, in the direction of the forest and tea garden with its high walls. No way was he trusting the other males to remain away from a female in heat, especially one throwing off such potent pheromones. Controlling leopards under those circumstances would be nearly impossible.

He caught her up, tossed her over his shoulder and began to jog toward the guesthouse. Every step hurt, and he knew by the way she clutched his shirt, dragging it up to expose the skin of his back, that she was in dire straits. He felt her tongue lapping at him. The pads of her fingers reached down the waistband of the trousers he wore. Each touch was pure fire dancing over his skin. He wanted her with every cell in his body. He was so completely tuned to her, he nearly missed the scent of the leopard stalking them.

He stopped abruptly as Temnyy raked at him, hissing a warning. Very gently he put Ashe on her feet. "I need you to get to the house right now," he said, shrugging out of his sports jacket. He caught the hem of his tee as he toed his shoes off. Ripping the tee over his head, he moved out into the middle of the rolling lawn that stretched between the two houses.

Ashe shook her head. "I can't, Timur. Don't ask me to do that."

He flicked her a cold gaze, noting the agitation she betrayed with the way her fingers twisted together repeatedly. "I wasn't asking. You fucking do as you're told." He counted to three and then stepped right into her, looking down at her face. Eye to eye. Breath to breath. His resolve only deepened. *"Now."* He couldn't watch her as he fought a leopard. Others might take the opportunity to try to take his female.

Ashe nodded, those long lashes fluttering. She turned and started to run back toward the guesthouse. She hadn't gotten more than a few feet when a large male leopard rushed from the heavy foliage around the garage. He cut off her escape and began a slow stalk toward her. Ashe skidded to a halt and raised one hand defensively to her throat. She looked to Timur for instructions.

"He's trying to force you to shift, baby," he said softly.

Timur didn't recognize the leopard, but knew by the scent that it was Gilbert, Evangeline's uncle. "Once your female is out, he would try to force her to mate with him. I've got this. The moment the fight starts, you get to the safety of the house."

He stripped the trousers from his body, his eyes never leaving his opponent. The man might be older, but his leopard was in good shape and had seen a few fights. The Tregre brothers might pretend to the world that they were beaten down and timid old men, but they weren't. This leopard proved that. He was fit and bore scars from numerous fights with other leopards.

"You know where the weapons are, and you know how to use them. If he comes through that door, you kill him. It's Evangeline's uncle." He needed her to know, man or leopard, either would try to force her compliance.

Timur called Temnyy and shifted almost instantaneously. Even as he shifted, he launched himself, running full bore at the leopard. He hit him with the force of a freight train, slamming into the cat's side, driving him back several feet before the leopard lost his footing and was down. Rolling. Snarling. Scrambling for a purchase in the soft dirt with his claws so he could drag himself to his feet.

Temnyy slammed into his side again, in exactly the same spot, hoping to crack the dense bones there. He raked viciously with his claws, tearing at the leopard's underbelly, teeth ripping at the nearest ear. He spat it out and clawed for the leopard's nearest eye. The entire attack had only been seconds, but he'd damaged his opponent immediately and severely.

He didn't back off as most leopards would. He was as ruthless and merciless as his human counterpart. More so. Shifters gave their rivals opportunities to run. Timur knew Gilbert would never have given Ashe the opportunity to say no. If she'd said it, no matter how adamant she was, the man would have forced her cooperation. His leopard would have forcibly taken her female.

The leopard rolled away from him, angling to his left, just as Temnyy knew he would. When the cat started to get to his feet, Temnyy was on him, landing hard on his back, deliberately going for the spinal cord, teeth driving deep at the back of the neck. The neck was thick with loose skin and old scars, but it didn't stop Timur's male. He was vicious in a fight. He was used to fighting for his life, fighting to the death, and he didn't hesitate.

Temnyy wanted the leopard dead, but, even more, Timur wanted the man dead. It would be one less enemy to keep track of. There was no doubt in his mind that Gilbert Tregre was one of the worst, and probably one of the most successful criminals. No one had ever suspected him. Even when he got caught red-handed, he'd acted his way out of his crime. He'd fooled Drake Donovan and an entire lair of law enforcement leopards.

"Stop. You have to stop." Evangeline rushed toward the two snarling leopards.

Fyodor caught her and held her back. Beau watched as Temnyy bit down hard into the neck of his brother's leopard, but he didn't say a word, nor did he try to shift. Christophe began to rip his shirt off, while Ambroise backed away from the two fighting cats.

"Don't," Fyodor commanded Christophe. "Timur, take control of your leopard and back off. Gilbert is finished. You're going to kill him."

Timur cursed under his breath. He'd only been fighting for less than three minutes maximum and already they were surrounded by others. Ashe, thankfully, had done as he'd asked and was safe inside the guesthouse. He had no choice but to stop Temnyy from killing Gilbert's leopard. He couldn't very well kill him in front of Evangeline, but it was going to happen and soon.

He forced Temnyy to let go of the other cat's throat.

Gilbert's cat lay panting and submissive, terrified to move one inch. Temnyy reacted the way all triumphant cats did. He snarled, paced, swiped his paw at his fallen challenger and then raced back to grip him in a suffocating hold. Timur took a firmer hold on his cat. Snarling, Temnyy once again complied, backing away.

When he got his leopard calm enough, he directed him toward the guesthouse and away from the humans. He wasn't feeling very humane himself in that moment. He wanted to rend and tear and rip into Evangeline's family. He wanted to snarl at his brother for stopping him from killing. Mostly, he needed to get to Ashe. Her scent had driven him crazy and Temnyy was even more so, in the throes of their females being in heat.

Deliberately, Timur shifted, going to his full height instantly, walking naked, his back to them, letting Evangeline's family see what they were dealing with. He had scars. Masses of them on his back, buttocks and thighs. They were from leopards as well as from whatever implement his father had thought would induce the most pain the fastest. Let them see that he'd survived all that.

They needed to learn respect. Temnyy was a vicious combatant, one that no other leopard should challenge unless they were prepared to die. He didn't fight to allow his enemy to come back another day. He fought to kill. He stalked into the house and slammed the door hard, letting his brother know he could go to hell. There would be no one disturbing him until his woman was completely sated and so tired she couldn't move.

She was waiting for him, the gun on the table beside her hand. She had stripped down to her bra and panties in anticipation of his win. He would talk to her about that later; right now, there was only one thing to do. He didn't stop walking once the door was closed. He stalked right across the room, knocking away the one chair blocking him with a swipe of his hand, clearing his path to her.

He went right up to her, caught the front of her bra with one hand and ripped down as he fisted her hair, tipped up her face and slammed his mouth down on hers. *Fuck. Fuck.* She was pure fire. The heat hit like a fireball, pouring down his throat and rushing through his veins to settle into a storm of flames in his groin.

He walked her backward until she was pinned against the wall and he could lift her, taking her left breast into his mouth, wanting to swallow her whole. He sucked hard, heard her cries, felt her fists in his hair, her body squirming against his. His settled her on his thigh, so she could rub all that fiery heat over him while he suckled. He worked her right nipple hard, feeling the flow of liquid every time he tugged or rolled. He raked with his teeth, bit down lightly, lapped with his tongue, used the suction of his mouth to drive her wild.

He was wild, feral almost, the adrenaline from the fight in his bloodstream, driving him to greater peaks of hunger and need. He was desperate for her, needing to hear her moans, needing her to surrender everything she was to him. He would take nothing less. His mouth moved from her nipples to the undersides of her breasts, determined to claim every inch of her. There would be no doubt who she belonged to before the night was over.

He used his teeth there, his tongue, sucking and then gently biting his way around her breasts and down her belly. Her moans and pleas added to the thundering roar in his ears. He slid his hands down her spine, taking her in, feeling every inch of her that he could reach. His woman. His heart jerked so hard in his chest he was afraid it would shatter.

He was on his knees, yanking her thighs apart, catching every drop of honey she had. Ruthless with his tongue, desperate for everything she was. Ashe. He was so in love with her he wasn't certain what to do with the overwhelming emotion that shook him to his very foundation.

Timur knew, in the throes of a female leopard's heat, sex was rough and hot, but he also knew his woman was sore. She had to be scared after what had happened with his challenger. He needed to find a way to temper the drive their leopards gave them.

She shattered twice and then he was taking her down to the floor, knowing he'd never make it into the bedroom. He framed her face with his hands and looked into eyes that were ringed heavily, eyes so amber they glowed at him.

"I never want you to think for one moment that I don't love you. That I'm with you for my leopard, Ashe. I'm with you for me." He brushed kisses over both eyes. He wished there was another word to use. People loved all kinds of things. Men said it to women everywhere, but then walked away. He could never walk away from her. He knew it would be impossible to lose the feeling that was so strong it shook him.

He guided his cock into her, determined to be gentle when his body was desperate to surge into her. He watched her face for any signs of discomfort. "Tell me," he commanded when she winced. When he stopped, she tried to push herself onto him. "I need to know what this feels like."

Her tongue moistened her lips. He groaned and kissed her. How could he possibly resist that invitation? When he did, he slipped a little deeper into her. She felt like silk wrapping around him tightly. Scorching hot. It was difficult to hold himself still.

"Good, Timur. It feels good," she whispered, touching his face, skimming her finger over his rough jaw. She let that finger move down his chest, as if she was just tracing his muscles.

His body reacted to the feel of her touch, but it was his heart that seemed in the most jeopardy. "Tell me everything."

"It burns, but in a good way. I feel like I'm going up in flames and only you can take the burn away. I don't know how something that feels so good can make me feel so desperate."

He kissed her, because he was feeling a little desperate himself. It wasn't easy holding back, not when everything in him insisted he let the fire consume him. He threaded his fingers through hers and drew her arms up above her head.

"Look at me, Ashe. Look at me while I move in you." He fought his body to give her slow. To give her gentle. Her eyes were wide open, staring into his. Her sheath clamped hard around his cock, scorching hot, the friction incredible, so that his entire body shuddered with pleasure. The way she looked at him shook him. Those amber eyes drifted possessively over his face, as if he was a good man, a white knight, the best man in the world.

"When you look at me like that, baby, I feel like I'm worth something." The admission came out against her mouth where he took her breath into his lungs.

"You're everything to me, Timur," she whispered back.

His heart turned over when he heard the truth in her voice. Her hips moved, rising to meet his, until there was no holding back for either of them. He was loving her with every stroke, every surge into her, every streak of lightning that he induced in her. Then they both were going up in flames and floating together. He kept his hold on her, fingers tight through hers while they drifted down.

He took her twice more, once bent over the kitchen table and once against the wall. He tried to be careful, but their leopards drove them and there was no going back from that. He took her into the bedroom, where he could press warm cloths between her legs in an effort to ease the soreness. She was small. He was on the larger side. Rough sex might sound great, and for him, felt great, but for her, no matter how good it was, the aftermath was something else and he didn't like it, nor did he know what to do about it.

"How are we going to let them run? Godiva wants out. How are we going to let them mate?" Ashe whispered, as if the leopards wouldn't hear them. "There are male leopards everywhere. Temnyy can't fight them all off."

Temnyy could and would, but Timur wasn't going to tell her that. "Tell her a few more minutes." He wanted to make certain Ashe had time to rest. He had a plan to let the leopards run, just not on this part of the estate. Not with so many guards out.

He stroked back her hair, enjoying just lying next to her, his body curled protectively around hers.

"Timur." She rolled over and propped herself up on one elbow. "Is there any way out of all of this? I know you're in deep, that it was something you were born into, but we don't need to be a part of it, do we?"

Her voice trembled and when she touched him, he felt the same tremor in her fingers. He wanted to give her everything and knew she was thinking of a future with him, a future with children.

"I'm sorry, *malen'kiy smerch.* For the first time in my life, when Drake Donovan laid the plan out for us, I felt like we were part of something worthwhile. I might still have to live dirty, but we're cleaning up the worst of the criminal lairs. That's what we do, Ashe, and I'm proud to be a part of it. Coming from a lair that was so violent and vile, seeing the cruelty of men driven by killer leopards, I felt shame at who I was, at what I was. Drake gave us a sense of purpose. He made us feel that those years we had behind us, years of being forced to do our father's bidding, would finally be of help to someone, maybe make up for some of the shit things we had to do."

Ashe leaned into him and brushed a kiss along the heavy muscles of his chest. "I'm not certain I understand what you mean. You told me, but tell me again. Make me understand so I feel that the two of us staying here, living with the cops coming at us and enemies everywhere, is worth it. You're worth it, but I have to know that the things you do are worth it as well."

She hadn't pulled away, and that gave him a sense of relief. She didn't react until she had all the information, and he loved her all the more for that. She'd need that a lot with him.

"Drake's idea was to take out the worst of the criminal leopards from the inside. Elijah Lospostos, like me, was born into a world of violence and crime. He inherited the mantle but didn't want it. By the time he realized it was impossible to get out, he'd met Drake Donovan. Drake runs an agency that goes anywhere in the world and retrieves kidnap victims. He also works with Jake Bannaconni to take down the worst criminals." He would explain it to her over and over until she understood what they were trying to do.

Ashe frowned. "If you're already working undercover, you could at least go to someone in law enforcement . . ." When he shook his head, she rubbed her finger along his jaw. "It's a way out, Timur. For all of you. At least the cops would be off your backs."

"That would be too risky. Sooner or later someone would be on a payroll and we'd be running for our lives. This way, we're in a close-knit group. We have to rely on one another. That group is growing faster than we anticipated. We were only supposed to go after leopards. The world of shifters has different rules than human law, and we handle the criminals accordingly, but now, it seems as if we have to make a decision whether or not to include humans we know are particularly ruthless and just plain fucked-up."

"Like Ulisse and his human trafficking."

He nodded, watching her closely, his heart pounding, adrenaline racing through his veins.

She bit down on her lower lip, her lashes fluttering against her cheek. "It's even more dangerous than if you were a criminal, Timur."

"I *am* a criminal, Ashe. The friends you're going to have

will be the wives of the men I trust. Our children will play with their children. There will always be bodyguards and guns and me telling you or the kids no to something you want to do."

She seemed more committed now, and interested, as if she was trying to figure out a way to help him, to help them all and find where she might fit in their world. She asked him questions, dozens of them, and he answered as honestly as he could. He found her interest settled him just a little more.

Ashe rose up on her elbows, looking him straight in the eye. "You're not just staying for your brother, are you, Timur? I need to know absolutely that you're committed to me, that if you had a choice, you'd go with me far from this life."

He had to think about that. Would he leave Fyodor? Would he leave his life here? What would he do? He wasn't capable of doing many other things. "I'm absolutely committed to you, Ashe," he acknowledged. Those, he knew, were the truest words he'd ever spoken. "As for the leaving this life and my brother, I honestly don't know. If I had to choose, I would choose you every single time. I'm not staying just for him. But if we left, we would be hunted for the rest of our days by both sides. More, this is my only chance to make a difference, to hopefully make something good come out of the bad I was born into."

He watched her closely to see her reaction. Ashe nodded her head. "Thank you. It was important to me that you told me the truth."

What did that mean? He didn't have time to find out because already, the next wave of heat was surrounding him. Flames licked at his skin and fire rolled through his body.

His cock rose and immediately she was there, her mouth bringing the conflagration to a roaring inferno. He forgot what he was telling her. Forgot everything but watching her swallow him, letting himself feel the absolute pleasure she gave him every time her mouth was on him.

She rolled over top of him, straddling him. At once he felt the heat of her center, burning his skin. "I need you again, and then Godiva needs Temnyy. Desperately, Timur." She fisted his thick girth and then slid right over top of him, engulfing him completely.

The breath left his lungs in a rush. She didn't wait, but began to move, grinding down, setting a fast pace, taking him deep, her muscles clamping down on his cock as she rode him. His hands went to her swaying breasts, working her nipples, watching her breath hitch every time he tugged or pinched. She was beautiful, leaving him astonished that she could be his.

There was no holding back, not when her breasts jolted and swayed with every powerful move of her hips. Not when her body undulated and seduced. Not when she was temptation and sin with every breath she drew. His mouth was everywhere, his hands claiming her. Then he took over, pulling out of her, flipping her onto her hands and knees and surging deep again. She screamed his name several times before he emptied himself into her.

Temnyy's need was just as urgent as theirs. He caught her hand and tugged her up, liking that his seed was on her thighs and inside of her. "We're going out the far window and making a run for the garage. Once inside, go to the Jeep."

"I need clothes . . ."

"What for? We're heading for the hill country. The estate is several miles wide and equally as long. We'll get them away from the sentries and let them run. We don't need clothes for that."

She didn't argue with him but shot him a mischievous look that sent his cock into a frenzy of need again. She was up to something. He went out the window first, and he waited for her. She was much smaller, and it was easier for her to slip through without making a sound. Timur thought it was good practice for her to sneak through an enemy's line. She didn't want to be caught naked and that gave her the necessary incentive to stay low and move fast.

He led the way until they were close to the garage and then stepped back and waved her ahead of him. He loved her ass. The way it swayed, the firmness of her cheeks, the little dimples just above the swell of them. When she made it to the door of the garage, he pressed close to her, patting her cheeks with firm, hard swats and then rubbing the pink handprints.

"Stop, you crazy man," she hissed over her shoulder. "Someone will hear."

"Do you think I care?" He knew he was experiencing the inevitable high one got from being in the throes of a leopard's mating ritual.

She cast him one more look of pure censure and then raced to the Jeep. Heat banded as Temnyy pushed close, but Timur refused to allow him to shift. He hurled himself into the driver's seat, pressed the garage opener and turned the key. There was no top on the vehicle and the wind rushed over them, cooling their bodies as he turned onto the narrow dirt track that led into the vineyard.

They passed two guards, both leopards who watched as they hurtled past. Ashe's laughter teased his senses. She could turn a situation such as this one, where their leopards tore at them and their bodies drove them, into pure fun. She held on to the bar and pulled herself into a standing position as he took them around the dark vineyard and up to the higher hills. He knew where every guard was stationed, he had been the one to position them, so he knew when they were outside the boundaries.

He slowed the Jeep, so she could feel the wind on her face and body. Her legs acted as springs, and her body swayed with the movement of the vehicle. She laughed again. "It's a perfect night, Timur."

It hadn't been, but now it was. Being with her made his entire life different. It gave him meaning and purpose. Before, he had thought maybe the work they were doing would make his world right, but it hadn't. There had been nothing at all to temper the violence. Now, there was Ashe.

The vineyards rolled with hills and then gave way to more trees. He parked the Jeep and watched as she jumped down and took off running. Her hair flew out behind her and every muscle rippled beneath her satin skin. He slid out from behind the wheel, keeping his eyes on her as he stretched and then he took two running steps and shifted.

Temnyy leapt after her as if shot from a gun. Ashe glanced over her shoulder, saw the large leopard, and her laughter and small squeal of alarm floated back to him. She had to stop to shift. She hadn't practiced enough yet and Timur made a mental note to make certain she did so as soon as possible. Sometimes the difference between life and death was just a few seconds.

The big male raced after his mate and caught up with her at the first edge of the trees. It was cool and quiet in the small grove and she was already exploring, running from tree to tree to rub her scent everywhere. Temnyy found Godiva just as tempting as Timur found Ashe. He paced beside her, scent-marking over every place she rubbed to tell the other males he was there, and she belonged to him.

They found several puddles, but mostly there were leaves and the occasional downed limb. She crouched, and he covered her, over and over, every fifteen minutes or so, throughout the night. They rested side by side. Sometimes Temnyy lay beside Godiva and other times he paced around her, restless and a little edgy, as if he'd caught the scent of trouble but could never quite tell where it was coming from. Then Godiva would be up again, and he would forget everything but his female in need.

Hours later, morning light began to streak through darkness, and Timur nudged at Temnyy, telling him it was time to return to the estate. He had left Gorya in charge of Fyodor's security, and there was a part of him that was a little anxious. He hadn't liked having Evangeline's family there while he was gone, but there was no way to tell Godiva her heat was coming at an inconvenient time.

The two leopards walked beside each other toward the outer edges of the grove. Tree branches overhead formed a cool canopy in the very early morning hours. Birds flitted from branch to branch and squirrels chattered. Temnyy bent his head to sniff at a lizard as it crossed his path. Something hit the bark of a tree in front of the leopard, slicing through fur right between his ears. The sound was just behind it, a distinct report that was unmistakable. At once the leopard reacted, jerking to one side, slamming into the smaller female, knocking her back toward the center of the grove.

Godiva didn't need another warning. She ran, staying low, moving into the shadows and finding grass where she could blend much easier. Temnyy stayed close to her and he too dropped to the ground.

The shot came from the east, Timur told his cat, falling into his calm resolve. *Leave Godiva here and work your way around so we can get the shooter.*

Temnyy relayed his impressions to his female. She stubbornly refused to remain hidden in the brush while he took chances. She was adamant that she could help.

Timur swore under his breath. Of course, Ashe would refuse to hide from danger. *Persuade her, Temnyy.*

He didn't have to tell the male cat twice. The leopard swiped his paw at his mate, a warning few female leopards would ignore. Then the big cat began to belly crawl through the grass. Twice more the high-powered rifle spit bullets, but the shooter was fishing, hoping the cats would break and run. Once, the bullet hit close to Godiva, but she didn't so much as flinch. The second bullet was farther away from both leopards.

Temnyy had plenty of experience moving in short grass without being seen. He had endless patience. He used the freeze-stalk method that was so successful, moving inches and coming to a complete halt. His eyes might be blue, but at that distance, they would be lost in a sea of spots. The cat had the perfect camouflage and he used it to his utmost advantage.

Timur had an idea where the shooter was and directed Temnyy toward that spot. It was a good distance away, almost to the other side of the grove. The male leopard took his time, unhurried by the sun coming up and light filtering through the grove. Fifteen minutes later, the cat heard a vehicle start up and then the sounds faded as if it had driven off.

Still, the leopard was careful, making his way to the blind in the tree where the shooter had been. Timur swore again. There was no scent. That pointed the finger at Evangeline's family, but there could have been a member of the hit squad they missed. He let Temnyy take his time, sniffing everywhere, following the tracks back to the place where a vehicle had been parked. The trail ended there. The SUV had driven off on the main road leading to the grove.

Timur shifted and tracked back to the tree where the shooter had been, closely examining the ground and then the tree itself. There were no shells left behind, but he found fur caught in the bark where a leopard had gone up the tree. That leopard had been Amur. He held the fur to his nose and inhaled. The scent-blocker had faded enough that he caught an elusive scent. He stiffened and took a long look around.

Temnyy, I'm going to throw this fur on the ground. You smell it. I want you to tell me if I'm wrong.

He placed the fur carefully in the root system of the tree and shifted, allowing his leopard to take over their form. The male took his time, but he knew they'd smelled that scent before, and just recently. The shooter had left his stench behind when he'd come to visit with the other cops. Anton Lipin had been sent from Russia by Lazar. There was no other explanation. He might have already been established in law enforcement, but he was on Lazar's payroll.

Temnyy made his way back to Godiva. She rose the instant she saw him, her tail twitching. The two leopards rubbed against each other and then headed back to the Jeep. Ashe was stumbling with weariness by the time she shifted and climbed onto the seat.

"It's light."

"I see that." Timur swung into the driver's seat, his gaze moving over her face and body. She had a few bruises on her, several red marks and one or two strawberries. It was the best he could hope for under the circumstances.

"We don't have any clothes."

"Baby, you're telling me things I already know. What's the big deal? We're still on the property, and I'll drive right to the back door of the guesthouse. We won't need to steal away out the window."

She heaved a sigh. "Who shot at us?"

"I'm not certain who he is in all this." It was a lie blended with the truth, and she was too tired to notice.

"He didn't leave clues behind, did he?"

"Sooner or later, I'll figure it out." He had a prisoner waiting to be interrogated. He'd know everything he needed when he was finished with the man.

The Jeep bumped over a few ruts and Ashe crossed her arms over her breasts and put her head back against the seat, closing her eyes. He wanted to gather her close and hold her to him. She looked completely worn-out. They drove through the vineyards, Timur avoiding the few workers that moved through the plants, checking to make certain there were no pests or damages. He circled away from the human soldiers and brought the Jeep behind the guesthouse.

Ashe appeared to be asleep, but she woke when he turned the key and the Jeep went quiet. She looked around her, blinking. "Amazing. We actually made it without anyone seeing us."

He got out and went around to her. "You're gorgeous, woman. I've never understood why a woman wanted to hide her body, especially from men. We like looking at you."

He opened the door and inhaled, just to make certain no one had been in the residence since they left it. The house smelled of sex. Of pheromones. Of leopard. Not the enemy. He stepped back to allow her inside.

Ashe walked straight into the kitchen to find a bottle of water. She drank the entire contents. Timur made another mental note to make certain he gave her water after their marathon sex sessions. He went on through to the bathroom, snagging his phone, and turned on the tap to run her bath. For the first time, he found himself anxious to get her to sleep so he could leave. He needed to find out everything there was to know about the man who had tried to kill them. He sent a warning to his brother and cousins that at least one sniper was in the area and active. He didn't give them the name, just to be safe. He would in person.

The others are arriving soon for a meeting. We need any information you can get from our friend. Their friend was their prisoner.

Timur scowled at his brother's text. Like he didn't already know that. *I have to take care of my woman first. She needs care, Fyodor. Our friend is still going to be there and the longer he waits, the more anxious and cooperative he becomes.*

How much time do you need with Ashe?

That set Timur's teeth on edge. Would Fyodor ever neglect Evangeline? The answer was no. Never. *As long as it takes. When do the others arrive?*

Jake sent the plane for them and it should be here by ten this morning.

Timur sighed. Ashe is asleep on her feet. As soon as she's down, I'll see to our friend. After that, I have no idea how long things will take. You can entertain our visitors while I talk with him.

Ashe wandered in. Up close, he could see more bruises forming on her skin. He skimmed his finger down one and tossed his phone on the sink counter. "I'm sorry, baby. I thought I was careful."

She glanced down at her body. "You were incredibly gentle under the circumstances. I just hope the two of them settle down for a few hours and give us a rest." She yawned. "I'm so sleepy I don't know if I can stay awake long enough to take a bath."

He caught her wrist and tugged when she turned back toward the bedroom. "If you fall asleep in the bathtub, Ashe, I'll put you to bed."

She wrapped one arm around his neck and leaned into him. "Thank you for being so sweet to me, Timur. I don't know what I expected, but you kept me from being afraid."

He frowned, unable to discern exactly what she'd been afraid of. "I think the shooter was after Temnyy. The initial shot was to take him out, not Godiva."

"I don't know about that, I guess that should have made me afraid, but mostly, it made me angry. Whoever was shooting at us was doing so from a distance. What a coward." She stepped into the bathtub and slid down until the hot water was up to her neck. "I meant I was afraid of Godiva and Temnyy getting together. It was . . . intense."

He turned off the taps and sank into the water with her, letting it soothe the aches in his muscles. "Leopard sex is always intense. It's never easy, baby, not even later, when she's not in heat."

"The leopards are still going to want to be together physically? I thought leopards only were with each other when the female was in heat." She ducked her head under the water to soak her hair, came up and slicked it back off her face and then leaned back against the porcelain. "My parents never talked about that side of it."

"We're shifters. We're not quite human, and they aren't quite leopard. We have different rules and different needs."

"I guess that makes sense, but seriously, they're going to have to slow down. I thought I was in good shape, but I feel like someone took a baseball bat to my body."

His heart stuttered. "You should have told me it was that bad."

"What were you going to do? Godiva gets hot and she makes me that way. I can't seem to control myself any more than she can. I don't know why I'm such a baby. Every other female shifter has to have similar experiences."

They weren't his woman. Women were different, and she had a small frame. His male was big. He was big. He dwarfed her in size the way Temnyy dwarfed Godiva. He should have considered that. *She's feeling battered, Temnyy,* he chided the male. *You should have taken more care with her.* He was really angry with himself, not his cat. It was his responsibility to take care of her and under the circumstances, with her heat driving them, he didn't seem to have much in the way of control.

His leopard ignored him. The cat was driven by his nature. "Those other women aren't you, Ashe. You're mine. I don't like you hurt."

Her lashes fluttered, lifted and those amber eyes were focused on his face. "You steal my heart, Timur, every single time."

She smiled at him, and he felt that pierce through his armor easily, mostly because she'd stripped him of every shield. He was left naked and vulnerable, completely exposed to her.

He didn't reply, but he did take the cloth and soap to wash her carefully. He rinsed her hair and then helped her stand. Drying her hair wasn't easy, so he just wrapped it in a towel while he dried off her body. She didn't try to help. She just stood there for him, looking as if she might fall over any minute.

"I'm in love with you, Ashe," he said. "I'm not offering you a lot in the way of white picket fences and social status, but I can tell you I'll love you with every breath I take. I know no other man will love you better."

Her amber eyes didn't leave his face. "I'm very grumpy in the morning, Timur."

"You are?"

She nodded solemnly. "And I'm a terrible cook. Worse, I have no real desire to learn. You know how they show the little woman with the apron in her kitchen waiting anxiously for her man to come home?"

"I've seen that, yes."

"That is never going to be me. If you're really, really lucky, I might make you a sandwich and even then, I can't promise that it will taste good."

"I see."

"I totally lied when I said I'd take cooking classes. That's never going to happen."

"I was fairly certain of that."

"There's more."

He picked her up, cradling her close to his chest as he carried her through to the bedroom. "I don't know if I can take more."

"You might as well know the worst."

"What is it?"

"I'm a terrible driver. I never really learned properly, and I've had several wrecks."

"Several?" He placed her in the bed and pulled up the covers.

She nodded solemnly. "Six. And three other near misses. One that might have been a wreck, because I rear-ended him, but he didn't want to exchange information."

Timur tried not to be alarmed. It was also difficult to keep a straight face. "I think we'll be getting you a driver."

"That might be best."

He lay down beside her, one arm locking her close. "Go to sleep." He kissed the back of her head. She didn't make a sound other than her even breathing.

16

TIMUR backed away from the mess that had been their enemy. He despised having to kill a leopard, especially one that had shifted in order to protect its human counterpart. The leopard had been particularly savage and in order to survive, Timur'd had to use lethal force.

There were blood spatters on his torn clothing and the shoes he'd hastily kicked off. Ignoring his men, he went straight to the shower. His clothes would be burned along with everything else that might provide any connection to the disappearance of one Gavyn Zherdev, young for belonging to a hit team, but no less determined. Gavyn had started out posturing, all bravado, like so many others before him.

Timur let the hot water pour over him, knowing it would wash away the surface blood from his skin, from his hands, but it would never touch what had seeped inside him. He pressed his forehead to the wall of the shower cubicle. His woman would take his reaction as proof of him not being psycho, but he wasn't certain. What kind of man could do the things he could do without ruining his heart or his soul?

Gavyn's bravado had given way to screams of defiance. Timur was used to that, so used to it he became bored by it, expecting it, knowing it was only another layer he had to peel away—and he'd done so. He was expected to extract the information that this man had. They'd needed to know everything he could tell them about the enemy's plan. He'd personally needed to know how much danger his woman was in.

Gavyn had originally come to kill Ashe. He was not to put a bullet in her head. He was to kidnap her, the team would use her, and then they would send her back to her grandfather in tiny pieces. He had been part of the original team sent by Lazar. His orders had been to keep her alive as long as possible, so she felt every bit of Lazar's wrath. Mostafa's granddaughter had to be taught a lesson, just as his son and whore of a wife had been taught.

Timur had needed to delve deeper, and he'd told Gavyn that. An entire hit squad after one small woman? So far at least five of their team had been killed. Would Lazar send six of his best men to do a job like the one he'd described? He always asked his questions in the same, soft tone, pacing, because these kinds of interviews always made his leopard restless.

Temnyy'd hated this man with every cell in his body. He'd wanted to get to him, rip him apart, devour him and then spit him out. This man had come to kill his mate's counterpart. That was not to be endured lightly. Usually, when Timur had to interrogate someone, at his command his leopard stayed as far away as he could, curling up, trying not to hear anything said or done. This had been different. This man had come to take something precious from him—his mate. That was not to be tolerated, and Temnyy had refused to stand down.

Timur had barely been able to control his cat, and the snarling posturing had been much more difficult than normal. He'd looked at his prisoner, heat banding over his eyes as Temnyy leapt again and again for the surface.

Stop. You are not making this any easier.

Give him to me. I will tear him apart.

I need information. Much more than this. Leave me alone so I can extract it.

Temnyy had refused to speak to him again, had just sent him a sulky, mulish snarl, but he'd retreated a short distance. Timur once more had turned back to his prisoner.

Lazar had gotten word that his son, Mitya, was there in the States and his nephews Fyodor, Timur, Sevastyan and Gorya were there as well. Immediately, Ashe had become Lazar's second concern. He no longer wanted her dead. Not yet. He wanted her taken alive and held along with Evangeline, so his nephews could see the women tortured, raped and killed. He was preparing a special death for them all.

Timur had paced away from Gavyn. He hadn't been able to kill him yet. He had to be careful. With his back to him, he'd asked who had given Lazar the information that his sons were close by. The answer hadn't surprised him, although the time it took to get the information had. Ulisse had sold them out to Lazar, seeking favor with his fellow trafficker. Right on the heels of that, Apostol Delov had confirmed they were alive and living in the United States.

Timur could have told Ulisse that a shifter like Lazar would never keep his bargains and his loyalty was only to himself. He'd given Gavyn much-needed water and let him rest for a few minutes, had let him think that there would be no more. When he'd approached again, he'd asked how they knew the layout of Fyodor's house.

Gavyn hadn't known where the information had come from. There'd been no reason for him to lie about that or hold back, and his voice had held the ring of truth. Timur had asked about opium. Yes, Ulisse dealt in opium and it was good product and there was plenty of it. Ulisse had finally revealed his source, after Lazar had refused to do business with him. The source was the Mercier Perfume factory in New Orleans.

How many snipers had Lazar sent with the hit squad? Gavyn had been adamant that there were no snipers sent. Lazar wanted them all alive. The orders had changed, and they weren't to kill any of them. Hurt them, yes, but not kill them. As soon as they had them secure, Lazar would come, but he wouldn't set one foot in the country until he knew all of them were scooped up.

There had been something in Gavyn's voice that told Timur he hadn't been lying, but knew more than he had said. Timur had let it go for the moment. He had to ask the right questions. There had been things Gavyn hadn't admitted.

Lazar had seen what Fyodor had done to the lair, and he was leery of them. Fyodor was a force to be reckoned with. He'd killed his own father, Lazar's brother, and then the other members of the *bratya* that had followed his father. Lazar had reason to be leery. He had helped to create the monsters, and now those monsters had turned on him.

Timur pressed both palms to the wall of the shower and watched the red blood turn pink as it flowed into the drain. He had spent the day before, as well as the night, with his woman and her warm, soft body. It was like sliding against satin, her skin amazing when he held her against him, or covered her with his own heavier, much harder body. The difference in the way their bodies felt amazed him. He knew he would always want to wake up next to her, his body tangled with hers.

When he was inside her, she surrounded him with the tightest silken fist imaginable. Scorching hot. A vise of sheer pleasure. She gripped and milked his cock until he thought he'd go out of his mind. There was no walking away from something that intense and overwhelming.

When he touched her, when he fucked her, when he made love to her with every breath in his body, it was always perfect. Every time.

He forced himself to keep his eyes open, to watch that blood slowly be swallowed by the drain. He needed to know what he did. To own it. In some ways, watching the blood swirling at his feet, mixed with water, was a tribute to the dead man. Gavyn Zherdev was now another ghost to haunt him. To keep him awake.

Could Ashe's soft skin and hot pussy combat a fresh kill? What about the haven of her mouth? He loved when her lips were stretched around his girth and she was kneeling in front of him, eyes on his, while he fed her his cock—while he watched it disappear down her throat. That might make him forget temporarily.

He shook his head and moved his hands down several inches, measuring her height. Holding both palms that height, he let the water finish washing what was left of Gavyn off of him. She had to save him, because without her, there was only this. Hell. He lived in hell. He had all his life and Ashe had given him a glimpse of paradise.

It wasn't the fucking. It wasn't her mouth, or her pussy or her soft skin. It was the laughter she shared with him. The way she looked at him, that softness in her eyes. More. She looked at him as if he were more than a killer. More than a machine. She looked at him as if he were a man and a good one at that. She gave him something no woman should ever give a man like him—her trust. All of it. Everything. He tasted trust in her kisses. It was there in her eyes when she knelt before him. When she offered him her body.

Timur groaned and his fingers curled into two tight fists. He hit the wall of the shower. A loud thud of protest. He was going back to her with Gavyn's blood on him. The water wasn't going to take it away, no matter how long he stayed in the shower. He had his answers, the truth of the large team of hit men, the truth he hadn't needed confirmed because he knew, not only in his gut but in his soul, Lazar had found them and that it was Ulisse who had betrayed them. Still, it had to be confirmed, and Gavyn had held out a long, long time.

Why? Timur turned toward the water spraying at him from every direction. Most gave up within the first fifteen minutes when Timur started on them. Gavyn had chosen his loyalties and he'd remained true to them, prolonging his life when his suffering could have been over in minutes. Just minutes.

It had taken far longer to find out about the man named Anton Lipin. The man was one of Lazar's most trusted men. He infiltrated every law enforcement agency with ease by using his Interpol identity that had been carefully constructed over the years. He'd been sent as soon as word had come in that Mitya and the others had been sighted. He'd taken over running the hit team. He had direct orders from Lazar and only he knew what they were. No one dared disobey him. Lipin was ruthless and thought nothing of killing one of his own men.

It had taken some time to get the information that Anton Lipin had served as a sniper in the military and was one of the most decorated soldiers among the leopards in Lazar's lair. He was responsible for more kills than any other.

Gavyn had been adamant that Anton would not have gone against Lazar's orders. Anton had served him faithfully for years. It was said that if you were talking to Anton, you were talking to Lazar. He wouldn't go against Lazar's orders.

The question nagged at Timur. Why would Anton try to kill Timur when Lazar had specifically ordered otherwise? He'd returned to the subject over and over, and Gavyn had remained certain that Anton wouldn't. Yet he had. Unless . . . If orders had changed in the short time between when the first hit team had been sent for to kill Ashe and when the second team was dispatched, could they have been changed again?

If Lazar had put out a hit specifically on Timur, Gavyn had known nothing about it, although the general consensus was if Timur was dead, it would be easier to get to Fyodor.

Cursing, Timur stepped from the shower, caught up a towel and wiped the droplets of water from his body. Naked, he drew on gloves and finished stuffing his blood-covered clothes and shoes in the bag lying on a narrow bench. The room was cement with several drains in the floor. Even the inside of those drains was cleaned after each use. Few people knew about the rooms below the house, but just in case, every precaution was taken.

Timur dressed and waved his hand toward Kyanite and Rodion. He didn't envy either man on cleanup duty. What was virtually a crematorium was located down there as well. The body and the clothes of anyone attending the interrogation would be burned and then every ash collected until not a single particle was left behind. Those ashes were then taken far from the estate and disposed of where no one was likely to find them, or if they did, have a clue what they'd discovered.

He climbed the narrow staircase to the hidden hallway leading behind the walls of the estate. Fyodor hadn't been the one to install those rooms beneath the house, that had been Antonio Arnotto. He'd had secret hallways and hidden rooms scattered throughout the mansion. He'd lived his life in the spotlight, appearing to be a shrewd businessman, but no criminal. There had been countless bloodstains in the room long before Timur even brought his first prisoner down those stairs.

It was interesting to him that Ambroise had immediately noticed the discrepancy in the measurement of the walls and that he'd told his brother about it. He'd drawn the entire layout of the house, and if he knew there were hidden passageways, he could have easily guessed where they were and where they led. All four of the Tregres were tied to the perfume business and the opium in some way. Christophe had worked there as a teenager, and Ambroise worked designing labels for them. Beau and Gilbert worked in distribution. All of them knew Charisse and Armande, the owners. There were ties.

Gavyn hadn't been able to tell him anything about that family or the opium other than that Ulisse was a distributor. Timur used the door in Fyodor's master bedroom rather than chancing stepping out where the others attending the meeting might see him and know where the hidden doors were. They were allies, but he didn't believe in taking chances with his brother's life.

Fyodor and the others were waiting for him. Jake Bannaconni and Drake Donovan were bent over a table, looking at a drawing. Joshua Tregre and Mitya Amurov sat in armchairs near the fireplace. Elijah Lospostos and Eli Perez stood talking together, just to the right of the fireplace. They all looked up when he walked into the room. Most of the bodyguards were absent, but Gorya and Sevastyan, as members of Fyodor's and Mitya's families, were also present. They looked Timur over quickly, knowing the kind of toll interrogating leopard prisoners took on a man.

Fyodor sat in a chair by the fireplace and didn't turn as his brother walked in. He just stared into the flames, his broad shoulders slumped.

"He found us at last, didn't he?" he asked in a soft voice.

Timur took the ice-cold bottle of water Gorya handed him. There was a wealth of a buffet spread out on a long narrow table at one end of the room, but his stomach wasn't up to eating.

"Yes. Apostol Delov was not the man who gave us up. He fished, but he didn't tell Lazar, afraid he wouldn't get the reward. Just by fishing, it confirmed what Lazar had been told. We knew it was coming, Fyodor. We wanted it to come. That was the entire reason for using your real name. You could have stayed Alonzo Massi and that would have bought us more time—maybe. Most likely not though, because you're easily recognizable. Your picture has been in newspapers, on television, even a time or two in a magazine because of Siena. He would have found you. This way, we know he's coming at us." Timur looked at his cousins. "At all of us. He particularly wants the two of you."

Mitya looked completely impassive. Sevastyan shrugged. They had known, just as Fyodor had, that Lazar would never rest until he found them.

"It didn't occur to me Evangeline would get pregnant so soon and if she did, there might be complications." Fyodor didn't look up.

Timur wished he had an answer. He stood in the middle of the room knowing he couldn't offer comfort to his brother, because the answer was, they surrounded their women with danger from every front. They held things back from them. They weren't good men and never had been, yet they refused to give up the women they loved. He wanted to believe that had everything to do with his leopard, but he was always honest with himself. Ashe was his. Born for him. Made for him. He'd lie. He'd steal. He'd kill over and over to keep her.

"We started down this path," Drake said, "with good intentions, having no idea how complicated it would get. We knew shifters indulging in criminal activity also became severely twisted. They had to be removed, and only we could do that. We're shifters and we have to police our own."

Timur didn't say anything. What was there to say? He knew he would never walk away and leave his brother to face the kind of danger he did every day without the best security possible—and Timur was that security. They were locked on to the path they'd chosen. They couldn't stop because it suddenly got rough. Nor, even if they tried to walk away, would they ever be free. They would be hunted for the rest of their lives.

"What of Evangeline's family?" Fyodor asked. "Are they in any way connected to Lazar?"

"Through Ulisse most likely, but that isn't confirmed," Timur admitted. "Ulisse is distributing opium, and Lazar wants his source. Apparently, the opium is sought after, a very good product. Lazar forced Ulisse to tell him where he got the product. Our raid on the convoy needs to be cancelled."

"I can get the evidence against Ulisse to the cops," Jake volunteered.

It was understood that an enemy like Ulisse, despite being human, couldn't be left to claw at their backs.

"Ashe and I were shot at in the grove just beyond the vineyard. He used the scent-blocker but left behind fur in the tree. Amur leopard. Definitely Anton Lipin."

Fyodor nearly came out of his chair. "You didn't tell me. What the hell, Timur? I would have sent men to help you."

"I didn't need help." Timur shrugged his shoulders. "I handled it."

"Like hell you handle it next time. You let me know what's happening *immediately.* I'm just as concerned for your safety as you are for mine," Fyodor hissed, his eyes nearly glowing.

Timur hid the sudden desire to smile. His brother rarely expressed his affection for anyone but Evangeline, but it was there in that spurt of anger. He nodded his head, not daring to use his voice because Fyodor would have heard the lie. No way would he contact his brother for help. If Timur was in danger, what kind of head of security would he be if he couldn't handle it himself?

"Anton Lipin was sent by Lazar?" Elijah asked. "He's Interpol?"

"He's running the team Lazar sent here. That also gives him access to the scent-blocker," Timur pointed out. The question still nagged at him. Why would Anton Lipin decide to deviate from Lazar's orders not to kill any of them? It made no sense for Lazar to change the orders at the last moment again.

Drake drummed his fingers on the table and then straightened up, facing them. "I took over the lair after I claimed Saria. It was a mess, and I mean a real mess. Most of the leopards were out of control. At that time, several of the men, instead of challenging me, came after me with rifles. If any of them are working with the Tregres . . ."

Joshua turned and looked at him impassively.

Drake waved a hand in his direction. "Sorry, Joshua. I keep forgetting you're a Tregre. Your uncles then, are up to no good. There's no question, and they're looking at Evangeline's bakery to add to their distribution. You can't let them near that place."

"That would happen over my dead body," Fyodor snapped.

"I think that's the point," Timur said. "Kill you. Kill me. They very well could convince Evangeline to allow them to work for her. She's a sucker for a sob story. She took in Ashe knowing we were both going to be angry with her."

"She knows better than to do something like that again," Fyodor assured.

"Lipin arrived to run the hit team," Timur continued. "He gave orders that instead of killing Ashe, they were to take both women prisoner. We were to be taken, but not killed. Lazar has something special in mind for us. On the other hand, then Lipin takes a shot at me." He was missing something important. His mind kept circling back to the fact that Lipin, for the first time, according to Gavyn, had disobeyed a direct order. Why?

"Lipin has to have recruited other leopards," Mitya said. "Leopards are a valuable asset they can't afford to just keep throwing at us. You've killed how many now?"

Timur nodded his agreement. "Not all the leopards

waiting for us in our home were Amur. There were definitely some from other lairs."

"Local?" Drake asked. "The Tregres have been in the swamp for years and know all the families. It was Charisse Mercier who developed the scent-blocker. Her mother originally was the one to extract opium and use the perfumes being sent out to distribute. Everyone was cleared."

"Maybe they were," Eli said. He was out of his chair now and perched instead on the arm. "But everything seems to lead back to this perfume maker and her factory."

"Her brother, Armande, tried using a firearm against me back before I took over," Drake said. "He's leopard, and that's a killing offense."

"Great," Timur said. "Who else might join Lazar's cause, given enough money? Because I'm betting his recruits are local. I've never met these men from your lair, Drake. I wouldn't recognize their scent. We disposed of them before you arrived. So, who else?"

"There were two brothers in that lair, both friends with Armande Mercier. Robert Lenoux, along with Armande, came after me with a rifle. I sent Robert to Borneo, hoping it would make him a better man. He didn't go and in fact, disappeared not so long ago. His younger brother, Dion, is convinced that someone killed him and hid the body. Robert was traced here, to San Antonio. Dion has been drinking a bit and he definitely can shoot. If he became convinced that Timur had anything to do with Robert's disappearance, he would go after Timur and never hesitate." Drake looked pointedly at Timur.

"You're looking at the wrong man," Timur said truthfully. He didn't so much as glance at his brother.

"Does he work for this Charisse?" Eli asked. "Is there a connection?"

"Just about everyone in the lair has someone in their family working for Charisse. It's a poor parish, without too much in the way of good solid work. Her company offers not only fair wages, but also benefits," Drake admitted.

"So that answer would be yes," Eli confirmed.

Drake nodded. "I believe the Tregres got Dion his job."

Timur frowned. There were so many connections to the perfume factory and the opium. "Joshua, what do you actually know about your uncles?" He was Evangeline's first cousin but had been raised in Borneo by his mother.

Joshua shrugged. "Not much. I do know they betrayed my father by telling my grandfather that he was running off with his wife and child. My grandfather killed my father. I also know, from my mother, that Evangeline's mother didn't die in childbirth or run off the way they tell the story."

"What happened to her?"

Joshua shook his head. "I don't know. My mother would never say. They were exchanging letters and a few weeks *after* Evangeline's birth, the letters stopped. She just cautioned me to stay away from the family, and I always have. Any family with that many secrets has too many skeletons. Probably real ones."

"I don't like Evangeline having anything to do with them," Fyodor said. "On the other hand, if she was my sister, I wouldn't want her to have anything to do with us, so that makes me a hypocrite."

"Or protective of your wife," Jake said.

"I think Christophe is a good man," Drake said. "From what I've seen of him and heard from my crew in Borneo, he pulled his weight and worked hard. But, and it's a big but . . . I can't say with certainty that he isn't involved in this up to his neck."

"He knew about the passageways in the halls," Timur pointed out.

"What about Ambroise?" Fyodor asked. "Is he dangerous? Can he handle weapons?"

Drake shrugged when they all looked to him. The

Tregres were from his lair and he was a man who kept close eyes on those under him. "Every Tregre can handle a weapon, including Evangeline. It's necessary. They hunted their own food. If they didn't go home with something, they didn't eat. I'd bet he can handle himself, but he just doesn't seem to be the kind of man who would plot to kill his sister and her husband."

"Which leads us back to that damn perfume factory and Charisse and Armande," Timur said. "We can't seem to get away from it."

Timur swept a hand through his hair, pushing the strands that had tumbled onto his forehead back. His hair was still wet from his shower. His gut was still in knots from having to interrogate and then kill a leopard. He made his way to the buffet and took another bottle of water from the ice bucket.

"Lazar sent the first hit team after Ashe. They had specific orders. Apparently, her grandfather made Lazar very, very angry. Our good friend Ulisse has a nice little side business with Lazar. They trade young girls back and forth. Ulisse sends them out of the country to Lazar, and Lazar returns the favor, sending girls from our homeland to Ulisse."

"Leopards?" Fyodor demanded sharply. "Ulisse isn't leopard."

"Not leopards. We have too few now for Lazar to use them that way. He gets young leopard girls from their fathers and sells them as he did Ashe's mother, for temporary use only. They are very young, from ten to fifteen. He doesn't like to let go of them any older than that because they might go into a heat cycle. He learned from the loss of Ashe's mother that he couldn't risk the girls being too old. No, the ones he sells or trades to Ulisse are wholly human."

"Ulisse betrayed us," Fyodor said. "He sat at my table and ate my food with my wife sitting opposite him, and all the time he plotted our betrayal."

"According to young Gavyn, that's exactly what happened," Timur confirmed.

Fyodor stood up, with a surge of flowing power. He stalked across the room, turned, and looked at his brother, sheer ice in his gaze. "I want him here if possible, Timur. I would like to talk to him myself."

Timur was silent. His gut tensed and then tied into a hundred tight knots. "Fyodor." Just his brother's name. He understood the need for vengeance. Ulisse was supposed to be an ally, not an enemy. They invited few people to their table, but Drake had decided to try to include him in their ring of power. It had been a mistake, one of many Timur knew would be made.

"When we agreed to take down organized crime," Elijah said carefully, "we talked only of leopards. Going after humans increases our danger tenfold. More. We can't take down everyone. Eli knows that."

Eli had been a DEA agent for years. He was also leopard, but as an agent he hadn't discriminated between leopard and human. Leopards couldn't go to jail and had to be destroyed, and he couldn't ever be caught doing that. He'd joined with Drake and Jake in their war against the shifters who used their abilities for criminal activity.

Fyodor shrugged. "If you want to give Ulisse a pass, that's up to you. This man betrayed me and my wife and family to our greatest enemy. He is involved in human trafficking, which we all agreed we wouldn't tolerate. Still, I will accept your decision."

Like hell he would. Timur knew better. The softer Fyodor's voice, the milder he sounded, the more pissed off he was, and he would definitely go after Ulisse.

"Don't be an ass, Fyodor," Elijah snapped. "No one is going to let that man go free. We'll take him down. We just need to be a little cautious."

"Why?" Timur asked.

There was silence and all of the heads of territories

looked at him. Drake's eyebrow shot up. "Why what, Timur?"

"Why do we need to be cautious? This man betrayed us. Every crime boss in the States has the right to go after anyone who betrayed them. I say we take him out fast and hard and let the others know what we did and why we did it. We treat it as two separate issues. I know he's in deep with the perfume factory and the opium. I got that information from interrogating the hit man and, believe me, by that time he was telling me the truth without hesitating."

Timur moved farther into the room, right into the middle of the men he considered to be powerful. "Ulisse is part of whatever this is against Fyodor and me. The Tregres want Evangeline's bakery to widen their distribution of opium. Ulisse gave us up to Lazar in order to incur his favor. If Lazar wants something, what does he do?" He turned to his cousin. "What does he do, Mitya?"

"He doesn't take no for an answer," Mitya said. "If he knew who Ulisse worked with, such as the Tregres, he would approach them and offer the deal of a lifetime. Of course, that deal would never quite come to pass. He always comes out on top."

"Right," Timur nodded. "Ulisse is already beginning to be worthless to him. He'll need another source for his trafficking, so who would he approach next?"

"Me," Elijah said, "although my views on the subject are fairly well known."

"Exactly," Timur said. "So, then who? If he has the Tregres in his pocket and they can give him the opium source, which has to be that factory and either Charisse or Armande, maybe both, then who to keep his most lucrative business going?"

There was silence. Fyodor let out his breath audibly. "Me. He'll approach me, but he'd need all his ducks in a row. He'd need to have Evangeline in his pocket. Either physically have her or blackmail her into making me cooperate. That's Lazar's style and his twisted revenge. He would want me to suffer, to think any minute he would kill me, which he would, once he found another to do business with."

"We're back to why Lipin tried to kill me," Timur said. "If Lazar wants to persuade Fyodor to do business, he wouldn't want me dead. Fyodor would be out for revenge."

They looked at one another, and then Timur shrugged. When there was no answer, he was forced to shelve it, but he knew the question would continue to nag at him.

Fyodor sighed. "You're going to have to question Evangeline's family, Timur."

Timur knew that was coming. Either way he was screwed. "All of them?"

Fyodor nodded slowly. "I don't think we have any other choice. We have to know which ones are in this, if not all of them."

"Ambroise is very . . . sensitive." Drake settled on the word. "He's more of a dreamy artist type than a gun-toting soldier."

"But he was a soldier," Fyodor said. "I asked last night at dinner and both of the Tregre boys served. One in the Army, the other the Navy. Ambroise was a Navy man."

"But he was in an office," Drake said.

"Are you saying there's no possibility that Ambroise Tregre is engaged in selling opium and that he isn't, in any way, helping his family to take over Evangeline's business at the bakery?" Fyodor's voice, for the first time, was confrontational. Timur had never heard him use that voice on any of their allies.

Drake shook his head. "No, I can't say that, Fyodor, but I did want Timur to understand the kind of man he's going to be questioning. He's going to have to handle him differently than he might Gilbert."

"What was that last night?" Eli asked. "Why in the world would that idiot think to challenge Timur's leopard for his female? They're a bonded pair."

"I don't think Beau or Gilbert understand what a bonded pair is, which means they were never with their real mate," Drake said.

That was interesting and something Timur hadn't considered. Most leopards outside the *bratya* lairs sought their true mates and lived with them. They sometimes hunted the world over. Wherever leopards thrived or lived in small pockets, they often could find females. Now that more and more were being integrated into society and lived in cities or near them, it was becoming much more difficult.

It was very possible the Tregres had married women with leopards, but those women weren't their true mates. If those men were more like their father than previously thought, men who thought women should serve them, and they had the crueler traits of their leopards, they could be very difficult to deal with. Add in cunning and shrewd, just as their father had been, and the two men would make vicious enemies.

"I'll be careful with him," Timur said, although what did that mean? That he wasn't going to pull off his fingernails one at a time or use shock therapy on the kid? If Ambroise's father could fool everyone into thinking he was not quite bright and beaten down by his father when he really was a mastermind, then the kid could be just like him.

"Evangeline doesn't have to know," Fyodor said.

"She'll know, don't fool yourself. Most likely, Ashe will know too." Timur wasn't looking for sympathy. This was his job. He didn't have to like it, but that came with the territory. "Hopefully, they'll eventually realize I do whatever it takes to protect them."

Joshua came out from where he'd parked himself in a corner. The light fell across his face and there was something there that Timur had never noticed before. Shadows maybe. Joshua was a hard man, the kind of man one didn't cross, but he'd always seemed a fair one. He was quiet and cool under fire.

"Beau and Gilbert are not the men they seem. I can only go by what my mother told me, and it wasn't much, but don't trust them for a minute, Timur. They fool people and it costs them. I know my father loved them both very much, and they betrayed him. I know my mother was afraid of them and afraid for their wives. She never elaborated, but I know she never wanted me to go near that family."

"I'll know if they lie," Timur assured.

"Will you?" Drake asked. "I wonder. If they've managed to fool everyone, that means they were fooling leopards. That isn't easy. They had to be able to tell lies and not have them heard."

"Ashe tells me there is a trick to that," Timur said. "One her father taught her."

"Great thing to teach your child," Eli murmured. "How to lie."

"I've learned to rely on other things besides my leopard for the truth," Timur assured.

Several of the men went to the sideboard and put food on plates. Timur reasoned that they thought the discussion over. He wasn't so certain. He had a wide range of suspects, but those suspects were all connected.

"What are we going to do about Ulisse?" Elijah asked, proving he hadn't forgotten the man who had aligned himself with Lazar against them.

"We've wanted Emilio Bassini to strengthen his territory. He runs guns, but despises human traffickers. He'd shut that end of the business down fast," Jake said. "If you take out Ulisse, you could propose to the council that Emilio take over his territory. That way, we wouldn't be spread so thin, and so far, we haven't been able to find anything on him to suggest that he's a shark in the water circling us for our blood."

"With Ulisse's businesses, that almost doubles Emilio's territory," Drake pointed out.

"True," Jake agreed. "But his financials are a mess. He's

weak and very vulnerable. If he wasn't allies with all of you, he'd be eaten alive by some of the other greedier bosses. He knows that. He would be more careful and perhaps even ask for your help, Elijah. In fact, when the council meets, you might offer that as a suggestion when you put Emilio's name in the ring to take over that territory, that you would be willing to help him sort out Ulisse's businesses."

"How do you want it done?" Timur asked the question to the room, but he looked at his brother.

"I want him brought here. I want him questioned, and then I want him to die here," Fyodor said. "I'll be in attendance and I'll ask him myself what he was thinking selling me down the river along with my wife."

"That's fair," Elijah said.

Drake shook his head. "Just kill the bastard and get it over with. You take too many chances, Fyodor. Nothing can be traced back to you. Kidnapping him and prolonging his life adds to the margin something could wrong. The less time you have contact with him, the odds go down that you could get caught."

"Also," Eli added before Fyodor could react, "there's always a good chance the Feds have him under surveillance. You don't want to get caught on tape. Let me nose around a little. I have quite a few friends that will give me the information. I feed them tips every now and then, and it works both ways."

"I'll need that information immediately, Eli," Fyodor said, "because I'm not waiting."

"What does that mean, Fyodor?" Timur asked. "My woman's leopard is still in heat. I can't just leave her alone."

"I'm not incapable of picking up this bastard myself," Fyodor snapped.

Timur sent him a quelling look. "Don't be an ass. I'll do it. I just have to time it right."

Fyodor nodded. "You're right. And you're right about Ashe. Of course, you have to be with her."

"She's sleeping now." Timur glanced at his watch. "This evening, after her leopard calms, I can pick up Ulisse. In the meantime, Drake, get Ambroise and Christophe back here. Christophe wants a job. He'll know by the end of our interview whether or not he thinks he can work for me. He'll come back for the chance at a job. You'll have to get creative to get Ambroise back here. Make certain to separate the brothers once you have them here."

"No problem," Drake agreed. "I'll get on that now."

"What about Beau and Gilbert?" Joshua asked. "When do you plan to get them here?"

"After I speak to Ulisse," Timur said. "I want to make absolutely certain they're the guilty parties, and I want to know what they want from Evangeline. We can pick them up after my interview with Ulisse. That's going to take some time."

Even if they cut off Lazar from Ulisse, Lazar would reach out until he found someone who would work with him and then he'd be a threat again to all of them. Still, as long as Lazar was afraid of them, and Timur was going to make certain his uncle was very afraid, then the man wouldn't make the trip to the States. He would bide his time and wait for the right opportunity. Timur just had to make certain that opportunity never came.

17

TIMUR stretched out beside Ashe, his body feeling as if someone had beat the living hell out of him. He remembered that same exact feeling from when he was a kid and his father had kicked the shit out of him, just to make him strong. The man didn't want a whining, whimpering candy-ass baby for a son. Kicking the shit out of him nightly was his way of making certain Timur became a man.

"Honey," Ashe murmured sleepily and turned to him.

"Go back to sleep, baby." He had pulled all the privacy screens to darken the house so she wouldn't wake with the sun in her eyes. He hadn't meant to disturb her, but he needed her. That bothered him, but not enough to stop him from lying beside her.

She didn't have a stitch on and he was fully clothed, but it didn't matter. Whenever he was near her, his body knew immediately who it belonged to, and it wasn't him.

"I didn't mean to wake you," he added when she continued to blink up at him with sleepy eyes. She looked drowsy and sexy all at once. Her hair was braided, but was far looser than when she'd woven the thick mass together. He couldn't resist brushing the tip of her nose with a kiss. "Really, baby, go to sleep."

Those eyes saw too much. He knew because she laid her head on his chest and wrapped her arm around him. "Tell me what's wrong, Timur, and don't lie. There's no need to. Whatever you're going to tell me isn't going to send me into some tailspin where I run for the hills. I made a commitment to you. My female is committed to your male. Just talk to me."

He sighed and stroked a caress down the back of her hair. His fingers caught in the braid and rubbed the silky strands together. "We think Evangeline's family is involved somehow with the hit men. With my uncle Lazar and a human trafficking ring. With selling opium, using a perfume factory to distribute and trying to get Evangeline to allow them to use her bakery the same way."

She was silent, her fingers swirling letters on his chest, beneath his shirt. He felt every stroke as if she was writing her name and it was sinking beneath his skin to brand his bones.

"I'll admit, I didn't much care for her father," she said slowly. "Her uncle was disgusting, trying to force Godiva to mate with his male. He knew I was with you, and yet he still did it. So, yeah, I can see that they're both maybe not the best men, but do you think they would really have anything to do with drugs and human trafficking and betraying her to Lazar? That's a big leap from just being disgusting."

"Unfortunately, I'm not the only one who thinks it, Ashe. There are signs that point to their guilt."

"That will be so terrible for her. What about her brothers? Do you think they're involved?"

"It's possible, but I don't have an answer for that."

She was silent again. He felt her every breath, as if the two of them breathed the same rhythm. It might have been an illusion, but he heard her heart beating in sync with his.

Just being with her soothed him. He stared up at the ceiling, wondering how his life could be so fucked-up, yet he had her. Ashe. A woman who walked into his life and gave him a sanctuary, a haven. It was no longer about her body. It was about her heart.

"You're head of security." She was puzzling it out, the way she did everything. "That means Fyodor is going to want you to talk to them. Question them, right?"

He didn't answer her. His fingers continued moving in her hair. His heart beat a little faster, thudding against his chest.

"Of course, that's what you have to do. Someone has to get to the truth. That's what you meant when you said you weren't that much different from the men who killed my parents, isn't it? But you're wrong, Timur." She turned onto her stomach, propping herself up on his chest so she could look into his eyes. "You aren't like them at all."

"Baby." He couldn't look at her. He refused to lie to her.

"No, you're not. You're trying to protect your brother and Evangeline. And me. Probably everyone. You aren't killing someone for money or for personal gain. You aren't following some crazy man's orders to hurt someone as much as you can just for revenge or some sick, twisted perversion of what a lair should be."

There was Ulisse and what he'd like to do to the man who had betrayed them all. Still, what was the point of finding his woman, being given that gift, if he didn't actually become a better man? That was up to him. She saw him this way. As the white knight charging up on his white steed—or in his case—leopard—to save the day.

"If I were to question these men, Evangeline won't like it. She's become . . ." He was at a loss for words. He didn't express how he felt often and certainly not about his brother's wife, but she had somehow become special to all of them. Mitya and Sevastyan as well. He didn't want to disappoint her or have their relationship strained. "She did something for all of us we never thought possible. Somehow, our leopards calmed in her presence. None of us had one shred of hope that such a thing would ever happen, but it did. Not just for Fyodor, but for all of us. You do the same, at least, that's what the others told me, but none of the other female shifters do that. Evangeline was our miracle. Hurting her would be . . ." He trailed off.

"I understand," Ashe said. She rubbed her chin on his chest. "Still, she has to be protected, especially from these men. They would hurt her more than any other. She loves that bakery, Timur. If they used it as a distribution center for opium, it would break her."

"It isn't going to happen," he told her.

She laid her head on his chest. "When do you have to talk to them?"

He glanced at his watch. "I've got some business to take care of. Drake is getting her brothers here first. I want to clear them so Evangeline knows they aren't in any way trying to hurt or use her."

She smiled. He felt her warm breath right through the weave of his shirt. "You came back to check on me and on Godiva."

He decided to be honest. "I came back because I needed to be with you, even if it was for just a few minutes." He didn't care if that made him too vulnerable.

"Whatever you need, Timur." She pressed kisses up his chest to his throat. "I am very much in love with you, as shocking as that is to me. I want to be whatever you need."

"You already are." He knew if he asked her, no matter that she was sore, she would let him have her. She'd welcome him, actively and without reservation, participate no matter how rough he got. She would slide down his body and give him a blow job if he asked her, and she'd do that all while looking up at him as if she adored him. "I needed to hold you, baby. Just feel my arms around you." That was the truth and his voice rang with honesty.

Ashe smiled at him and once more settled her head on his chest, ear over his heart, while both arms went around him. They lay together for at least ten minutes, before she drifted off to sleep again. He held her for another ten after that.

Temnyy, can we leave them for a little while? He knew his leopard would feel precisely where Godiva was in her heat cycle.

For a few hours, Temnyy conceded reluctantly. His mate might be sleeping, but he didn't like being away from her where he couldn't get to her quickly, especially after the challenge from the outsider the night before.

Timur almost wished the cat had told him differently. He moved out from under Ashe carefully, whispering to her to go back to sleep when her lashes fluttered and she made a soft sound of protest. He stretched after he stood, staring down at her the entire time. His woman. She was soft, and yet she had pure steel running through her. She would stand with him and she'd do whatever it took to protect their family. She was the right choice.

NO crime boss ever really thought they were going to get hit in broad daylight, especially if they knew, as Ulisse did, that they were under surveillance by the Feds. The team had spread out, each coming in from a different direction. They were good at disguise and blending in with neighborhoods. This one was upscale and gated. Ulisse had neighbors and he made certain to fit into the neighborhood. His yard, a very large one, was well manicured, with wrought iron gates and cool green foliage surrounding the huge home.

His electricity had been giving him problems on and off for the last hour, appearing to short out. When the call went out, the household was assured that a truck would arrive within a two-hour time period. Just shy of that, it rolled up to the parking area, the logo perfectly displayed, and two men jumped out, both dressed in overalls and carrying two boxes containing tools. Both wore baseball caps with the logo of their place of work. At the door, they presented their ID to the security guard who asked for it. They were let inside.

Six minutes later, a carful of kids, teens living in the neighborhood, sped through the streets as they did every day after getting out of their private school. As they came around the corner just in front of Ulisse's neighbor's house, another vehicle came around from the other side. The two cars collided. As they were going at a good rate of speed, the crash was loud. A horn got stuck, airbags deployed, girls screamed and chaos ensued. The driver of the other car leapt out and confronted the driver of the teens. Neighbors poured out of houses.

Outside cameras were pointed in the direction of the wreck. The doors of the surveillance van parked down the street opened, and two men rushed over to see if they could help the crying victims. The front door of Ulisse's house opened and the two men in overalls emerged from the house and walked back to the truck. Both men got in and the truck was started, but they seemed to be looking at the accident with some surprise. After a couple of minutes, three security guards emerged and went up to the truck. After a brief conversation, they waved and walked across the street to the dark sedan that had been parked there for the last couple of hours. They drove away.

"What the fuck, Timur? Couldn't Fyodor just call me without all the melodrama?" Ulisse demanded.

Timur sent the traitor a small shrug. "You know him. He's secretive. That's how he stays alive. Besides, he was worried about the threats his informant heard against you. Whoever it is has a plant on your security force. We find out who, you can take care of it. In the meantime, you have the two you absolutely trust." He glanced in the rearview mirror to make certain the car followed. Rodion was in the car with the two men.

"Your text caught me by surprise," Ulisse admitted. "Although, come to think about it, I've interrupted conversations between a couple of the newer soldiers. I walk into the room and they stop talking immediately. If it's one of them I'll cut off his cock and feed it to him." He glared out the window. "Emilio actually had the balls to ask me to incriminate myself because he thinks I might be informing the Feds. He got hit twice. I've got a lot riding on his shipments getting through. He better not be behind this."

"I doubt if Emilio would take on someone of your caliber, Mr. Mancini." Timur added a little bit of deference to his voice. Just enough. He wasn't a man given to speech and Ulisse didn't know much about him. Timur always made certain to fade into the background when the heads of the various territories were in the same room with Fyodor.

Ulisse nodded. "Elijah maybe. He'd have the balls, but not the reasons." The man fell silent until they entered a warehouse. As soon as the car behind them entered, Timur indicated for the crime boss to get out of the truck. "We're switching cars. The Feds can track both these vehicles through the city and if we want to bring anyone to you, we don't want a trail of cameras picking up your every move."

"Clever. Fyodor thought of everything."

Timur shrugged. "He's a careful man and a good businessman. A man to have on your side."

Ulisse threw him a quick glance as if trying to discover whether or not Timur was trying to convey something to him. Timur wasn't looking his way, but sent a quick meaningless smile to the two security guards with Rodion. They were already at the black SUV with tinted windows. Timur slid behind the wheel and Ulisse got into the front passenger seat. Rodion took the very back seat with the two security guards in the middle seat. Essentially, if Timur gave the signal, Rodion would kill both guards instantly. He hoped that wouldn't happen as he didn't want to drive around with two dead bodies in the car.

He drove as sedately as possible until Ulisse accused him of driving like an old lady. Again, he just shrugged. "We don't give cops reasons for stopping us." The car swept up the drive leading to the Arnotto mansion. Ulisse looked out the window. "You have a massive amount of security and fire power." Everywhere he looked a man was stationed with a semiautomatic visible.

The crime boss stepped out of the car, his two guards flanking him immediately. Timur led the way around the house toward a side entrance. "I'm not to take any chances with your life. There've been too many attacks recently so I stepped up security on Fyodor, and now, with this threat to you, he wanted it doubled."

He led the way down the hall to the small, hidden door leading to the cement rooms down below them. It was cool in the hall and he led the way, staying in front of Ulisse while his two guards stayed right behind him. "This meeting room is protected. Elijah has one in his home as well. No way can the Feds record a word, no matter how good their equipment." He walked right into the first room and turned back to face Ulisse.

Ulisse's smile faded and a dark scowl took its place. "What the fuck?"

Behind him, Kyanite kicked the door closed, stepped behind the guard nearest him and slit his throat. Rodion did the same with the second guard.

Ulisse tried to pull a gun, but Timur stepped into him and slapped him so hard it rocked the man backward. Timur followed and repeated the slap a second and then a third time until Ulisse was against the wall. Timur spun him around and slammed him face-first into the concrete wall. He was leopard strong and every slap, his grab and the way he shoved Ulisse, took its toll on the man. Timur patted him down, removing weapons and brass knuckles and his cell phone. Only then did he turn him around and, grabbing him by his shirt, forced him to walk to the chair bolted to the floor in the middle of the room.

"I don't like traitors." Timur spat on the ground at the crime boss's feet. "I don't like that you sold out my family thinking Lazar would give you a better deal when he sent you young girls to sell. There's not much about you I do like, so if I were you, I'd tell me whatever I want to know immediately, because I know more ways to hurt you then you can imagine."

"You're making a mistake . . ."

Timur shook his head. "I don't make mistakes. You got greedy. You wanted to be Elijah Lospostos. You wanted his power and the respect the council gives him. They give him respect because he doesn't sell out his friends the way you did. Lazar Amurov is my uncle. I've known him since I was a boy. He's cruel and vicious and loyal only to himself. He would have eaten you alive."

"I don't know what you're talking about . . ."

Timur's slap knocked out two teeth. Ulisse nearly choked on his lies.

The crime boss could only stare in horror at the bodies of the two men he'd brought with him, the only two men who knew who had sent him a message. Fyodor had texted him that an informant had said there was a threat against him and one of his security guards was involved. He was sending Timur to get him. Tell no one else, especially his guards, other than his most trusted. Bring them with him. It had been that easy.

Fyodor opened the door and stepped through. He glanced down causally at the two dead men and then walked around them to pull up a chair opposite Ulisse. He was a good distance away so as not to get a speck of blood on his clothing. His silence made Ulisse turn even whiter, his eyes rolling in his head.

"Tell me about the Tregre brothers. Beau and Gilbert. How did you get involved with them?"

"Fuck you, I don't know . . ."

Timur punched him, three to the face and several more to his gut. He used half the strength the leopard gave him, but that was harder than any human could hit. He stepped back. "I could go at this all day. A week. A month. I haven't gotten started. I have my tools laid out, drills, the electrical shock, that's always fun. I know you've seen the results. I can pull all your teeth. That's fun for you as well but you'll still be able to answer me. Have some fuckin' dignity."

Ulisse spit blood over and over. He sat up slowly. "They came to me. They were the ones who came to me. Said they had a sweet deal going and wanted to expand. I heard them out. They made sense." He spat more blood.

"They brought you the opium, and you sent it out of the country. To Lazar. You already had the pipeline to him through the trafficking. No one traffics without Lazar's fingers in it somewhere," Timur said. "So, you used that same pipeline."

He nodded. Coughed. Spat more blood. "I think you broke something in me."

"How did you get the idea to sell our family out to Lazar?"

"I asked Beau why he didn't take such a sweet deal to his son-in-law. Evangeline is his daughter, so why didn't he go to Fyodor instead of me? I wasn't going to get caught in something Fyodor wouldn't touch. He said there was family trouble in Russia and Fyodor wouldn't do business there."

Timur glanced at Fyodor to see his reaction. "You just took it on yourself to point the finger at us?"

"I told Beau that I did business with Lazar Amurov and that Lazar put out feelers, that he's got them all over for Mitya, Fyodor, you and the others. Beau mentioned to me that sooner or later someone was going to tell him where you all were, which is true."

"Why would Beau say anything at all to you about the family? All he cared about was the opium getting through."

He spat again and tried to look at Timur through his swollen eyes. "Both Beau and Gilbert liked to be paid bonuses. I didn't get the opium unless I supplied them with girls from time to time. They knew Lazar supplied the girls to me because the girls told them."

Timur's stomach dropped. He couldn't imagine what Fyodor was feeling right at that moment. Evangeline had escaped from this family of vile leopards because her grandfather had a reputation of hurting, even killing, women. Now, if this was true, and Ulisse couldn't possibly fool a leopard—which meant it was—her father and uncle were the same.

"Did they supply Lazar's hit team with scent-blocker?"

Ulisse frowned. "They gave me something to give them, yes, but it didn't make any sense to me. Said no one would know they were there. They had the entire floor plan of the house drawn out and said a window in the den would be left unlocked."

Timur glanced at his brother. Beau and Gilbert had come to the house with Ambroise, but they hadn't taken a tour of the house. Ambroise had been the one to ask and be shown around the house with Evangeline. Had Beau or Gilbert left the poolroom long enough to find and unlock a window in the den without being seen? His team would have escorted them if they'd left that room.

"How many snipers did Lazar send after us?"

Ulisse shook his head, groaned and coughed again, this time gurgling. "He doesn't want any of you dead. Not before he gets here. He had a few men here and then sent more after . . ."

"After?" Timur prompted.

"Just fuckin' kill me, you bastard," Ulisse said.

Timur stalked to the tool chest and brought it back to place it on the floor near Ulisse's feet. "You make me have to get this shit out, I'm going to use it on you," he threatened. He kept his tone as cold as ice and just as casual, as if he didn't care one way or the other.

Ulisse swore in his native language, but when Timur started to open the toolbox, he shook his head. "After I told him about Fyodor and Evangeline."

"What about them?"

"How he was so gone on her. He sent the others after that. He told me she wasn't to be killed, none of you were."

"So why the snipers?"

"I'm telling you, there were no snipers."

Timur heard the ring of truth in his voice. If Lazar hadn't sent snipers then Anton Lipin had acted against orders. Why? He spent the next half hour repeating questions and circling back to the sniper, but it was clear Ulisse didn't have any more information for them.

He spent another hour getting the exact pipeline Ulisse used to send girls to Lazar and how he got the ones from Lazar. From there he needed to know if Emilio was involved with trafficking or if he was part of the conspiracy to take down Fyodor. Ulisse's face was smashed and unrecognizable by that time and he wasn't capable of lying. Emilio wasn't a part of any of it. Ulisse hadn't wanted to cut him in.

Fyodor finally nodded, and Timur didn't hesitate. He slit Ulisse's throat and moved tiredly away from the man who had been a crime boss a good part of his life.

"Now we know for certain Evangeline's father and uncle are up to their ears in this mess. If anything, they created it. They went after her bakery and sold us out to Lazar." Pulling off his gloves, Timur tossed them onto the floor where blood pooled.

"I don't know how I'm going to tell her. She was so happy her family came to dinner last night, particularly her brothers."

"We don't know if they're in any way involved."

Fyodor heaved a sigh. "You're going to have to find that out, Timur." He hesitated. "I'd like to question them myself."

"You know that's not a good idea. If they're guilty, it won't matter to Evangeline. She wants family. If you're the one telling her every member of her family betrayed her, she isn't going to like you very much." Timur wasn't about to let Fyodor ruin his relationship with Evangeline. He didn't want his bond with her broken, but what choice was there? They had to know if her brothers were involved in the conspiracy against them.

Fyodor stood up slowly. "Thank you, Timur."

Timur didn't acknowledge the expression of gratitude from his brother, but it meant something to him. He left the room to the others to clean and get rid of the bodies. He needed a break. Some time with his woman, even if he just watched her sleep. He took a shower and let the warm water pound his sore muscles and then he went to her with more blood on his hands.

He stood over the bed just looking down at her sprawled out, arms wide, legs out, like a pinwheel, or a star, no covers, the thick braid unable to cage that wealth of hair.

"What are you looking at, handsome?"

She didn't move. Didn't open her eyes, but she knew he was there and she sounded a little amused.

"I'm looking at what's mine."

"You sure about that?"

"Absolutely sure." He poured confidence into his voice.

"Then why am I alone?"

"Letting you sleep, *malen'kiy smerch*. If I'm with you, I'm in you."

Her soft laughter was muffled by the sheets, but the sound moved through him in spite of that. The notes were melodious and tugged at his heart. Deeper. Settled in him. He pulled his shirt from his body and tossed it aside, looking down at the wide expanse of satin skin. The line of her back was beautiful, the curve of her butt, enticing. Her legs, shapely. Just looking at her caused that burn to start.

A slow burn was something for him to savor. With a leopard's heat involved, his need of her was brutal. Harsh. This was different. Little flames licked at his skin. His blood turned thick and hot, but moved slowly through his body to settle in his cock so that the ache became familiar and yet new at the same time.

He kicked his jeans aside and sank down onto the bed beside her. She didn't move, not even to give him room. He drew a line up her side, from the curve of her hip, over her ribs to the enticing swell of her breast.

"I missed you." She made it a confession. "I woke up and didn't like being without you."

He rubbed the cheeks of her bottom. "I don't want you waking up without me."

"Put your hand between my legs. Feel what you do to me."

He did as she said. She was hot and slick.

"That's me waiting for you. She's still asleep. No leopard, Timur. Just me."

His heart contracted. "Turn over, baby."

She didn't move. "Is it always going to be like this? Me waking up craving you?"

"I hope so. I want you to always want me. I know it's going to be that way with me. I think about you every minute I'm away from you. Even when I shouldn't be."

"Was it bad?"

"I shouldn't tell you. I should keep you as far from my business as possible."

She did turn over, drawing her knees up, but keeping her legs spread wide. Her eyes were on his face, seeing too much. Seeing into him. "No, you shouldn't keep your business from me. I can feel how heavy a burden it is and I want to make it better. I don't need or want details. But you can tell me if it was bad. There can't be harm in that."

"Then, yes, it was bad," he conceded.

"I can give you a massage. It can be a sensual one," she offered. "But a massage might help. We can find ways that I can help you." She wrapped her fingers slowly around his cock, her thumb sliding over the large crown. "I want to do that for you."

"I need the taste of you in my mouth, Ashe. I want to taste every inch of you." He had a bad taste, a coppery one, that wouldn't disappear, as if he'd somehow gotten blood inside him and it wouldn't come out. He knew only Ashe with her sweet, giving nature could remove it.

He framed her face with both hands and rubbed his lips over her forehead. Her breath was warm on his wrists as he kissed her eyelids and then the tip of her nose. He rubbed his nose along hers, savoring the feel of her. The sweetness of her. The way she gave him every single thing he asked for without reservation. His mouth took hers.

That was her gift. She gave herself to him. All of her. Every inch, not just physically, but mentally and emotionally. She trusted him with her when he didn't deserve that enormous gift. He kissed her over and over, losing himself in the hot haven of her mouth. Kissing Ashe was a paradise in itself. Hot. Wet. Fiery. Her taste was exquisite. Perfection. He chased after it, needing more. Greedy for more. She gave it to him.

He kissed his way from her mouth to her throat, using his tongue to take the taste of her skin into his mouth. She was soft and warm and tasted like heaven. He took his time, kissing her along her collarbone, taking the shape of her into his mouth, on his lips, into his mind where he mapped that image, etched it there for eternity into his brain.

He kissed his way to the curves of her breasts. His tongue slid over them, tracing them so he could commit that feeling to his brain. His teeth scraped gently, as if he could take part of her into his bloodstream and keep her there.

"Timur." Just his name, but need was there. Hunger. Her body moved, hips undulating, trying to get him to cover her.

"Let me," he whispered. "Let me have this."

Her eyes moved over his face. She saw every line etched deep there. She saw whatever it was she needed from him to let her know this was important to him. Not just important—it was as essential as breathing air. She nodded, and pressed her hips to the mattress.

He rewarded her with another long, slow kiss, so that fire burned through both of them. He let it happen, taking those flames and savoring them. He didn't allow the need building in both of them to stop his exploration. His claiming. He kissed the tips of her breasts and then spent time learning every curve, slope and peak. He used his mouth. His teeth. His tongue. His hands and fingers. Committing her to memory.

He registered every ragged pant. Her gasps that sent a rush of heat arrowing to his groin. The moans that sounded like music. The soft little cries that vibrated through his cock. Her hands moved over his shoulders, alternating between massaging his muscles, rubbing his skin and biting down with fingernails. Every touch sent waves of emotion straight to his heart. Sometimes the connection was so strong, he feared his heart couldn't take the intensity.

He kissed his way along her ribs on either side, tracing them with his tongue, feeling her hands move to his head, fingers curling into his hair. She held on as if she might lose him, or she needed an anchor. He wanted it to be for both reasons.

His mouth blazed a trail to her belly button. He spent time there, wondering how he'd ever neglected it. He found the way she jerked under his tongue and teeth intriguing. She was sensitive there, and he slid his hand up the inside of her right thigh to the junction of her legs to feel how hot and slick she was.

"You're so ready for me." He murmured the words against the soft, satiny skin of her belly. Deliberately, he rubbed his chin through the tiny curls on her mound. He hadn't shaved and the shadow on his jaw was bristly.

"I'm always ready for you, Timur. I seem to be going around in a constant state of arousal."

He pulled her thighs farther apart. "Do you?"

"Yes."

The acknowledgment hissed out when his tongue swiped across that slick entrance, gathering the honey that was all his. All for him.

"The other night, at the dinner table, before my female made her presence known to everyone, I was fantasizing about sliding under the table and having you for dessert. The way you smell, Timur, that amazing scent, all man, drives me crazy."

His cock jerked hard at the idea of Ashe sucking him down at a dinner table. His dinner table, not someone else's, but he liked her fantasy. "Tell me more."

He didn't want to talk, but he wanted to hear her. Every word. He wanted to indulge himself. He wanted to feast on her taste. To devour her. This wasn't for her, to drive her to the very edge, this was for him. All for him. He fastened his mouth around her, his tongue stabbing deep. Her hips bucked, and he locked her down with one arm so he could use his fingers in his pursuit of treating himself.

"The other day, when we were sitting in chairs in front of the fireplace and I had a blanket over me. I was sitting on your lap, remember?" Her voice was strained.

How could he forget? He'd been as hard as a rock and they weren't alone. He made a sound, but he didn't stop what he was doing. He might never stop.

"I had my dress on and no panties."

He knew that too. He'd been the one insisting no underwear under that long, flowing dress. He'd hoped the air would ease her soreness. That had backfired on him. He'd been so aware of the fact that she wore nothing under that dress that he'd fixated on it and his cock had been hard for what seemed hours.

Just to punish her for making him ache so much, he pushed two fingers deep and used his thumb to stroke her clit as he lapped at the honey spilling out of her.

"I couldn't stand it. You were so hard and your hand was right under my breast. I used my fingers . . ."

He lifted his head. His own fingers plunged in and out of her while he stared at her, devouring her with his gaze, making certain she was aware of his displeasure. "You got yourself off?" How had he not known? They hadn't been alone and he'd been aware of his own discomfort.

She nodded, her small teeth biting into her lower lip. There was no remorse in her eyes. None at all. Just that mischievous look that drove him insane with lust. "I did. Right there with everyone in the room."

"You put your fingers inside you?"

She nodded again, and this time he could see the answering hunger in her, stark and raw.

"Do it now. For me."

She obeyed him instantly, sliding her fingers down her belly slowly and then letting them curve over her mound until two disappeared. "It feels better when your mouth is there."

He yanked her fingers from her and licked them clean. "Next time you decide to get yourself off, I want to know you're doing it."

Kneeling between her thighs, he pressed his cock to her. In his fist, he felt heavy and thick, like a steel rod with no give in it. He watched as he pushed the crown deeper, watched as her body began to slowly swallow his. It was sexy and remarkable. Sensual and sinful. Her lips stretched to accommodate his girth, just as her mouth did when she took him down. He loved her body and the way she strained to accept every inch of him.

"What does this feel like to you?"

"Possession. Belonging. Yours. It burns, but in a good way. You're going too slow though. I need you to . . ." She tried to force him to take her faster, to impale herself on him.

"This is mine. For me this time."

She stopped moving immediately. "I'm sorry. I did promise you that, and I meant it. Whatever you want. However you need me. I want to give that to you."

Already she'd given him so much. The coppery taste was gone and in its place was all Ashe, that sweet spice that was her. He felt her everywhere. He had her in his heart. In his mind, he had her in his body. Now, she surrounded him like a living flame, squeezing him tightly, stroking his cock with those small, strong muscles.

He didn't let the feeling overwhelm him or drive him. He took his time, savoring her, registering each separate layer of beauty she gave him. Taking everything in. The love on her face, the adoration in her eyes, the way her breasts swayed with every movement of his body, the ragged little pants that nearly destroyed his ability to keep his body from letting the fire consume them both fast.

"You're a fucking miracle, Ashe. What you give to me."

Her gaze never left his face, even when her smile turned to a hitch of shock as he surged deep and then held himself still. "Anything, Timur."

He believed her. His woman. He took a breath and began to move in her, wanting her to feel his love with every stroke. "I'm not good at relationships, baby. I'm going to fuck things up often, so what I want is patience. I want to give you so much back that in those times, you'll remember and you'll have patience with me."

If it was possible, her face softened even more and her eyes went watery. "I think I can manage that."

He took his time for another few minutes, wanting to feel every grip of her sheath, that silken fist strangling him. And when he couldn't take it anymore, he got down to business.

18

AMBROISE Tregre wasn't taken downstairs to the rooms below the house. Timur didn't want him to know anything about those rooms unless it was necessary. The man had an eye for detail and a memory that allowed him to draw anything he saw. Timur didn't need that room hanging on a wall of a gallery someday. If it became obvious that Ambroise was part of the Tregre conspiracy, he would be taken to that room never to leave.

It was after midnight when the two brothers arrived back in San Antonio after having driven back to New Orleans. A plane had been sent for them and both, thankfully, had gotten aboard without needing weapons to persuade them.

Ambroise paced the length of the den. He didn't look at Timur but looked up and down the walls, along the floorboards and up to the ceiling. "Something is wrong, isn't it?" he asked abruptly, coming to a halt in the middle of the room. "You're here talking to me instead of Fyodor because you're head of security, not because you're his brother."

Timur nodded, studying the kid. He was older than Evangeline, but he looked younger. He was nervous, but not necessarily scared. He clearly wasn't aware this meeting was life or death for him. Timur didn't enlighten him. Sometimes, it was easier to get information by not asking a question, but waiting to hear what the other person had to say. He waited in silence.

Ambroise sighed. "We're never going to be free of what comes with our name. My grandfather was a vicious murderer. He liked to beat men and women equally, because it made him feel powerful. Unfortunately . . ." He trailed off and shook his head.

Timur waited. Hands in pockets. He leaned against the wall, ankles crossed, looking as if he would be at a disadvantage if a fight ensued. Ambroise had a leopard. That meant he would be fast and could easily leap the distance to Timur. Timur wasn't in the least bit worried. Temnyy was fast and experienced. Ambroise's leopard wouldn't stand a chance against him.

"My father and Uncle Gilbert, over the years, have begun to act like my grandfather did. I could see a change in them right after his death. Maybe it was there all along, and they were just better at hiding it than my grandfather. I left for school. I couldn't breathe there. I don't live at home and haven't for years. When I heard *Pere* planned to try to persuade Evangeline to let him help with her bakery, I wanted to be here to see what he was proposing. He got into some trouble a while back, and I didn't want that to touch her."

Timur wasn't going to waste time. "I know about the drugs, and it looks as if he's back in that business. What I don't understand is why you drew a map of your sister's house, so that any enemy she had, including your father, would know the entire layout."

Ambroise looked horrified. "Wait. No. I drew it for Christophe. He isn't an enemy. He couldn't be there and her house is so cool that I wanted him to see it. No one else . . ." He trailed off and closed his eyes. "Uncle Gilbert went to the apartment we share in New Orleans. Like I said, we don't live in the swamp anymore. When Christophe came back from Borneo, he needed a place to stay, so I had him stay with me. The drawings were at our place. Uncle Gilbert came over one morning for something, and I was in the shower. Christophe was already gone."

"Would there be an advantage to your father if Evangeline died?"

Ambroise frowned. Shook his head. "No. What would there be? She's married. Everything she has would go to her husband."

"Was there ever insurance or papers signed giving her father whatever she had?"

Ambroise was silent for a few moments. "He has insurance on all of us. I signed a legal document giving him everything if I died before I went to college. I think Christophe did as well, before he left the country. I don't know about Evangeline. It wasn't like any of us had anything."

Timur would bet his last dollar Evangeline had as well. Beau Tregre had sold out his daughter and her husband because he already knew he couldn't control her. He'd made his pitch, but it had been more to appease his conscience than because he thought she'd give him an "in" to her bakery. He wanted it to expand his opium business.

"Thanks, Ambroise," Timur said. "I need to talk to Christophe. Fyodor and Evangeline are in the sitting room. You can meet them there."

Ambroise went to the door, hesitated and then turned back to him. "My brother and I both have had suspicions that our father killed our mother. Once, when Christophe asked, he said she committed suicide. Uncle Gilbert said our grandfather killed her. When I asked *Pere*, he said she ran off. He told most outsiders she died in childbirth, but she didn't." He didn't wait for a response and left the room.

Christophe was waiting in the poolroom. He put the cue he'd been using in the rack and went straight to the large stone fireplace at the opposite end of the room from the table. "Is Evangeline all right?"

Timur nodded, studying the man's face. He was fit as only a shifter could be. In his prime, every muscle honed to its greatest strength. He looked like a man, unlike Ambroise. The two brothers couldn't be any different. There was a delicacy to Evangeline that was also in Ambroise. Timur didn't see that anywhere in Christophe, but his eyes were like his sister's. Same shape. Same thick crescent of lashes. He could see the resemblance when he looked for it.

It was a good tactic, asking questions first. Timur wasn't going to let him get away with it. If one of the brothers was guilty of helping his father, Christophe seemed much more likely to be that person. Except . . . Timur thought he was the stronger of the two boys. He wouldn't bend under pressure. Still, that meant it would be his choice to join with his father.

Timur remained silent. Christophe stared at him and his eyes changed color, going gold. Timur found himself staring at the man's leopard. It was close to the surface. Very close. Either Christophe had called it close because he intended to fight his way out of the room, or he wanted the cat close just to be safe.

"My leopard would tear yours to pieces," Timur cautioned. "You've had some fighting experience, but nothing like mine. That's the only warning you're going to get, so keep him under control."

Christophe blinked and the cat had subsided. Timur didn't believe for a moment that it had retreated far. Evangeline's brother glanced toward the door and then back at Timur, clearly sizing him up. He sighed. "What do you want?"

"Tell me about your father."

"That's what this is about. What's he done?"

"You tell me."

"How the hell would I know? He and Uncle Gilbert are just as fucked-up as my grandfather was. I got out of the family home as soon as Ambroise was clear. I mean the *day* that boy was accepted into a school, I took him to get an apartment and I got a job away from the swamp. I didn't go back except to see friends, and when Drake took over the lair, I asked him to send me anywhere and he did."

"Tell me about the drawings of the house. How did it come about that Ambroise drew those for you?"

Christophe held up his finger. "Don't you even try to implicate Ambroise in anything. If those drawings were used, it wasn't his doing. He's an artist. He has his head in the clouds half the time. I couldn't come to the house and he wanted me to see how beautiful Evangeline's home is. In fact, he even had sketched a few pictures for her to put up on the walls. He did it for me, to reassure me that she was all right."

"You deliberately brought up the fact that there was a discrepancy in the measurements and your brother had noticed them."

Christophe heaved a sigh. "Yeah. I know. He'd mentioned it in front of *Pere* and Uncle Gilbert. I wanted you to know. I should have kept my mouth shut, but something just didn't sit right about them being there. *Pere* had no interest in Evangeline. He never had. I grew up with him, and he rarely mentioned her. Half the time I thought he'd have forgotten her existence if Ambroise and I hadn't reminded him she needed food. Why would he suddenly take such an interest in her?"

"You tell me what you think."

There was a long silence. Christophe shook his head. "Whatever he wants from her, he's up to no good. *Pere* has always been the leader between the two of them. Uncle Gilbert's bullshit move to challenge you for your mate got him in trouble."

"Why do you think he did that?"

Christophe shrugged. "I gave up a long time ago trying to understand either of them. We were in survival mode. Ambroise and me. I was always afraid I'd have to kill them. I've answered your questions and I've admitted that my family is fucked-up, but you haven't told me anything." Belligerence crept into his voice.

"I don't have to tell you anything, Christophe. You're up here in this nice room and I'm treating you with kid gloves. You could be in another room with cement floors and drains. You think about that before you decide you want to work for your sister's husband. You think your family is fucked-up, you haven't even begun to see what that can look like."

They studied each other for a long time in silence. Timur let it stretch between them. He was certain Christophe was as innocent as Ambroise. In the end, it was Evangeline's brother who relented.

"If you know what Uncle Gilbert and *Pere* were doing here the other night, I would very much like to know as well. She's my sister. We might not have grown up together, but she's still mine. My family."

Timur weighed the risks. In the end, he shrugged. Christophe was family—his family through Evangeline. If he was guilty, he'd kill him, but if he wasn't, he'd do whatever he could for the man.

"I suspect he's set your sister and my brother up to be murdered. He's running opium again as well. There's more, but I think you get the picture."

Christophe swore and turned toward the door. Timur glided between the man and the exit. "That's not how we're going to handle it."

"Maybe not you, but I've had enough. He all but destroyed Ambroise. I've uncovered evidence that he murdered my mother. Or at least someone did. He's never going to cop to it. He and Uncle Gilbert are up to no good out there. I went out to the swamp when I knew they were both in town. I smelled females. More than one. I scented blood. A lot of it. I couldn't find bodies or live women. When I was there, no woman was ever brought to either of their homes, but I've been gone awhile."

"He'll be brought to justice. That's Drake Donovan's job as leader of his lair. If he comes after Fyodor or Evangeline, that will be my job. You need to stay clean."

"You don't understand what it's like to live knowing your entire family is fucked-up. I'm afraid of what I'm going to be. I've got those genes. Ambroise has them. Hell, Evangeline has them. None of us should have children, that's for damned sure."

"I do know what that's like. My father and grandfather were very similar to yours. I worry about Evangeline and Ashe all the time and any children we might bring into this world. What I do know is this, Christophe: there seems to be a difference between a true mated shifter and one who chooses not to mate with the woman he's supposed to be with. Leopards can drive their human counterparts to vicious, cruel acts, and I believe we can do the same to our leopards. They need their mate, and evidently, so do we."

Timur poured a drink for Christophe and handed it to him. "Take Ambroise somewhere safe for a few days. I'll let you know when this is over. It should be very soon."

"Let me help."

"Not this time. Evangeline needs family. I can't worry about keeping her brothers safe while I'm trying to keep her alive."

Christophe drank the small finger of scotch and then placed the glass carefully on the table beside the decanter. "There must be some way I can help."

Timur indicated the chairs on either side of the stone

hearth. Christophe sat across from him, leaning toward him, determination on his face.

"I want you to really think about what you know about your uncle Gilbert. It wasn't a smart move for him to challenge me. He wasn't drunk. It seemed more of an act of desperation."

Christophe frowned and shook his head. "I swear, I have no idea why that man would be that stupid."

Gilbert's seemingly ridiculous challenge nagged at Timur in the same way Anton Lipin deviating from his orders bothered him. It was clear that Christophe couldn't shed any light on either strange incident. He switched subjects.

"Tell me about your father's and uncle's friends."

Christophe shook his head. "They aren't friendly. No one goes to our home there, and other than working for Charisse and Armande, and they're packing and sending out the boxes through the mail so they aren't really around anyone, they have little contact with others. I know they were able to get Dion Lenoux a job with Armande in the factory. Sometimes they'll do that, but it's rare."

Timur tried to think how he could word the question to get Christophe to give an answer that he needed. "Who manages the perfume factory?"

"Armande is in charge of everything business. He gets the accounts and oversees everything in the factory. Charisse is very picky about how things look, so Armande makes certain that every box of soap and perfumes going out looks exactly how she wants it to look. Armande oversees all of that."

"How do you know?"

"I've known both of them for years. Charisse is different. She lives in a world of scents. She grows flowers, hybrids, you know, and comes up with all sorts of products that sell like hotcakes. She would stay in her greenhouse or the lab forever if she could. Especially since the truth about their mother came out. Her mother was involved with my grandfather and actually was as mad as a hatter. Seriously. She was a serial killer. Charisse just kind of disappeared into her work, and Armande took over running things."

"Do they need money?"

"Not when I worked there. I was a kid when I worked there, and it wasn't for me, but that's how I know the workings of the factory. I also know a lot of the people who work for Charisse and Armande."

"If opium was being packaged in the boxes being sent out, would either or both of them know about it?"

"No way would Charisse know unless she happened to go into the factory for some reason when they were packaging that shit. Then, knowing her, she'd probably zero in on the smell right in the middle of all those other smells. She never goes there anyway because there are too many people. She's really isolated herself."

"Would Armande package opium with the perfumes and soaps and allow that to be distributed worldwide? In other words, would he be part of your father's drug deals?"

Christophe shook his head and then stopped. "If Charisse was threatened, then yes, he'd do whatever it took to protect her."

Timur stood up. "Why didn't you ask Joshua for a job? He's your uncle."

"Two reasons. I want to get to know Evangeline. Working for her husband seemed the perfect opportunity. And Joshua took over Rafe Cordeau's territory when he disappeared. I didn't want any part of that."

"I see." He gestured toward the door. "Take Ambroise and find a safe place to hole up for a couple of days, until you get a text from Fyodor stating it's safe to come here. We'll talk about jobs then. Don't ask questions and don't jump to conclusions. Above all else, don't talk to your father or uncle. Make yourself scarce."

Christophe nodded, and Timur left him to find Fyodor.

It was nearly five in the morning and he'd been away from Ashe far too long. He was going through withdrawal. Besides, when he felt like shit, which he did after questioning Evangeline's brothers, he wanted to hold her. To feel like he wasn't covered in filth.

Fyodor gestured toward a chair when he walked in. He closed the door behind him and gratefully sank down onto the leather. There were two bottles of ice-cold water sitting on the small end table beside the chair. He picked one up and removed the lid.

"Both those boys are clean, Fyodor, but her father is dirty as hell along with her uncle. They're running drugs, and I believe they've set her up to die so they can inherit the bakery and get insurance money. Even though you're married, she hasn't changed her will, and her father gets everything, especially if you happen to die as well."

"No, he doesn't," Fyodor said. "First of all, he's dead and just doesn't know it and secondly, when we got married, we took care of all that. Even if he succeeded, he wouldn't inherit anything from her."

Timur filled him in on everything Evangeline's brothers had told him, and his own conclusions. "Lazar has his top man here. Lipin is Interpol. He's always worked for Lazar, apparently always done everything Lazar said, yet it appears he went against orders when he took a shot at me. That bothers me, Fyodor."

Fyodor shook his head. "Lazar could have changed his mind and given the order to kill you. It's possible we're reading the situation wrong and he'd go to Joshua Tregre to try to complete his pipeline again and then he wouldn't need us. It stands to reason that he might think, because they share a name, that Joshua would be like his uncles."

Timur put his feet up on an ottoman and stared into the fireplace, every muscle in his body aching. "Did you or anyone else talk to Gilbert after I left with Ashe? Ask him why he would challenge me for her?"

"Beau got him into the car and out of here very fast. Evangeline was upset and I didn't pursue it. I should have, Timur. That's on me."

Timur pressed the bottle of water to his forehead, letting the cool drops of condensation seep into his skin. "We're taking out Lazar's leopards. He can't afford to lose many. We don't have that many in any of the lairs. He can't see that by killing the women, we're getting fewer and fewer replacements. He needs his leopards."

"He's recruiting locally."

Timur shrugged. "Drake will go through that lair, and this time he won't be so nice. He'll do it quietly. You know Lazar isn't going to come here himself, although it's possible Rolan will try to usurp his position. They're always in competition and he'll hate the fact that Sevastyan is working as Mitya's security. You know Lazar will throw that in Rolan's face."

"We knew it was coming. We'll have time to prepare," Fyodor said.

Timur could hear the weariness in his brother's voice. "I think Christophe might be an asset to us, but he won't come in if he thinks you're dirty. You'd have to bring him all the way in." He ran a hand through his hair and glanced at his watch. She hadn't texted him to say her female needed his male. He would have welcomed that from her, even though he knew she needed the rest. Her body needed a few days to recover.

"Ashe is tough as nails," Fyodor said. "She doesn't look it, but she is. I watch her with you, Timur, and she's all about you. She pays attention. She's quick. She's a good match for you. I'm happy for you."

"She's . . . unexpected." Timur stretched and put his head back, to stare up at the ceiling. "She—" He broke off again. Not even to his brother could he say, *She turns me inside out.* He wasn't that kind of man. He might like to read poetry and secretly write it, but no one was ever supposed to know that about him. He certainly couldn't admit to flowery, romantic expressions when he was the man his brother counted on to destroy his enemies.

Fyodor laughed softly. "Believe me, Timur, I understand. If I tried to explain how I felt about Evangeline, or describe her to someone else, I wouldn't have the words either."

"Who knew? Who knew this would happen for us," Timur said. He couldn't just sit there; although he was very tired, he was feeling too much. She did that to him. He jumped up and began to pace. "She was the last thing I expected."

"Where is she from?"

"That's how small a world the leopard world really is," Timur said. "Her father is from somewhere in Greece. Her mother was from one of our lairs. Lazar sold her mother, at fifteen, at an auction in Greece. The grandfather, Mostafa is the surname, bought her for his son. The son was supposed to use her for a while, pass her around and then send her back to Lazar. He would put her with one of his men to provide sons and then they'd kill her."

Fyodor sat up straight, slightly shaking his head. "Lazar had his hands on Ashe's mother at one point? That is a small world."

"She's from one of our lairs, Fyodor. I don't know which one. It wasn't ours."

"Trust Lazar to get the most use and the most money out of one of our women. Someone needs to put that man out of his misery. Hopefully, it will be one of us," Fyodor said. "I used to think he was invincible."

"Maybe not invincible, but he sure as hell made a pact with the devil."

"How did Ashe end up here in the States?"

"Her parents fell in love and her dad was rich enough to get them out." Timur told Fyodor about Ashe's parents being true mates, falling in love and escaping their mutual lairs.

"You'd think Lazar would try to acquire Ashe to take her mother's place as a breeder in the lair," Fyodor said. "Why send a hit squad? The first few men were here to kill her. Lazar sent a bigger crew after us later, right?"

Timur nodded, shoved his hands in his pockets and went to the window to look out. He loved the night. Everything about it. That stemmed from all the times he'd crawled away from his father, broken and bruised, into the sanctuary of the darkness.

"From what I've gathered, Lazar and old man Mostafa had a falling-out. Mostafa had changed his mind when he heard his son was dead and wanted his granddaughter alive. Lazar got pissed and decided Mostafa wasn't getting his hands on Ashe. Lazar would kill her first, or if he could kidnap her, treat her to the same fate he'd had in mind for her mother."

"Evangeline's pregnant, and there's a part of me that worries what I'm passing down to our children. Our father. Sevastyan's father. Rolan and Lazar. Our grandfather. Where does it end?"

"I don't know," Timur said. "Christophe was just saying the same thing to me. His grandfather was, father and uncle are, cruel and vicious. Of course, we have to worry that one of our children could turn out the same way, or that we could somehow become like them."

"I haven't talked to Evangeline about it, but I know there's a part of her that's worried as well." Fyodor rubbed his temples as if he was getting a headache.

"Every single shifter, male or female, who has gone mad and turned into a vicious killer has refused to be with their true mate. They don't take care of their leopards. They deprive them and hunt with them. They allow them to crave human blood. If you mistreat your cat, eventually, you'll feel the effects."

Fyodor sighed. "I know that firsthand. My leopard is still fierce and always out for blood. Evangeline has tempered him. She quiets him and if I give him a chance to run with his mate nightly, he's much more content. I don't feel the effects of his bad temper nearly as much as I used to. In fact, now that I'm really thinking about it, the difference is night and day. I had to install steel bars on the doors and windows to keep him from escaping while I slept. That's how vicious he was. I've never once worried since I've been with Evangeline."

"It's strange how Evangeline and Ashe both are some kind of leopard whisperer. I've been around the wives of the others and my leopard still raged. When I first met Evangeline, I was shocked that he settled when he was close to her. Mitya and Sevastyan and Gorya all said theirs did as well. Now if they're close to Ashe, that happens. Don't you think it's strange that we're brothers and our women both have some trait that calms other leopards?"

"We're both lucky bastards," Fyodor agreed. "My leopard still gives me hell when Evangeline isn't around."

Temnyy had been nearly uncontrollable at times, raking and clawing for freedom, demanding blood. Raging against every human Timur came into contact with. He understood exactly what his brother meant. Now that he had Ashe, his leopard was much more amenable. Of course, he'd been out running with Godiva every night and having sex. That had tired him out and put him in a far better mood, but if they were away from their females too long, Temnyy was back to his storming, wild ways.

"My leopard is much happier with Ashe in our lives." Why was it so much easier to reference his cat rather than just tell his brother that the woman had changed his life forever? He couldn't imagine what it would be like without her now. He wanted Fyodor to know what Ashe meant to him. Why couldn't he just say it? That he loved her with every breath he took?

"We're going to have to come up with a better plan to

protect them," Fyodor said. "I worry that Lazar or Rolan will decide to plant a bomb in the bakery."

"They won't," Timur said, utterly confident. "They both want personal revenge. Hands-on. They'd like to torture us themselves. They won't come here until they know they're safe from us. They won't make a move like that against us. The team was sent to take us prisoner, not kill us. I think the idea was to keep us in this house and then Lazar would arrive and take it over."

"That sounds like the bastard."

"Ashe wants to rent the shop next to the bakery and then put the two shops together. I told her you owned the building." Timur paced across the floor. Restless. Unable to stay still. "I didn't want her to be disappointed if you thought it wasn't a good idea."

"It isn't just me who owns those buildings, Timur. You own them as well. *We* purchased them. You, Gorya and me. We're in this together. Your names are on this estate. You want to live here, we'll make it happen. In fact, I'd prefer that."

Timur nodded. "I did tell her that. Ashe likes Evangeline's house."

"So did Evangeline, but I convinced her to live here. There's more room for the leopards and we can watch over our women much easier here than spread out. Evangeline's house is a nightmare to defend. She bought it because it's cute and feminine and it was in that quiet little cul-de-sac with a very large park behind it so her leopard could run if she emerged. Our enemies could come at you from a dozen different ways, and it's also very public."

Timur nodded but said nothing. He wanted to give Ashe the world. Anything she wanted. He'd find a way to make the house work if that was her choice.

"You could persuade her by saying you were keeping me safe. And Evangeline. That's even better. She really likes Evangeline."

"Everyone likes Evangeline." Timur paced the length of the room. "I would expand the guesthouse if I was going to stay. I know there's a workout room here, but I'd want to put in my own as well as a few other amenities for Ashe." He couldn't believe he was considering it.

The estate was enormous, with plenty of room for the leopards. Groves of trees provided an arboreal highway for the cats. There was a full-sized pool and tennis courts. A spa that was not only well-equipped, but at any time, day or night, a massage therapist would come the moment they were called. There were any number of cars to drive, gardens and just about anything else a man—or a woman—could want.

"I would want privacy. I like to walk around in the nude when I'm at home."

"That isn't news to me," Fyodor said. "Do whatever you want to the house to make it right for the two of you, or build another one. There's a nice site just beyond the tea garden. You want that, we could have a house built immediately. If we build from the ground up, we can put in additional safety features, like a panic room, and escape routes for humans or leopards."

Timur liked that idea. He turned back to his brother and nodded. "That sounds good. I'll talk to Ashe about it and see if she likes the idea of designing our own home." Just saying that aloud gave him satisfaction. It would be their home together. They could have children. He would see to it that his children had a happy childhood and there was no chance that the cruelty and viciousness of his own father would ever touch them.

"Do you worry about what kind of father you're going to make?" Timur asked.

"All the time," Fyodor admitted. "I've been watching men like Drake and Elijah, even Jake Bannaconni. They're good with their children. I figure I can follow their lead, and if I get into trouble, I'll ask them questions."

Timur thought it was a good plan, especially since Evangeline was already pregnant and expecting twins. By the time Ashe and he had children, Fyodor would, hopefully, already know what he was doing and Timur would just follow his example. The entire question of having children and whether or not he was going to be a good father eluded him.

"After what we saw happen with Jake's woman, do you worry that you could lose Evangeline in childbirth?" Even as he voiced the question, he thought of Emma standing in a doorway, blood dripping onto the floor, a look of panic on her face. She'd nearly died. If that happened to Ashe . . . He had to shut down that line of thinking or he'd be doing the panicking.

"I think about it every day," Fyodor admitted. "I go to bed thinking about it and wake up the same way. She's so sick, in the bathroom all the time. She can barely hold down water. Already she has been severely dehydrated several times. Jake has this nurse that took care of Emma when she was pregnant and I've hired her to watch over Evangeline."

"Is Evangeline's life in danger?" Because if it was in danger, what the hell was Fyodor thinking letting her continue to be pregnant? Maybe having children wasn't such a good idea. Timur did his best to shut down panic. They couldn't lose Evangeline or Ashe.

Fyodor scowled and drummed his fingers against his thigh. "I worry and she says I'm being silly and that quite a few women have the problem she's having and they get through it. I read the statistics on it. There's not a lot of help other than IV fluids, which the nurse gives her. There's some medication, but so far, she hasn't had much relief."

"Is it true that birth control doesn't work on shifters?"

"It doesn't work during a heat cycle." Fyodor met his brother's eyes. "Don't even think about dictating whether or not you're going to have children. Think about all the things they give up for us. All the things we force them to do, the friends they can't have and the danger they're in. Don't be stupid, Timur, and try to take away something so fundamental as having children. You'd find yourself without a woman fast."

"Maybe she won't want them."

"Good luck with that. And what about you? Do you want children?"

He'd never dared to hope that he could have children. Never. Sometimes, he'd fantasize about having his own woman and there was sometimes a baby in her arms, but he hadn't really believed it would ever happen for him. Now there was Ashe and he wasn't going to lose her.

"Don't hold her too tight," Fyodor cautioned. "Sometimes, with Evangeline, I have to tell her that I need to know she's safe. That she won't disappear and nothing is going to happen to her. I'm lucky that she understands I'm having one of those days. Sadly, I have them often, but she gives me that. At least talk to Ashe before you handcuff her to the bed so you know where she is and that she's safe."

"I'd be more likely to handcuff her to me," Timur said. He needed to be with her. Maybe it was the talk about their women and their safety that had him so uneasy. He needed to get this done so he could lie in bed beside her and listen to her breathe. There was something very soothing about hearing Ashe breathe.

"I curl my hand around her throat so her heart beats right into my palm," Fyodor confessed as if he could read Timur's mind. "Even that isn't enough. I can hear my own heart beating right over top of hers because I'm terrified living with the idea that I could lose her."

Timur knew what he was talking about. He knew what real terror was. He'd grown up in a monster's household. He'd had no chance at life. None. His father had beaten humanity out of him in his hope of creating a dark, twisted being that would be useful to him. Even after he'd gotten out, he'd take that legacy with him. He couldn't escape who he had become. But none of that held a candle to the soul-deep terror that came with even the thought of losing Ashe. Ashe was a light shining right into him. If he was going to write poetry again and enter it into his secret journals, every poem would be about her.

"We're going to have to kill Evangeline's father and uncle," Fyodor said abruptly. Rage crept into his voice and there in the darkness, his eyes glowed with a crimson fury. His leopard stared at Timur through Fyodor's eyes. The dangerous cat was very close to the surface. He probably had been prowling there, his temper smoldering as man and beast turned over and over in their minds the danger to Evangeline and where it came from.

"I'm very aware of that," Timur agreed. "In part, by killing them, we'll also be cutting off the opium line to Lazar. With Ulisse gone, we've also cut off his trafficking. He'll have to start hunting around and that might mean he'll make an approach to Joshua, or if we're lucky, you."

"I'm not killing them because it will help us with our plan to get Lazar and Rolan into the United States where we have the chance at wiping them off the face of the earth. I'm killing them because they betrayed Evangeline. *My* Evangeline. No one touches her. No one sets her up. That's why they have to die."

Timur agreed wholeheartedly. He loved his sister-in-law. She had managed to make them all a family. That family included his cousins, Mitya and Sevastyan and Gorya. All of them were protective of her.

"She can't go into work." Timur made it a decree. "Now that we know the danger is to her, above anyone else right now, she's got to stay where we can protect her."

"I'm well aware of that. She's so sick, day and night, vomiting. Scares the hell out of me. This was one of those times I had a talk with her and explained, if she wanted to continue this pregnancy, there were certain things I needed.

One of them was for her to stay home. I've already told Ashe that I'm not going to allow Evangeline to go to work. She volunteered to open the bakery for us."

Timur froze right in the middle of the floor. Air was trapped in his lungs because he couldn't exhale. His heart nearly stopped. "She's at the bakery right now? Alone?"

"Of course, not alone. What do you take me for? She's yours. That means she needs to be protected. I sent Gorya and Jeremiah with her."

Two men. Gorya was good, but Jeremiah was still learning. He didn't have the instincts that came with experience. Heart pounding, Timur tried to quiet his chaotic brain. Something nagged there. Anton Lipin in the grove shooting at him. Ashe wasn't in danger from Lazar or Rolan because they'd completely wiped out the teams sent to get her. But there was Evangeline's father and uncle. The uncle who had challenged Timur for her.

She had only two men guarding her when Timur had kept a full six-man team on Evangeline. He wanted to punch his brother. Temnyy roared with rage.

"You should never have allowed her to go," Timur bit out, already turning away.

"I realize that now, Timur, but at the time Evangeline was so sick, throwing up again, and I had to call the nurse to give her fluids. I was so worried and she was crying, worried about her bakery and Ashe volunteered to go. I wasn't thinking clearly. Ashe was very insistent, and I had the place checked out thoroughly. I sent Gorya with her. We've concentrated the threat on us mainly." Fyodor was on his feet. "Shit. They'll be expecting Evangeline to be there."

Timur was already out of the room. He didn't much care what Fyodor said. Timur whipped out his phone and group texted, alerting the guards to drop whatever they were doing, secure the house and guard Fyodor and Evangeline.

Apparently, Fyodor was texting frantically as well, demanding half the men go with Timur. He wasn't waiting for them, no matter what his brother ordered.

He chose one of Fyodor's toys, a sleek Ferrari that had belonged to Antonio Arnotto. Siena didn't want any of her grandfather's collection of cars and had gifted them to Fyodor, along with the estate, on his wedding day. It was a gorgeous car, but more than looks, it had speed and handling that was hard to beat.

She was there with only two guards. Gorya—his cousin who had been through too much for any one person to manage in a lifetime—and Jeremiah, a boy becoming a man. He wasn't quite as fast yet as the others. He didn't have experience with killer leopards—cats trained to need violence and blood the way most people needed air.

Timur texted as he drove. Over and over. Gorya didn't answer. Neither did Jeremiah. The beginnings of panic settled in his gut. He breathed deeply to overcome it.

19

"UM, Ashe, that's the third time you've set off the fire alarm," Jeremiah announced. He hadn't moved from where he was perched on the edge of a table, eating cookie dough. He clearly wasn't planning on doing anything about it.

She tried to glare at him over her shoulder as she frantically waved a towel to clear the smoke, teetering on a chair at the same time. "You might help, you cretin."

He shrugged. "There is no help for you. None. Zero. I surrender to the absolute ineptness that is you."

Gorya caught Ashe around the waist with both hands and lifted her off the chair. "Stay down." He took the towel from her. "And you, quit eating that and help out."

Jeremiah shook his head. "Evangeline made this cookie dough. It's the only decent thing to eat, and I'm starving. We've been here for two hours already with just the blackened ruins of what is left of a once-great bakery. May it rest in peace."

Ashe threw a blackened croissant at him and, with deadly accuracy, hit him in the head.

Jeremiah was unfazed. "Does Timur know you can't cook?"

"This is *baking*," she hissed. "It's an entirely different thing."

"You didn't answer the question." Jeremiah spoke with exaggerated loudness as if she wouldn't be able to hear him over the blaring of the fire alarm.

The alarm was unnecessarily loud and she was definitely talking to Evangeline about it. Why would anyone need to have some idiotic piece of technology blaring so loudly one could barely think? It was no wonder she messed up a few recipes.

She dumped the tray of black croissants in the trash along with the other two hours' worth of her attempts. "Evangeline must be a baking genius or something. Who does this? And why?"

"The why is easily answered," Jeremiah said. "For me. I need to eat. If there isn't anything else she's left overnight, then I claim this dough. If you try to actually bake cookies, you'll just fuck those up and then I'll starve."

"If I had a gun, I'd shoot you right now," Ashe declared.

Jeremiah ignored her and scooped another spoonful of dough out of the large round metal bowl Ashe had pulled out of the walk-in refrigerator. Evangeline prepared dough for pies and cookies ahead of time. Ashe had left those for last, hoping to get the harder items she'd have to bake from scratch done first. She'd followed the recipes *exactly* but the results were disasterous. Okay, maybe not exactly. Maybe once or twice she'd lost her place or put in one spice instead of another. In her defense, they looked alike.

"Have you considered a career in assassination? You could just poison people," Jeremiah offered, licking the spoon.

"Don't you *dare* put that spoon back in the dough. That

is unsanitary. You'll be the one poisoning the customers." She reached to yank the mixing bowl from his hands.

He caught the other side of it and jerked it to him, holding it protectively like a mother might a baby. "You're going to put the cookies in the oven, that will kill any germs I might have. I need this after sampling your vile concoctions. I've been traumatized, and my stomach is devastated beyond belief. Sheesh, woman, I'm not certain Fyodor should allow you into their family with the carnage you've wrought on these poor helpless baked goods."

"There's a reason you don't have a girlfriend," Ashe said, and dumped the rest of the trays of blackened croissants into the trash.

"How do you know I don't have a girl?" Jeremiah scowled at her.

She yanked the bowl of cookie dough from his hand. "You wouldn't dare be so mean. You lack the ability to be supportive."

Marching over to one of the two long islands in the center of the room, where she'd laid out the recipes, she slammed the mixing bowl down onto the metal top with a little too much force. The sound was loud enough to make her wince.

"Leave her alone, Jeremiah," Gorya said again. "He's working on his vocabulary, just in case you haven't noticed. He might shut the hell up if you acknowledge his good word usage."

Jeremiah snorted. "I'd do better if she'd quit setting off that fucking alarm."

The fire alarm went silent abruptly, removing the blaring and very annoying noise. Gorya had unscrewed it and unhooked wires.

"It isn't entirely my fault that the stupid fire alarm keeps going off. It's highly sensitive. Evangeline needs to change the setting or something."

Gorya groaned, shook his head and walked to the other

side of the room, keeping his back to her. Jeremiah wasn't so polite.

"Change the settings? As in you have a fire alarm but you set it for quiet? On vibration maybe? If there's smoke the entire building might vibrate?"

"Shut the hell up," she snapped. "I'm trying to concentrate. If I don't get this right, we'll be a bakery without any goods. I can pretend we're sold out of everything else, if I at least have these cookies."

"Ashe." Gorya came back to stand beside her. "Why don't we just clean up in here and keep the bakery closed for another day or so until we see if Evangeline gets better?"

"I promised her I would help her," Ashe said.

She looked around the room. Pots, pans and dirty dishes were piled high. Flour coated the floor and was on nearly every surface. She didn't even know how that had happened. The cute little torch that she was supposed to use delicately had nearly started a fire. The worst was, she really had been working hard. Very hard. She had absolutely nothing to show for it but a very messy room that looked like it would take a cleaning crew of twenty or so to put it right.

Ashe wasn't given to crying. She just wasn't, but she felt the burn behind her eyes and hastily turned away from both men. She'd never had any interest in cooking or baking, but she'd always thought it would be easy enough if she just put her mind to it. She'd done that. She'd really tried, but not one single thing she'd made had come out right. She certainly couldn't sell any of the goods she'd done, not in Evangeline's exclusive bakery with its really great reputation. Not even the one sponge cake that had sort of turned out. It was a little lopsided, but the taste was right. Okay, *very* lopsided, and caved in completely.

"She'll know you tried," Gorya said. "We'll help you clean up."

Jeremiah hopped off the table and went straight to the pile of dirty dishes. "No worries, I'm good with soap."

She knew he was trying to make her feel better by volunteering to help clean up but that meant she didn't look as stoic as she hoped. She must look close to tears. That was just plain humiliating.

"I'm going to try this last thing. These are Fyodor's favorite cookies. If nothing else we can bring them home with us if they don't turn out and we decide we can't open. I'll get them on the trays to bake and while they're baking I'll make the caramel cages that she puts over some of them."

"You go ahead and try—" Jeremiah broke off. "You do that," he corrected. "I'll start the cleanup."

Ashe took a deep breath. She could do this. For Evangeline. For Timur. She didn't want all of his men laughing at him behind his back, making fun of him because she couldn't cook. She had learned one thing from this horrible experience. Well, maybe two. She *detested* baking and all things to do with kitchens and she hated the sound of fire alarms.

She wasn't going to get distracted. It wasn't like she had to keep track of ingredients. Evangeline had already done that. Of course, she was going to put the other ten things she'd ruined that Evangeline had in the refrigerator out of her mind and just think of these cookies as her first attempt. They were going to be perfect.

Very carefully, she laid out the cookies on the trays. Dozens of trays. She made certain each cookie was perfectly shaped. Each time she cut the dough with the little circle or star, she ended up with rough edges, but she smoothed them meticulously. She refused to think of time marching on, or the bang of the dishes as Jeremiah rinsed them and put them in the dishwasher.

"They look good," Gorya observed.

"I've got the ovens exactly the right temperature this time," she said, nervously checking the ovens for the fifth time. "But look anyway, just to be certain, Gorya." She was *not* asking for Jeremiah's help again. She'd tried that before and he'd been a Neanderthal.

"If you're looking for three fifty, you're right on target," Gorya said.

She glared at Jeremiah over her shoulder and gave a little sniff of disdain. Very, very carefully, she carried one tray at time to the ovens and shoved them in. She'd tried before to carry two trays of tart pastries and had dropped them upside down on the floor of the kitchen. She might have been tempted to try to save them, but not in front of Jeremiah, who had laughed like a hyena, or Gorya, who'd kept a straight face and crouched down to help her pick them up from the flour-and-sugar-covered floor.

"You know, the first trays are going to be done before the last ones," Jeremiah called helpfully.

She almost dropped the tray she was inserting into the second oven. There were racks in each oven, evenly spaced, but Evangeline had said something about the middle racks she couldn't remember.

"Shut the fuck up," Gorya snapped. "She's doing fine."

Ashe tried not to look anxious. "Do you think he's right?"

"Set the timer. These are going to be great," Gorya assured.

"I think I'm falling a little in love with you," she said and sent Jeremiah another glare over her shoulder as she set the timer.

Jeremiah was completely unfazed by her glare. He didn't drop dead and he didn't wither on the spot.

"Now I just have to make the caramel cages." Even she heard the trepidation in her voice. She had messed up every single thing that required her to mix any ingredients and this looked very hard. Like expert hard.

"I'll help," Gorya said.

"I won't," Jeremiah called from where he was spraying

water over pots and pans. "I'm going to sit back and watch the show."

She resisted throwing a knife at him, but she imagined it while she studied the recipe. She had to read it three times before the image of Jeremiah pleading for his life faded. That was the problem, her mind just wouldn't stay on mundane things like baking.

"This looks difficult, Gorya."

"One step at a time. First step."

She took a deep breath, and measured out sugar, corn syrup and water into a large, heavy-bottomed saucepan and turned on the heat. "It's supposed to be medium-high, whatever that means. Is it medium, or is it high? Why don't they just say so you don't have to guess?" she groused, chewing her lip. She was sweating. Actually sweating.

"I've got it," Gorya said and adjusted the heat.

"I know there was a candy thermometer around here somewhere." She looked around a little helplessly. "I'm supposed to insert it and cook the sugar until it reaches three hundred and eleven degrees. Insert it where? What does that mean?" She pushed back her hair with her forearm. She wasn't about to contaminate her sugar concoction.

Gorya found the thermometer and put it in the saucepan. Ashe breathed a sigh of relief as she stirred the sugar. "It's hot in here, isn't it?"

"It's the ovens," Gorya said. "We've got them all on and that's heating the room."

She could have kissed him. It wasn't that she was overheated because she was so nervous. There was no way she was ever doing this again. Fyodor would have to hire a qualified baker. Was it a baketress? Was there such a thing? She *had* to keep her mind on what she was doing. She looked at the recipe again.

"I have to wait for it to get to the hard crack stage. What's that?" She looked at Gorya for advice.

"Babe, I have no idea what that means," he admitted.

"Those cookies smell good though. Really good. I think you did it this time."

She wasn't about to point out that Evangeline had done it. The dough had been prepared the night before and left in the refrigerator. Of course, so far she hadn't messed them up like everything else.

Ashe sent Gorya a smile, still carefully stirring. "I hope so. Could you open the back door and let in some cool air? Or do you think it will mess up the sugar and it won't get to the hard crack stage, whatever that is."

Jeremiah burst out laughing "Hard crack stage? That sounds like you're cooking up some kind of drug instead of candy."

She spun around, hands on her hips. "That's it. I'm kicking you out." She pointed to the door. "Now. Go away."

"Come on, Ashe. You finally have cookies in the oven that smell like they aren't the charred remains of zombies. I need sustenance. I'll be good."

"No, you won't." She knew he wouldn't, but he did look hangdog. That particular expression was going to get him out of trouble for certain. She felt sorry for any woman who fell in love with him.

Gorya laughed at her. "I knew you'd give in as soon as he gave you that puppy dog look."

He moved easily between the two metal islands locked in place in the center of the room, striding toward the back door. The two metal surfaces had been immaculate when she'd arrived in the kitchen. Now, they were a mess. She had no idea how they'd gotten that way. She'd never seen them like that when Evangeline was baking. Even when she rolled out dough and flour covered the surface, they never looked like this. She imagined she might have to buy the bakery new islands, they were that bad. It might be better than having to clean them.

She bent over the recipe, frowning as she found and laid out the small domes to use to make the cages. Some were flatter than others, but she began to coat each of them with cooking spray.

"Thoroughly coat," she murmured aloud, over and over.

"Is the record stuck?" Jeremiah asked, turning toward her, laughing.

A blast of cool air swept through the room and she gasped, dropping the spray can and hurrying to her sugar, afraid it would ruin it. As she turned to run, out of the corner of her eye, she saw Gorya crumple to the ground like a rag doll. The sound of a muffled gun was simultaneous. She knew instantly the weapon had a silencer on it. Contrary to popular belief, silencers didn't completely stop the sound of a gunshot. Her father had fired bullet after bullet from various guns until she could tell him what they were just by the sound.

"Jeremiah!" She yelled to him as she sprinted toward the fallen man. He was closer and already his head was turning toward Gorya, who was sprawled half in and half out of the kitchen.

Jeremiah got to him first, stepping to the side of the door and reaching with one hand to snag the shoulder of his shirt. Up close, Ashe could see blood spreading fast across the pale blue material until it was the only color she could see.

"Get back!" Jeremiah yelled as he jerked hard to pull Gorya in.

The shooter clearly was behind the Dumpster to the left of the door and had shot at a close angle. He fired again and Gorya's leg jerked. Then Jeremiah was falling back, still dragging Gorya. Ashe saw blood on Jeremiah's shoulder and pain clearly etched into every line of his face. She leapt across the doorway, took hold and shut it as Jeremiah managed to get Gorya all the way inside. She slammed the lock into place and then pushed the rolling trays in front of it, taking the time to lock them in place. They were light and wouldn't hold for long, but it was all she had.

Whirling around, she saw immediately that Gorya was in trouble. "Jeremiah, get on your feet. You have to help me." She poured authority into her voice. She could see he was in shock from the pain. She reached for Gorya. She was leopard, and she was strong. Her parents had taught her all kinds of skills and made certain she trained daily.

Miraculously, Jeremiah got up, swaying, but up on his feet. With his good arm, he helped her drag Gorya to the far end of the room where the small bathroom was.

"There's a first aid kit under the sink. You keep him alive," she ordered. "I'll hold them off. Call for Fyodor and Timur. Tell them we'll need a helicopter. He won't make it waiting for an ambulance to get him there."

"Ashe," Jeremiah started.

"Don't argue. You're a mess." She slammed the bathroom door shut and raced back to the two metal islands Evangeline had as her workstation. They were long and sat in front of the door leading outside. Both were on rollers. She unlocked them and rearranged them, leaving enough room for the door to open. Sooner or later they were going to get inside. She guessed by the sounds outside it would be sooner. She put them wide enough to block either side of the door, forcing whoever came in to go down the middle between the two islands. She locked them in place.

She knew Jeremiah would call for help so she didn't waste time there. Instead, she looked around the kitchen for weapons. There were plenty. She had been trained in guerrilla warfare and hand-to-hand combat. She knew how to call up her leopard to use her skills in fighting, and she knew how to run like hell when the situation demanded it. This time, there would be no running. She had to protect the two wounded men. Ashe raced around the kitchen, preparing her battleground.

When she was done, she hit the light switches, not that it would do that much good if she was facing leopards, but she liked the cover of darkness. She knew where everything was, but she stayed very still, crouching low just in front of the two islands, with her chosen arsenal. The scent of burnt sugar permeated the air. Running, she added another cup of water and more sugar, just dumping it in the pan. She left the burner on.

She didn't have time to make a survival gas mask; in the fifteen minutes it would take to make it, this fight would probably be over. She glanced down at her watch to note the time. She had no idea how many were in the alley, but there was more than one shooter.

Gorya had been shot at an angle, the distance close. The shooter had definitely been hiding behind the Dumpster.

Jeremiah had been shot from a completely different angle. He'd protected himself from the shooter behind the Dumpster, but that had exposed him to someone on the roof of one of the buildings across the alley. Even as she was figuring out how the two men were shot, she sprayed water on the windows from the hoses at each of the three sinks. It was long range for the one on the other side of the room, but the sprayer was fairly powerful and it hit dead center. She didn't want a river, just enough.

The flour was next. She threw it at the windows, coating them, one after another, sending a prayer to the universe that it would stick. At least it would cut down on the attackers' vision. She hurried back to the front of the two islands and waited, counting her heartbeats. She didn't have to wait for long.

A volley of bullets came through the window, shattering the glass. She waited, counting her heartbeats. The breath moving in and out of her lungs. Her hands were steady as something hit the back door hard, jarring the tall rolling trays.

"They're coming through in another minute, Jeremiah," she called out. "I'll hold them off as long as possible. Keep Gorya alive no matter what."

Timur loved Gorya. She knew the two cousins had been

raised as siblings, and Gorya might as well have been Timur's blood brother for how close they were. He wasn't dying. Not today and not by cowards ambushing him.

"He's bad, Ashe," Jeremiah called. "I should be out there and you in here."

She ignored the macho male bullshit that demanded a wounded man protect her when she was perfectly capable. "I was trained for this, by my parents." She tried to reassure him, hoping his ego wouldn't have him abandoning Gorya to cover her unnecessarily. "I'll call you if I need you. Just keep him alive."

The door shook, and the blow sounded even louder. She was tempted to go unlock it so it wouldn't be destroyed. She looked around the kitchen. She'd pretty much already single-handedly managed to destroy Evangeline's beautiful little kitchen—without the intruders. The door shuddered again and burst inward, narrowly missing the two islands that formed a hallway.

A hail of bullets laid down cover and the first assailant burst through the door, his gun in his arms, finger on the trigger. He was already looking left to right as he stepped forward right into the corridor she'd set up. Behind him, a second man followed in tight, standard formation. She had counted out the seconds of the blasts of the guns. When the first man stopped firing, she stood and threw the knife she'd pulled from the block, all in one motion.

The knives weren't balanced, but she was used to that. Not a single knife her father had made her practice throwing for hours on end, every day throughout her childhood, had been balanced. She hit the first man right in the throat, and as he started to go down, she threw the second knife and dove for cover.

The first man gurgled horribly in the dark. The second man yelled, his voice trembling with shock and pain. She'd hit him, but he was spraying the room with bullets. A few came close, but he had no real idea where she was. She could tell by the way he was yelling that he was hurt, but she didn't know how badly.

She tossed a long-handled metal spoon right into the shelves of pots and pans. It made a terrible racket, enough to draw the fire from the injured man. Bullets hit Evangeline's prized collection of cooking pots and saucepans. Ashe crawled on her belly, using toes and elbows to propel her forward.

Her target had climbed over the metal table. She'd covered each tabletop with a mixture of oil and jalapeño juice. He'd slid on his back across the oily surface, thinking to use it to get closer to his target. The jalapeño juice came into contact with any bare skin he had. He started cursing. She silently thanked Evangeline for making her jalapeño muffins for early morning workers.

Ashe could see drops of blood dripping onto the white flour on the floor as he came closer. She waited until she was certain he was right on the mark she'd made and then she was up, the handle of the pot containing the boiling sugar and syrup in her hand. She threw the contents in his face, stepped forward and wrenched at the gun in his hands.

She found herself looking at a leopard. A very, very angry one. If he'd allowed his leopard out, he wouldn't have been able to hold on to the gun. He flailed around, screaming as the sugar attached to his skin, burning. As he tried to scratch it off, the jalapeño juice on his fingerless gloves added to the fierce burn, but he wouldn't release the weapon.

She heard the spit of another gun, and a bullet just cut across her temple. She caught up the fryer as she whirled around, flinging the contents at the man with the sugar burns. He screamed as the donut oil hit him square in the chest, neck and face. She kept him between her and the other gunman.

"Dave, drop to the floor, drop to the floor!" the other man yelled.

Dave's leopard glared at her, struggling with his crazed counterpart to shift into his cat form, but Dave wasn't thinking clearly and wouldn't release the weapon, fighting the burns and the leopard at the same time.

She counted to herself. Her father had drilled it into her that if she was using a human shield, a member of the opposition, it would take no more than ten to fifteen seconds before his friends would most likely shoot him to get to her. She dropped to the floor and heard the shot. David dropped, his screaming abruptly cut off. She found herself staring into his eyes and watched as the leopard's life in him faded as well.

Ashe went for his gun. Somehow, when he'd dropped to the floor, his gun had fallen under his body. She tried to get him off of it, but three bullets hit the stove behind her, forcing her to roll away from him. She chose to roll toward the butcher block of knives. It was still sitting right where she'd positioned it, on the floor, just behind the left island.

Bullets hit the floor to the left of her, but she kept going, feeling a little desperate. She had no idea what was happening in the bathroom, whether Gorya or even Jeremiah was still alive. She didn't really know how badly Jeremiah had been wounded. Her hand closed on a knife and she pulled it from its resting place in the butcher block.

She took a deep breath, let it out and then tossed a smaller knife toward the saucepan that lay just feet from her. Instantly bullets hit all around it. She stood and threw, all in one motion, registering her enemy even as she was straightening her body. It was instinct more than anything else that gave her such true aim. Instinct and years of practice. He went down hard, the knife protruding from his throat. She closed her eyes when she heard the gurgles that told her he was dying.

When she opened her eyes, she was looking directly at the door. Her heart nearly stopped when she saw a leopard stick its head cautiously through the doorway. She could use all the survivalist tricks in the world, but the odds were stacked in favor of a killing machine like a leopard. Even a gun . . . She looked toward the dead body of David. She knew exactly where his weapon was.

She recognized the leopard. This was Evangeline's uncle Gilbert. He'd challenged Timur's leopard for her. Ducking back into cover, heart racing, she called to her leopard. *Godiva, I know you despise this leopard, but I need you to be at your most alluring.* Her hands went to her jeans. She stripped fast and shifted.

Godiva shook herself and then chuffed. Deliberately, Ashe directed her toward David's body. All the while she rubbed her scent on everything she could find, spreading her pheromones, the last stages of her heat, but no less potent or tempting as when she'd first gone into her cycle.

The male came around the island, its yellow eyes staring at her. Deep inside Godiva, Ashe shivered. She felt as if she was looking at pure evil. Her heart thudded and she had to fight to keep herself from directing Godiva to run. There was no fighting this male. He was bigger and stronger and she was very inexperienced. But she had other skills.

Godiva swished her tail and spread her tantalizing scent toward the male as she made her way to David, one sultry step at a time. The male came around the other side of the island to cut her off. Godiva swiped her paw at him but then chuffed seductively, still moving, positioning herself right in front of David's body.

Ashe knew where the gun was. She could even see a small part of it. Godiva crouched invitingly. The male took the bait, rushing toward her. Godiva's paw reached beneath David's body, hooked the weapon with her claws and pulled it out. Instantly Ashe shifted partially, her entire upper body. It was sickening, and difficult to concentrate, but it was the only thing she could think of to save them both. She turned, shocked that the leopard was so close. She felt a blast of hot air, and the creature lunged.

She fired, point-blank, over and over, emptying the gun into the leopard's brain and throat. She couldn't stop pulling the trigger, not even when the cat was dead on the floor right in front of her.

"That wasn't a smart move, Ashe," Beau Tregre said from the doorway. He held a gun on her and his hand was rock steady. "Now you have no weapon. Why don't you shift fully and come here?"

"Screw you," she hissed, shifting. "I'm not going anywhere with you." She looked around. Her clothes were just a few feet from her and she walked over to them and picked up her jeans.

"Where's Evangeline?"

"I can't believe you're planning on killing your own daughter," she snapped. "What kind of asshole are you?" She yanked up her jeans and glanced at him. He was staring at her breasts. Deliberately she picked up her top but didn't put it on. Let him be fascinated while she figured out a plan.

"She's safe. She isn't here this morning, bad luck for you."

Beau swore and gestured for her to walk to him. She shook her head.

"I'm going to kill you right where you stand."

"I don't think you are," another voice said. Timur reached around him and took the gun from Beau's hand. "Step inside."

"There might be more," Ashe warned, yanking on her shirt. She ran toward the bathroom. "Jeremiah and Gorya have been shot."

"We've got medics on the way. We have to get rid of these bodies. They're all leopard. I've got a crew coming right after me. Fyodor sent an army."

Timur nudged Beau. "Where did you get your recruits?"

Beau shrugged. "Not everyone was happy to work for my nephew. It seems that Joshua can be a real hardass. He doesn't let his men have fun anymore. They were happy to work for me." He smirked. "A couple in Drake Donovan's lair hate him as much as I do. I've got a good business. A great one. Armande Mercier will do anything I tell him, just to keep his sister safe. Rafe Cordeau and I had a deal to run opium through his pipeline. When Rafe disappeared, I went to Ulisse. Now he seems to have disappeared. I can offer you the same deal I had with them."

"Why did Anton Lipin take a shot at me in the grove?"

Beau shrugged. He looked surer than ever because Timur hadn't immediately rejected his offer. "I have no idea."

Beau shrugged again. "What do you think? Let's do business. We can double what we're doing if we have control of the bakery as well."

Timur shot Beau Tregre without another word. He felt nothing when he did it. Not elation, not anything at all. This man had tried to kill his own daughter. He would have eventually killed his sons for money. He was cruel, vicious and corrupt. Timur looked up at his woman standing there. She was amazing. *Amazing.* And she was his.

It was Temnyy who saved his life. The cat leapt toward the surface, forcing his muscles to contort, fur bursting through skin. He toed his shoes off as he ripped at his jeans, peeling them off his legs fast. Not fast enough, but when the huge male leopard hit him, he was half leopard, half human.

The leopard hit so hard it drove him to the ground. He heard Ashe scream as if at a distance, but pain had blossomed and spread through him. Instinct had him rolling, trying to protect his neck, throat and front from the teeth and claws of the big cat. His shirt had ripped to accommodate the change, the thick fur protecting him as teeth drove for his spinal cord, but he couldn't shake the leopard and get his legs from his jeans. It required one second, a fraction of a second, but he didn't have that.

Godiva hit the male hard, coming in from his right side and driving him off Timur. Instantly he had the jeans gone and was able to shift completely, whirling around to face his opponent. Godiva's momentum had taken her to the open doorway and she went right on out the door so there was nothing at all between Timur and his opponent. He'd never seen the large leopard before. It was in good fighting shape and had obviously seen battles. It was an Amur, beautiful and distinctive. He knew then he was facing Anton Lipin.

Temnyy raged, his lips drawn back, ears flat, snarling, fierce and ready to fight. He growled at his opponent, and then took a step toward him with a screaming roar of fury. The two cats stared, each waiting for the other to make a single move while they growled and spit, showing their displeasure and hatred of each other.

They launched themselves almost simultaneously, meeting in midair, trying to wrap each other up, gripping with their front legs, while their back legs sought to do the most damage possible, ripping and slicing at bellies and genitals. Anton's leopard was every bit as vicious as Temnyy. They came down, locked together, rolling, legs tearing at each other. They hit the island, and for a moment were trapped there, big bodies bending at impossible angles, utilizing their flexible spines.

Temnyy broke away, rolled to his feet, leapt into the air and attacked before Anton's leopard could climb to his feet. Gripping with his front legs, Temnyy held him fast while he sank teeth deep and ripped and tore with his hind legs. He couldn't get a good enough hold to kill him, so he did as much damage as possible to weaken him.

The two leopards broke apart, eyed each other for a short growling session and then Anton launched his big male into the air. Temnyy rose to meet him, slashing with razor-sharp claws at the exposed belly. It was luck more than just plain skill that allowed him to hook claws deep and rip his opponent open.

Anton's leopard howled in pain, falling to the floor as blood instantly covered his belly. He lay on one side panting, agony forcing his human to take his place in order to spare the animal suffering.

Timur made certain there were no weapons close as he shifted back to human as well. He lifted his gaze to his woman standing in the doorway before checking out the dying man. She had to be all right. There was blood on her, but she was standing, head up, just looking across the mess that had once been an immaculate kitchen. She tossed him his jeans and he dragged them on before switching his attention to Anton. The man was in a bad way. Even if Timur wanted, he couldn't have saved him.

Anton looked up at Timur. "You don't know what you have. What she does. Let her come to me. Sit by me." There was pride on his face, and in his voice, but not in his eyes. The plea was there. "She calms him. My leopard. She makes him settle. He's never had that. Not once in all these years."

It was that simple—or that monumental. Anton Lipin cared for his leopard, and like all leopards in the fucked-up lairs, his had been viciously abused and trained to be savage. Out for blood. Cruel. Every bad trait possible had been encouraged and brought out. In doing so, there was no rest for the human counterpart.

Timur fought for his breath as he reached a hand toward his woman. His men were pouring into the alleyway and bakery, spreading out, making certain that every threat was gone. They needed to do damage control outside, in the alleyway, making certain those shop owners who might be arriving early saw nothing that would alarm them.

Ashe went to him, compassion in her eyes as she glanced down at the man who had nearly killed Timur. Then her gaze was sliding over her man, touching on every slash, cut and rising bruise. She brushed his face with gentle fingers. His hands were on her, sliding over her, noting every drop of blood. She had a gash in her temple and another along her shoulder. There was a tear in her shirt. She was barefoot and dusted in what looked like flour. She was the most beautiful sight he'd ever seen.

"Beside me," Anton said. "Close. For him. He has needed a rest, and there was never one for him."

Timur sank down onto the floor beside the dying man. Oddly, he identified with him. That very well could have been his fate—asking his enemy to help his leopard as they passed from the world. Like Timur, Anton had been born into that world of violence. He'd given his allegiance to the head of their lair, as they were taught almost from their first breath. He'd lived a life of pure hell, forcing his raging leopard to be among prey every minute while he lived his double life as an Interpol agent and enforcer for Lazar. He'd done his duty, just as Timur had. They'd just chosen different sides.

Ashe sank down beside him, taking his hand, but leaning toward Anton. There was no animosity on her face. She didn't really understand—no one who hadn't lived their life could—but she still had that compassion in her Timur had come to rely on.

"He needed you," Anton explained. Blood bubbled around his lips. He coughed.

Timur could see his leopard staring at Ashe. He tightened his fingers around her hand. It felt small, which was deceptive, because she was a very strong woman. She reached with her other hand and laid her palm very gently on Anton's face and stared back at the leopard. She didn't move until the light had faded completely from his eyes. Then she turned to Timur and buried her face in his chest and wept.

He got to his feet, taking her with him, holding her close. He knew they had to clean up the evidence fast, get each of the bodies out and burned before anyone tipped off the cops. Silencers muffled sound on a gun, but didn't entirely get rid of it. An early morning shopkeeper might have heard something. Guns or leopards, it didn't matter. Fortunately, it was still very early and dark, so no one else appeared to be moving around the back side of the shops. So far, no one had come into the back alley.

Jake Bannaconni had sent a helicopter for the two injured men, along with medics who could work on leopards. He'd established a small, private hospital for them on property he'd purchased, and Gorya's and Jeremiah's would be the first two surgeries performed there.

Timur's men swept in, rushing toward the bathroom where Ashe directed them. Timur took his time, stepping around each of those lying on the floor in the midst of what looked like bloody flour. He took Ashe with him, keeping her face pressed close. He had no idea why he was protecting her from looking at the dead bodies when she had killed them and he was very proud of her, but instinct had him doing just that.

More men poured in. These began wrapping bodies in tarps taken from vans and removed them quickly.

"You did very well, baby, but I have to see Gorya and Jeremiah. Jeremiah texted all the details, and the surgeon told him how to keep Gorya alive." He could hear the tightness in his voice, but mostly he felt it in his heart. He loved Gorya as a brother. They'd grown up together, protecting each other from his father. They'd made pacts, taken blood vows to always have each other's back.

Ashe looked up at him, her fingers gently touching his face. "He's strong."

Timur knew that about his cousin. Gorya was one of the strongest men he knew. Fyodor, Sevastyan and Mitya were all strong. They had to be in order to have survived their lairs and their fathers.

"What the hell did you do to this place?" he asked as he picked his way through the rubble that had once been a state-of-the-art kitchen. Evangeline had started with a few good necessary big items, like her ovens, but her husband had recently replaced everything with top-of-the-line ovens, refrigerators, freezer, warmers, dishwasher, anything he could give her to make her life easier. "It looks like a war zone."

"Oh no, I left the stove on." Ashe hurried to turn off the stove and caught up with him as he stepped into the bathroom.

The medics were working on Gorya, getting him ready for transport. His face was leeched of all color. In fact, if anything he looked gray. The floor was slick with blood. Jeremiah had blood all over him. He was awake and had two men crouched beside him, hooking him up to all kinds of lines.

"Gorya?" Timur asked abruptly.

One man glanced over his shoulder. "Touch and go. We've got to get him to the doc right now." He looked at the two with Jeremiah, one eyebrow lifted.

"Get him in the bird and we'll be right behind you," one said. "Go."

Timur touched Gorya's hand as his cousin was taken out. He turned back to watch the men working on Jeremiah. The kid attempted a grin of all things.

"Your woman's a badass, Timur," he said. "She can't cook worth shit, but she's a total badass."

Timur nodded and crouched beside the younger man, taking care to stay out of the way of the two men strapping him to the gurney. Very carefully, he removed the gun from the kid's fist.

"Don't ever cross her," Jeremiah warned. "She knows more ways to kill a man than I do. Seriously, boss, don't do it."

"No worries, Jeremiah," Timur assured. "I have no intention of crossing her."

"She's inventive when it comes to killing men." He beckoned Timur closer and waited for him to bend down.

He looked left and right to make certain no one would overhear him. “You’re so lucky, man. She’s a total babe,” he whispered. “She’s a *man*killer, and that’s hot as hell.”

Timur looked up to meet Ashe’s eyes. His stomach dropped the way it always did when he looked at her. All those strange somersaults. She smiled at him, making it worse. She might not be able to bake him cookies, or cook his dinner, but he didn’t give a damn. She was perfect.

20

TIMUR stared out the window into the night. Every breath he drew into his lungs brought Ashe in as well. She lay facedown, sprawled out on the bed, her favorite position. She looked like a star with her arms wide and her legs spread apart. Her head was turned toward him, but her eyes were closed. She had that beautiful sated look he was coming to know on her face.

He loved the way she looked at him, especially when he made love to her. She always looked a little shocked when an orgasm swept through her. Every time. She also looked at him as if he were the best man in the world. How that happened, he didn't know, especially when he brought her nothing but danger. He was determined to spend the rest of his life making certain that look never turned to disappointment.

He sighed. She was a warrior. She wasn't going to ever sit at home with a dozen kids, happy to never know what he was up to. She would insist on knowing. The moment she thought there was danger, she would lock their children in a safe room and go on the offensive.

She'd defeated three of Rafe Cordeau's leopard soldiers. They were men with terrible reputations, men who enjoyed using their leopards to hunt humans in the swamp, mostly prostitutes, but occasionally an enemy of their boss. Beau had recruited them when Rafe was killed, knowing their proclivities, allowing them occasionally to continue by using the girls he got from Ulisse.

His woman, Ashe Bronte Mostafa, had kicked their asses. She'd used weapons she had available to her, leaving Jeremiah armed so he could hold off anyone who got past her. Ashe had done that. She'd made her decisions quickly and she'd been efficient. The entire battle hadn't lasted a full five minutes. She'd noted the time. That meant she'd made four kills in under five minutes. One had been in leopard form.

His heart still pounded every time he thought about her going up against Gilbert Tregre and his leopard. The man was evil and his leopard even more so. She'd tried to gloss over the telling, knowing he wasn't going to like how she'd done it, but she was alive, and that was what mattered to him. She'd been quick-thinking and courageous, and she'd stayed alive.

Anton had answered the question of why Gilbert Tregre had challenged Timur for Ashe. Like Anton, Gilbert had been close enough to Ashe that he felt the difference in his leopard and wanted to give him that gift of calm. Had he just realized Evangeline could do the same thing years earlier, he might have been a different man, or he might have been a worse one. They'd never know.

They'd closed the bakery for a couple of months stating they were expanding. Building was in progress. That meant replacing the floors that would have evidence should they ever be under investigation. Putting the two shops together allowed Fyodor and Timur to build in more defenses besides just bulletproof glass in the front. He should have replaced the windows in the kitchen when he'd replaced the front of Evangeline's store.

"Come to bed," Ashe murmured sleepily without opening her eyes.

"I like looking at you." He wasn't lying. He loved looking at her.

"I like feeling you next to me."

He laughed. He couldn't help it. Joy always welled up when he was near her. "You sleep like a starfish, all spread out. It isn't like I can fit."

"You fit perfectly."

"Don't try seduction. I've already taken care of you tonight. Twice. You're becoming insatiable," he teased.

"If that's the only way I can ever get you in bed with me, I have no choice then."

The laughter in her voice felt like velvet rubbing caresses over his skin. How did she do that? How did she make him feel so happy? What had really changed? He was in a dangerous job, with cops believing he was a criminal. If the criminals found out what they were doing, there was no place in the world any of them would be able to hide for long. None of that mattered because Ashe made it better.

He settled on the edge of the mattress, his palm on the curve of her right cheek. He spread his fingers wide. "You make my life so much better."

Her lashes fluttered and then lifted. She angled her head so she could look at him. "I'm so in love with you, Timur."

"I live in a very dangerous world, *malen'kiy smerch*. You might be my little badass tornado, but we'll have a family. You're going to get pregnant, and our children will have to go to school with other children whose parents won't want you or them around their families. Money can buy a lot of things, baby, but the looks they'll give you won't be nice. They'll whisper behind your back . . ."

"I've thought of that," she admitted. "Mostly, after talking to Evangeline. I grew up away from everyone, so I have no reference to what it would be like in school. She didn't either, and she's worried for her children. She asked me if I thought it would be a terrible thing to homeschool them. At the time, I said it was a distance in the future and we should cross that bridge when we came to it. Still, it made me think."

"What did you think?" He began a slow massage. Her skin was always so warm and inviting. She never moved away from him or denied him touching her. He loved that about her.

"I didn't know what to think. I really didn't miss going to school because I never went. I didn't miss having other children around. I was too busy. When I got older and went out on my own, I had to catch up socially. All the books in the world don't prepare you, but I did it. Evangeline said there are other women, wives of some of the other men. She likes them and says I will too. They'll have children. Our children can be friends."

He bent his head to press a kiss to the small of her back. "You're absolutely right, they will have children, and we can make certain they get together."

"What are you going to do about your uncles? Lazar and Rolan?"

"Nothing. Not right now. We've gotten word out to all our friends to watch them and every entry point we know they use to get in and out of the States. We'll be prepared, but the more time we have, the better that will be."

"You don't sound worried."

"I'm not. Their greatest weapon is a leopard. Leopards are scarce. We killed not only his top man, but several of his best soldiers. We also destroyed the leopards who had joined with Beau and Gilbert, which meant his local recruits are stamped out. If we missed any of them, Drake is bound to ferret them out. He's that pissed. He isn't likely to miss anyone or anything this time around. And Joshua is looking closely at all the men who had originally worked for Rafe

Cordeau. Neither Lazar or Rolan is going to chance losing any more of their assets until they're stronger. That means alliances. We're working on a plan."

"What if they just decide to kill all of you and get it over with? They could put a hit out on you."

"We would know immediately. He would have to go to someone like Elijah. There is no way he knows Elijah, or Joshua, for that matter, is working for the other side. In any case, baby, we're safe for a while. They might not make their move for a long time. Or they'll decide to come after us immediately. I have no control over either choice. At the moment, they're in Russia and we're here. All we can do is prepare and keep our eyes open."

"I suppose you're right. They just feel a little like a sword hanging over our heads. That has to be the way my parents felt their entire lives."

Living with a sword hanging over his head was the way *he'd* lived his entire life, and it felt natural to him. "I wish I could have met them. I would have thanked them for teaching you how to defend yourself. You probably saved Gorya's life. Possibly Jeremiah too."

She made a face. "Jeremiah needed someone to shoot him."

He laughed and she joined with him. "You two fight like brother and sister."

"Don't ever tell him, but I kind of feel like he's my brother," Ashe admitted.

"Has Fyodor told Evangeline about her father and uncle?"

"Yes. Yesterday. We've had work crews in tearing up the place just in case those damn cops come around looking for Evangeline's pastries. Speaking of, what was up with all the charcoaled croissants they had to throw in the Dumpsters?"

She leaned over and bit his wrist. He retaliated by smacking her bottom, not that it did much good—she just laughed.

"Don't *ever* say the word *croissant* in front of me again, Timur. And just so you know, if someone tells you baking is far easier than cooking, don't believe a word they say. I told Evangeline she was a liar, a straight-up liar."

He leaned down and kissed her cheek, right where his handprint was. "The word *croissant* is stricken forever from my vocabulary."

"It had better be stricken from Jeremiah's as well," she said. "And do we have to have fire alarms? I really hate the things.

"Absolutely we do." He nuzzled her back with his chin and then planted a trail of kisses from her shoulder to the dents just above the curve of her buttocks. "I forgot to tell you."

"What?" She half lifted her torso up, but he pressed her back down with a hand to the middle of her back.

"Armande confessed everything. Beau threatened his sister. He said he was terrified they'd kill her if he didn't cooperate."

She frowned. "Do you believe him?"

"I'm not certain. I don't know what to think about him. It's Drake's problem. He'll interrogate him and decide what to do. We're out of that."

Timur wrote a short poem on her back. Nothing fancy or flowery, just the way he felt, like waking up to sunshine. She didn't realize that every dirty Fed or cop that came at them was going to be put in the ground. They had no choice if they wanted to live. They couldn't be blackmailed. They had to appear dirty even to the men working for them outside their close circles. It was the only way to stay alive.

"What about Christophe and Ambroise?"

"Fyodor is handling that, which is a very good thing. I've got other things on my mind."

"What other things?" She eyed him suspiciously.

He stroked a caress over her bottom and then shifted his body, sliding between her widespread legs. "This kind of other things." He hooked his arm around her waist and pulled her to her knees, one hand at the nape of her neck so she stayed with her head on the mattress. "I know how you can't go without me for more than"—he glanced at the clock—"an hour and fifteen minutes."

Her laughter was muffled by the sheets. "You're so right. Feel me."

He did as she said, slipping his hand between her legs to find her slick and hot, just the way she was every time he did it. "Now you've got me in a dilemma. Do I feast on you? I'm pretty hungry. My woman refused to cook dinner to-night."

"You know darn well I can't cook, and you only asked to tease me. I wouldn't want you to go hungry though." She wiggled her bottom at him.

She was so beautiful she took his breath. He laid his fore-head against all that soft skin, skin that was his because she gave it to him. Her gifts were priceless. When he married her, and that was going to be soon, she was going to get the book of poetry he had written for her. Every word was what he felt about Ashe Bronte Mostafa, soon to be Ashe Bronte Amurov. That was such a better fit with her exotic name.

"I want your mouth," she demanded.

He found himself with a silly grin on his face. "Then you don't get to move. The moment you move, I take it away."

She heaved an exaggerated sigh. "Apparently you want to play one of your many silly sex games."

She loved his games and he knew it. "*Sexy* games," he corrected. "And just so you know, I'm so in love with you too. So much so, baby, that we're getting married as soon as the doc gives Gorya the okay to attend our wedding." Before she could answer, he began one of his favorite things—devouring her.

Keep reading for an excerpt from

VENGEANCE ROAD

The next book in the Torpedo Ink series
by Christine Feehan
Available February 2019 from Jove

BREEZY Simmons leaned against her pickup for a moment, staring at the large building that housed the Torpedo Ink Motorcycle Club. Her heart beat so hard in her chest she was afraid she might vomit. The world spun uncontrollably, and she quickly leaned down, putting her head between her legs, taking deep breaths. She caught a glimpse of two men on the other side of the compound as her head went toward the asphalt, and she didn't recognize either of them. That made her pounding heart sink.

She couldn't possibly have the wrong club. This *had* to be them. She was running out of time and options. Drawing big gulps of air into her lungs, she slowly righted herself and took another cautious look around. The two men stared at her from across the parking lot. She was careful not to look at them too long. She didn't want them coming anywhere near her. She needed to get in and out very fast.

The Torpedo Ink compound was extremely large and had

a high chain-link fence surrounding it. There was even razor wire up on top of the fence, making the place look like a fortress. The rolling gates were wide open, and she'd driven her truck right inside, parking as close to the clubhouse as possible. She deliberately left the door to her beat-up pickup open and the engine running. Hopefully no one recognized her and she could get in and out of the building quickly, once she ascertained these were the right people, the ones she was looking for.

In the early morning hours the club was just beginning to stir. Clearly they'd partied hard over the weekend. In the enormous side yard, the one with the beautiful ocean view, she could see the embers in the fire pits glowing as the breeze stirred them up. A man with his back to her watered them down with a hose. He wore a tight tee and jeans, but no colors. Still, she knew this was the home of the club that called itself Torpedo Ink. She sent up a silent prayer that this was the right one.

There were empty bottles strewn around the grass and on the ground to the side of the building in the wide expanse of open field. Cars, motorcycles and trucks were scattered around the parking lot, although no one parked where the club did. Their motorcycles were lined up neatly and a prospect watched over them. He sat on the curb looking at her. She was parked too close to the precious bikes, but she didn't care—although it had drawn the attention of the prospect.

Another long line of motorcycles was parked a short distance from the clubhouse and a prospect watched over those bikes as well. He looked at her without much interest, which indicated to her that these bikes belonged to a visiting club. He wasn't as interested in protecting the grounds as the prospect closest to the clubhouse.

She had to get this over with. Just being in such close proximity to an MC made her sick. The fact that she knew what had gone on at the party made her even sicker. That this might be *his* club, and she had to risk running into him made all that far worse.

Breezy squared her shoulders, dragged the envelope off the seat and turned all in one motion. The prospect was on his feet. If she knew for certain this was the right club, she would have thrust the letter into his hands and left, but she was guessing from a process of elimination.

She purposely hadn't kept track of him, especially when she'd heard, a year after she left, that eighteen members of the Swords had set up the international president for assassination and had allegedly wiped out a number of members and disappeared. She knew who those eighteen members were immediately and, knowing them, she knew it was possible when others said it wasn't. She'd run as far from the life as she could and now she was pulled right back in.

The parties. The violence. The utter disregard and disdain for women. She shut that down fast and walked with brisk, purposeful steps to the club. She yanked open the door and went right in. It smelled just the way she remembered. Booze. Sex. Weed. Her stomach lurched. God. *God.* She couldn't stand walking into the clubhouse, let alone anything else.

The common room was enormous. One side held a long, curving bar; in the center of the room were tables and chairs, and the other side had several couches and armchairs. Sleeping bodies were everywhere. A woman picked up bottles and put them into a garbage bag, dumping paper plates in along with the other trash as she moved through the mostly naked bodies strewn around the floor. She glanced at Breezy but didn't say anything. She kept picking up trash as if on automatic pilot. Breezy remembered what that was like. She could have been that woman.

She didn't recognize any of the men that she could see lying on the floor or slumped in the chairs, and her heart sank. She paused by the bar, her gaze going from one face to the next. Half naked or naked men and women were draped in chairs around the room or on the floor. Most snored softly, but one woman was busy going down on a man with wild blond hair and ice-blue eyes. Three teardrops were tattooed like drops of ice dripping down his face.

He slumped in a chair, looking almost bored, his eyes at half-mast as the woman knelt at his feet, her mouth busy, while another one kissed her way up his chest. Across from him, a second man who looked exactly like the blond, obviously his twin, watched, his fist around his impressive and somewhat intimidating cock. The one with the teardrop tattoos indicated to the woman kissing his chest to go to his watching brother with a jerk of his chin. She immediately dropped to her hands and knees and crawled between the thighs of the other man.

It was them. The right club. The men she had searched for. She'd found them. She recognized the twins and her heart kicked into overdrive. How could she *not* recognize them? They were gorgeous men. As cold as ice, but beautiful. The one with the tattoos—Ice had been his name—suddenly lifted his gaze and met hers. Her heart stuttered at the recognition she saw in his eyes.

She slapped the envelope onto the bar.

"Give that to Steele."

She turned to go, her gaze sliding around the room once more.

At the sound of her voice, three women stirred in the far corner of the room, their sleeping bodies pushed aside by the man who lay under them. The movement drew her eye. He half sat, shoving at the dark hair spilling onto his forehead. It was thick and wild, a little out of control. He blinked drowsily at her. Her heart faltered. Stopped. They stared at each other, and her stomach lurched.

Breezy threw dignity to the wind. She ran. Fast. She heard the sharp whistle following her, but she had already flung herself into her pickup and thrown it into reverse, her foot stomping on the gas pedal. She pressed down hard, and the truck roared as it backed all the way through the rapidly closing gates. Men poured out of the clubhouse—she could see them through her windshield when she glanced at them—but they were mostly naked, and the gates had closed behind her with a loud clang. She was on one side, the side of freedom; they were on the other, those gates holding them in. For once, luck was on her side.

She backed straight into the street, thankful it was so early and there was no traffic. Throwing the pickup into drive, she nearly spun out of control as she overcorrected, before straightening out and taking off toward Highway 1. She had a plan, just in case, and she was grateful she'd made that plan. Her entire body trembled, so much so that it was difficult holding on to the steering wheel. But she did so, her knuckles turning white.

Why did it hurt? He'd made it very, very clear she was nothing to him. Another club girl. No, lower than that. A whore. One her family pimped out. A drug mule. Nothing. She was nothing. She'd thought he was her world and all the while he'd been plotting to take down her family's club. She'd loved him. He'd used her and then thrown her away, shattering every dream, every hope she'd ever had.

Her vision blurred, and she swiped at her eyes, furious that he'd made her cry again. That he *could* make her cry again. She'd cried enough tears over him. The liar. He was just like all the others in the clubs. Women were nothing to them. Nothing. They used them. Humiliated them. She'd been born into that life, but she didn't have to stay there. She wasn't that girl. Not anymore. Not ever again.

She pulled off onto the little narrow dirt road she'd scouted earlier, just in case she was recognized. She knew they'd come after her; after all, she was the daughter of their mortal enemy. She drove the truck as far down as the narrow road allowed, right into a thick grove of trees. Brush rose up all around once she pulled off the road. The narrow track had long since been abandoned and it was overgrown with shrubbery, vines and trees. She parked, hastily got out and covered the pickup with the branches and vines she'd cut earlier in preparation.

When she was positive the truck couldn't be seen from any angle, Breezy crawled through the driver's window, reached into the back and pulled a blanket around her. She couldn't stop shivering. Even her teeth chattered. She let herself cry, but she did so silently, and she told herself she wasn't crying for lost dreams or heartache. She had so little chance of being successful, and yet she *had* to be. There was no room for failure. None.

She closed her burning eyes and leaned her head back against the seat, trying not to think about Steele. She didn't know any other name for him. She'd only known him as Steele. She should have realized that if you'd been with a man for a year and he hadn't told you his given name, he wasn't into you. But she'd been young and desperate, and he'd been the white knight. She'd been so stupid. She hit her head on the back of the seat multiple times, wishing she'd been smarter. Wishing she'd been born into another family. Another life. Wishing time hadn't run out on her.

It took only a few minutes until she heard the roar of pipes as motorcycles moved in force down the highway. It sounded like an army was coming after her. Out of stark fear, she slid down farther on the seat. It was going to be a long wait until night. She'd had no choice. She knew clubs. She knew on a Sunday morning, after partying all night, they would be sleepy, and she'd have her best chance at getting away if she was discovered. She also knew that she didn't dare go out on the highway until nightfall. She hadn't slept in nearly forty-eight hours and this would be her only chance for a long while. She closed her eyes and willed herself to stop thinking about things she couldn't control and go to sleep. It didn't work, but she tried.

* * *

LYOV Russak, known as Steele, the vice president of Torpedo Ink, whistled loud and long, raising his hand high, and pushed his way through the soft flesh of women to spin his finger in a circle, indicating to Absinthe, who manned the monitors, to close the gates fast. He shoved his way free of the women, cursing in his native language as he got to his feet.

Her voice. He'd never forget that voice. Breezy Simmons. *His* Breezy Simmons. The girl that had forever made him a sick fuck who still, to this day, thought of her, dreamt of her and pretended every woman he was with was her. That was how truly fucked-up he was.

He had never confessed to his brothers that he had somehow, inadvertently or not, become the very thing they despised. The thing they hunted. He was ashamed of that. Ashamed, not because of the terrible mistake, but because he couldn't get the way she felt wrapped around him—and his cock—out of his mind. It was nearly all he thought about and that made him the sickest fuck out there.

She was even more beautiful than he remembered. She'd matured. Her figure had matured. He'd just caught a glimpse of her, one small glimpse, but his body had recognized her almost before his brain had. All that thick, tawny hair; those large green eyes. So green it was like looking into an emerald sea. His entire body clenched.

The Demons had come for the weekend, bringing their women with them, and the two clubs had partied hard. He'd drunk too much, the way he usually did at these events. He'd indulged far too much with women, the way he also did at these events. The endless cycle that got him nowhere because he fucking lived in hell. The woman who could have changed all that was leaving. Walking away from him—again. No, make that *running* away from him. It wasn't happening, and he didn't care how much of a monster that made him. She wasn't getting away from him twice.

Across the room, Ice and Storm were pushing women off their cocks and rising to their feet. Keys and Player untangled themselves from the women they'd been with and rushed the door with the twins. Steele was right behind them, practically shoving them out of the way just in time to see the gates slam shut, effectively stopping pursuit as her truck backed out onto the street in a furious rush.

"No. *Fuck* no." He swung his head toward the prospects. "Get after her. Don't fuckin' lose her. I mean it. You stay on her."

It was definitely Breezy. She was older. Three years older now, but it was her. She'd stared at him in absolute horror, and he couldn't blame her. What the *fuck*? He'd looked for her covertly, after Torpedo Ink had completed their mission and taken down the Swords' president and weakened their club, but she'd dropped off the face of the earth. That had been the plan—for her to disappear—but he always thought he'd be able to find her. And he'd tried. God, but he'd tried.

When he'd driven her away, he'd told himself he wouldn't look for her, that he'd let her go. He'd lost that battle with himself, not that it did him any good. He had searched, over and over, but he hadn't found her. Now she'd walked right into his lair and he wasn't about to let her get away again.

"She left something for you, Steele," Ice said, shoving his hand through his hair. He shook his head absently at the woman who tried to drape herself over him. "Sorry, babe. Time to leave."

"I could stay with you," she whispered, her hand sliding down his belly toward his cock.

He gave her a friendly slap on her ass as he expertly avoided her hand. "Sorry, babe. Need you to get on home, wherever the fuck that is."

Ice turned away from her, striding across the room to the bar where he'd seen Breezy put something. He picked up the envelope and turned it over. It was plain white. No writing on the outside.

Steele took it out of his hand and went striding out of the common room to the hall where their private rooms were. He needed to get dressed fast and get on his bike. Find her. He had to find her. He hesitated as he grabbed a pair of jeans. He couldn't go to her stinking of other women. She'd know. She'd smell them on his skin. Urgency made him yank up his jeans and drag a shirt over his head. She already knew. She'd seen the women piled on top of him. He could explain later. Right now, the most important thing was to make certain she didn't get away. He grabbed his colors and slid into them, feeling whole the moment he put them on.

Ice, Storm, Maestro, Keys and most of his other brothers joined him as he ran out of the clubhouse to his bike. The Demons had rallied, news sweeping through the compound that something was up, and they were supportive of their new allies, immediately offering help. Player was already directing the search, sending bikes in various directions. The prospects had said they'd seen her truck turning south, toward the Bay Area, so that was the direction he was going. Absinthe had gotten her license plate number off the camera continually sweeping their parking lot.

Steele threw his leg over his bike and had it roaring within seconds. Then the wind was in his face and his brothers were at his back as he tore down the highway looking for his woman. He'd been the one to end things, and it had been ugly. Really ugly. Deliberately ugly. He'd said things to drive her away—and she'd gone. She'd managed to take pieces of him with her. She'd stolen those pieces from him, and he'd known, when she'd left, he wasn't going to get them back.

He'd been angry. He'd been afraid for her. He'd been so shocked that just by being with her, he'd become everything he most despised in the world—a predator. It hadn't mattered how it happened, he'd only known it couldn't continue and he'd sent her away. No, he'd driven her away.

He increased his speed, straightening out curves and hurtling down the highway as fast as he could travel without putting himself in the ocean. He was risking doing just that, but to find her, to see her again, the risk was worth anything. Then Keys and Maestro slid up next to him, moving in perfect unison with him, and he realized he wasn't risking just his life—he wasn't alone. His brothers were with him every step of the way. Lately, he'd come to realize, Keys and Maestro guarded him the way Reaper and Savage protected Czar. He didn't need or want it, but they stuck to him like glue. He slowed a fraction, just enough to be safe as they searched for the one woman he knew had cut out his heart and kept it.

BREEZY slept fitfully, waking at the smallest sound, such as a branch scraping across her rust bucket of a pickup. It sounded like a saw rasping over the paint and it yanked her out of her dozing over and over. She climbed out of the truck only when it was absolutely necessary and she had to use the bushes. Each time, she forced herself to drink more water. She'd given up eating, but that only made her feel slightly faint. She wasn't hungry anymore, but her thirst persisted in spite of her desire to ignore it. She drank water, and that meant more trips outside the truck, which meant she was at risk.

She watched the fiery ball of the sun begin its drop into the sea. The sky turned all shades of golden and then orange, and spread through the low clouds drifting overhead. She had to admit, as sunsets went, it was pretty spectacular. She could have settled here in Northern California. She didn't like big cities, and this area was far from that. Truthfully, she needed to be in a city, to disappear. There, no one cared about or noticed a waitress working in a diner. In a smaller town, like Caspar or Sea Haven, everyone would notice.

She had been so careful, keeping her head down, working, doing nothing else. Just staying off the radar and as far from the club life as possible. Still, she'd been pulled back despite everything she'd tried to do to prevent that from happening. The life was insidious, and once in, it seemed there was no way out.

She was crying again, and that always gave her a vicious headache and annoyed her. She had stopped crying three years earlier after she'd spent weeks giving herself headaches and little else. She had stopped, gotten back on her feet and taken care of business. She'd been proud of herself for every accomplishment. Then her world fell apart and she had no choice but to make certain Steele got that letter. Everything depended on him getting it and following the instructions. That was important and yet she knew following instructions was a very un-Steele-like thing to do. She didn't even know for certain whether it would matter enough to him that he'd do it for her.

The sun plunged into the sea and she immediately began preparations for leaving. It was nearly time. She climbed out of the window and began removing the branches and vines from around her pickup. She had to back the truck straight along the road for a good thirty feet before there was a wide enough area for her to turn around.

She made it the thirty feet without using her lights, as the darkness was only just becoming inky streaks running through the very dim light. As she started up the road, heading away from the ocean and toward the main highway, she saw that a small tree had fallen across the dirt track. It didn't surprise her, given the wind. Fortunately, the round trunk looked more like a sapling than a mature tree, one she could handle by herself.

Sighing, she turned on her headlights to illuminate the area, so it would be easier to shift the fallen tree. Pulling gloves out of her glove compartment, she pushed open her door with the soles of her boots and slid out. She was tired, afraid and anxious to be gone from Torpedo Ink territory. Just the thought of that dangerous ride along the highway was terrifying. She planned to take the Comptche-Ukiah

Road leading away from the coast. It would take her off the highway. They probably thought she hadn't done any research or planned ahead—after all, she was a stupid female to be used for carrying drugs or weapons, or prostituted out on behalf of the club. She couldn't actually *think*.

Bitterness nearly choked her. She detested MCs and all they stood for. She crouched, took a breath and reached down for the trunk. The moment she had her hands on the tree, arms reached around her, caught her wrists and yanked them behind her back. She rose up fast, throwing her head back to try to come in contact with her attacker's head. He grunted when she smashed into his chest, but he had already secured her wrists with zip ties.

"How many times did I tell you to look around? You forgot all my training, babe."

Furious, and more than a little scared, she spun around and tried to kick him the moment he let her go. She *had* forgotten, damn him. He blocked the kick hard, numbing her leg when he defended himself by striking down on her shin to deflect the blow. She tried again, and he blocked her a second time with equal power.

The breath hissed out of her lungs and she bent forward as far as she could, drawing her hands up as high as possible, intending to slam them back down as she came upright fast in order to break the zip ties. He'd taught her that as well. Before she could straighten, his hand was on her back, holding her down.

"Breezy, you'd better calm down before you get hurt."

Her breath hissed out of her lungs. "Go to hell, Steele. You have no right to lay one finger on me."

"That's not exactly true, sweetheart, and you know it," he said.

"I'm not part of your club. I'm not part of your life in any way. Just get the hell away from me."

He didn't let her up, his palm pressing her down while he texted one-handed. "You always were a smart little thing. I looked at the tapes we had of your ride." He sounded derisive. "Babe. Really. You're driving a shit truck. It's a rust bucket if I ever saw one. There was no way it could have gotten that far ahead of us, even if we were a minute or two behind, which the prospects were. That meant it was a process of elimination on which road you'd turned off onto. I also remembered you as being extremely patient when you need to be. That meant you were going to hide out until nightfall. It gave me plenty of time to track you down."

"Let me up."

"Ask nice."

For one moment, she was afraid she might spontaneously combust—and not in a good way. She stayed quiet. He had to let her up sometime.

"I'm not real happy with you."

Staying quiet went right out the window at the bite in his voice. "I really don't care whether you're happy or not. Let. Me. *Up.*"

"You ask nice. You don't want to play hardball with me, Breezy, because you won't win. Not when I'm this pissed. Didn't have much to do when I found the truck but wait for you to wake up, so I read the fuckin' letter."

Her heart jerked hard. Fear shot through her and she went very still, no longer resisting or struggling to get free. If anything, she tried to make herself smaller, frozen like a little mouse with a big predator about to pounce.

"I read that fuckin' letter eighteen times, Breezy. *Eighteen.* I showed some restraint by not going near the truck because I might have strangled you. I still might."

His palm moved up her back to settle slowly around the nape of her neck, his long fingers curling around either side of her throat. "You get how really fuckin' pissed I am with you?"

"You get how I really fucking don't care?" she spat back. Let him kill her. She was dead anyway. "You threw me out, Steele. I begged you to let me stay with you. It was humiliating, and I still did it. Then I begged you to go with me when it was obvious you wanted me gone. You made it abundantly clear that I was nothing to you. A whore for the club that kept you warm at night. I can repeat verbatim what you said to me, if you'd like. So don't get all self-righteous on me."

The fingers tightened, digging into her throat. The thumb pressed into her chin. His other hand bunched her hair in his fist and slowly pulled her to a standing position. She stared up at his set features. He was even more gorgeous than she remembered, and she dreamt of him every night. *Every* night. That made her a masochist.

Unlike most of the others he rode with, he had few scars on his face. They were mostly on his body, covered with ink. She knew every scar, every tattoo. She had traced every one of those scars and tattoos with her tongue. With her fingertips. She'd memorized them until they were etched so deeply in her brain, she could have drawn them and gotten every detail perfect.

She wore his tattoo on her skin. He'd had his friend ink her for him, a tattoo of his design, right across the top curve of her butt, an intricate pattern that she always thought was beautiful. She had a love/hate relationship with that tattoo. The ink beads dripped down onto her buttocks, both cheeks, but high up; the intertwining lace wove his name there declaring her his property. His. She'd loved that. It had meant something back then. Now, not so much.

She had been shaking, and he'd held her hand and whispered to her, beautiful, loving things, things that had made her laugh or want to cry with happiness. All the while his friend Ink had tattooed the custom design on her. It had felt intimate. Loving. She often thought of that day and the way, for the first time in her life, she'd felt important and loved by someone.

"Untie me."

He shook his head slowly. "You're coming back to the clubhouse with me."

She flinched. She couldn't help it. She didn't want to go anywhere near that place again. "Once was enough, Steele." There was sarcasm in her voice. Maybe bitterness. "One look, one smell and I knew I was so finished with that life. You managed to fall right back into it once I was gone, or were you still participating while we were together? I should have known it would take more than one woman to satisfy you. You always had such an appetite." She made that sound as nasty as she could manage.

She didn't look away from his glittering midnight-blue eyes. She'd always thought he had the most beautiful eyes, ringed with all those dark lashes. The color of his eyes was unusual in that they were so dark one had to stare at them a long while before realizing they were actually blue. His hair was wild and always out of control. When it was longish, it was decidedly unruly, falling into his face, but it didn't make him look young. Nothing took the cold from his eyes.

She found that his friends, the ones he mostly ran with in the club—and at that time they'd all been riding with the Swords—had eyes that were flat and deadly. She'd been young enough and stupid enough to get a thrill from that. Now, she just knew they weren't good people and she didn't want any part of them.

"Did you come here to kill me? To kill Czar?"

If her hands hadn't been tied, she would have slapped him right across the face. She'd risked everything to warn him. To warn Czar. And some man named Jackson Deveau she'd never even met. She'd risked *everything* just to do the right thing. "Screw you, Steele. Yeah, that's exactly what I did. I came here and left you a letter detailing how I planned to kill you all." Sarcasm dripped from her voice.

In the distance she heard the sound of pipes as two Harleys approached. She saw their lights once they rounded the bend. There would be no escaping from this if Steele didn't let her go. She raised her gaze to his once more. "You know what the stakes are. Let me get out of here. If I can't . . . "

He shook his head. "You aren't going anywhere, Breezy. We're going to put this before the others and take a vote."

Horror swept through her. "We're not something to *vote* on, Steele. What's wrong with you? Just let me go. I warned you. I warned Czar. It's up to you to warn this Deveau."

Steele transferred his hold to her elbow and she closed her eyes and took several deep breaths. Her only hope was to convince Czar she was no threat to anyone. The others had always followed Czar's lead, even within the Swords club, much to the chagrin of the president of their chapter. Czar had been the enforcer and very trusted. No one suspected, not for one moment, that he—and the others—were plotting to assassinate the international president and bring the club to its knees. Of course, she was gone by then. Long gone.

The motorcycles reached them. She recognized Maestro on one with Keys riding behind him. Ink was on the second bike. Her heart sank. She shook her head, trying not to feel desperate. A few hours could cost her everything. She looked up at Steele again and caught him watching her. She should have known. Steele could be so completely still, it felt like he could disappear. His energy would get so low that you could forget he was in your space. He never missed anything when he was like that. He took in the smallest detail.

He wasn't a particularly small man either. He was a good six feet, all muscle, but not bulky about it. The definition was there, and not an ounce of fat. When she'd been with him, she'd been self-conscious about the softness around her tummy, but he had assured her time and again that he loved every inch of her body. She remembered how he'd looked at her with those cold eyes, just watching, as if any second something would happen and he didn't want to miss it. He wasn't looking at her that way now. Now, it was more like he was about to shred her to pieces. He didn't have to; he'd already done it long ago.

She remained silent when he nodded toward the truck. What was there to say? She started toward it, Steele pacing along beside her, one hand on her arm as if he feared she would bolt for the cliff and toss herself over it. That wasn't likely, but she clearly had made a mistake. She should have just shot him and then made her escape.

He yanked open the passenger door, put his hands on her waist, lifted her and tossed her easily onto the seat. Slamming the door again, he indicated his bike, telling Keys without words that the keys were in the ignition. His Harley was big. It was powerful. It was hidden in the brush just as cleverly as her truck had been. He'd been the one to teach her self-defense moves. How to break out of zip ties. How to hide her vehicle if there was a need. Always to have a plan. He'd warned her repeatedly that she had to pay attention to her surroundings.

She pressed her head against the seat and closed her eyes, keeping them that way even when he shoved the seat back and took the driver's position.

"You should have told me."

Breezy glanced at him. Steele. He could always make her heart flutter and butterflies take off in her stomach. Always. He did so now in spite of everything and she hated herself for that. For being weak.

"Let's just get this over with. Is Czar waiting? Because I want out of there as fast as possible."

"He's waiting, but you aren't going anywhere. You may as well understand that right now. The Demons are already gone. They cleared out this afternoon. We're all set to deal with this as soon as we get you back to the clubhouse."

"The Demons take all your women with them?"

"Breezy—"

She cut him off. "We aren't together. We never really were. You made that very clear, Steele, so there's no need to explain yourself. You like sex. I get that. You like all kinds of sex. I get that too. I was one of the ones serving your needs, I certainly know your . . . appetites."

His expression hardened. "Don't fucking pretend we

weren't on fire together, baby. Right now, hating me the way you do, you still want me. You think I can't tell when a woman wants me?"

"I'm certain you know everything there is to know about sex and women wanting you, Steele. You make an art of it. All of you do. My body may remember what it was like with you, but so does my brain. You're bad news. I thought the Swords were bad, but you were worse. Far, far worse. At least they were up-front in the way they treated me. My father turned me into a whore when I was fourteen. He told me straight up it was the only way I was worth anything to him or the club. He made me carry drugs and service other clubs to cement deals. I was so low, he let them beat the shit out of me right in front of him, but at least I knew what I was to him—to my brother and every other member of that club. You made me think I was worth more than that to you."

She couldn't stand looking at him, so she turned her head away and stared out the window into the night. She'd gone over and over every single detail of her life with him, looking for signs that she should have caught along the way to prove that it had been a charade. A complete sham. She'd just been so young and stupid.

"Breezy, come on, baby, it wasn't like that and you know it."

"Don't. Don't, Steele. I'm not that same girl. You saw to that. I'm not naïve anymore. It may take hard lessons, but they get through. You made yourself clear and I heard every word. I made a life for myself and . . . " She broke off, her lungs seizing. It took a few minutes to find a way to breathe again. "Did you really assassinate the international president of the Swords? That's what the rumor mill is saying. The Swords hate you more than any other enemy and there's a price on every one of you."

"He had the biggest human trafficking ring in the world, Breezy. He was even allowing his clients to use and kill men, women and children on his designated freighters and bury their bodies in the ocean. He had to go."

"Czar joined first. And then one by one, the rest of you." She made it a statement. They'd joined the chapter in Louisiana, the one her family belonged to. Czar had risen to power fast. He was that scary, and Habit, the president of the chapter, had relied on him heavily. Whenever Czar had recommended a prospect, Habit had been more than happy to oblige him. Each man had been as cold as ice and equally as deadly. They'd made the chapter extremely strong.

"That was the plan."

"You rode with them for three years before you sent me away." One of those years he had been a prospect, and he'd just watched her. A year of them dancing around each other. Another year he had been with her. She'd been his old lady. His woman. No one else dared to touch her or try to use her for anything in that year. She'd been safe for the first time in her life. And then . . . he'd told her the truth. He hadn't wanted her anymore. He had never wanted her in the first place. She'd known all along her father had given her to him with the idea of currying favor with Czar and his very strong companions. Her father had wanted to be part of that.

"Five years Czar was with them. I rode with the Swords for four years." He turned off Highway 1 to Caspar. "A fucking lifetime."

"You spent four years with them, another year after you sent me away, and yet you could so easily betray them?" She knew he could. He'd spent a year with her and she hadn't meant anything to him.

"They're all scum, Breezy. Every last one of them."

She couldn't help it. She glared at him. "And you aren't? You rode with those men, pretended to be their brother and then put a bullet in them? You killed a bunch of them, didn't you? You and your friends."

"Yes, we did," Steele replied evenly, without one iota of

remorse. "I'd do it again in a heartbeat. Believe me, baby, I don't lose any sleep over it."

"I'm sure you don't." She was equally sure he didn't lose any sleep over her either. There was evidence of that when she found him lying naked under three women.

"You're avoiding every subject but the one we need to talk about."

The lash of anger in his voice sparked her own. She wanted to swing around on the seat, put her boots up and slam them right into his chest. Drive them right through his black heart. She sat very still, blood thundering in her ears.

"You need to let me go. I've worked this all out. All I asked from you was to follow the plan. That's it. In all this time, that's all I've asked. I know you're busy with your parties, Steele. That's clear. But maybe this once, for a few days, you can skip getting drunk in order to be ready in case you're needed. I'm going in first and taking all the risk. Maybe your three women can take turns giving you blow jobs and keep you happy while you wait to see if I get killed or not."

He slammed on the brakes, gave her a hard look and jumped out of the cab. She watched him round the hood and toss the keys to one of the prospects, and then he was yanking open her door. He caught her chin in hard fingers, forcing her head up so she was looking into eyes glittering with sheer anger. "If you think I'll let you go into that hornet's nest, you've got another think coming. He's *my* son. I'll be the one going to get him."

#1 *NEW YORK TIMES* BESTSELLING AUTHOR

CHRISTINE FEEHAN

"The queen of paranormal romance...
I love everything she does."
—J. R. Ward